Praise for An

'Hocking hits all the commercial high notes . . . She knows how to keep readers turning the pages' *New York Times*

'A fast-paced romance . . . addictive' *Guardian*

'[*Wake*] wil please fans and likely win new ones . . . the well-structure d st ry and strong characters carry readers' *Publishers Weekly*

'Drew [illegible] and kept me hooked . . . cracking pace' *Sunday Express*

[illegible] e is no d ying that Amanda Hocking knows how to tell [illegible] d [illegible] keep readers coming back for more. More is exactl [illegible] y will be looking for once they've turned the last page' *Kirkus Reviews*

'F [illegible] teries, realistic characters, and lots of action . . . [illegible] great book. A worthwhile read' *RT Book Reviews*

' [illegible] ffectively melds myth and contemporary teen [illegible] mily, young love, and mythology all combine [illegible] -read paranormal suspense story that will [illegible] aiting new instalments' *Booklist*

'Amanda Hocking has a gift for storytelling that will grip readers and keep them wanting more . . . Entrancing' *LibraryThing*

'Explosive and interesting . . . a nice, smooth story with unique mythology and lovable characters. I thoroughly enjoyed it' *Teen Bookworm*

'Pure imaginative brilliance! *Wake* is full of thrills, eerie suspense, and mystery . . . incredibly difficult to put down' *Book Faery*

'Real and vibrant. A brand-new series that reawakens everything we love in underwater mythology, *Wake* by Amanda Hocking will certainly leave you with the desire to pick up more of her titles' *A Cupcake and a Latte*

'An amazing story . . . ravishing yet explosive. I am enthralled by the amazing characters and fast-paced plotline. The thrill of the water, the history that propels the reader deeper, *Wake* is awesome!' *Books with Bite*

'Amanda Hocking is like a breath of fresh air in the young adult paranormal market' *That Bookish Girl*

'A wonderfully adventurous and dynamic series, full of high intrigue, mythology, paranormal lore, romance, and suspense. I, for one, can't wait to be swept away in the new world of the Watersong' *Fallen Angel Reviews*

'Amanda Hocking has such an easy and elegant way with her language – her stories just seem to flow well and her words dance. This is going to be another series that I'll fall for. I absolutely cannot wait to see where she takes us with the next book'

Into the Hall of Books

'Great chemistry . . . plus a family history that just makes your heart ache, and you've definitely got a recipe for a fantastic new series. Get your hands on this now!' *YA Books Central*

Available from Tor by Amanda Hocking

THE TRYLLE SERIES

Switched

Torn

Ascend

THE WATERSONG SERIES

Wake

Lullaby

Tidal

Tidal

AMANDA HOCKING

TOR

First published 2013 by St Martin's Press, New York

First published in Great Britain 2013 by Tor
an imprint of Pan Macmillan, a division of Macmillan Publishers Limited
Pan Macmillan, 20 New Wharf Road, London N1 9RR
Basingstoke and Oxford
Associated companies throughout the world
www.panmacmillan.com

ISBN 978-1-4472-0574-6

1 3 5 7 9 8 6 4 2

A CIP catalogue record for this book is available from the British Library.

Printed and bound by CPI Group (UK) Ltd, Croydon, CR0 4YY

Tidal

ONE

Domination

Gemma loved the way it felt when he kissed her, and his mouth was hungry and eager on hers. He didn't appear that strong—though when he crushed her to him like this, she could feel the firm tone of his muscles under the thin fabric of his shirt—so it was as if his passion made him stronger.

It wasn't that Kirby was a particularly great kisser. Gemma had made a decision to stop comparing everyone to Alex or the way he kissed, because they would all come up short. But even without Alex in the mix, Kirby wasn't the top contender.

Still, there was a reason that she'd gone out with him a few times, and that all their dates ended up in the backseat of his old Toyota. They hadn't done much more than kiss, and Gemma wouldn't take it any further.

What kept her coming back to Kirby wasn't love or his kisses. Her heart still longed for Alex, and only Alex. But she couldn't be with him, and she couldn't sulk around the house anymore. Or at least that was what Harper and her dad kept telling her.

That was how she'd ended up here with Kirby, giving in to the physical moments with him that somehow felt both wrong and completely right.

Even if she were still just human, Gemma would've found this fun. Kirby was sexy and sweet, and he made her laugh. But the siren part of her craved this, almost demanding the physical contact.

The truth was that she was getting restless. Thea told her that would happen if she didn't eat. Technically, she only needed to eat once before a solstice or equinox, but the longer she went without feeding, the more agitated and irritable she would become.

There were a few tricks to staving off the hunger. One of them was frequent swimming, which Gemma did as often as she could. Another was singing, but Gemma was too afraid to try that. She didn't want to accidentally enchant anyone.

The third wasn't so much about denying the hunger as giving in to it. And that was what she was doing with Kirby. Kissing him to keep from biting him.

When he kissed her deeply, pushing her back against the seat of the car, something stirred inside her. A warm heat in her belly spread over her, making her skin flutter, like when her legs transformed into a tail.

The siren wanted to come out, and there was something strangely wonderful about holding it back. Gemma was in control, not the monster, and as Kirby kissed her neck, she stayed firmly on the line between siren and human.

It wasn't until his hand began sliding up her skirt, running along the smooth skin of her thigh, that Gemma silenced the siren lust within her. Her skin stopped fluttering, the heat inside her went cold, and Gemma sat up, gently pushing Kirby off her.

"Oh, I'm sorry," Kirby said, still breathing heavy, and moved back from her. "Did I go too far?"

"You know the rules." She gave him a small shrug and straightened out her skirt. "I won't go any further than that."

"Sorry." He grimaced and brushed his dark hair off his forehead. "I got a little carried away. It won't happen again."

She smiled at him. "It's fine. I know you'll stick to the rules better next time."

"So there will be a next time?" Kirby asked.

He was kneeling on the seat, his blue eyes sparkling. Kirby was handsome in the way models were—smooth, lean, chiseled—but he had a real kindness about him.

The way he treated her probably had more to do with her siren appeal than how he actually felt about her. She hadn't used her song on him, so he wasn't a love slave. But her appearance had its own power, one that was hard for guys to ignore.

Kirby was a few years older than she was, but she'd seen him around school. Even though he was attractive and popular, he never bullied other kids. In the short time they'd been kinda dating each other, he'd never said a mean word about anybody, and it never occurred to him to challenge her.

That was what kept Gemma coming back to *him*. He was safe.

She liked him, but not too much. Whatever magical spark it was that made her fall in love with Alex was completely missing with Kirby. When she was with him, she was completely in control—of her emotions, of the monster, even of him. She would never hurt him, and he could never hurt her.

"Yeah, there will be a next time," Gemma told him, and he broke out in a wide grin.

"Great. I don't think I could ever forgive myself if I blew it with you."

"You'd be surprised by the things a person can forgive themselves for," Gemma said under her breath.

"What?" Kirby asked.

"Nothing." She shook her head and forced a smile. "How do I look?"

"Gorgeous, just like always."

Gemma laughed. "No, I meant, is my makeup messed up? Does it look like I've been making out in the backseat of a car?"

Kirby leaned in, inspecting her hair and makeup, then kissed her quickly on the lips. "Nope. You look perfect."

"Thanks." Gemma combed a hand through her dark waves of hair, the streetlight shining through the windows and hitting the golden highlights that coursed through it.

"So we're still sneaking around, then?" Kirby asked, leaning back in the seat and watching her smooth out her skirt and straighten her top.

"We're almost done," she said. "Tomorrow I am officially ungrounded."

"That's kind of a bummer," Kirby said, and she shot him a look. "There's something kinda hot about sneaking around, worrying about getting caught."

Gemma laughed, and Kirby closed his eyes as if relishing the sound. She was careful that she never sang around him—she didn't want to put a spell on him. But her voice and even her laughter had an effect on him.

"Look at you, pretending to be a bad boy," she teased.

"Hey, I'm pretty tough."

He flexed his muscles, and she leaned over and kissed him. He put his arms around her, trying to pull her in for a longer kiss, but she broke away from him.

"Sorry, Kirby, but I really gotta go," Gemma said. "My dad's probably waiting up for me as it is."

"Lame." Kirby sighed, but he let her go. "I'll see you at rehearsal tomorrow?"

"Of course." Gemma opened the car door and slid out. "See ya."

She shut the door behind her and jogged down the block toward her house. When Kirby dropped her off, she always made him park around the corner so her dad couldn't peek out the front window and catch them making out.

As she went past Alex's house, she kept her eyes fixed on the sidewalk, refusing to look up at it. It didn't do any good to see if his car was in the driveway or if his bedroom light was on. He didn't want to see her anymore, and that was the way it had to be.

Her own house looked dark, which she took as a good sign. Brian had to work early in the morning, so hopefully he'd already gone to bed. When Gemma opened the front door, she tried to be as quiet as possible.

But as soon as she closed the front door, a table lamp clicked on, and Gemma nearly screamed.

"Oh, my gosh, Harper." Gemma put her hand to her chest and leaned back against the door. "What the heck was that?"

"I wanted to talk to you," Harper said.

She'd turned their dad's chair so it faced the doorway and sat in it with her arms crossed over her chest. Her long dark hair was up in a messy bun, and she wore her old ratty pink pajama pants, which really ruined her imposing look.

"You didn't need to hide out in the dark like a maniac." Gemma gestured to the lamp sitting on the table next to Harper. "You scared the crap out of me."

"Good."

"Good?" Gemma rolled her eyes and groaned. "Seriously? It's gonna be one of *those* talks?"

"What do you mean, '*those* talks'?" Harper asked.

"The kind where you lecture me on everything I'm doing wrong."

"I'm not lecturing you," Harper said defensively. "It's just . . ." She took a deep breath and tried to start over. "It's after ten o'clock at night, and play rehearsal was supposed to end two hours ago. You're lucky that Dad is trusting you again, but *I* know that rehearsal doesn't run that late."

"Because Daniel is narcing on me," Gemma muttered and stared down at the worn rug on the floor.

"Daniel is not 'narcing' on you." Harper bristled at the accusation. "I know because I drove past the theater, and nobody's cars were there. And based on the amount of eyeliner you're wearing and the ridiculously short length of your skirt—"

"It's not ridiculous," Gemma said, but she pulled down her skirt.

"—I can only assume that you're running around with some boy," Harper said. "Do you know how dangerous that is for you? Of course you do. The sirens kill boys—you've seen it."

Gemma stared at the floor. She still hadn't told her sister about how she'd killed a guy before. He'd been assaulting her at the time, and that had incited Gemma's transformation into the monster. But the real reason she'd killed him was because she had to. In order to survive as a siren, she had to feed.

Over the past four weeks, since Gemma had returned home and they'd struck a deal with Penn, Harper had come to suspect that murdering boys was how the sirens ate. She'd never asked Gemma directly if she'd killed anyone, so Gemma had never told her. But Harper must've known that if Gemma hadn't killed anyone already, she'd have to soon.

"It's not like that." Gemma sighed. "He's just a guy that I'm working with in the play, and we've been hanging out. It's no big deal."

"Some guy?" Harper raised an eyebrow.

"It's Kirby Logan," she said.

"He's nice." Harper seemed to relax a bit, probably remembering him from high school. "But that doesn't mean you should be hanging out with him. He's too old for you—"

"Seriously, Harper?" Gemma scoffed. "I'm a mythical monster, and your issue is a three-year age difference?"

"No, it's actually—" She stared up at Gemma. "There are a million reasons why you shouldn't be sneaking around with Kirby, and one of them is his age, another is that you just had a major breakup with Alex, but none of those really matter. The only one that counts is that you know you shouldn't."

"This is such bullshit." Gemma hit her head back against the door. "You and Dad are the ones that have been saying I need to get out of the house and do something and stop sulking. So I finally decide to do something. I joined the play last week, and I'm making friends, and now you're telling me it's wrong?"

"No, Gemma, that's not what I'm saying." Harper was doing her best to keep her voice low so it wouldn't wake their dad. "You were just sitting around the house in your pajamas. You weren't getting up until two or three in the afternoon. You weren't showering or eating. I wanted you to do *something*."

"And I am, but you have to cut me some slack," Gemma said. "I can't swim in meets anymore because I'm now supernaturally, freakishly fast, so it's not fair to everyone else. It's not even fair to me. I worked hard to be as good as I was, and now it doesn't matter what I do."

"Of course it matters what you do," Harper said quickly, her tone softened now.

"I meant with swimming," Gemma said. "I gave up swimming, I had to give up Alex, and I might have to give up you and Dad—"

"We'll find a way to fight this," Harper said for the millionth time that summer.

She'd cut her off, but Gemma was glad she didn't let her finish her thought. Gemma had been about to say that she might have to give up her life, but she hadn't really talked to Harper about it yet.

The sirens were running out of patience, and although they hadn't specifically told Gemma, she suspected that they were looking for a replacement for her. It was only a matter of time before they found one and then got rid of Gemma.

"I don't know who I am anymore," Gemma finally said, barely holding back the tears in her eyes. "I gave up everything I loved. So I need you to let me figure it out, okay?"

Harper let out a long breath. "Okay. But please be careful."

"I always am," Gemma lied and turned around to hurry up the stairs so she wouldn't have to talk anymore.

Once she was safely in her room, she put her hand over her mouth and let herself cry softly.

The past month, while Gemma had been sinking deeper into her depression, Harper thought it was mostly over Alex, and that was partially true. Giving up her dreams of being an Olympic swimmer, coming to terms with the fact that she was a murderer, and letting go of all the plans and hopes for her entire life was the rest of it.

Over and over again, Gemma had been asking herself, *What would you do if you only had a matter of weeks to live?* Because weeks sounded right to her. She didn't think the sirens would tolerate her or Capri for much longer than that.

The problem was that Gemma still hadn't been able to come up with an answer. What she really wanted to do—spend time with her parents, Harper, and Alex, on the beach, swimming all day and night—was impossible.

Now she had to come up with a second choice. So far the only thing she had was kissing Kirby and pretending like everything was going to be okay.

TWO

Obsession

The wind blowing off the bay helped cool his bare skin against the heat of the sun as he pulled into the harbor. Daniel eased *The Dirty Gull* into the dock. Once it was stopped, he hopped off the boat to tie it up.

He'd barely made it through the knot when he heard the splash of water behind him, and he sighed deeply. He didn't even have to look over his shoulder to see it was her. By now he could almost feel her watching him.

Daniel may not have fallen under the sirens' spell the way other guys did, but he wasn't completely oblivious to their charms. Penn had a presence about her, one that defied all sensibilities. The air seemed to change when she grew closer, with a new electricity churning through it.

As he'd been coming over to the mainland from Bernie's Island, he thought he'd seen Penn trailing him. He couldn't be certain of it, but almost every time he was out on the water, he thought he saw her shadow just below the surface of the water—the dark outline of her fish form as she swam alongside the boat.

Sometimes he could chalk it up to seeing things, but when Penn appeared on the dock like this, it only confirmed his suspicions. She was stalking him.

"Nice day for a swim?" Daniel asked.

He glanced back just long enough to ascertain that Penn wasn't wearing a bottom to go with her bikini top and quickly looked away.

"You're going to get arrested if you don't cover up," he told her as he stood up.

Penn snickered. "I doubt that. I've never been arrested for anything."

From the corner of his eye, he saw her pull out the tiny bottom. She'd had it rolled up in a little ball and carried it in her bikini top.

Daniel climbed back onto his boat. A T-shirt was lying out on the deck, and he pulled it on over his head. Penn clicked her tongue in disappointment, and he went belowdeck to grab his shoes and socks, the small door swinging shut behind him.

Since he'd moved onto Bernie's Island, his former living quarters were much more sparse, but that made it harder for him to find his shoes. In transit, they'd moved about, and now they actually had room to slide underneath the bed.

Once he grabbed them, he turned to hurry back onto the deck. He didn't trust Penn to wait outside without getting into something.

When he pushed open the small door leading back up to the top, he almost ran right into her. She stood at the top of the stairs, her long black hair dripping wet down her tanned skin, and her dark eyes sparkling at him.

"Aren't you going to offer me a towel?" Penn asked, her voice like velvet.

"Why are you on my boat?" Daniel asked. "I don't recall inviting you on."

"I'm not a vampire," Penn said with a subtle edge to her words. "I don't need an invitation."

"I don't have any towels on board anymore," Daniel said, answering her question.

He went up the stairs, and since she hadn't moved, he pushed past her. Her skin felt hot through his T-shirt, and as he brushed up against her, he heard her inhale deeply. That wasn't what creeped him out, though—it was the strange growling sound.

There was something inhuman about it, and it had a prehistoric quality to it. It was a small noise, one that Penn had seemed to make unconsciously, but it was enough to make his skin crawl.

"I still can't decide what I'm going to do with you," Penn admitted with a sigh. "One minute, I can't wait to devour you, and the next, I'd much rather sleep with you."

"Why do you want to do anything with me?" Daniel asked. He sat down on the seat at the edge of his boat and pulled on his shoes.

"I don't know," she said, and that seemed to upset her.

Daniel looked up at her, squinting in the bright sunlight, and she leaned back against the bench across from him. Her legs were stretched out long before her, and she tilted her head back, letting her hair hang over the edge of the boat.

"Are you familiar with Orpheus?" Penn asked.

"No." He'd finished putting on his shoes and leaned back. "Am I supposed to be?"

"He's a very popular figure in Greek history," Penn said. "He's renowned for musical ability and poetry."

"Sorry, I don't read that much poetry," Daniel replied.

"Neither do I." She shrugged. "I never read much of his, anyway. But when I was with him, he'd all but stopped writing and he'd given up his music and went by the name Bastian. The 'mythology' says that he died after the death of his wife, but the truth is that he only changed his name and gave up his old life."

"So he's like you, then?" Daniel asked. "Immortal or whatever?"

Penn nodded. "He is. But unlike sirens, who gained their immortality through a curse, he got his from being blessed. The gods were so pleased with him and his music that they granted him eternal life."

"Why are you asking me about this guy?" Daniel asked. "What does he have to do with me?"

"Nothing, probably." Penn crossed and uncrossed her legs. "We were very close for a while, Bastian and I. He was one of a handful of immortals who was immune to siren song. All the gods and goddesses were unaffected by it, but many of the other immortals—humans who gained eternal life from either a curse or blessing—still succumbed to it.

"But not Bastian." She stared off, something wistful flitting across her expression, but she quickly erased it. "Anyway. I thought maybe you were a relation of his."

"I'm fairly certain that nobody's immortal in my family tree." He stood up. "Listen, Penn, it's been great, but I really have to get to work. I have—"

Before he could finish his sentence, she was upon him. She pushed him down so hard, his back slammed painfully into the bar. Then she leapt on him, straddling him. She squeezed her thighs tightly against his sides so he couldn't move.

One of her hands was pressed against his chest, the razor-sharp fingernails poking through his shirt and digging into his flesh. The other was on his neck, but this one was almost caressing him, her touch soft and gentle.

With her face hovering right above his, her lips nearly touching his, her black eyes stared right into him. She leaned in closer, pressing her chest against his, so his shirt would be left damp.

"I could eat your heart right now," Penn told him in a provocative whisper, and she stroked his cheek gently, her fingers running along his stubble.

"You could," Daniel agreed, meeting her gaze evenly. "But you're not."

"I will, though." She studied him for a moment. "Eventually."

"But not today?" Daniel asked.

"No. Not today."

"Then I need to get to work." He put his hands on her waist, and when she didn't react with clawing or yelling, he lifted her up and set her on the seat next to him.

Penn pouted. "Work is so drab."

Daniel shrugged. "It pays the bills."

He'd moved away from Penn to the edge of the boat and was about to step off when he felt Penn's hand clamp onto his wrist. She moved supernaturally fast, and it was hard for him to get used to that.

"Don't go," Penn said, and it was the pleading in her words that made him pause. She knelt on the bench next to him with a strange desperation in her eyes. Hurriedly, she blinked any emotion away, trying to recover with an uneasy smile that was probably meant to be flirtatious.

"I have to," he insisted.

"I can pay you more," she said, her tone almost comically breezy.

For all her attempts at trying to seem nonchalant, her grip on his wrist had only tightened. It'd gotten rather painful, but Daniel refrained from pulling it free. He didn't want her to know that she was hurting him.

"What would you need me to do?" Daniel asked.

"I could think of something." She winked at him.

He rolled his eyes and finally yanked his arm free. "I've told them I'd build the sets for the play, and I'm a man of my word. They're expecting me."

"A fence," Penn said hastily as Daniel climbed off his boat. She stayed behind, leaning on the rail so she faced him. "You could build a fence around my house."

"What do you need a fence for?" he asked, waiting on the dock to see if she had any good reason for it.

"What does it matter to you why I need a fence? I just need one."

"I have my hands full already." He turned away from her.

"Ten grand!" Penn called after him as he walked away. "I'll pay you ten grand to build me a fence."

Daniel laughed and shook his head. "I'll see you around, Penn."

"We're not done yet, Daniel!" Penn shouted, but he just kept walking.

THREE

Alterations

"Stop that," Marcy said as Harper began emptying the overnight drop box at the library.

"What?" Harper turned back to face her with a stack of worn Harry Potter novels weighing down her arms.

"Working," Marcy replied tightly, and Harper rolled her eyes.

"Edie's been back for weeks. You have to be used to it by now," Harper said, but she let the door to the drop box slam shut, leaving a small pile of books behind.

Marcy was kneeling on her chair and leaning so far forward on the desk, she was practically lying on it. Her dark eyes stared out from behind her glasses with a manic intensity as she watched the front door of the library.

"I'll never get used to it," Marcy insisted.

"I don't even understand what the big deal is." Harper set the books down on the desk.

"*Move,*" Marcy hissed and waved her off, because Harper was apparently blocking her view of the front door.

"You know that's all glass, right?" Harper asked, motioning to the door that sat in the middle of the large windowed library front. "You can see through all of that. You don't need your eyes locked on the door like a laser beam."

"*Pfft*," Marcy scoffed.

Harper moved to the side anyway, since it was easier to get out of the way than try to use logic on Marcy. "She won't be here for another ten minutes, so I don't understand why you're so freaked out already."

"You don't get it," Marcy said, sounding gravely serious. "If I'm not busy the entire time she's here, if I even spend *five* minutes sitting behind this desk, Edie will immediately launch into some story about her honeymoon, and she won't stop talking about it."

"Maybe she's doing it on purpose," Harper said. "You've worked here for, what? Like, five years? And in all that time combined, you've maybe given two honest days of work—until Edie got back from her honeymoon. Now you're a busy little bee. Maybe she's finally found a way to motivate you."

Marcy shot her a look. "I need to watch for her, so the second she comes in I can haul ass and do anything that isn't being around her," she said. "I get that she had a really amazing time exploring the world or whatever, but . . . it's, like, I don't care. And I don't know how she doesn't get that."

"Feigning human emotion has never been your strong suit," Harper said and started scanning in the books.

"What are you doing?" Marcy asked.

"Checking these in, so you can run and put them away the second Edie gets in."

"Awesome." Marcy gave her a rare smile and looked over at her. "You kinda look like crap. Are you not sleeping again?"

"Thanks," Harper said sarcastically.

"No, I just meant, did something happen last night?" Marcy asked.

"Nothing more than usual." Harper let out a deep breath to blow her dark hair out of her face. She stopped scanning the books and turned to Marcy. "Gemma's seeing some guy."

"Some guy?" Marcy raised an eyebrow. "I thought she was still in love with Alex or whatever."

Harper shrugged. "I don't know. I mean, she probably still loves him. That's why I don't know why she's sneaking around with someone else. It just seems ridiculous."

"Isn't she still grounded?" Marcy asked.

"Today's her first official day being ungrounded," Harper said. "She's been hooking up with this guy she met at play rehearsal, and then she stays out all night with him doing . . . I don't even know what. So I was waiting up for her last night."

"Well, if she's grounded, why didn't you just tell your dad about it?" Marcy asked. "He'd ground her again and make her quit play rehearsal."

"I don't want her to quit the play. She needs to be doing *something.*" She rubbed her temple.

In fact, Harper preferred that Gemma stay in the play. Daniel had taken the job at the play partially because he needed the work, but it also meant that he could keep an eye on her. So every night, for a few hours, Harper knew that Gemma was safe. She just wished that Gemma would start making better choices where boys were concerned.

"I get that she's going through this totally insane thing, but I don't know how bringing another person into the mix will make it any better," Harper said. "She broke up with Alex because she knows how dangerous it is for sirens to be around boys, and now she's dragging in another boy."

"I thought the only reason the sirens cared about Alex was because he was in love with her," Marcy said. "They probably won't give a crap about some random boy, unless he falls in love with Gemma, too."

"I don't know." Harper's shoulders slumped. "I don't even know what the sirens want anymore. They've been here for *weeks*, and nobody's figured out anything. We still have no clue how to break the curse. They don't know how Alex is able to love Gemma, or why Daniel is immune.

"I'm supposed to be leaving for college in two weeks, and I have no idea what the hell is happening or how to help Gemma, and I just want to scream or rip my hair out." Harper groaned in frustration.

With working full-time, getting ready for a college she wasn't even sure she was going to anymore, worrying about her sister, trying to find a way to battle evil mermaids, all while making time for a new relationship, Harper was nearing her breaking point.

Marcy snapped her fingers suddenly, causing Harper to jump in surprise.

"Duh!" Marcy announced. "You should talk to Lydia."

"What?" Harper asked.

"I've been meaning to tell you," Marcy said. "But I keep forgetting. This whole Edie thing has my mind all messed up."

"You really need to get over the Edie thing, Marce," Harper said. "She's your boss, and she's going to be around for a long time."

Marcy sneered at the thought of dealing with a supervisor again, and then she continued on with her story. "So I was on Facebook the other night—"

"Wait. You're on Facebook?" Harper interrupted. "Since when? I thought Facebook was the antithesis of everything you stood for."

"No, I said getting on Facebook and posting pictures of my cat with hilariously misspelled phrases in all caps was the antithesis of everything I stood for," Marcy corrected her. "And sometimes I use Facebook. I like playing the games where I water plants all the time, and I talk to old friends."

"There really is just so much I don't know about you," Harper said.

"Yeah, there is," Marcy agreed. "But the point is, I was talking to this old friend of mine. I'd completely lost touch with her, but it turns out she owns a bookstore up in Sundham. She'd definitely have some books that might help you out with the sirens. Plus, she's pretty knowledgeable on all that kind of stuff."

"Like what kind of stuff?" Harper asked tentatively.

Marcy shrugged. "Hunting vampires, slaying demons, raising the dead. That kind of thing."

"She can raise the dead?" Harper was too weary to hide her skepticism.

"No, *she* can't," Marcy said defensively and swiveled in the chair a bit. "But she knows a lot about it, if that was something you were into."

Harper went back to scanning the books and tried to think of a tactful way to let Marcy down. Whenever Marcy did even the slightest thing for somebody other than herself, Harper tried to reward it.

"Look, Marcy, I appreciate what you're trying to do. It's really very considerate. But—"

"But what? You have a better lead to follow?" Marcy asked

pointedly. "Or any other leads or ideas? Any clues at all?" Harper pursed her lips but didn't say anything. "Exactly. My idea may be a little out there, but it's better than no idea."

"You're right," Harper relented and offered Marcy a grateful smile. "Are you busy this weekend? If the bookstore's open, maybe we could go then."

"Yeah." Marcy nodded. "You should get used to making the trek up to Sundham anyway, since you're going to college there pretty soon."

"*If* I go to college," Harper reminded her.

"Oh, crap, here she comes," Marcy said.

She jumped off the chair, grabbed the stack of books that Harper had checked in, then dashed from the desk to put them away. All this happened within the few seconds it took for Edie to open the front door and come inside.

"Hello, girls," Edie said brightly as she strode inside.

Edie was the kind of woman who somehow managed to be beautiful and dowdy at the same time. She was tall and thin, with blond hair, high cheekbones, and full lips, and considering she was over forty, she'd aged astonishingly well.

But she hid under long flowing skirts, overly drapey tops, and layers of beaded jewelry. Her eyes were a lovely blue, but they were barely visible behind her thick calico glasses.

"Hey, Edie," Marcy said. Since Marcy was so short, the stack of Harry Potter books went up to her chin, and she was nearly tipping over as she turned back to continue speaking to Edie. "Love to chat. Gotta run. Books to put away and all that."

"And how are you doing this lovely morning?" Edie asked Harper as she walked behind the desk. She dropped her oversized purse on the desk, and it jingled loudly.

"Fine," Harper lied and wouldn't meet her eyes.

"Are you feeling okay?" Edie asked, concern filling her voice, and almost absently she touched Harper's face. "Your skin is cool, so at least you don't have a fever."

"I just haven't been sleeping that well," Harper said and stepped away from Edie.

She didn't have a reason to move, except that she didn't want to be that near Edie's scrutinizing gaze, so Harper turned away to straighten some forms sitting on the desk.

"Troubles at home?" Edie asked.

"Nope, just good old-fashioned insomnia."

"You know what will fix that right up?" Edie asked. "Tea. I know it sounds cliché, but it really works! I'd never been much for it, but when we went to England, they had it with every meal. Now Gary drinks it every night. He can't sleep without it."

"I'll keep that in mind," Harper said.

"You really should." Edie leaned back against the desk and crossed her arms loosely in front of her. "There are just so many different things you can learn from other cultures. Gary and I came back from our honeymoon so much healthier and wiser than we were before." Edie launched into a lengthy list of new facts she had picked up on her travels.

Marcy peered out from behind a bookcase at Harper, as if to say, *I told you so*. But Harper already knew she was right. She just couldn't fault Edie for her somewhat incessant prattling. She'd found such intense happiness, and she wanted to hang on to it for as long as possible. Harper couldn't blame her for that.

"That is true," Harper said when Edie paused to take a breath, trying to cut off her train of thought. She turned to face her and smiled as brightly as she could. "Hey, Edie, my dad forgot his lunch again, and I was wondering if I could leave a bit early for my break so I could bring it down to him."

"Of course you can," Edie said. "But I have no idea what he'll do when you go away to college. Then again, I have no idea what *we'll* do, either."

Harper didn't say anything to that. She hurried into the office to get her dad's sack lunch out of the minifridge before Edie could regale her with more tales of her magical time spent abroad.

When Harper went outside to get into her car, she glanced across the street at Pearl's Diner. Since the sirens had moved back to town in July, she'd gotten used to spotting Penn, Lexi, and Thea hanging out in the booth by the window, drinking milkshakes. Penn had this awful way of staring at passersby the way a lion stares at a gazelle.

Today the booth was empty, and there was some relief in that. Even though they had come to some type of understanding, Harper didn't like talking to the sirens or seeing them in any capacity. They were evil, and they made her skin crawl.

Unfortunately, her relief was short-lived. As she walked closer to her car, she saw the long, bare legs draped over her hood, and Harper slowed her steps. She briefly considered going back to the library, but she refused to run from the sirens anymore.

Lexi sat back on the hood of Harper's Sable. Her head was tilted back, so her long golden hair cascaded down onto the windshield. The short skirt had ridden up high on her thighs, and the hot metal of the car should've burned her skin, but Lexi didn't seem to notice.

"Can I help you with something?" Harper asked as she walked around the front of the car to the driver's-side door.

"Nope," Lexi said with her usual melodic lilt. "Just getting some sun."

Harper unlocked the door and opened it. "And you just happened to decide to tan on top of my car?"

"Yep."

"I'm leaving now, so you might want to move," Harper told her and got inside.

Lexi made no attempt to move, though, not even after Harper started the car. If it weren't for the people walking by or watching from shop windows, Harper would've sped off with Lexi on the hood of the car. If she hurt Lexi, that would just be icing on the cake.

But people were watching, and she'd be liable to get arrested if she deliberately threw Lexi off her car and then ran her over. So instead, she revved the engine and rolled down the window.

"Lexi, come on," Harper said, trying to sound as forceful as she could. "Get off the car. I've gotta go."

"Don't get your panties in a bunch," Lexi said. "All you had to do was ask."

She sat up straighter, then turned back to look at Harper through the windshield. Lexi lifted up her sunglasses, revealing that her normally aquamarine eyes had shifted into the odd yellow-green of an eagle. Her lips peeled back in their usual seductive smile, but her straight teeth had been replaced by jagged fangs.

Harper swallowed hard, then honked the horn loudly in response. Lexi laughed—a light, lyrical sound—and her features shifted back to their normal stunning state. As Lexi slid off the hood, she was still laughing, and Harper sped off as fast as she could.

While there had been an uneasy truce with the sirens over the past few weeks, they hadn't exactly been leaving Harper or Gemma or even Daniel alone. Lexi especially had a habit of popping up and reminding them of exactly what kind of monster she was.

It was as if the sirens wanted to remind them not to get too comfortable, and that at any moment they could snap and kill anyone they wanted.

As she drove down to the docks, Harper tried to shake off her encounter with Lexi. By now she should be used to it, but those razor-sharp fangs chilled her every time she saw them.

When she reached the docks, she parked her car as close as she could get and took a deep breath, stifling what was left of her chill. On her way, she walked past the space where Daniel used to keep his boat.

He didn't dock there anymore because he didn't live on his boat. Daniel had been staying out at Bernie's Island, and he kept *The Dirty Gull* at the boathouse. He used it to get back and forth across the bay, but he docked it somewhere else for a cheaper hourly fee.

When she went down to the docks where her father worked loading and unloading barges, she usually went to the foreman's office, and he would summon her dad. This time, before she had a chance to even reach for the door, Alex opened it and stepped outside of the office.

"Oh, hey, hi!" Harper said, trying much too hard to sound cheerful.

"Hey." Alex wouldn't even look at her.

He'd started working at the docks a few weeks ago, and Brian had told Harper about it, but she had yet to actually see Alex here. In fact, she'd hardly seen him at all since he'd broken up with Gemma, and she was a little surprised by how he looked now.

Working at the docks doing hard labor had made a visible difference. He wore gray coveralls with the sleeves rolled up above his elbows, and the fabric strained against his biceps. His shoulders appeared broader than before. In the last few months Alex had looked more toned and muscular, but now he was downright buff.

His heavy work gloves stuck out of the back pocket of his coveralls, and his hands looked cracked and rough. Before, the only calluses he'd earned would come from playing video games, but in a short amount of time his hands had already come to resemble Brian's.

Alex averted his eyes, staring off at a barge behind them. His brown hair was longer, almost shaggy, and his mahogany eyes were stormy. Harper wasn't sure if it was from working out in the sun all day, but his face appeared harder. Something had changed in him.

"So how is . . . um, how are things?" Harper fumbled. "Do you like working here? My dad says that you're doing good."

"It's fine." He stared down at his steel-toe boots and didn't elaborate.

"Good, good." Harper held up Brian's lunch. "I was bringing my dad his lunch."

"I ate lunch already."

"Yeah?" Harper asked. "Cool. Cool." She glanced around, hoping to see her dad or anyone who could breathe life into this conversation. "How long have you been working here?"

"Three weeks."

"Yeah? Good. Yeah. It's a good way to save money for college."

"I'm not going to college," Alex replied matter-of-factly.

"What?" Harper leaned in, hoping she'd heard him wrong

over the noises of the dock. "You're going to Sundham University. Aren't you?"

"Nope."

Harper was confused by his sudden change of heart. For years now, Alex and Harper had been planning to go to the same college. They were going into different fields, but if they were moving to a new town, they thought it'd be nice if they knew someone. Plus, Sundham was close to home for both of them.

"What about all your plans?" Harper asked. "What about the meteorology and astronomy stuff?"

"I'm just not that into it anymore." His mouth twitched as he watched the barge slowly pulling into the bay. "I'm working here now."

"Yeah." She smiled, trying to appear accepting, but really she was worried about him. "So, did Dad tell you that Gemma's in a play now?"

"I don't care about Gemma or what's she doing," Alex snapped, with an undercurrent of hatred so raw that Harper flinched.

"Oh. Sorry."

"Look, I should really get back to work." He glanced over at her, looking at her for the first time, and then instantly looked away. "It was nice seeing you."

"Yeah, you, too. And if you ever wanna hang out . . ." Harper said, but he was already walking away. "I'm right next door. You can call me anytime!" He never even looked back at her.

FOUR

Paramount

After their conversation on Tuesday night, Gemma had been avoiding Harper. It had been a day and a half, so Gemma knew she'd have to start speaking to Harper again soon, but she wanted just one more lecture-free morning.

Gemma purposely slept in late, waiting to venture out of her room until after Harper had left for work. Then she got up, did a few chores around the house, and planned to get ready so she could leave for play rehearsal before Harper got home from work.

Of course, she did manage to squeeze in a half hour of *Judge Judy*, which was her latest vice. While spending the past month moping around the house, Gemma had gotten addicted to daytime television. While she'd mostly kicked her habit, *Judge Judy* was the one show that remained.

After it ended, she took a shower and got dressed for the day, but she'd left the TV on. When she came downstairs, pulling her hair up in a loose ponytail, she saw that the regularly scheduled programming had been interrupted by a news bulletin, and her heart dropped.

She'd been coming down the stairs, taking them two at a time, but she slowed as she walked into the living room.

The handsome young heir to a multimillion-dollar fortune had gone missing without a trace, and every media outlet seemed to be covering it incessantly.

"Here's the top story of today, Thursday, August fifth. Authorities have found what they believe may be Sawyer Thomas's yacht off the coast of one of the Bahama Islands," the news reporter was saying. "Again, this hasn't been confirmed yet, but the footage you are seeing is live. The diving team is searching the yacht, but so far there is no word as to whether there are any bodies on board, but there doesn't appear to be anyone alive."

The screen showed a beautiful beach, white sand with clear blue water. A large boat had capsized just offshore. Helicopters were swarming overhead and several smaller boats were surrounding it as divers in black suits descended.

The crawl along the bottom was rehashing all the information about the case. *Sawyer Thomas, 25, has been missing since the 4th of July. The Thomas family is offering a $2 million reward for any information leading to his whereabouts.*

As the divers continued searching the wreckage, a picture of Sawyer popped up in a box in the corner. It appeared to be fairly recent. He was smiling widely, the top few buttons of his white shirt were undone, and his blue eyes were dazzling, even in a picture.

That was when Gemma turned off the television. His face haunted her nightmares enough that she didn't need to be reminded of it while she was awake.

Gemma hadn't killed Sawyer—not with her own hands—but she felt responsible for his death just the same. He'd been kind to her, so she'd been trying to help him escape the sirens. But she shouldn't have intervened. If she'd just left him alone, maybe he would still be alive.

Of course, Lexi was completely psychotic and had ripped out Sawyer's heart without any real provocation, so there was a good chance that she would've killed him eventually. That didn't change the fact that Gemma hadn't saved him or taken him with her when she ran away. She knew he was in danger, and she didn't do enough to help him.

Gemma wished the manhunt for Sawyer would hurry and turn up something, not only so she wouldn't have to keep seeing his face everywhere, but so his family would have some closure.

She'd considered calling the tip line, but what could she tell them? That she'd seen a monster rip out his heart underneath the fireworks? She didn't even know what had become of his body.

After Lexi had killed him, she'd kicked him into the bay. But since he hadn't turned up on the beach or in a fisherman's net, Gemma assumed they'd done something with him. Maybe they'd dragged him farther out to sea, maybe they fed him to sharks, maybe Lexi ate him. Gemma didn't know, and honestly, she didn't want to know.

The capsized yacht had probably been the work of the sirens, maybe to cover up the murder, or maybe it had just been an accident when they took the boat on a joyride. Lexi had been gone for a few days last week.

Gemma swallowed back the lump in her throat and pushed Sawyer from her mind. If she wanted to get out of here before Harper got home, she had to hurry, which meant that she didn't have time to cry about Sawyer. Besides, she'd already cried over him plenty of times this summer, and it had done nothing to help him or herself.

The Paramount Theater was in the center of town, only a few blocks away from the Capri Public Library and Pearl's Diner. It was a bit of a distance to walk, so she'd left early enough so that she'd have plenty of time to get there. Her car still wasn't working, but Kirby would give her a ride after practice.

It was an old theater, built in the early 1900s. It'd been popular when it had first been built, but over time people had gradually lost interest. The Paramount closed and became run-down. Then about twenty years ago the town had started a revitalization project and began to fix it up.

Gemma's mother had actually been part of the crew that restored the theater. Nathalie didn't know anything really about building repair, and from what Gemma understood, Nathalie's help had been limited to painting, cleaning, and fund-raising. But she'd worked very hard, and eventually the Paramount was returned to its former glory.

The marquee out front would light up at night. Right now it simply proclaimed THE TAMING OF THE SHREW, AUGUST 27 in all capital letters. Opening night was just over three weeks away, and then they'd do four shows over the course of one weekend. It wasn't Broadway, but it was something.

A poster on the front of the building was done in an old playbill style. They'd put all the actors' names on it. Thea was listed right below Aiden Crawford. They should technically share the top billing, since they played the leads Katherine and Petruchio, respectively, but Aiden had the bonus of being the eldest son of Mayor Crawford, the most prominent man in Capri.

Thea had joined the play first, and Gemma had followed at her suggestion. Thea'd apparently always loved the theater, but Gemma had mostly auditioned to keep close to Thea. Not only so she could find a way to reverse the curse, but to keep an eye on the sirens. Besides, it was good for Gemma to do something to keep herself busy.

Gemma walked past the ticket booth and the main doors, and she went around the side of the building to the door that led to the backstage area. Since she'd left so early, she was one of the first ones there, but that usually seemed to be the case.

Tom Wagner, the director, was already there, and so was Daniel, but he'd probably already been there for hours. Daniel had been tasked with re-creating the Italian Renaissance. Gemma knew that he had his work cut out for him, and she'd seen him laboring backstage on the beginnings of elaborate sets since she'd been cast in the play a week ago.

When she came in, Tom was sitting on the stage, his legs dangling over the edge, with a script lying next to him. His dark hair was slightly disheveled, and the top several buttons of his shirt were undone. In an abstract way, Gemma was aware that he was attractive, and his soft British accent definitely helped support that idea.

"Bianca." Tom smiled widely when he saw Gemma. He insisted on calling everyone by their character's name, but that was fine by Gemma. "You're so prompt. I wonder if your costars will catch on to that."

"I don't think punctuality is contagious," Gemma said.

He laughed. "No, I don't suppose it is."

She hopped up on the stage next to him—carefully, since she was wearing a skirt and didn't want to reveal too much. Out before her were rows and rows of velvet seats. The walls had been made to appear as old brick, like the walls of a castle. The ceiling above them had been painted a dark blue like the early night sky, complete with small lights poking through for starlight.

"Are you having any problems with your lines?" Tom asked.

"None so far," Gemma said. "But I haven't memorized them all yet."

"For shame," he told her with a smirk. "By now I would've thought you'd memorized all the words in the play, not just yours."

A clunking sound came from behind them, and Gemma looked back over her shoulder to see Daniel picking up a tool off the stage. She waved at him, but he only nodded and smiled, his hands full of tools and wood.

Within a few minutes the rest of the actors, along with the assistant director, began filtering in. Kirby was the next to arrive. He smiled at her, but he was careful to keep his distance.

Gemma told him that she didn't think they should display any kind of public affection because she didn't want the other actors to talk or Tom to get angry with them for not focusing enough. That was part of it, but it wasn't the whole truth.

After what had happened with Sawyer, she didn't want the sirens to know about any boys she was dating. She trusted Thea, but if Lexi found out about Kirby, she'd probably do something to him just to mess with her.

Gemma didn't think she'd hurt him, not since Lexi, Penn, and Thea had all promised not to hurt anyone in Capri. But she knew that Lexi loved to play games, and Kirby didn't need to deal with that.

Thea arrived a few minutes late, but the very last person to arrive was Aiden Crawford. He played the role of Petruchio, the boisterous gentleman intent on taming the shrew, Katherine, for his wife. He was a good match for the character, since he was confident bordering on cocky. He was foxy enough that most people seemed to overlook his arrogance.

Once everyone arrived, Tom got rehearsal under way. Gemma rehearsed a few scenes with Kirby, who played Lucentio, Bianca's most valiant suitor. But when they got to a scene that was apparently a bit too complicated for Aiden to follow, Tom excused Gemma and Thea from the stage so he could focus on helping Aiden.

They sat in the middle of the theater, on the plush red velvet seats. Theoretically, they were supposed to be running lines together, but they were really just watching the boys scramble onstage as Aiden, Kirby, and another actor continued to botch their lines.

"This is the third time I've done *The Taming of the Shrew*," Thea said. "But I'm usually Bianca. Penn was Katherine once, but she didn't enjoy it that much. She prefers situations where she's revered, not tamed."

"That makes sense," Gemma said. "Have you been in a lot of plays, then?"

"Hundreds. Probably thousands." She leaned back farther in her seat. "I'm showing my age now, but television and radio, these are such new concepts. In the several millennia before that, the only way we had to entertain ourselves was with plays and stories.

"I've done opera before, but that's a bit tricky." Thea motioned to her throat. "The whole siren-song thing can turn an audience into a frenzied, obsessed mob."

"That doesn't sound all that pleasant."

"No, it's really not," Thea said. "I'm just glad they're not doing a musical. I so needed something to get me out of the house, but I won't sing in front of crowds anymore."

Tom appeared agitated by something Kirby had said and yelled at him. Not berating him, exactly, but it seemed a bit more harsh than Gemma would've thought the situation required.

"He's really taking this seriously," Thea said as they watched Tom give very forceful stage direction. "That's weird for such a small-town production."

"This is kind of a big deal," Gemma said. "He's, like, a real director. Not Broadway, but he's done some bigger productions. He's not from here."

"I suppose the British accent gave that part away," Thea said. "But how is this a big deal? Is this town super into Shakespeare or something?"

"This play is part of Capri's big At Summer's End Festival," Gemma explained. "The activities kick off on August twenty-seventh and go all week until Labor Day. There's a carnival, a parade, a cook-off, and a Miss Capri contest."

"Weird." Thea wrinkled her nose. "You seem to have an awful lot of festivals here."

"It's because it's summer and we're a tourist town. We have to milk it for all it's worth, and then when the tourists go home, the town closes up. The festivals stop."

"You cannot tell Lexi that," Thea said. "She would freak out."

Gemma chewed her lip, and then turned to Thea. "How much longer do you think you're going to stay here?"

"It's hard to say." Thea lowered her eyes.

"You're getting restless, all of you are," Gemma said. She paused, but Thea didn't bother to contradict her. "You haven't found out anything supernatural or helpful about Alex or Daniel. Have you?"

"I never really thought that Alex loving you was all that supernatural," Thea said, and just saying it like that opened the still-fresh wound in Gemma's heart. She tried to keep her expression neutral as Thea went on. "My theory is that Alex had already fallen in love with you before you became a siren. That's how he got around the curse."

"Did you tell Penn that?" Gemma asked.

"No," Thea said. "I thought the curse needed some reevaluating, that maybe we'd been denying things that were true. I just wanted to talk Penn into staying here so we could figure things out."

"And what have you found?" Gemma asked, but she thought she already knew the answer. If they'd had any major breakthroughs, any life-changing pieces of information, Thea wouldn't be sitting in the theater preparing for a play.

"Nothing." Thea's husky voice sounded soft and sad. "I don't know where else to look. And Penn's lost interest." She stopped, correcting herself. "Well, she's lost interest in Alex, anyway."

That was a relief, but that was what Gemma had suspected. She hadn't spoken to Alex since they'd broken up, but she'd found out from Thea that the sirens had had a few conversations with him. None of them had sounded too terrible, mostly because Penn found Alex simple and boring.

Penn had her sights set on somebody else entirely, and Gemma turned her attention to him. Back past where Tom was instructing Aiden and Kirby, working quietly so as not to disturb them, Daniel was crouched down, with the blueprints for the sets spread out on the stage.

The sleeves of his flannel shirt were rolled up far enough that the black tendrils of his tattoo reached out from beneath one. He ran a hand through his dirty blond hair absently. His jaw was set firmly in thought, the dark line of his stubble like a shadow across his face.

While Penn's interest in Daniel was growing more apparent, neither Gemma nor Daniel had really told Harper about it. She was aware that the sirens were trying to figure out the source of his immunity, but that was all. Gemma thought it would be better if Harper had one less thing to worry about.

"Maybe . . ." Thea sighed and tossed her long red hair back over her shoulder. "You need to try harder, Gemma."

"What?" Gemma turned to face her.

"Penn and Lexi won't stay here forever." Thea's green eyes were serious. "And I would like it if you left with us. So you need to try harder to get along with them."

"Thanks, but . . ." Gemma shook her head. "I don't want to go with you."

"I know you want to break the curse, and if you find a way, good for you," Thea said. "I mean that honestly. If you can find a way out of this that doesn't involve my death, then more power to you. But if you can't, then you should find a way to make this work."

"Thea, I can't." Gemma swallowed hard. "I can't be a siren."

"You already *are*," Thea told her emphatically. "And if it comes down to being a siren or being dead, you should pick the siren. It's not as bad as it seems."

"If it comes down to it, I'll think about it," Gemma said finally, but she wasn't sure if she would. "But you really don't know a way to break the curse?"

"Not one that doesn't end up with us all dead, yourself included." Thea shook her head. "And I can assure you that being a siren is better than that."

"I'll try and get along with Penn and Lexi more," Gemma allowed. "But if you know anything about breaking the curse, will you tell me?"

"Assuming it doesn't kill me or my sisters, yeah, I will." Thea turned back to the stage, and her tone sounded brighter than it had a few moments ago. "We're not leaving just yet, anyway. I know I'm definitely finishing this play."

"You really like acting?" Gemma asked, glad to be off the subject.

Thea laughed. "This whole curse started because we were so obsessed with performing for an audience that we weren't doing our jobs. I don't like it—I *love* it."

"Kate?" Tom was saying from the stage. "Kate? *Katherine?*"

"Oh, right, that's me," Thea said.

"Would you care to join us onstage, please?" Tom asked.

She was on her feet in an instant. "Yes. I'm coming." As she slid past Gemma out toward the aisle, she said, "Told you I was used to being Bianca."

Thea went up onto the stage, apologizing for not coming sooner, and Gemma realized that Thea really did care about this part. The only time Thea had appeared even remotely happy since Gemma had met her was when she was onstage, and there was something captivating about her. Even though she was just running lines with Aiden, who usually missed his cue and fumbled his words, it was hard for Gemma to take her eyes off Thea.

In fact, she was so entranced by Thea's performance that she didn't notice that Penn had sat down in the row behind her. Not until Penn leaned forward on the back of the seat next to her and spoke.

"What is Daniel doing hiding way in the back while Thea hogs the stage?" Penn asked, and Gemma jumped. Penn laughed, loudly enough to cause everyone to look back at her. "Did I frighten you?"

"You know it takes more than the sound of your voice to frighten me," Gemma said, giving her a thin smile.

"You say that, but we both know the truth, don't we?" Penn asked and winked at her. "And you didn't answer my question."

"Daniel's building the sets." Gemma sat back in the seat. She'd been leaning forward as she watched Thea's performance, but she knew Penn wouldn't let Gemma be interested in anything other than her.

"That's dumb." Penn looked genuinely disgusted by this fact and watched him as he walked across the stage, disappearing behind the curtains as he exited stage right. "He should be starring in it. He's way better-looking than that loser up there."

She pointed to Aiden, who Gemma had already realized wasn't the best actor in the world, but he was definitely hot. He had sandy blond hair, blue eyes, and a bright smile. But apparently Daniel's unshaven look and hazel eyes appealed to Penn more.

Gemma knew that wasn't exactly the case—it wasn't so much about the way Daniel looked. He may have been attractive in his own right, but Penn's interest stemmed from the fact that he was immune to her siren song. So he talked back to her, he challenged her, he formed his own opinions.

And after spending centuries being unable to have a real conversation with a guy, it was no wonder that Penn found Daniel incredibly fascinating.

"I don't think it matters to Daniel whether he's good-looking or not," Gemma said. "He doesn't like acting. He wanted to work on the sets."

Penn scoffed. "That's ridiculous. I thought he was acting in this thing. I didn't know he was just building the damn sets. I'm starting to think he's an idiot."

"Because he's good at carpentry?" Gemma asked.

"No, yesterday I offered him ten thousand dollars to build a fence around my house, but he turned me down because he was working on this play," Penn said. "If he was acting, that makes sense. But I can't imagine they're paying him anything close to that."

"Where did you get ten thousand dollars?" Gemma asked, glancing over her shoulder. "You don't work." Penn shrugged and didn't answer her. "And that's not even your house. That's somebody else's house you conned them out of."

"I live there now, so it's mine," Penn said simply.

"I don't even know why you want to spend time with Daniel." Gemma turned around and crossed her arms over her chest. "He's not that great."

"I don't want to spend time with him. I'm just trying to find out what's going on with him. That's all."

"This whole siren thing has turned you into a terrible liar," Gemma said. "You fall back on that song and your voice, so you don't even try to be convincing anymore."

Penn turned to face her, glaring at her with dark eyes. "Gemma. Shut up. You're annoying." She paused before leaning forward and whispering in her ear, "I'm already looking for your replacement. It's only a matter of time before you're dead."

Her heart pounded dully in her chest as Penn confirmed Gemma's worst suspicions. A few moments ago she'd told Thea she would try to get along with Penn, but she'd already known it was futile. No amount of ass-kissing would change the fact that Penn wanted her dead and gone.

"Why are you even here?" Gemma asked, ignoring Penn's threat.

"I'm here to pick up Thea. I dropped her off for practice, and I'm supposed to take her home."

"Practice doesn't end for another half hour, and that's assuming it doesn't run late."

Penn let out a long, irritated groan. "Whatever. I'm going to wait outside for Thea." She stood up. "Because you're horrible, and I kinda hate you."

"I know. The feeling's mutual."

Once Penn was gone, Gemma sank in the seat and rubbed her forehead. Mouthing off to Penn wasn't the smartest thing to do, but it was hard to stop. Besides that, Penn would probably kill her either way, and at least right now Penn seemed too preoccupied to care that much.

That should've been a good thing, except that Gemma knew what was distracting her. Penn had her eyes set on Harper's boyfriend.

FIVE

Distractions

Penn sat in the cherry-red '67 Cadillac convertible across the street from the Paramount Theater, waiting for her sister. She'd left the top down hoping for a breeze, but it didn't do much to battle the heat. The sun was starting to go down, and it was cooling off very slowly.

It wouldn't be so bad if she could at least figure out how to use her iPhone. There was supposed to be some game with violent birds that was addicting, but she had enough trouble turning the damn thing on, let alone flicking poultry at pigs.

She could master the language, the slang, the fashion, even the ever-changing roles of women in society. But technology continued to baffle her. Driving a car and changing the channel were about the best she could do.

Part of that was because it all changed so quickly. It wasn't that long ago that computers were the size of rooms, and now one fit in the palm of her hand. In her lifetime, it felt like a blink of an eye.

The rest of it was simply that she didn't care to learn. Since the moment she'd become a siren who could enchant people to do her bidding, she'd surrounded herself with servants. As a mortal, she'd been a servant herself, working as a handmaiden for the spoiled goddess Persephone, and she'd spent that entire time vowing she'd never do anything like that again.

So for most of her life she'd had others doing all the things for her that she didn't want to do. In the old days, that meant literally having people to dress her and wash her hair, but then it had just become the cleaning and getting the door. In her mind, it was still the servant's job to answer the phone.

Now everything was so convenient it didn't make sense to have someone draw her a bath, not when she could simply turn the handle on the faucet. It was quicker and easier for her to do it herself.

Except when it came to damn phones and computers and anything of that kind. The term "tablet" only confused and irritated her more. Mankind had worked for so long to get away from writing on cumbersome tablets, only to come back to them when pen and paper were still readily available.

Fortunately, Lexi was much more technologically inclined. That was the best part of having her around. She seemed like a moron, and most of the time she was, but she could also rewire the house if she needed to.

She'd been the one who had bought Penn the iPhone. Though "procured" might be a better word, since none of the sirens had actually *earned* money a day in their supernatural lives. They charmed, they conned, they took what they wanted.

So far, Penn had concluded it would be more fun to throw the phone at the wall than spend another second trying to find this ridiculous bird game. She was just about to do that when she heard laughter from across the street and peered over her sunglasses to see people exiting the theater.

Gemma walked out with some boy from the play. He was cute enough in an ordinary way, but Gemma probably thought he was dreamy, and that made Penn want to gag.

The only person in the whole entire thing that Penn would even think about sleeping with would be the director, but she'd always had a thing for men in positions of power, even the smallest amount.

The director came out last, talking to Thea for a few seconds before they parted. Thea started walking across the road.

Penn had been watching the director, momentarily distracted by the dimple he had on one cheek when he smiled, and she quickly looked around. Everyone had left by then, even Gemma, but Penn didn't particularly know where Gemma went. She'd probably just gone back to her dirty little house with her dull sister.

Just when she'd resigned herself to having missed him, she saw Daniel come out of the back door of the theater.

"Looking for someone?" Thea asked as she climbed in the car.

"No," Penn lied. "What were you guys doing in there? Rehearsal took forever."

"We ended on time," Thea said. "I told you that it went until eight."

"Like I remember everything you say." Penn tossed her cell phone in the backseat and started the car.

Daniel glanced both ways before crossing the street, a few cars down from where Penn had parked. As he walked nearer to the car, Penn called out, "Hey, Daniel."

"Penn." He smiled thinly at her and seemed genuinely surprised to see her. He'd been walking by, but he stopped and stepped closer to the car. "Nice ride."

"Thanks." She pushed her sunglasses up so he could get the full effect of her dark eyes. "Want a lift?"

"I don't think there's much room," he said, referring to the tiny backseat.

He put both of his hands on the door and leaned down, but he kept his distance. The top buttons of his shirt were undone, so she could see the scant hair on his chest, and something about that enticed her more than any amount of bare flesh had before.

"You can always sit on my lap," Penn offered.

"I think you're going for sexy with that, but that doesn't seem like it'd be sexy or safe driving," Daniel said. "So I'm gonna have to pass."

"I could sit on your lap," Penn said, trying her most seductive smile.

He lowered his head, looking away from her, and laughed darkly. For a second she was thinking he might actually say yes, that he'd finally take her up on one of her offers, but when he looked up, she saw the denial in his eyes.

"I'd rather walk," he said simply and stood up.

"I'll see you around, then," Penn said as he stepped back from her car.

"Oh, I know you will." Daniel turned around.

"You could at least be less obvious when you stalk Daniel," Thea said as Penn watched him walking away, and then Penn glared at her.

"I'm not stalking anybody, so shut up," Penn said, then threw the car in gear.

Penn drove through Capri, barely acknowledging street signs or stoplights. She lived by the theory that people would move for her, and they often did. Sometimes she'd get a honk or someone shouting at her, but she'd just turn and smile at them. That was her solution to most problems.

"Penn, come on," Thea said, looking at her directly. "This is all about Daniel."

"What?" Penn laughed, but it was weak. "That's stupid."

"Penn, you can't pretend with me. I know you." The wind was blowing through Thea's red hair when she turned to her. "I'm probably the only one in the whole world that really knows you. And you're obsessed with that guy."

"I'm not!" Penn insisted. Then she groaned and shook her head. "It's not an obsession. I just . . . I can't figure it out."

"Maybe there's nothing to figure out."

Penn stopped at a stop sign at the edge of town, thinking that over for a minute. A car pulled up behind her and honked at them, but she was oblivious.

"No, there's something there," she said finally, and turned the corner, beginning the ascent up the hill to the top of the cliff. "Do you think he's related to Bastian?"

"Bastian?" Thea asked, sounding strangely out of breath.

"Yeah, Bastian, or Orpheus. Or whatever name he's going by now. Last time I saw him it was Bastian."

"That was . . ." Thea swallowed. "That was three hundred years ago."

"Exactly," Penn said. "Maybe he's had kids or something since then. I should try to find him." She lowered her voice, almost muttering to herself. "Although I haven't been that good at finding anyone lately."

Thea shook her head. "You haven't seen or heard from Bastian in centuries. And it wasn't like the last time you talked to him turned out so great."

"That's true." Penn mulled it over for a second. "He's probably dead by now anyway."

"Right," Thea said. "And I'm sure Daniel is of no relation to him."

"But there's something about him." Penn slowed to take the curves on the steep incline. "He's . . . captivating."

"I don't find him all that captivating."

"Yeah, well, that's probably because you're a lesbian," Penn said.

"What?" Thea turned to face her, her mouth agape. "I'm not a lesbian. Where did that even come from? And even if I were, what would that matter?"

Penn shrugged. "It doesn't matter. It's just that Gemma is the only person you seem to ever want to spend time with. I mean, when was the last time you even kissed a guy?"

"I don't need to go around hooking up with strangers."

"Yeah, you kinda do. It's the core of who we are. You're denying your very nature."

"You and Lexi do what you want, and I don't condemn you for it."

Penn scoffed loudly. "Yeah, right! All you do is sit in your ivory tower and judge us. Sorry we're not as perfect as your new BFF."

"You picked her, Penn. Remember that. Gemma was your choice. And if you don't like her, that's on you."

"I know," Penn agreed. "But I have good news. I think I found the solution."

"The solution?" Thea asked tentatively.

"Yeah. You know I've been looking for a replacement, and I think I found one," Penn said. "She's in some dinky little town in Delaware called Auburnton or something like that. I don't know. But you should come meet her. I think you'll like her."

"You've already introduced yourself to her?" Thea asked.

"Yeah, I wanted to make sure we found the right girl," Penn said. "She doesn't know I'm a siren yet, but she'll be a good fit for us. Much better than Gemma, anyway."

"That's what you said about Aggie!" Thea shouted back. "You said Gemma would be so much better than Aggie, and now you're ready to kill Gemma without even giving her a chance."

Penn scoffed. "I've given her plenty of chances! She's been ungrateful and horrible and just . . . awful since she turned."

"She's only sixteen, and this is all new to her," Thea insisted. "You've got to give her a chance. She's like a puppy, and she just needs some time to be housebroken."

"I told you as soon as I found a new girl I was getting rid of Gemma," Penn said. "I don't know why you're arguing with me about it now."

"I thought it would take you longer and it would give Gemma a chance to fit in better," Thea admitted.

They were surrounded by loblolly pines, and the air smelled of the trees and the ocean. Thea stared dejectedly at the trees as they went by.

When Thea spoke again, she'd softened, her rough voice sounding gentle. "Gemma's not *that* bad."

"You've got to be kidding me!" Penn laughed. "Because of her, we're stuck in this crappy little town."

"Really?" Thea arched her eyebrows. "You're trying to tell me that you're letting the new girl boss you around? That's your excuse for staying here?"

"No. I'm not saying that. I'm staying here because *I* decided that it would be easier for us until I could find a replacement for Gemma."

Thea waited a beat before asking, "And what about Daniel?"

"What about him?"

"Once you find the replacement and Gemma's out of the picture, we're just going to leave?"

They'd reached their house at the top of the cliff. It was more rustic than Penn normally liked, but it was the nicest house that she could find in Capri. It was a log cabin, but the kind with high ceilings, a chandelier, and granite countertops.

Penn pulled in the driveway and turned the car off, but she stayed inside. Thea didn't get out, either, probably because she knew better than to walk away if Penn wasn't done with the conversation yet.

"Of course," Penn said firmly. "Daniel has no bearing on any of my decisions. He's simply an oddity of nature, a curiosity that's giving me something to play with until we can get the hell out of here."

"Say what you want, Penn, but remember that I've seen you in love before."

"Like I would be in love with some dirty human like that? Gross." Penn grimaced. "Just to prove to you that you're wrong, when I do find a replacement and we get rid of Gemma, I'll get rid of Daniel."

"You'll get rid of him?" Thea asked.

"I'll rip out his heart and eat it in front of you. I wouldn't be able to do that to someone I was in love with."

"I didn't ask you to do that." Thea had turned away from Penn again, staring emptily out at the trees surrounding the cabin. "And you'd be surprised what you can do to the people you love."

SIX

Fairy Dust

As soon as they got close to Bernie's Island, an intense nostalgia washed over Harper like a wave. She'd been afraid that she'd lost the wonderful love for one of her favorite places on earth, but it was all coming back.

Daniel moving out to the island had helped her forget about the night they'd come out here and found Bernie McAllister eviscerated in the trees. She'd managed to shove that image deep down inside her, burying it beneath all the happy memories of her childhood spent out here with Bernie and her sister.

As they pulled up to the dock, which was hidden among the trees that grew out into the water, Harper breathed in deeply. The island was almost overgrown with bald cypress trees and pines towering above them.

Instead of taking *The Dirty Gull* into the boathouse, Daniel tied it off at the dock. He'd have to take Harper home in a few hours, and it would be easier this way.

He got off the boat, and held his hand out for Harper, helping her.

"Do you see that?" Daniel let go of her hand to point down at the dock.

"What?" Harper looked down at the warped gray boards beneath her feet. "Does it need to be replaced or something?"

"No. Well, yeah, probably, but that's not what I meant," Daniel said. "I mean, do you see where your feet are? You're standing on the island now."

"Technically I'm on the dock, and that's not part of the island," Harper teased.

He sighed. "It's close enough. And you remember our agreement?"

"I do." She smiled up at him. "Once we're on the island, no talking about sirens or Gemma. It's just the two of us tonight, without any distractions."

Since moving out to the island, Daniel had been picking up more jobs to cover the cost of rent, and Harper'd been working extra shifts at the library to save up for college. And whenever the two of them did manage to get the same time off, something with Gemma or Brian or the sirens always seemed to come up. They'd hardly had a moment alone together in the past month.

So Daniel had come up with a plan in which they'd both leave the world behind for a little bit—or as much as Harper could leave it. With everything going on with her sister, she'd never really be able to let go.

"I do reserve the right to leave my phone on and accept any incoming calls, or make any, if I feel it's necessary," Harper said.

"I'll allow it. But only in case of an emergency."

"Fair enough."

"Now come on." Daniel stepped backward but he held out his hand to her. "It's Friday night, and we're going to enjoy ourselves."

She laughed and let him take her hand, his rough skin somehow feeling so perfect against hers. They walked on the narrow path up to the cabin, with creeping Charlie threatening to overgrow the worn dirt path.

The trees were tall and thick enough that the sun streamed through in thin shards. When an ocean breeze blew through the trees, the sunlight seemed to dance on the ground. It was the peacefulness, the odd silence and seclusion of the island, that gave it this wonderful air of magic.

It was so easy to imagine that fairies or other woodland pixies were flitting among the trees, and as a child Harper often had. Bernie had always aided in these fantasies, telling both her and Gemma all kinds of stories filled with fantasy and wonder when they were young.

Once Gemma had found a blue wing of a butterfly. What had happened to the rest of the insect, Harper had no idea, although she was certain that Gemma had done nothing to hurt it. She'd brought the wing over to show Bernie, and he'd crouched down, examining it with careful precision.

"You know what this is, don't you?" Bernie had asked in his warm cockney accent and pushed up the brim of his hat.

"No. What is it?" Gemma asked. She couldn't have been more than six at the time, so it must've been on one of the occasions when Bernie was babysitting them before their mother was in the accident.

Harper stood behind her sister, watching over Gemma's shoulder as Bernie gave his explanation. They were behind the cabin, by the roses that Bernie's wife had planted. He refused to trim the bush or cut it back, so it had grown into the largest rosebush Harper had ever seen.

The flowers themselves were massive and a vibrant purple. Each one was nearly twice the size of her fist, and they were so fragrant. When the breeze blew through it in the summer, the sweet perfume of the roses overtook everything else—the scent of the pine trees, the sea, and even the creeping Charlie.

"This is a fairy wing," Bernie said as he examined the blue wing, turning it carefully in front of his face. "And from the looks of it, I'd say it was from a Bluebelle Fairy. They fly over the flowers that are about to bloom, sprinkling their dust on them, and that's how the flowers blossom."

"There's no such thing as fairies," Harper said. Even then she was too old to fall for his stories.

"There most certainly are," Bernie said, pretending to sound offended. "When my wife was alive, bless her soul, she'd spot fairies all the time. That's how come her rosebush always has the biggest, brightest flowers on it. The fairies are taking care of it for her."

Harper didn't want to contradict him more, mostly because she knew that he was just trying to have fun with Gemma. But part of it was because even though she knew better, she still believed him—or at least she wanted to.

"Gemma knows I'm telling the truth," Bernie said and handed the wing back to Gemma. "She's probably seen the fairies, haven't you?"

"I think so." She held the fragile wing delicately and stared down at it. "They come in colors other than blue, too?"

"Oh, they come in every color you can imagine," Bernie said.

"Then, yes, I've seen one." Gemma sounded more confident and nodded her head vigorously.

"Next time you'll have to point one out to your sister, won't you?" He had looked up at Harper then and winked at her.

"Hey, where'd you go?" Daniel asked, drawing Harper back to the present.

They'd reached the cabin, which looked about the same as the last time she'd seen it. The structure was over fifty years old, and while Bernie had kept it up as best he could, in the last few years it had really begun to show its age.

Daniel had obviously cleaned it up some, replacing the shattered front windows and a log that had rotted out. He left the flowering ivy growing up over the far side of the cabin, small purple and blue blossoms on it, but he'd trimmed it back from the windows and the roof.

"Sorry." She smiled up at Daniel. "I was just thinking."

"About what?"

"Bernie used to say there were fairies out here," Harper said, and she turned to survey the wind blowing through the trees. The way the shadows and the light played together, as well as the birds and butterflies flitting through the trees, it was easy to imagine that she saw them now.

"Did you believe him?" Daniel asked, watching her as she stared out at the trees.

"I didn't, not then." She shook her head. "No, I did at first, but then I grew out of it and stopped playing make-believe." Harper looked back at Daniel. "But now I wonder, maybe there really are fairies."

"What makes you believe in them now? Did you see one flying around?" He glanced up, scanning the skies for any signs of one.

"No." She smiled, but it was pained and fell away quickly. "With everything we've seen lately, it's made me realize that there has to be more than meets the eye. There have to be so many creatures that we don't even know about."

"I know," he agreed and stepped closer to her. "Isn't that wonderful?"

"How is that wonderful? I think it's scary."

"You're missing the beauty of it," Daniel said. "There's so much magic in the world, so much more than I'd ever even believed there could be. We've only just seen the tip of it. Pixies, gnomes, even unicorns and dragons. Who knows what more is out there?"

"You're only listing the nicest parts of the fairy tales," Harper said, looking up at him. He was so close to her, they were nearly touching. If she breathed in deeply, her chest would press against his. "What about the monsters?"

"Dragons aren't the nicest parts of the stories," Daniel countered, and she smiled crookedly. "But you don't need to worry about the monsters. I'll protect you."

A breeze came up, bringing the sweet scent of the roses with it, and a lock of Harper's hair came loose and blew in her face. Daniel brushed it back, but let his hand linger on her cheek for a moment as she stared up into his hazel eyes. The way he looked at her made heat swirl in her belly.

She was hoping he'd kiss her, but instead he dropped his hand and took a step back.

"Are you ready to come inside and see what I've done with the place?" Daniel asked and moved backward to the cabin door.

"What did you do?" Harper asked, tilting her head.

He smiled. "Come here and you'll see."

SEVEN

Anniversary

When Daniel had moved out here two weeks ago, Harper had helped him, but she hadn't been able to visit him since. Then, the house had been in disarray as he tried to unpack and fix up some of the damage the sirens had left.

He leaned back on the front door now, reaching behind himself to turn the handle, and he stepped backward with it as he opened it. Harper stepped inside cautiously, unsure of what to expect.

She'd expected him to clean it up but she hadn't known he would redecorate. The walls had been left their natural wood color, but Daniel had painted over them with a varnish, making them look brighter, cleaner, and more modern.

The countertops in the kitchen had been old and cracked, and he'd replaced them with dark stone counters. Bernie's old furniture had been traded in for a soft couch, and for a coffee table Daniel used an old steamer trunk.

Somehow he'd managed to make the place look fresher and more contemporary, yet still maintain its rustic, seaside appeal.

"This looks amazing," Harper said and turned around to look

at him. "How did you do this? How could you afford all this stuff?"

"I've got my ways," Daniel said. "I did some work for people and collected hand-me-downs and thrift store stuff. Then I just put it all together."

"This is incredible." She looked around the cabin again. "You're really good at this. The sets for Gemma's play are going to look *amazing*."

"I know." He smiled. "So do you wanna hear what I have planned for our anniversary dinner?"

"It's not really an anniversary dinner," Harper said, mostly because she felt a little silly celebrating a one-month. "That was technically two days ago. I think. We did decide that we officially started dating on the Fourth of July, right?"

"Right. It sounds more romantic that way." Daniel grinned. "We kissed, and then there were fireworks, and we've been together ever since."

She laughed. "There were literally fireworks."

"That's the point," he said. "Now go have a seat. I'm making you dinner."

"You're making me dinner?" Harper tried not to look skeptical. "I thought you said you couldn't cook."

"I can't. Now go have a seat."

He put his hand on the small of her back and gently pushed her over to a small table that separated the kitchen from the living room. A tablecloth was draped over it, with two white candles set in the center.

"So how is this gonnna work, then?" Harper asked after she sat down. "You making dinner if you can't cook?"

"I have a very simple plan," he said as he went back to the kitchen.

"You don't have to do this, you know." She leaned on the table, watching him open the fridge.

"I know. I want to. I wanted to do something nice and normal."

"Normal?"

He took out a large Tupperware bowl. Harper could make out green leaves with red cherry tomatoes on the side, like he'd cut up and mixed together fresh salad greens earlier. He set the bowl on the counter, then went over to the cupboard.

"Yeah," he said and pulled plates out of the cupboard. "I've never really gotten to take you out on a proper date. The one time I did take you out, it turned into a battle with sirens."

"We're not supposed to talk about that," she reminded him.

He smiled. "Right. Well, you know what happened anyway."

"So . . . why does this mean you have to cook for me?" She propped her chin with a hand and fought the urge to get up and help him. It felt wrong having someone else wait on her.

"It doesn't. But it's something that guys do," Daniel explained.

"I can cook for you."

"I know you can. You've done it before, and the food was very tasty, thank you." He smiled at her, then dished out the salad onto plates.

"I can help you, at least," she offered.

Daniel stopped what he was doing so he could face her directly. "Harper, I want to do something for you. Will you let me do that?"

"Yes. Sorry." She smiled sheepishly and tucked her hair behind her ear. "I would love it if you made me dinner."

"Thank you."

"So . . . what are we having?" Harper asked.

Daniel carried two plates over to the table. He set one down in front of her and one at his place across from her. Fresh arugula, spinach greens, cherry tomatoes, and cucumbers were the only things on her plate so far.

"Well, I thought we'd start with a salad, with homemade vinaigrette," he told her. "It's my grandmother's recipe, and it is delicious."

"Ooh, sounds intriguing."

"It is." He went back into the kitchen and grabbed a small decanter of the vinaigrette from the fridge. "Then, for our next course, I thought we would have a bowl of Pearl's famous clam chowder."

"Pearl paid you in a bucket of soup again, didn't she?" Harper asked as he sat down across from her.

"She did, but it's amazing," Daniel admitted. "For dessert, I have not one but *two* flavors of ice cream. Is your mind blown yet?"

She smiled. "Yeah, it kinda is."

"So, yeah. That's my dinner." He stared expectantly across the table from her. "What do you think?"

"I think it sounds wonderful, and I appreciate the thought you put into making it. It's very sweet."

"Sweet enough to earn me a make-out session after supper?" Daniel asked with an arched eyebrow.

She pretended to think it over. "Depends on how full I am."

"We could always skip the soup," he suggested, causing Harper to laugh. "The salad might be filling enough."

Harper dug in, eating a mouthful of salad, and nodded. "This is really good."

"Thank you," he said, sounding a little relieved. "The vegetables are fresh from the garden out back. It was a bit overgrown when I moved in, but I think I've got it under control now. The dressing is really simple, and it's one of three things I actually do know how to make."

"Your gramma taught you how to make it?" Harper asked between bites.

"She did, yeah." He nodded. "She passed away a while ago. I was really close to my grandparents. They basically raised me and my brother."

"What about your parents?" She watched him for his response.

"What about them?" Daniel asked and didn't look up from his food.

"You never really talk about them."

"Oh." He poked emptily at his food for a few seconds before going on. "There's not a lot to tell. My dad was a drunk, and he wasn't the nicest guy. He used to beat up on my mom and stuff. He finally left when I was ten. I thought things would get better after that, but they didn't."

Harper had been about to take a bite, but she stopped. Daniel hardly ever talked about his family life or his childhood, and she hadn't any idea that he'd grown up in an abusive home.

"Why not?" Harper asked finally.

He shook his head. "I don't know. It was weird because my mom was so miserable when he was around, but it was like, after he left, she didn't know what to do when somebody wasn't telling her what to do or putting her down."

"I'm sorry to hear that," she said and took another bite, mostly so Daniel wouldn't think that she didn't like his meal.

"It's okay. Eventually she found someone to fill that void, and they got married. My brother died, then my grandparents died and left her some money. She didn't see any reason to stick around here anymore, so she and the new husband moved out to Vegas."

"And you stayed here?" Harper asked.

"Well, I wasn't exactly invited to join them, but I don't think

I would've gone anyway. My boat's here, and that's about the only thing I really owned. And I grew up here, so . . ." His voice trailed off.

"I'm glad you stayed."

He looked up at her finally and smiled. "Me, too."

They finished their salads, and moved on to dinner and dessert. Harper tried to wash the dishes, but he wouldn't let her. He insisted that it was a romantic evening, and the cleaning could wait until tomorrow.

Daniel let her pick the movie from his rather modest collection, and she chose *Edward Scissorhands.* It wasn't her favorite, but given a choice between that and *Jaws, Mad Max*, or *The Godfather,* she thought it seemed like the most romantic.

They started out sitting on the couch next to each other, but it wasn't long before Daniel was lying on his back and Harper was curled up with him. Her head was on his chest, and he had one arm wrapped around her.

Normally, Harper would lie awake in bed for hours before she could fall asleep. Her mind would race through all her concerns, almost all of them involving Gemma, sirens, or college, and when she was really in a mood, she could stay up all night worrying about her mom, her dad, Alex, Marcy, really anything and everything.

But something about being with Daniel like this, feeling safe and secure as he held her to him, the sound of his heart beating slowly under her ear, was putting her to sleep.

For his part, Daniel had been working incredibly hard over the last few weeks. When he wasn't at the theater trying to get the set together or doing odd jobs, he was fixing up the house.

So within minutes both of them were sleeping soundly on the couch.

She woke up first, and she knew she should've felt some panic at waking up in a strange place, but she couldn't muster the anxiety. Lying with Daniel felt too good. Besides, the clock on his wall said it was only a quarter after eleven, so Gemma probably wasn't even home yet.

He was still asleep, but he must've woken up at some point because the television was off. The only light was the moon pouring in through the open windows. It wasn't full yet, but it was bright enough that Harper watched him sleep for a minute.

If he woke up and caught her, she'd be incredibly embarrassed, but he looked so peaceful and handsome as he slept. His unshaven scruff made him ruggedly sexy, and she had a feeling that if he shaved it completely, he might look too pretty. His skin was smooth, and his mouth had a sexy, sinful quality to it.

The urge to kiss him overtook her, and she decided that she'd better wake him first. They hadn't had their after-dinner make-out session yet, and to set the mood, she wanted to wake him in the right way.

"Daniel?" she whispered in his ear, doing her best to sound sultry and seductive. *"Daniel?"*

He didn't stir at all. Not even slightly, and she was speaking right into his ear. She instantly began to panic, and she couldn't tell if he was breathing or not. When she'd fallen asleep she'd heard his heartbeat, but had she heard it a few minutes ago when she awoke?

"Daniel?" Harper asked again, and by now she was certain that he'd died while she was asleep. "Daniel?"

He moved his head. "Hmm?" He turned to look at her, opening his eyes slowly, and she let out a deep breath. "What?"

"You didn't hear that?" she asked. She sat up a bit, and he moved his hand to her back.

Daniel still appeared groggy and didn't seem to completely understand the situation. It must've been apparent that she was upset, because he rubbed her back to comfort her.

"What?" Daniel asked, becoming more alert.

"I was saying your name. I was whispering right in your ear."

He furrowed his brow. "Why were you whispering in my ear?"

"I was trying to wake you up all romantic-like."

"Aw." He smiled. "That's very sweet of you."

He tried to pull her down, either to kiss her or so she'd lie with him again, but she resisted. She was still confused and anxious.

"Yeah, but why couldn't you hear me?"

"The accident." He sat up a little bit, since he'd begun to realize that Harper wasn't going to let this go.

"You mean the boating accident you were in with your brother?"

"Yeah. It messed up my back. I don't have complete range of motion in this shoulder, and I have all these nifty scars." He rolled his right shoulder, trying to show it didn't move so well. "But it hurt my ears, too. It didn't damage the outer part, but it messed something up so I can't hear certain octaves. I'm not deaf, but just some stuff I can't hear."

"Did it mess up both ears?" Harper asked.

"Yeah, the right is worse than the other." Daniel motioned to the ear she'd been whispering in. "I almost lost my hearing completely in it, but I had a surgery, and it's pretty much fine now. The other one was never that bad to begin with. But there's a nasty scar running across the back of my skull. If I ever go bald, it'll be gross."

"Why didn't you tell me this before?" Harper asked, and she

knew her tone was more pointed than she wanted it to be, but she couldn't help it.

"I showed you the scars before," he reminded her.

"But you didn't tell me about your hearing." She sat up completely now, pulling away from him, and that only made his confusion deepen.

"I don't know." He shrugged. "I didn't think of it. Why does it matter?"

"That's got to be it. The sirens, Daniel. That's probably why you're immune to them."

She leaned down, kissing him on the lips, and he wrapped his arms around her, pulling her against him. He moved, rolling her over so she was on her back, and he kissed more deeply. Harper felt the scruff of his face on her cheeks, and something about it seemed so perfect. The way Daniel kissed her summed him up perfectly—a little rough on the edges, but so sweet and sexy.

Abruptly, Daniel pulled away from her and sat up straighter, looking around the room. "What was that?"

"What?" Harper smiled, thinking that he was teasing her about when she whispered in his ear.

She had her hand on his chest and slid it up, meaning to pull him back down to her, but then she heard something, too. For a few moments, she'd been lost in his arms. But now she heard it—a wet thwacking sound as something slammed into the front door.

"Stay here." Daniel got up, managing to move both quickly and calmly while fresh panic spread out over her.

Harper stood up and looked around, hoping to catch a glimpse of something through the windows of the cabin, but she saw nothing. "Did you see anything?"

"I don't know. Just stay here," he repeated and walked to the front door.

"Maybe you shouldn't open the door," Harper suggested. "At least not if you don't know what it was."

"I'm sure it's nothing," Daniel said.

Harper lagged behind him and grabbed the poker from next to the fireplace. Daniel may not be cautious, but she wasn't about to open a door unprepared. Not when she knew what kind of monsters could be out there.

"You're out alone on an island," Harper said. "It's either a wild animal or the sirens, and either way, it's not safe."

"I'll be fine," Daniel insisted. He smiled reassuringly at her, then turned and opened the front door.

Harper gripped the cold metal tightly in her hands, preparing to strike Penn or Lexi dead if they were on the other side of the door. But when it opened, Harper saw nothing.

"Oh, good," Daniel said as he stared down at the ground. "It's only fish."

"Fish?" Harper moved closer to him so she could peer down and see what he was talking about.

Two huge bluefish lay at Daniel's doorstep. Or at least they appeared to be bluefish, but it was hard to tell, since they'd been thrown at the door with such force that their guts had splattered out, leaving droplets of blood and viscera all over the side of the cabin.

Harper was about to ask him what that was about, but then she saw it—a gigantic black feather floating through the air. Rather fittingly, it landed right in a small puddle of blood, the black veins of the feather appearing almost iridescent in the moonlight.

"Penn," Harper said. A chill ran through her. "Do you think she was watching us?"

"It's hard to say." Daniel rubbed his hand on his forehead. "Well, I should get you home."

"A siren throws dead fish at your house and your only reaction is to take me home?" Harper gaped at him.

"It's getting late." He turned back toward her, but he wouldn't meet her eyes.

"Daniel, I'm not just gonna leave you here like this," Harper insisted.

"Harper, it's fine," he said. "Penn's just messing around."

"Just messing around?" Harper scoffed. "She's clearly threatening you. She could still be out here now."

"No, she's not." He shook his head. "If she wanted to hurt me or you, she would've. This is just a stupid prank. It's the siren equivalent of egging my house."

"Daniel, I think it's a bit more serious than that." Harper stared up at him for a while before exhaling deeply and letting her arms fall to her sides. "Fine. You can take me home. But only if you're sure you'll be safe out here."

"I'm sure." He smiled and kissed her gently on the mouth. "I can take care of myself."

Daniel took her hand and led her down the trail back to the boathouse. The earlier magic of the night had faded away. The trees around them felt imposing, and the moonlight shining through them made the branches look like arms reaching out for her.

EIGHT

Cliff Diving

After weeks of it sitting immobile in the driveway of her house, Brian had finally gotten Gemma's beat-up Chevy running again. He'd refused to work on it until after Gemma was ungrounded so she wouldn't be tempted to take it.

It was just in time for Gemma's Saturday visit out to see her mom. With college rapidly approaching, Harper was picking up as many shifts as she could at the library. She usually had Saturdays off, but with Edie back around, Marcy had been more than happy to give up days to her.

Harper had begun talking about not going off to college, saying it was too dangerous to leave Gemma now, but Gemma wouldn't hear of it. As far back as she could remember, Harper had been talking about going off to school and becoming a doctor.

Well, maybe it hadn't been as far back as she could remember, but it definitely had been after their mom's accident. Harper had spoken with the neurosurgeon a lot while Nathalie was in the hospital, and she'd been preoccupied with the field ever since.

Everyone had made it clear how much work and dedication it

required to become a doctor, and even if she did all the work and the schooling, there was still no guarantee that Harper would ever be one. But she hadn't been deterred. If anything, it had only made her work twice as hard.

There had been many nights when Gemma had woken up to go to the bathroom, and Harper would still be awake, studying for an exam or working on her homework. She'd been working part-time since she was fifteen, on top of school and keeping the household running.

Gemma knew how badly her sister wanted this, and she refused to take it away from her. If Harper didn't go to college this year, she'd lose her scholarships and her place in the premed program. It would throw off her entire future and ruin everything.

After all the things Harper had already given up for her family, Gemma wouldn't let her give up anything else.

As she made the twenty-minute drive out to Briar Ridge, Gemma tried to think of arguments to convince Harper to go. All the logical ones wouldn't really work because they were stuck in a totally illogical situation.

It would've been nice if she could have asked Nathalie for motherly advice, but she didn't have any. She was in a good mood, chatting away about all sorts of things, and it was a little hard for Gemma to get a word in edgewise.

Gemma had tried to tell her about the play she was working on, because Nathalie had been somewhat of an actress in her day. That was how she'd gotten involved in the Paramount Theater restoration in the first place. Nathalie had wanted a place to perform.

But Nathalie couldn't focus today. No matter what Gemma asked her or said to her, the conversation would veer in some bizarre direction. Her current obsession was a BeDazzler she'd gotten, although her lack of hand coordination presented a problem in her using it properly.

Somehow Gemma managed to escape the visit without any new jewels stuck to her clothing. Seeing her mother was always a little draining, and that only exacerbated the watersong.

When she went awhile without swimming or got too far away from the sirens, the ocean would call to her. It was like music in her mind, but the stronger it became, the more obnoxious and even painful it could become. The watersong had given her horrible migraines when she first became a siren and was refusing to swim.

The air conditioner in her car was broken, so hot August air was blowing in through the windows. The watersong had gotten to an irritating level. Not to mention her hunger was beginning to gnaw at her. She'd need to go on a date soon. The physical contact could help stave off her hunger before things got completely out of control and she ended up hurting someone like she had before.

Sirens craved four things—singing, the ocean, eating, and physical contact with boys. So kissing helped keep her appetite suppressed, as long as she kept herself in control.

But since she didn't have any plans with Kirby, she'd have to settle for a swim. It would help her blow off some steam, quell the watersong, and even curb her appetite a little.

Right before she made it to Capri, she turned off the main drive and went up the winding road that led to the top of the cliff where the sirens were staying. Gemma didn't particularly enjoy spending time with the sirens, but she had to do things with them sometimes. Not just to keep the watersong quieter, but to keep the peace.

She needed to act the part of a dutiful member of Penn's little clique, at least some of the time, so Penn would be less tempted to go back on their deal about staying in Capri and not killing anyone, including Gemma.

Besides that, Gemma wanted to check up and see what the sirens were up to. She knew they were trying to figure out if there was anything supernatural going on in town other than themselves, but she didn't really know how forthcoming Penn would be if she found anything.

When she pulled in front of the sirens' house, she didn't see Penn's car. That didn't mean anything, except that Penn probably wasn't here, but that was a good thing. Gemma got out of her car and rang the doorbell.

She was just about to leave, deciding that nobody was home, when Thea opened the door. Her red hair was pulled back, and that was the first time Gemma had seen her with her hair up.

"Hey, Gemma." Thea leaned on the doorframe. "What brings you up here?" She nodded at the car behind Gemma. "Other than that heap. How did that even make it up the hill?"

"My dad just fixed it, and it's running pretty well," Gemma said, getting defensive of her battered old Chevy. "I thought I'd check and see if you maybe wanted to join me for a swim."

"Sure." Thea shrugged. "It's just me here, and I've been practicing my lines for the play for a while. I can use the break."

Thea stepped away from the door, and Gemma followed her inside. Penn had complained that the houses in Capri weren't nice enough, but Gemma thought this place was pretty swanky. The downstairs was an open concept, and the second floor was a loft above. The only walls on the main level were around the bathroom, the pantry in the kitchen, and the fireplace in the center of the house.

The house was situated almost right on the edge of the cliff, not that far away from where Gemma and Alex had gone, back when they were seeing each other, to talk and make out. From the living room she could see almost the entire bay, including Bernie's Island and a large part of Capri. The house was aimed toward the south, but if she stepped out on the cliff, she could almost see all the way up to the Achelous River, which was a few miles north of the bay.

"It does have a great view." Thea sighed and stood next to Gemma, who'd wandered to the back of the house to take it all in. "I'll miss it when we leave."

"Really?" Gemma asked and looked over at her. Thea appeared strangely wistful for a moment, but she tried to hide it.

"Maybe 'miss' is too strong a word," Thea said as she walked away from her. "I'm going upstairs to change into my swimsuit."

"But you'll miss this?" Gemma turned to watch Thea climb up the stairs to the loft above, where the bedrooms were. "A drab place like Capri?"

"I thought you liked it here," Thea said, her voice bouncing off the pitched ceilings. She'd disappeared out of Gemma's sight, presumably getting her suit on. "You're always wanting to stay here."

"That's different. My friends and family are here," Gemma said. "And you've been all over the world and seen all kinds of exotic places. I can't imagine this would be in the top ten, or even the top fifty places you've been."

"I haven't been as many places as you'd think," Thea said. "We can never be that far from the ocean, so everywhere we go has to be a seaside town. Beaches, I've seen hundreds. To me, exotic would be an open prairie, land that goes on and on without any water in sight."

Gemma sat down on the edge of a sofa as she waited, still staring up at the loft even though there was nothing to see.

"But there still have to have been more beautiful places than here," Gemma said.

"Of course there are." Thea's voice was muffled a second, but when she spoke again, her voice was clear. "The coast of Australia is probably my favorite. They have the most gorgeous reefs there. I've swum there thousands of times, and it's always changing and always beautiful."

"I'd love to see that," Gemma said.

"Maybe you will." Thea appeared at the top of the stairs, now in a dark brown bikini. "But the ocean's the ocean anywhere you go. The water's just as wet here as it is anywhere else."

"So then what could make you miss this place?" Gemma asked. "What makes Capri special?"

Thea breathed out deeply and came down the stairs much more slowly than she'd gone up them. When she reached the bottom, she finally answered.

"It's not the most beautiful or entertaining place we've been, that's for sure," Thea said. "Penn thinks there might be some kind of supernatural draw, but I don't know if I believe that."

"Why did you come here in the first place?" Gemma asked, realizing that the sirens had never told her how they'd ended up in town.

Thea shook her head and wouldn't meet her eyes. She hesitated before speaking, almost as if she were holding something back. "It was just a stop on the coast. We never planned to be here this long."

"But you have stayed," Gemma said. "And you want to stay longer. Don't you?"

"Oh, I don't know." Thea walked away, going out to the back door, so Gemma got up to go after her.

When she went outside, Thea was standing right at the edge of the cliff, her toes almost hanging over it. Anthemusa Bay spread out before them. Boats were floating on the water, looking so small from the distance.

"All the places blur together eventually," Thea said finally. "Even the beauty of the ocean, eventually it becomes . . . redundant. It's not *here* so much as *now* that I want to stay in."

"What's great about now?" Gemma asked.

"It probably seems terrible to you. Your whole life is in upheaval. But for me, this is the calmest things have been in a very long time. Penn is more sated. Lexi is miserable, but that matters less. Lexi's bitching and whining have nothing on Penn."

Gemma nodded knowingly. "When Penn's unhappy, she makes everybody unhappy."

"That's an understatement. She makes life a living hell."

"So she's happy here?" Gemma asked.

Thea shrugged. "She's preoccupied, and sometimes that's about as close to happy as she gets."

"You're talking about Daniel?" Gemma debated about saying anything more on that, but she decided she should tell Thea. That didn't mean that word wouldn't get back to Penn, but if Thea thought it should, then maybe it should. "I talked to Harper this morning, and she thinks she figured out why he's immune."

Thea turned her head sharply. "Really?"

"Yeah. Harper was with Daniel last night, and he couldn't hear her whisper or something," Gemma said, almost reluctantly telling Thea the story. "Five years ago, he was in an accident, and it messed up his hearing. He's not deaf, but certain octaves and tones are out of his range."

"So he's deaf to whatever makes the siren song enchanting," Thea said. She sighed and pulled the hair tie out, making her red locks fall free.

"Are you going to tell Penn?" Gemma asked.

Thea looked at her for a long moment. "I should . . . but I won't. And I advise you not to, also. If she hasn't solved that mystery, it might keep her interested in staying in town." She gave Gemma a knowing look. "That might keep you alive longer."

"She told me she's looking for a replacement." That was the first time Gemma had said it aloud, and the reality of it hit her harder than she'd thought it would.

She hadn't told Harper about it—she refused to. Her sister already knew too much and was too wrapped up in the drama of her life. Gemma thought the best way to protect her was to keep her out of the loop. The less Harper knew, the better.

That didn't change the fact that the very real threat of Gemma's death was looming in the not-too-distant future, and it was hard for her not to throw up when she thought about it too much.

"I'm trying to hold her off, Gemma," Thea said. "Penn *thinks* she found the right girl, but she's being cautious. There's still some time, but not much."

"Can't you just tell me how to break the curse?" Gemma asked, almost pleading with her.

"Gemma, honestly, don't you think if I knew how to break the curse, I would've done it by now?" Thea asked. "I wish I could have a better solution for sure. I wish I knew the magic answer to make everything easy and wonderful, but I don't. I'm trapped in the same mess you are."

"I know, but . . ." Gemma trailed off and ran her hand through her hair. "I just don't know what to do anymore."

"Enjoy this life for as long as you have it," Thea told her simply.

Thea slipped off her bikini bottoms and tossed them back on the cliff. Then she dove off the edge, her arms pointed out in front of her as she fell toward the waves crashing below her.

That was the apparent end of the conversation, so Gemma followed suit. She kicked off her sandals and panties, so she was left in her sundress. Unlike Thea, Gemma preferred swimming in a dress instead of a swimsuit. That way she had all her lady bits covered when she reemerged from the water, since the tail transformation ripped off suit bottoms or underwear. Thea had jumped right from the edge, but Gemma liked a running start. She went back to the cabin, then raced to the edge and leapt off.

The fall to the ocean below was exhilarating. The wind blowing past her was so loud, she couldn't hear anything else. Her dress whipped around her, and her stomach flipped several times before she finally crashed into the water.

The first few moments after she hit were painful. It wasn't as bad for Gemma as it was for Thea, because she'd missed all the rocks that lined the face of the cliff. Thea had to have slammed into some of them, but by the time Gemma made it into the ocean, any signs of Thea's injuries were gone. She was just a beautiful mermaid, flitting about the water.

Within seconds of hitting the water, Gemma felt the change running over her. The flutter of her skin as it turned from flesh into iridescent scales. The water running over her made her skin feel electric. Every wave, every splash, every movement charged through her.

While Thea had waited for Gemma to join her in the water,

she turned and swam ahead. Gemma raced after her. They left the bay, moving away from where there were so many people who could spot them, and then they really began to play.

They moved together, swimming around one another almost as if they were dancing. They'd dive deep, then race back to the surface as quickly as they could so they could leap, flying through the air before splashing back into the ocean.

In these moments, when her entire body was tingling and joy was rushing over her like a tidal wave, Gemma couldn't feel any anxiety or fear or worry. She actually became incapable of it. The only thing she felt—the only thing that mattered—was the ocean.

NINE

Sundham

The campus lawn was filled with maples, and the rather imposing brick university was partially obscured by the foliage. The fall semester hadn't started yet, so it was quiet. A Latin inscription was above the door, but Harper, Marcy, and Gemma were too far away to be able to read it.

"This does not look like a bookstore," Harper said after Marcy had pulled her Gremlin over on the street in front of Sundham University.

"It's on the way," Marcy said and turned down the stereo.

An eight-track of Carly Simon had been the soundtrack for their forty-minute drive from Capri, with the last fifteen minutes almost on full blast because Gemma had requested it to drown out the watersong.

Harper didn't exactly know what the watersong was, and Gemma hadn't really articulated it. All she knew was that the farther Gemma got from the ocean, the more obnoxious the song would get. This was apparently the farthest Gemma had gone since she'd become a siren.

"It's really pretty," Gemma said, leaning forward from the backseat.

"Yep, it looks the same as it did in the brochures, and it even looks the same as it did when I went to a college visit last year before I applied to go here," Harper said. She turned away from the campus to glare at Marcy and Gemma. "I know what the school looks like."

"Just thought it wouldn't hurt to remind you," Marcy said.

Marcy exchanged a look with Gemma and shrugged.

"Nice try, Marcy," Gemma told her and leaned back in the seat.

"So you guys have been conspiring?" Harper asked, looking from one to the other of them.

Neither of them replied, and Marcy put the car in gear. It sputtered angrily and jerked backward, then drove forward.

"This isn't going to turn into a tour of Sundham, Delaware, is it?" Harper asked. "You're not going to try to show me all the sights in hopes I'll come here?"

Marcy glanced up at the rearview, apparently meeting Gemma's eyes for some kind of confirmation. Harper leaned over the seat to look back at her, and Gemma sighed and stared out the windows.

"Just take her to the bookstore," Gemma told Marcy.

"Seriously?" Harper groaned and laid her head against the headrest. "You guys know that my issue with going to college has nothing to do with the town itself or even the college? I think Sundham and the university are perfectly fine. That's why I picked here in the first place."

"We were only trying to remind you how good your choices were." Gemma faced her. "We thought maybe if you saw how awesome things were here, you'd be more enticed to go."

"How did you even get involved with this?" Harper asked, turning her attention to Marcy. "You don't want me to leave. Then you'll have to spend all your time with Edie."

"Yes, it's true, it would benefit me if you lived in Capri forever, doing all the work that I don't want to do," Marcy admitted. "But it may surprise you to learn that I'm not the most selfish person on the planet. I know it's in your best interest to go to college, so when Gemma asked me to help her convince you, I said sure."

Of course Harper wanted to go. She'd worked her entire life for this. But it was for the same reason that Gemma was trying to convince her to go that Harper didn't want to go—she loved her sister too much to stand by and let her destroy her life.

"The drive went by so fast, didn't it?" Gemma asked when it had been a few minutes since Harper had said anything. "If you were speeding, I bet you could make it back to Capri in less than a half hour. That's really not much time. If something happened, you could be back like that."

"Let's just go to the bookstore," Harper said. "Maybe we'll figure out a way to break the curse, and then this will all be a moot point."

Marcy did as she was told, driving through town. If Harper had been looking around, she probably would've thought it was quaint—wide streets with potted flowers hanging from old-fashioned lampposts.

But she didn't look. She just slouched in her seat while Marcy sang along absently to "Take Me as I Am."

The car jerked to a stop abruptly, and Harper had to brace her hands on the dashboard to keep from flying into the windshield.

"What happened?" Harper asked as the Gremlin fell silent. "Did your car just die?"

"No, my car didn't die. She would never die." Marcy glared over at Harper. "My dad bought her used when he was sixteen, and he gave her to me when I turned sixteen, and she hasn't died once in the past twenty-nine years."

"Twenty-nine years?" Gemma asked. "How is that even possible? My car is, like, fifteen years old, and I can't keep it running."

"It's all about proper maintenance and love," Marcy said. "I love Lucinda, and Lucinda loves me."

"Your car's name is Lucinda?" Harper asked.

"My dad named her. Now get out of the car. We're here." Marcy opened the driver's-side door and got out.

Harper looked out the window to see where it was that they were. They'd parked in front of a quirky little place nestled in between a flower shop and craft store.

The sign above the arch had CHERRY LANE BOOKS written in huge letters, and it creaked and groaned, even when there wasn't a breeze. The wood was dark gray, nearly black. The bookstore's front window was tinted too dark to see through.

Harper got out, and since the car was a two-door, she held the seat forward so Gemma could get out. She glanced around, admiring the neighborhood. Every other place on the street had cheery storefronts with bright colors, flower boxes, and signs in the window supporting the football team.

"Hey, Marcy, why is this called Cherry Lane?" Harper asked and pointed to the street sign at the end of the block. "This is Main Street."

"It's a reference to 'Puff the Magic Dragon,'" Marcy explained. "It was Lydia's favorite song when she was a kid."

"Are you sure it's open?" Harper asked as they walked toward the door.

The sign hanging on the door said CLOSED SUNDAYS. Sunday had been the only day that both Harper and Marcy had off, and Gemma didn't have play rehearsal.

"I called ahead. She said she'd open it for me today."

Marcy pushed open the door, and the bell above it chimed when she stepped inside. The scent of old books and incense wafted over Harper as she followed.

At first it seemed like a normal bookstore, with brightly colored displays of the new Danielle Steel book and a section of movie tie-ins, but, even from where Harper stood near the front door, she could tell that it held something darker in the back.

"Lydia?" Marcy called and started heading back to the dimly lit back corner of the store. "Lydia?"

"Are we supposed to follow her?" Harper asked Gemma quietly. Her sister just shrugged, then went after Marcy.

Harper had expected to see cobwebs clogging every corner, but there weren't any. The walls were lined with books that looked about a thousand years old, except for one shelf that was filled with tarot cards, dead flowers, and weird stones. Naturally, that was where Marcy stopped.

"I don't know where Lydia is, but the stuff that you're looking for, it would be in this section." Marcy gestured around her at the shelves overflowing with seemingly ancient texts.

Since Harper didn't know exactly what they were looking for, she began to scan the shelves. Gemma crouched down, picking up a flesh-colored book below the weird stones. Harper ran her fingers against the spines of the books, and they felt worn and soft beneath her fingertips.

She spotted one that had no words on it—only a weird symbol. It looked familiar to her, so she plucked the book down and flipped it open. The pages felt like they might disintegrate in her hands, and it smelled distinctly of dirt.

"My god, where does Lydia get these books?" Harper asked, genuinely awed by what she found. "I think this is written in Sumerian."

"What's that?" Gemma came over to see what the fuss was about. Since she was shorter than Harper, she had to crane her neck a bit to read over Harper's shoulder. "That's not a language. Those are just shapes and symbols."

"That's how it was written," Harper said. "It's a dead language."

"How do you know it?" Gemma asked.

"I don't *know* it. Like, I have no idea what any of this is saying. I kind of recognize some of the symbols." Harper ran her hand along the page. "I took an elective last year, Advanced Languages of the World. I thought the Latin part would help me with medical terminology."

"So then . . . that doesn't say anything about sirens?" Marcy asked.

"Probably not, but this is *really* old," Harper said and carefully put the book back on the shelf. "You can't just go pick that up at a garage sale or any old used book store."

"I told you this wasn't any old used book store," Marcy said.

"Many of the books I get come from private dealers who wish to remain anonymous," came a voice from behind them, and Harper whirled around to see a petite woman walking down the aisle toward them.

She looked to be in her mid-twenties, with black hair kept in a short pixie cut, which suited her, since she reminded Harper of a pixie. Her dark brown eyes appeared almost too large for her face, especially considering how delicate her features were. Her clothes were pastel and chiffon, looking much less goth than Harper had imagined the owner of this establishment would look.

"Hey, Lydia," Marcy said, her voice the same monotone it always was, so Harper couldn't really tell how happy she was to see her friend. "These are the people I was telling you about, Harper and Gemma."

"You must be the siren," Lydia said, instantly focusing her attention on Gemma.

TEN

Cherry Lane

"Um . . ." Gemma appeared unsure how to reply to that and looked embarrassed. "Yeah, I guess. I am."

"Cool." Lydia smiled widely. "I've never met a siren before."

"Well, here I am." Gemma shrugged.

Lydia bit her lip and her eyes sparkled. "You wouldn't want to sing for me, would you?"

"No, that's not a good idea," Harper answered quickly.

"Yeah, it's not really safe," Gemma agreed. "It can get out of hand."

"I understand. I know it's extremely dangerous." Lydia waved her hand. "I shouldn't have asked anyway. You'd think I'd have learned my lesson after the werewolf."

She pulled back her shirt to reveal her slender shoulder. A red scar in the shape of a large dog bite wrapped around it. Harper was content to look at it from where she stood, but both Gemma and Marcy leaned in to get a better look.

"Cool," Marcy said.

"So does that mean you're a werewolf now?" Gemma asked after Lydia had pulled her shirt back up.

"Yeah, I'm all, like, *rawr.*" Lydia made her hands into fake claws and pretended to growl, but she started laughing almost instantly, a light tinkling sound that reminded Harper of wind chimes. "No, no, that's not how werewolves work. It's a whole different process."

"Really?" Gemma asked. "How does one become a werewolf?"

"Well, it's, like—" Lydia started to explain, but then she saw Harper's annoyed expression and stopped. "Sorry. You guys didn't come here to talk about werewolves, did you?"

"I didn't come here for that, but I kinda want to talk about it now that you brought it up," Gemma said, her tone getting a touch sulky because she knew Harper didn't approve of that as a conversation topic.

"You're not missing much," Marcy said. "Werewolves are boring."

Lydia leaned forward and lowered her voice, like she was telling them a secret. "They kinda are."

"See?" Marcy asked.

"Anyway, you're sick of being a siren and want to break the curse. Did I get that right?" Lydia asked. "Or did one of you want to become a siren?"

"No, no, no," Harper said and waved her hands. "No more sirens. None."

"Yeah, we definitely want to break the curse," Gemma said. "And not have more sirens. In fact, if we can find a way to kill the sirens that already exist, that'd be great."

"You don't know how to kill the sirens?" Lydia raised an eyebrow. "So you don't know how you can die?"

"I know some ways," Gemma said. "But I don't know how I can be murdered."

Lydia crossed her arms over her chest and leaned back, studying Gemma. She did it for so long that Gemma became uncomfortable and began to squirm.

"That leaves you vulnerable to attack, doesn't it?" Lydia asked.

"Yeah, it does," Gemma said.

"We hadn't thought of that before, but thank you for putting it in my head now," Harper muttered.

"Do you know how to kill sirens?" Gemma asked.

"Unfortunately, no, I don't." Lydia looked genuinely sad and shook her head. "If I'm being honest with you now, I don't know very much about sirens at all."

"Well, what do you know?" Gemma asked.

"That you can sing the most captivating song and enchant sailors, but I'm assuming it extends to all people and not just those that operate ships," Lydia said.

"That's accurate," Harper said. She leaned against the bookcase, watching Lydia as she talked.

"And that sirens can transform into either mermaids or birds, depending on what I read."

"Both, actually," Gemma said.

Lydia's eyes widened. "You can do both? Wow." She laughed again and clapped her hands together. "That's amazing. That has to be so exciting."

"It does have its downsides, though," Gemma said, refusing to get caught up in Lydia's exuberance.

"Oh, you mean the cannibal part?" Lydia wrinkled her nose. "That would be disgusting."

Harper looked over at her sister, and Gemma swallowed hard

and lowered her eyes. Based on the fact that the sirens had torn apart Bernie McAllister and Alex's friend Luke, Harper had figured that the sirens were eating at least some of them.

Plus, she'd read about the cannibalism in the mythology books. Gemma hadn't mentioned it, though, so Harper never brought it up. She didn't think Gemma had hurt anybody. Gemma would do whatever she needed to do to survive, but not at the expense of somebody else.

"Yeah, that would be the part I'm avoiding," Gemma said quietly.

"I don't mean to be mean, but if you don't know that much about sirens, how can you help us?" Harper asked.

"I don't know how much *I* can personally help you, but I might be able to direct you towards some information," Lydia said.

"Where?" Harper asked.

"Well. Okay." Lydia held her hands up. "Let me explain first. Back in the day, there were all these powerful, magical beings that roamed the earth freely.

"The population of regular mortals—like you and me"—Lydia gestured between herself and Harper—"expanded more rapidly than that of these other beings. I'm guessing it's for the same reason that ants multiply at much faster rates than blue whales. We were small and expendable, bottom of the food chain. We died all the time.

"Many of these other beings were immortal—or at least appeared that way to humans," Lydia went on. "In fact, your average human began naming these more powerful beings, and oftentimes those names included terms like 'gods' or 'goddesses.'"

Lydia waved her hands. "Anyway, humans had a way of annoying these so-called deities. So the gods and goddesses would do things like trick them or curse them. But in order to make a curse real and take effect, the terms of the curse have to be written down."

"The terms of a curse?" Gemma asked.

"Yeah, kinda like when you lease a car or click the box 'yes' to agree to the terms of service on iTunes," Lydia explained. "In order for it to be valid, there has to be a contract."

"So you're saying that somewhere, the specifics of the siren curse are written?" Gemma asked.

"Right, it would have everything spelled out," Lydia said. "Like what a siren can and can't do, how to kill a siren, and how to break the curse. You know what? I'll show you one."

Lydia slid in between Gemma and Harper and went farther down the aisle. In lieu of a ladder, Lydia apparently preferred to climb up the bookcase, using the shelves as rungs.

"Do you need help?" Harper offered, since she was at least half a foot taller than Lydia.

"Don't worry," Lydia replied cheerfully. "I got it."

Lydia grabbed something from the top shelf, then dropped to the floor. She held up a thin, battered book. The cover had completely fallen off, and it was held together by a rubber band wrapped around it.

"This is the one for Dracul, and it lays out the vampire curse," Lydia said as she took off the rubber band and opened it.

Harper leaned over to get a look. The pages were falling out, and the lettering had faded so much it was all but illegible. It was written in a cursive that Harper didn't understand but there were a few pictures alongside it, showing a stake through the heart.

"I can't read it," Gemma said.

"Of course you can't. It's in Romanian," Lydia said. "But vampires aren't your problem, are they?"

"No," Gemma said, sounding somewhat dejected.

"Good. Then you don't need to read it," Lydia said and flipped through the book.

"Who wrote this?" Harper asked and pointed to the faded pages.

"This exact one here, I don't know." Lydia shook her head. "But the original curse was crafted by Horace, I think, because this Vlad dude *really* pissed him off, apparently."

"So this tells you how to break the curse?" Harper asked.

"Well, no." Lydia closed the book and turned around to face Harper, Gemma, and Marcy. "There is no way to break the vampire's curse, except by killing them."

"Wait, wait. But you said in order for the curse to work, it has to be written down somewhere?" Harper asked.

Lydia nodded. "Right."

"Then why don't vampires just destroy this book?" Harper asked. "There would be no more curse."

"Okay, first of all, every vampire over about a hundred years old would turn to dust if the curse was suddenly lifted," Lydia explained. "The curse extended their natural life, and without the curse, they should all be dead many years over.

"And second, if you destroy this book, it won't matter, because there's at least a dozen more books out there just like it," she finished.

Harper considered this, then asked, "What if you destroyed all the books?"

"You can't," Lydia said. "You could probably destroy most of them, but the original one, the one that Horace wrote the curse on, he would put it on something indestructible, because he wouldn't want his curse to go away that easily."

"Something indestructible?" Gemma asked. "Like what? A stone tablet?"

"No. Stone can still be shattered, crushed up into powder," Lydia said. "It would be anything that he's given indestructible properties."

"So . . . magic paper?" Harper asked.

Lydia shot her a look. "If you want to oversimplify, then yes, magic paper."

"Why isn't that written on magic paper?" Gemma pointed to the vampire book Lydia was holding.

"It doesn't need to be, because the original is kept somewhere safe," Lydia said. "When you look at more common curses, like vampires and zombies, or like really common, more basic spells, like turning someone into a toad—"

"Okay, yeah, we'll say everyone knows that," Harper muttered.

"It's in about a thousand grimoires," Lydia said. "Somewhere there is a master grimoire, and all the spells and curses are written down on 'magic paper.' But the more specific the curse, the fewer copies there are."

"So when talking about something like a siren, how many copies do you think there are?" Harper asked.

"Considering there can never be more than four sirens in existence at any given time?" Lydia asked. "I'd guess there's only one copy."

Gemma sighed. "And you wouldn't happen to have it, would you?"

"No, I don't. But I can make a guess who does." Lydia smiled brightly. "*Them.*"

"You think the sirens have it?" Harper asked.

"Of course. My understanding is that the sirens are relatively hard to kill. They wouldn't want the instructions on how to destroy them just floating around. I'm sure the head siren has it."

"But they're partially aquatic," Gemma pointed out. "They move through the water. How could they carry paper with them without it being destroyed?"

"It's 'magic paper,' remember?" Lydia said. "It's been granted properties that make it indestructible—meaning it can't be destroyed, not by water or fire or nuclear holocaust."

"Have you seen Penn with any kind of book?" Harper asked Gemma.

"No, I don't think so." Gemma furrowed her brow. "When I moved with them before, Lexi carried a large bag with her, but I never saw what was inside it."

"It's probably not a book," Lydia said. "I mean, the sirens are from Greece? Talking the second or third century? I'm thinking you're looking for a scroll, probably made from papyrus."

"So what you're saying is that we need to find a scroll made of magic papyrus, written in ancient Greek, that may or may not be in the possession of a bloodthirsty siren that does not want us to find it?" Harper asked dryly.

"I never said bloodthirsty. Are they bloodthirsty?" This seemed to excite Lydia, for some reason. "Wow. That's crazy. I always thought sirens would be nice."

"They're not," Harper said.

"Even if we do find it, there might not be a way to break the curse," Gemma pointed out. "Like the vampire curse, there's no way out except death."

"That's true. That is a possibility," Lydia said.

"What if we destroyed the scroll? Would that undo the curse?" Harper asked.

"Theoretically, yes," Lydia said cautiously. "But you won't be able to."

"I can try," Harper insisted.

"Yes, you can try," Lydia agreed with some reluctance. "But many people have tried over the last . . . well, since the beginning of time. And almost nobody ever has."

"Almost nobody," Harper said. "So somebody has?"

"There're always exceptions to the rule," Lydia said. "But I have no idea how they did it, or how you can destroy this one."

"Is there anything more you can tell us about the sirens?" Gemma asked.

"Not offhand, no. But I'll keep my eyes open for anything," Lydia said.

"Thanks, Lydia," Marcy said. "You've been a big help."

"Yes, thank you very much." Harper smiled gratefully at her. "We really appreciate it."

"No problem." She smiled. "Stop by anytime. Any of you."

"Thanks," Gemma said, but she sounded much more deflated than she had before they arrived.

"Oh, hey, Marcy," Lydia said as she walked them to the door. "If your uncle gets any more pictures of the Loch Ness Monster, be sure to send them my way."

"I will," Marcy promised, and then they stepped outside.

After the darkness of the shop, the sunlight felt almost too bright.

The heat was also a bit shocking. Harper hadn't realized how cold it had been inside the bookstore until she felt the warmth outside.

"How do you know Lydia?" Harper asked Marcy.

Marcy shrugged. "I just know people."

Once they were in the car, Harper let out a long breath. She wasn't exactly sure how she felt after that visit, but at least they had a course of action. They were looking for something specific. They could find it. They could solve the curse. Ending this whole siren business felt like a real possibility for the first time in a while.

"That went pretty good, I think," Harper said.

"I guess," Gemma said from the backseat, but she sounded awfully sullen.

"Is something the matter?" Harper turned around to look at her.

"No, everything's fine. The watersong is getting to me, I think," Gemma said, but she just stared vacantly out the window.

ELEVEN

1741, Marseilles

In the mansion in the south of France, Thea lay in bed long after her handmaidens had come in and opened her curtains. Sunlight spilled in through the large windows of her bedroom, but she lay curled among the blankets.

"Thea?" Aggie asked, and without waiting for a response, she threw open the large bedroom doors, causing them to slam against the wall.

Thea ignored her sister and pulled the covers over her head, burying herself.

"Thea, you've been in bed all day, and you stayed in bed all day the day before that, and the day before that," Aggie said.

The bed moved as Aggie climbed into it, crawling over to where Thea lay in the center, and she pulled back the covers. Aggie stared down at her, her warm chestnut eyes filled with concern, and she sighed loudly.

Aggie was fully dressed in a luscious pink gown adorned with lace and fabric shaped into flowers. Despite her attire, she hadn't put on a wig, so her long brown waves cascaded down to her shoulders.

"Are you sick?" Aggie asked.

"Of course I'm not sick," Thea said with a voice like silk. She rolled onto her back so she could stare up at the ceiling instead of at her sister. "We're incapable of falling ill."

"Then why are you lying in bed all day?" Aggie asked. "There must be something the matter with you."

Thea didn't have a very good answer for that. For the past five weeks they'd been living with a duke in the south of France. Everyone assumed that Thea and the other three sirens were his courtesans, and they let them think that. It was easier than explaining what they really were.

Since they'd come here, Thea had slowly begun to lose interest in all the things she used to love doing. Even swimming with her sisters was losing its appeal. The only thing she really wanted to do anymore was lie in her bed.

"It doesn't really matter what's going on with you," Aggie decided and scooted back on the bed so she could get up. "Penn and Gia went to town today, and they've brought a guest over for dinner. You need to get dressed and come down to eat with us."

"I'm not hungry," Thea said.

"It doesn't matter if you're hungry or not." Aggie walked over to Thea's wardrobe and looked through it. "Penn made it perfectly clear that this wasn't a question. She wants to impress him."

"Since when does she try to impress men?" Thea asked as she grudgingly sat up. "And don't we already have enough men here to entertain her?"

The duke shared the house with his two brothers, and that

alone should've been enough for Penn. That didn't include all the servants and friends of the duke who were constantly visiting his home on the edge of the Mediterranean.

"No, it's not a mortal," Aggie said as she pulled a gown from the wardrobe. "He goes by Bastian now, I believe, but he used to be called Orpheus."

Thea grimaced. "*Orpheus?* The musician? Isn't he supposed to be our nemesis? That's what Homer wrote, wasn't it?"

"Perhaps. Homer wrote many things that weren't true." Aggie carried the dress and laid it out on the bed. "Now come. You need to hurry. Penn will be angry if you keep them waiting."

"Why does she even care about this man?" Thea asked, but she did as she was told, slowly sliding to the edge of the bed so she could stand.

"She thought he might know where Father is," Aggie explained.

"Nobody's ever going to tell us where Father is," Thea mumbled as she pulled her nightgown over her head. "And how does she even know who this Orpheus person is if he's going by the name Bastian?"

Aggie held the dress open for her, and Thea stepped inside of it. She pulled it up, slipping her arms through the sleeves. Once it was on, she turned around and held her red hair out of the way so Aggie could begin lacing it up.

"She recognized him," Aggie said. "We've met him before. It was many years ago, back when we still lived in Greece."

"So it was *many, many* years ago," Thea said.

It had to have been at least a thousand years since they'd last lived in Greece. Immortals such as themselves had lived somewhat happily there for a while, but eventually they'd come to feel unwelcome, and they had dispersed all over the world.

"You must remember meeting him." Aggie tightened the waist, causing Thea to exhale roughly. "We went to a performance of his where he played the harp and sang the most beautiful song."

Thea shook her head. "I can't remember. Most of our lives have become a blur of random men, and it's hard to isolate one."

Aggie had finished, and she took Thea by the shoulders, forcing her to turn around and face her.

"What is going on with you?" Aggie asked.

"Nothing." Thea smiled thinly at her. "Everything is wonderful."

"You're lying. And we will talk about it later, but for now, you need to pretend that everything really is wonderful," Aggie said. "For whatever reason, Penn wants to impress this Bastian, and you need to be at your best."

"I will do everything I can," Thea assured her.

Aggie led the way down to the parlor room. As they walked through the halls, servants scattered. All of them lived in fear of the sirens, and that was as it should be. Only the duke and his friends seemed oblivious to their true nature, but that was as Penn wanted it. She kept her siren song focused on them, so they would give freely to her.

Before they even reached the parlor, Thea could hear Penn laughing. It wasn't the seductive laugh she used to get what she wanted, which seemed to be the only laugh she was capable of around men. This was her actual laugh.

Gia, the fair-haired Ligeia, sat on a chair, watching Penn and Bastian with bemused interest. Penn stood nearby, her hand to her chest as she smiled and stared up at him. Her eyes seemed to sparkle, and there was a lightness in them that Thea had never seen before.

When she came into the room, Bastian had his back to her. She was surprised to see that he wasn't wearing a wig. The sirens themselves rarely wore the powdered wigs, finding them itchy and unnecessary, but most other people of standing insisted upon them.

"And the farmer kept insisting that I pay for the chicken," Bastian was saying, and Penn laughed again. "But after all that, there wasn't a chance that I would pay a single denier for it."

Gia giggled but without the same fervor as Penn, who was apparently so interested in Bastian's story that she didn't notice her sisters entering the room. In fact, she didn't see them until they had walked over and were almost standing directly behind Bastian.

"Oh, I'm sorry, Bastian, my sisters have arrived," Penn said as she pulled her eyes from him and motioned to Aggie and Thea. "You recall Aggie and Thea, don't you? Though they went by Aglaope and Thelxiepeia back then."

He turned around, finally looked back at them. The second she saw him, it all came back to Thea.

Hundreds of years ago, she'd seen him perform. It had been in a great stadium, and Thea had been seated near the back with her sisters. Penn had seemed bored, too busy flirting with the gentleman in front of her to pay attention to the man onstage.

But Thea had been unable to take her eyes off him. The songs he played were the most beautiful she'd ever heard, and she spent most of her days listening to Gia sing—Gia, whose voice and song were so lovely and powerful she could enchant any living creature into doing her bidding.

After his performance, it had been Thea who insisted they speak to him. She'd dragged her sisters through the crowds until they finally found him. They spoke only a few words, mostly because Thea was too tongue-tied to find the right words, and then he'd walked away, leaving with his wife.

That memory had almost escaped her until she met his blue eyes, and then it all came flooding back. Somehow, he seemed even more handsome than she remembered him. Dark black hair, broad shoulders, and a smile so amazing, it took all the air from her lungs.

While Bastian greeted Aggie, Thea did her best to keep her composure. She smiled politely to keep her mouth from hanging agape.

"Thea," Bastian said when he turned to her. He took her hand, and she desperately hoped that he couldn't tell she was trembling. He bent down, kissing her hand as she did a small curtsy, and she had to remind herself to breathe.

"I believe I do recall you," Bastian said, once he'd let go of her and stood back up. He smiled crookedly, creating a small dimple in his smooth skin. "You enjoyed my performance."

"Bastian, everybody enjoyed your performance," Penn said with a light laugh.

"That is true," he admitted and turned back to her.

"I'm sure dinner is ready by now," Penn said. "Shall we go down?" She wrapped her arm around his, so he'd escort her to the dining hall.

Thea lagged a few moments behind, preferring to walk with Aggie and Gia. She didn't know exactly what was going on, but one thing she knew for certain—she had a very big problem.

TWELVE

Bonds

After rehearsal, they'd had their first rough fittings. The play was set during the Italian Renaissance, so the costumes were elegant and elaborate, especially since the director, Tom, required perfection and authenticity.

Gemma had gone down into the dressing rooms, where the costume maker had her try on a muslin gown for fit and structure. Once she'd had it on and measurements had been double-checked, she'd been allowed to change back into her street clothes and go home, but she lingered behind.

Throughout the theater's restoration, the dressing rooms had mostly remained untouched. They were small brick boxes shoved in the basement. They'd been painted white to brighten them up, but the paint was chipped and peeling.

The hallway outside the dressing rooms wasn't much better. It hadn't been painted at all, and the ceiling had exposed pipes and ventilation. All four of the dressing rooms had stars on the doors, painted with names of famous movie stars, like MARILYN and ERROL, for ambience.

But that wasn't what had Gemma meandering in the hall. She'd been the last one to have a fitting, so she was alone in the basement, admiring the photographs that lined the walls. All of them were black-and-white eight-by-tens and they had been taken either during the Paramount original heyday or shortly after it had reopened.

The one that Gemma had stopped in front of was of her mother. It had been taken years ago, before either Gemma or Harper had been born, maybe even before Nathalie had married Brian.

Nathalie was standing just to the side of the stage, holding a bouquet of roses. She wasn't looking at the camera; rather, she was staring at something just to the right of her. Her long hair was pushed to one side, and she had a crooked smile that somehow looked beautiful.

Based on her outfit, Gemma guessed that Nathalie had been playing Blanche in *A Streetcar Named Desire*. It had been a simple blue dress that ended up torn by the end of the play, but Nathalie had really loved her performance in it, so she'd kept the dress for years.

"There you are," Kirby said, and Gemma glanced over to see him walking down the hall toward her. "I've been waiting upstairs for you to come up, but you never did."

"I got a little sidetracked," Gemma said, and she pointed to the photograph in front of her. "That's my mom."

It took a few seconds for Kirby to pull his gaze away from her and look over at the picture. When he finally did, he nodded his approval.

"She's pretty," he said, but Gemma hadn't expected a different answer. Her mother was tall and elegant, with beautiful eyes and a serene smile.

"She was a very talented actress, too," Gemma said.

"Like, professionally?" Kirby asked. "Was she on television or movies?"

"No, she was an accountant." Gemma laughed at the juxtaposition. "But in another life, she would've been a model or an actress. She decided to have kids and get married instead."

"That sucks," Kirby said, and Gemma shot him a glare. He immediately looked down, his blue eyes wounded and apologetic.

"That does not suck," Gemma corrected him before turning back to the picture. "She loved my dad, and she loved my sister and me. She chose to be with us because we made her happier."

"Oh." He ran a hand through his dark hair and braved looking up at her again. "Did she die or something?"

"*Or something*," she said quietly. "She was in an accident nine years ago. She's still alive, but it's not the same."

"I'm sorry," Kirby said, and it sounded like he really meant it. He reached out to touch Gemma's shoulder, and she didn't brush away the gesture.

"I went to see her the other day, and I tried to tell her that I was in a play," Gemma said. "The last time I acted was when my kindergarten class did *Three Billy Goats Gruff*. I remember my mom being so excited back then."

She was surprised to feel tears swimming in her eyes, and sniffled to keep them back. Kirby had let his hand fall, but he stayed close to her, in case she might need him for comfort. But the truth was, she barely even noticed that he was still there.

"I thought she might get excited again," Gemma went on. "Mom always had such a light in her eyes when she talked about the plays she was in. But when I told her, she didn't even know what I meant.

"She used to walk around the house reciting Shakespeare and Tennessee Williams and Arthur Miller." Gemma let out a deep breath and shook her head. "But now she didn't know what I was talking about, and she didn't care."

Then, in a small whisper, she added, "She barely even remembers me."

"Hey, come on." Kirby tried to put his arm around her, but she stepped away from him.

"Sorry." Gemma wiped at her eyes and forced a smile. "You don't need to see me like this."

"I don't mind." Kirby smiled at her. "Why don't we get out of this dank basement? I'll give you a ride home."

"Kirby, no, that's okay." Gemma shook her head. "You don't need to do that."

Yesterday, while she'd been with her sister and Marcy trying to figure out how to break the sirens' curse at the bookstore, Kirby had been calling and texting her. She'd turned her phone off so she could focus, but when she finally turned it on, she saw that she had six new texts and two missed calls.

That was when Gemma decided that this had gone far enough. It was one thing to have fun with Kirby to pass the time, it was another thing entirely to actually become involved with him. Penn and Lexi would eventually take notice of him, which could become very dangerous for him.

Besides that, she was still in love with Alex, and she'd never love Kirby. Not that Kirby would ever love her, either. Whatever he felt for her was probably nothing more than siren-induced infatuation, and she didn't want him getting hurt over imitation emotions like that.

So she decided that she needed to end things with him.

Unfortunately, she'd been so busy trying to figure out where Penn might store a secret scroll that she hadn't thought of exactly how she would break things off with Kirby.

It wouldn't have been so bad if she'd been able to make any progress on finding the scroll. Her best ideas so far were to talk to Thea about it or search the sirens' house. Penn and Lexi had been home all day, and at rehearsal she'd been unable to get Thea alone, since she was always surrounded by the actors in the play.

And that left Gemma standing outside the dressing rooms, trying to find a way to let Kirby down gently.

"It's really no problem giving you a ride," Kirby said. "You're on my way home."

"I know, but I thought I'd walk tonight," Gemma said. "It's such a nice night."

"I could walk you home," Kirby offered.

"Kirby, the thing is, you're a nice guy, but . . ." She let out a long breath when she saw his expression fall. "I just got out of a serious relationship, and I need to focus on the play, and there's so much going on in my life. I don't think it's fair to you if we keep hanging out."

"It's fair," he said quickly. "It's totally fair. I'm fine with it. If you're busy, you know, I can give you space."

"Okay, well, I need a lot of space," Gemma said. "Like so much space that we're not talking or hanging out outside of the play anymore. At all. That kinda space."

Understanding washed over his face, and he swallowed hard. "Did I do something wrong?"

"No." She smiled sadly and shook her head. "You were perfectly wonderful."

"Then . . . can I at least walk you home tonight?" Kirby asked. "Like, to say good-bye?"

"Gemma?" Daniel asked. He'd appeared at the bottom of the stairs at the end of the hall. "Is everything okay down here?"

"Yeah, everything's fine," Gemma assured him.

"Good," he said, but didn't move away. "Everyone else has gone home for the night. So . . . Kirby, why don't you head on home?"

"I was going to walk Gemma home," Kirby said.

"Why don't you take the night off, Kirby? I'll make sure she gets home safe," Daniel said. "I've gotta swing by her house anyway to see her sister."

Kirby looked over at Gemma, probably hoping that she would fight for him to take her, but she just shrugged and shook her head. Truthfully, she was relieved to get out of it. Kirby was harmless, but that didn't mean she wanted to spend the next half hour turning him down.

Kirby lowered his eyes and nodded. "All right. See you later, Gemma." He turned and walked down the hall.

Gemma waited until after he was gone before she smiled gratefully at Daniel and walked over to where he waited for her.

"Thanks," she said. "You saved me from a really, really awkward walk home."

"You're only saying that because you don't know what *I* have planned for conversation. I'm going to talk about all sorts of uncomfortable things." Daniel smirked.

"So you're really gonna walk me home?" Gemma asked as they walked up the stairs together.

"Damn straight I am," Daniel said. "Do you have any idea what your sister would do to me if I left you to walk home unguarded in the middle of the night?"

"It's, like, nine o'clock," Gemma pointed out.

"You think that matters to Harper?" Daniel asked. "It's dark. That constitutes 'middle of the night' to her."

When they reached the top of the stairs, instead of going back up to the stage and through the auditorium they turned and went out the back door. Daniel held it open for her as Gemma stepped outside into the warm night air.

As soon as she stepped outside, Gemma could feel it. There was no real way to explain it. It was like something in her blood was magnetized. When the moon was full, it pulled to her, the way it pulled the tides, and the ocean seemed to call to her more loudly than normal.

"I should go swim tonight," Gemma said, as she breathed in deeply.

"Why don't you go home first?" Daniel asked. "I'm sure if you're going for a night swim, Harper would feel much better about it if she were there."

"Yeah, I will," she agreed almost reluctantly. Not so much because she didn't like swimming with Harper, but because it meant she'd have to wait longer to go.

Over the past few weeks, when she had to swim, she'd sometimes take Harper with her. More often she would go with Thea, and on the very rare occasion she'd gone with all three of the other sirens.

The agreement that Gemma had made with Harper was that she'd never swim alone again. As much as Harper didn't like the sirens, like Gemma, she'd come to trust Thea. So she thought it was safer for Gemma to be around Thea than to be alone.

"If I asked you a question, would you answer me honestly?" Gemma asked as she and Daniel walked along the sidewalk.

"I would try," Daniel said uncertainly. "But I usually don't lie, so it's a pretty safe bet that I'll be straight with you."

"Are you working on the play because of me?" Gemma asked, looking up at him to watch how he responded. "Did Harper put you up to it?"

"You're asking if Harper wanted me to babysit you," Daniel said, stealthily avoiding her question. "She never really used those words."

"But she did ask you to?" Gemma pressed.

"Actually, no, she didn't," he said. "But I knew it would make her feel better if she knew you were safe. And it's not like I would be happier if something bad happened to you."

"It's not like you'd be happier?" Gemma laughed. "Don't lay the concern on too thick."

He smirked and ruffled his already disheveled hair. "You know what I mean. You're a nice kid. I don't want anything bad to happen to you, but I don't want you getting the wrong idea."

"There's no wrong idea to be had, which is nice. You're one of, like, two guys that I can actually be myself around." She sighed. "It's really just you and my dad at this point that *aren't* leering at me."

"As your sister's boyfriend, I can do double duty as brother-in . . . boyfriend-in-law?" He cocked his head, trying to come up with the right expression, before shrugging and moving on. "Anyway, if there's anybody you want me to beat up for you, let me know, and I'm on it."

"Thank you." Gemma smiled. "I appreciate the sentiment."

"I don't look that strong, but I make up for it by being tall," Daniel said, and she laughed.

She glanced over at him, and he'd sold himself short. While Daniel was indeed on the tall side, he looked strong, too. He mostly wore button flannel shirts or faded T-shirts—the standard outfits of hipsters and handymen alike—but through that, she could see his thick biceps and broad shoulders. Plus, she'd seen him without his shirt on, and she knew that he was pretty ripped.

"Penn told me she offered you ten grand to put up a fence around her house," Gemma said.

"That she did." He scratched on the scruff under his chin. "I turned her down, obviously."

"Obviously?" She looked up at him. "That's a lot of money to turn down."

"It is, but I'm sure it's blood money," Daniel said, without looking to Gemma for confirmation. "And it's probably not in my best interest to spend that much time around Penn. All the guys in her life end up dead."

"How is it going with that?" Gemma asked.

"With Penn's somewhat obsessive interest in me?" Daniel asked and exhaled deeply. "It's all about walking a very fine line of not pissing her off and not leading her on."

"And you're not attracted to her?" Gemma asked. "At all?"

"No." He laughed and looked appalled. "Not in the slightest. Are *you* attracted to her?"

"*No.* Why would I be attracted to her?"

"Exactly. You were implying that she was so beautiful that any logic or reason or actual desire I might have would be overridden by her physical appearance," Daniel said. "Since we're both immune to her song or whatever supernatural hold it is she has on people, the same would be true for you."

"That makes sense," she said finally. "Have you told Harper about Penn's little crush on you?"

"I've downplayed it as much as I can," Daniel admitted. "She knows some, but not the full extent. She doesn't need to worry about it."

"No, I get that. I haven't told her much, either." Gemma sighed. "It's better that way sometimes."

They rounded the corner of the block, leaving the businesses in the center of town for the residential neighborhoods on the edges. A small brick retaining wall ran next to the sidewalk, and Gemma climbed up, walking on it with her arms out like she was walking a tightrope.

"Since we're being honest, can I ask you something?" Daniel asked.

"Of course," she said, but she slowed her steps and glanced over at him.

"The question is a bit weird, and I'm not even sure you'll know the answer." He shoved his hands in his pockets and stared down thoughtfully at the sidewalk. "But when we found you, after you'd run away with the sirens, how did Harper know where you were?"

Gemma's forehead pinched with confusion. "It was because of the newspaper. Weren't you the one who showed her?"

"No, I know how we found the town," Daniel said. "We knew the general location. But as soon as we saw that house, she *knew* you were there."

"What did she tell you?" Gemma asked.

"Not a lot, actually. I asked her a couple times about it, and she's always very vague. She won't say anything more than that she just knew."

"That's how, then." Gemma shrugged. She'd come to the end of the wall, so she jumped down and landed on the sidewalk next to Daniel.

"I didn't understand before, but now that you put it that way, I get it," he said dryly.

He'd stopped walking, so she did, too, and she turned to face him.

"Harper told you about the accident, right?" Gemma asked. "The one that happened when we were kids, and how my mom has a brain injury from it?"

"She has mentioned it, yes, but she doesn't say much about it," Daniel said.

"In her defense, there really isn't a whole bunch to tell. Mom was driving Harper to a pizza party, and a drunk driver sideswiped her. It hit the driver's side, so Mom got the worst of it, but Harper was hurt, too," Gemma explained.

"Her injury basically amounted to a bad cut on her leg." Gemma ran her hand six inches up and down her thigh to demonstrate. "She has a gnarly scar now, which is why she never wears short-shorts and hates to put on swimsuits."

"Okay," Daniel said, like he was trying to follow what Gemma was saying but did not understand the connection at all.

"Well, anyway, while that was happening, I was at home with my dad," Gemma said. "We were sitting in the living room, and I was coloring, and I remember just having this overwhelming panic. I don't even know how else to explain it. I was suddenly just *terrified*."

"Like a panic attack?" Daniel asked.

"Something like that." Gemma nodded. "But then I got this really sharp, intense cramp in my leg." She motioned to the same spot on her leg that she had for Harper's scar.

"So you're saying that you felt it when Harper got hurt?" Daniel asked.

"I know it sounds crazy, but then again, after everything we've been through lately . . ." She trailed off and shrugged. "I don't know why it happens, and I really can't explain it. But since I've become a siren, I think it's gotten more intense."

"How so?" Daniel asked.

"Before, I could only feel it when something really bad happened, like a car crash. But I knew when she was in trouble at the Fourth of July celebration and Penn had found you guys." She gestured to him. "And she found the house I was staying in."

"Hmm," he said after a minute, since there was nothing more he could really say.

They started walking again, but they didn't talk about anything of substance the rest of the way. They mostly just talked about Tom and how he was a little nuts. A few houses before they'd reached Gemma's, she stopped short.

"What?" Daniel asked, looking down at her.

"If I tell you something, will you promise not to tell Harper?" Gemma asked.

"What is it?" Daniel asked, his eyebrows crinkling in concern.

"No, you need to promise. Before I tell you anything."

"Okay." He glanced toward her house, as if expecting to see Harper lurking about, then turned back to Gemma and nodded. "I promise."

"I'm not . . . telling Harper everything." She chose her words carefully. "And I'd like it if you did the same."

"What do you mean?" Daniel asked.

"Harper has her whole life ahead of her," Gemma said. "She has all these great plans for herself, and she has you, and she has . . . everything. And there's a very good chance that no matter what she does to help me, I won't have a future. At least not one where I'm not a monster."

"Harper told me that you were making progress," he said. "I thought you'd found a lead on a way to break the curse."

"I don't know if it's really a lead, but I do know that I don't have much time left." She took a deep breath. "The point is that I want Harper to have her future. She needs to go to college, and she won't if she doesn't think I'm safe. So I need to pretend that everything is okay, even if it's not, and I want you to help me."

"You want me to lie to my girlfriend and put you in danger so she'll leave?" Daniel summed it up.

Gemma nodded. "It's in her best interest. She'll be safer if she's gone, and she has a much better chance at a happier life."

Daniel considered this and eyed Gemma. "I'll make a deal with you. I'll go along with you and try to shield Harper from the worst of it, on one condition—you tell me *everything*."

"Why?" Gemma asked.

"Somebody needs to have your back. I get why you want to protect Harper, but you don't need to protect me," Daniel said. "We got a deal?"

"Okay. Deal."

"Good." Daniel smiled. "Now you can start by telling me what you meant by not having much time left."

"It's . . ." She looked away from him and was surprised to find tears swimming in her eyes. "Penn thinks she found a replacement."

"For you?" Daniel asked, and Gemma wiped at her eyes and nodded. "What does that mean?"

"It means she plans to kill me and use my blood to create the potion to make a new siren to take my place." She smiled to keep the tears from falling. "And if I don't break the curse soon, I'm dead."

"Hey, don't cry."

He put a hand on her shoulder, almost awkwardly at first, but when she started crying, he wrapped an arm around her and hugged her roughly to him. She wept softly into his chest, giving in to the sadness for a few minutes before she let the embarrassment take over.

"I don't want to die," Gemma said, her words muffled into his shirt.

"Good," Daniel said. "That's a good start. Now, what do you need to do to live?"

"Get along with Penn, and find the scroll." She'd stopped crying, so she straightened up and wiped at her eyes. "Sorry. I didn't mean to blubber like that."

"No need to apologize. No blubbering occurred," he assured her with a smile. "I can help you keep Penn happy, at least for a little while. The scroll is the thing Lydia told you guys about yesterday?" Gemma nodded. "Harper told me you didn't know where it was."

"I don't," she admitted. "I want to check their house, and I need to talk to Thea and see what she knows."

"Okay. So do that," Daniel said. "Like, immediately."

"They're at home right now," Gemma said. "I think it'd be better if I checked their house when they're not there, and I want to do that before I talk to Thea. She said she'd do everything to help me just short of getting herself killed, and if I find the scroll and break the curse, it might kill her. So she would hide it from me."

Gemma realized what she'd said and swallowed hard. Over the past few weeks she and Thea had become closer, and Gemma even considered her a friend. But to save herself—to break this curse—it could mean that Gemma would have to kill her, or at the very least Thea might otherwise have to die.

"So you think you could get into the house tomorrow?" Daniel asked.

"Maybe. Thea has play rehearsal, and if I skipped it, I could get into the house, assuming that Penn and Lexi aren't there," Gemma said.

"Okay, how about this: You go scope out the house. If Penn and Lexi are home, I'll come up with some kind of distraction," Daniel said. "I don't know what yet, but I can come up with some reason to get Penn out, and Lexi tends to follow her around like a puppy. Then you get in and do your search."

"That sounds like a plan." Gemma smiled up at him. "Thank you."

Daniel smiled back. "It's no problem."

She started to walk back toward her house, then realized he wasn't following. "Aren't you coming over?"

"Nah, I don't think I should," Daniel said. "You should go swimming with Harper, and if I come over, she'll want to hang out with me."

"Are you sure? I could always go swimming another night." That was what she said, but she didn't really mean it.

"No, you go. Have fun. Spend time with your sister. I'll talk to her later," Daniel said, taking a step back away from Gemma. "Tell her I say hi, though. And don't forget to call me if you need me tomorrow."

Gemma knew she should try harder to stop him—he'd walked her all the way here—but she didn't. Once he was out of sight, she turned and jogged back to the house, already thinking of arguments to convince Harper to go swimming with her.

THIRTEEN

Vacillation

After Gemma got home from play rehearsal, she all but insisted Harper swim with her. Harper had refused as much as she could, but she knew that Gemma would go without her.

Because of the transformation that happened whenever she hit salt water, Gemma preferred swimming at night when there were fewer witnesses around, and Harper couldn't fault her for that. So she put on her swimsuit and took Gemma out to the bay.

They went out past the beach, where the soft sand became jagged rocks lining the shore. The paved parking lots for the crowds were replaced by a forest of bald cypress trees. Harper parked on a dirt road as close to the water as she could drive.

Gemma led the way, walking delicately from one rock to another, and Harper was careful to copy her footing so she didn't stumble or cut her foot on a sharp rock. When they reached the water, Gemma waded out first, and within seconds Harper saw the moonlight glinting off her tail.

She was much faster than Harper, but she waited for her, literally swimming circles around her. Harper never felt as uncoordinated as she did when she swam with Gemma. Her normally elegant strokes seemed more like clumsy dog-paddling compared to the way Gemma glided through the water.

She almost hated to admit it, but there was something awesome about swimming with Gemma when she was a mermaid. The grace and beauty Gemma had was truly stunning.

"Harper, hang on," Gemma commanded, floating in front of her in the water.

"What?" Harper treaded water next to her.

"Grab my shoulders," Gemma said, and when Harper hesitated, she goaded her on. "Come. Trust me. Just hang on to my shoulders."

Gemma turned with her back to Harper, and tentatively Harper gripped her sister's wet shoulders.

"Now what?" Harper asked.

"Now hold your breath," Gemma said with a laugh, and then she plunged into the water, dragging Harper down with her as she swam quickly.

Just when Harper was beginning to fear she might drown, Gemma pulled her back up, out of the water and through the air, before they came crashing back down again.

Being with Gemma out in the ocean, seeing her when she was in her element, actually broke Harper's heart. To know that Gemma had found someplace where she belonged so completely, and that she couldn't really stay there.

The night may have been magical, but Harper knew that wasn't all there was to the curse. If it was, she would gladly let Gemma relish it for the rest of her life. But that wasn't the case.

In the morning, both Harper and Gemma seemed to wake up with a renewed zest to find the scroll. Gemma may have been unable to get into the sirens' house or get a second alone with Thea yesterday, but she was determined to search today. She wouldn't tell Harper what it was, but Gemma assured her that she had a plan to get into the house alone.

For her part, Harper had spent most of the day at work looking up anything she could about curses and sirens and ancient scrolls. The Capri Public Library wasn't well stocked in books of the occult the way Cherry Lane Books was, so she hadn't really come up with anything yet.

But she was certain they'd find something soon. They had to. Until they did, though, Harper couldn't leave for college. She had to see this thing through. But if she didn't go to college, she'd have to tell her dad about it.

When she came home from work, she cleaned up the house. Harper stared out the kitchen window as she washed the dishes. She was staring at Alex's house, but her mind was a million miles away. She heard the front door open and close, followed by her dad's work boots clomping on the floor. A minute later, Brian appeared in the kitchen behind her.

"Hey, sweetie," Brian said, picking absently through the mail that Harper had left on the kitchen table.

"Hey, Dad." Harper finished rinsing off the last plate, then shut off the tap and turned around to face him. "How was work?"

"Same old, same old." He shrugged and opened up a bill. "How was your day?"

"Pretty good, I guess." She leaned back against the counter and watched him read the bill. He cursed under his breath and shook his head. "Is it bad?"

"Don't worry about it." Brian set it down, then looked up at her and smiled. "What were you saying about your day?"

"Nothing really." She smoothed out her ponytail and smiled at him. "Are you hungry? Do you want something to eat?"

"I'm not in grade school, Harper," he said, bemused. "I don't need a snack."

She laughed, but it sounded nervous. "I know."

"Did you need something?" Brian asked, narrowing his eyes at her. "You look like you need something."

"Nope." She shook her head hard. "Uh, no. Um, well, I guess . . . I was wondering how things were going with Alex."

He opened the fridge and grabbed a bottle of beer before responding. "At the docks, you mean?"

"Yeah, I was just wondering how he was working out," Harper said, hoping her dad didn't see through her attempts at small talk. She couldn't just tell him about her change of plans for the future as soon as he walked in the door.

"He's a good worker." Brian twisted the cap off his beer and took a long drink. "He doesn't say much to me. He never really did, but now it's even less. He was always a quiet kid, and weird. Still is. Just quieter and weirder."

"He's not 'weird,'" Harper said. "He's just . . . reserved."

Brian leaned back against the kitchen table. "Do you know why Gemma and Alex broke up?"

Harper lowered her eyes and shook her head so forcefully her ponytail whipped her in the face. "Nope."

"I feel like it was something bad," Brian said. "Something happened between the two of them."

"Maybe it just, like . . . I don't know." She shook her head again.

He watched her for a moment, then said, "I thought she might tell you."

"No, it's teenager stuff." She shrugged. "You know she's secretive."

"Yeah." He took another drink of his beer. "Did she tell her mom?"

"What?" Harper looked up, surprised to hear Brian even mention Nathalie.

"I don't know." He looked away, but not before Harper noticed how pained his blue eyes looked. "She always liked talking to her mom, so I wondered if Gemma still told her things."

"Um. Yeah," she said finally, nodding. "Sometimes I think she does. She knows Mom will keep her secrets."

"Yeah, Nathalie will. Whether she wants to or not." He took a deep breath, then stepped back from the table. "There's something I want to talk to you about. Why don't you have a seat?" He motioned to a chair.

"It's a have-a-seat kind of talk? What is it?" Harper asked, already panicking.

"Just sit down," Brian said, taking his own seat at one side of the table. "I wanted to talk to you first, before your sister. She's at play rehearsal tonight, right?

"Yeah, until eight or so." Harper sat down across from him, literally sitting on the edge of her seat. "Dad, you're really kinda freaking me out. Can you just spit it out? Are we losing the house?"

"What?" Brian was confused, then appalled. "No, we're not losing the house. Where would you get that idea?"

"I don't know! It sounds bad."

"It's not bad. You worry too much. You know, you worry more at the age of eighteen than I do at forty-one. You're gonna give yourself an ulcer or have a heart attack if you're not careful."

"Dad!" Harper said, barely able to contain her anxiety any longer.

"All right, all right." He held up his hand and took a deep breath. "Um . . . I think I need to go see your mom."

Harper waited a beat, staring at her father blankly. "You want to visit Mom? That's your bad news?"

"I told you it wasn't bad news, but . . ." Brian wouldn't look at her when she spoke, and that didn't help to ease her fears. "I've been thinking about a lot of things lately, and I need to see her again before I make some decisions."

"What kind of decisions? What are you talking about?" Harper asked.

"Harper, I told you there's nothing you need to worry about. I want to see Nathalie, and I wanted to go with you and your sister. Are you both going this Saturday?"

"Um . . ." She stopped to think. "Yeah, I think we are."

"Okay, then. Can I come with you?" Brian asked, finally looking up at her.

"Yeah, of course you can. You can go see her anytime you want. She's your wife."

"I know that." He began to peel the label off his bottle, and more quietly he repeated, "I know."

"That's all you wanted to talk about?" Harper asked, confused as to why he wanted her to sit down for something relatively painless.

"Yeah." He nodded, then lifted his head. "Unless you needed to say something."

"I do, actually." She took a fortifying breath before beginning. "There's something I've been needing to tell you . . ."

"You're not pregnant, are you?" Brian asked, nearly cutting her off.

"Dad! What? No. Of course not." Her eyes were wide. "Oh, my god, Dad. Daniel and I've been together, like . . . No. We're not even . . . Dad. Just no." She couldn't help herself and began to blush.

"Good, because babies are wonderful, but not until you're ready," Brian said, sounding relieved. "They're a lot of work, and you have all that college ahead of you."

She saw her in, so she said, "That's what I wanted to talk to you about."

"College?"

"Yeah, I was thinking about maybe holding off another year."

"Harper Lynn Fisher, you are going to college," Brian said firmly.

"I know, Dad. I'm just thinking it might not be the right time."

"Is this about Daniel?" He narrowed his eyes and his expression hardened. "If he's holding you back, I will get rid of him."

"Dad, stop. Get rid of him? Are you in the Mafia?" Harper asked in disbelief. "And this has nothing to do with Daniel. I've never let a boy interfere with my future before. Why would I start now?"

"Then what is this about?" Brian asked, his tone carrying an edge of confusion and irritation.

"I just think it's not the right time," she said simply.

The real reason—that Gemma was a siren—she couldn't tell her dad. He'd never understand or believe her. And even if he did, what good would it do? Harper was already driving herself crazy with worry. Brian didn't need to go through that, too, not when there was nothing he could do.

"If it's about money, Harper, we can do this." He leaned forward on the table. "You've got those scholarships, and you'll lose them if you don't go. I've got some cash put away, and you've got loans lined up. We'll make it work. You don't need to worry about it."

"No, it's not about money."

"Then give me one good reason why you shouldn't go," Brian said.

"Gemma." Harper gave the most honest answer she could. "There's something going on with her."

"I'm glad that you love your sister so much, but she is not your child. She's not your responsibility. She's mine. I'll take care of her. The only thing you need to concern yourself with is getting ready to leave for school. The rest of us will be fine."

She sighed. "There's stuff that you don't understand."

"Understand this—I have not worked forty-plus hours a week for the past nineteen years for you to throw your future away. Everything I have done, I have done so you and Gemma could have a better life than what your mom and I had. This is what we both wanted for you, and it's what *you* want for you. I don't care what the reason is for not going. There isn't one good enough."

"But Dad . . ." she said, but she was already giving up trying to convince him.

"No buts, Harper. You are going to college. And that's final."

FOURTEEN

Minotaur

"If I were a magic papyrus scroll, where would I be?" Gemma asked herself as she stood in the entryway of the sirens' house.

For once, she'd actually lucked out. Harper had let her borrow her car—something Harper very rarely let her do—and when Gemma'd arrived up at the sirens' house, Penn, Lexi, and Thea had been gone. Thea was at play rehearsal, but she had no idea where Penn and Lexi were, so she had to get her search under way as quickly as possible.

The house was nice, but it wasn't really large. That made it easier, because there were fewer places to look.

Gemma did a cursory search of the kitchen, opening cupboards and drawers, but while she inexplicably found a drawer filled with lacy panties next to the fridge, she saw no sign of a scroll or any other important papers. The pantry was stocked with canned goods and a broom, but nothing else exciting.

The rest of the downstairs was about the same. What little storage space they had in the living room was filled with movies and more lingerie. They had to have the most extensive collection of sexy undergarments outside of Victoria's Secret.

She'd made it two steps up the stairs to the second floor when she heard an odd flapping sound coming from outside. Her heart dropped, and she slowly turned back around. Through the windows she could see Thea just touching down on the driveway—her massive wings beating behind her.

Thea hadn't shifted fully into her bird form, so she still remained human, aside from the giant wings sprouting from her back. The wings were a gorgeous scarlet, shimmering in the sunlight, and the flapping caused her skirt to flutter up for a moment. The wings folded up behind Thea as she walked toward the house, and by the time she reached the door, they had disappeared into her flesh.

Gemma thought about hiding or trying to sneak out the back door before Thea spotted her, but at the last second decided against it. During her quick search, drawers were left open and lingerie had been tossed about. It wasn't like she had enough time to cover it up, and Thea would probably guess that she'd been the one ransacking their house anyway.

When Thea opened the door, she didn't seem that surprised to see Gemma, but then, she'd probably spotted Harper's car in the driveway.

"Looking for something?" Thea asked, surveying the state of the house.

"What are you doing home?" Gemma countered, trying to hold off answering the question until she figured out what she wanted to say. "Shouldn't you be at play rehearsal?"

"When I saw you weren't there, I knew you were up to something." Thea sat down on a chair in the living room and leaned back, putting her feet up on the coffee table across from her. "So I left early to find out what it was."

"How did you know I would be here?" Gemma asked.

Thea shrugged. "I didn't *know*. I just had a hunch. And with Penn and Lexi out of town for the evening, I thought I'd better follow up on it."

"Where are Penn and Lexi?" Gemma asked.

"Gone." Thea rested her green eyes squarely on Gemma. "So, are you going to tell me what exactly you're looking for?"

Gemma debated on how to answer before finally deciding to go with the truth. "The scroll," she said as she descended the steps.

"*The* scroll?" Thea arched an eyebrow but appeared otherwise unfazed. "You say that as if I should know which one you're referring to."

"The one with the curse written on it." Gemma sat down across from Thea and tried to play it as cool as Thea was. "It has everything the curse entails, what the rules are, maybe even how to break it."

The side of Thea's mouth curled up in an amused smirk. "I can assure you that it has no way to break the curse on it. Although I can see why you'd find some of the other information interesting, particularly how to kill a siren."

"So . . ." Gemma licked her lips. "You do know what I'm talking about."

"Of course I do." Thea laughed. "Did you really expect I wouldn't?"

"No, I guess not," Gemma admitted. "But I thought you might lie about it."

"I have no reason to lie. If you already know, what's the point?"

Thea tilted her head. "Though I am curious. How did you find out about it?"

"I have my sources," Gemma replied quickly.

Thea may have been Gemma's closest friend at this point, but that didn't change the fact that she was still a siren. She wasn't about to give up Lydia or Marcy's name, in case Penn or even Thea decided to retaliate later on.

"Well, whoever your sources may be, if they told you the scroll is the key to breaking the curse, they've misled you," Thea said.

"Maybe," Gemma said. "But why don't you let me see for myself?"

Thea laughed, throwing her head back as she did. "Oh, Gemma, please."

"What?" Gemma asked. "Why is that so funny?"

"Your arrogance." Thea subdued her laughter but smiled broadly. "You presume that you can solve a puzzle that we've spent hundreds of years analyzing. Do you really think me and my sisters are that stupid?"

"No, of course not," Gemma said in a hurried apology. "Penn may be many things, but stupid isn't one of them."

"Then what do you think you'll see that we haven't already seen?" Thea asked.

"I don't know. Maybe nothing," Gemma admitted. "But I have to try. My only other option is giving up, and I won't do that. Not until I've exhausted every avenue, and until I see this scroll for myself, I still have one more path to explore."

Thea shook her head. "That's not the only option. You can embrace this life. There are parts of being a siren that are truly wonderful."

"Don't try to sell me on it, Thea," Gemma cut her off. "I just want to know where the scroll is."

"Why do you think I would tell you?" Thea asked.

"You told me you would. You said you'd do whatever you could to help me."

"*If* it didn't end up with me or my sisters dead," Thea corrected her.

"You think that if I find the scroll, it will kill you?" Gemma asked.

"Not exactly." Thea stood up and started walking over to the kitchen. "Would you like something to drink?"

"No, I'm fine." Gemma turned in her chair to watch Thea. "What do you mean, 'not exactly'?"

"I don't know how much you really know about the scroll." Thea opened the wine fridge located in the kitchen island. She debated a few seconds before pulling out a bottle. "It's supposed to be indestructible."

"I had heard that," Gemma said.

"And it is, as far as I know." Thea pulled out a corkscrew, then shut some of the drawers that Gemma had left open. "At various times over the centuries, other mortals have tried to destroy our scroll. Even Aggie went through a phase where she tried to burn it."

"But it didn't work?" Gemma asked.

"Nope." Thea uncorked the wine and pulled out a glass. "Are you sure you wouldn't like a glass?"

"No. I make a point of not drinking anything from a siren," Gemma said wryly, and Thea smiled.

"That's probably a good rule." Thea poured herself a large glass of wine and took a long drink before continuing on. "We're not the only cursed creature in the world, as I'm sure you can imagine. And almost all of them have tried to break their curse by destroying their scrolls."

"None of them have succeeded?" Gemma asked.

"Depends on your definition of 'succeed.'" Thea walked back to the living room. "But very, very few have managed to destroy it."

"So you're saying it is possible?" Gemma asked.

Thea sat down across from her again, crossing her legs and setting the glass on the coffee table. "Have you ever heard of a minotaur?"

"I think so. It's like half man, half bull, right?" Gemma asked.

"Sort of," Thea said. "The original minotaur was Asterion. I never met him, but I've heard that he was an incredibly gorgeous young man, and Pasiphaë fell in love with him. She was already married to King Minos, despite being a rather powerful goddess in her own right.

"The king found out about his wife's adultery and threatened to behead her lover, so Asterion broke off the affair. Pasiphaë became enraged and cursed him to have the head of a bull," Thea explained.

"Why the head of a bull?" Gemma asked.

"I'm not sure exactly, but I was told it matched his other . . . *appendages,*" Thea said carefully, and Gemma wrinkled her nose. "Pasiphaë went on to have many other lovers, and if they tried to end the affair, she cursed them to the minotaur form and locked them away in a labyrinth so that they could never escape."

"That sounds terrible," Gemma said. "But what does that have to do with your scroll?"

"It was terrible, and I'm getting to my point," Thea said. "Eventually Pasiphaë died, and someone set the minotaurs free. But it was a terrible way to live. I met one once, and they truly were hideous creatures. Monstrous bulls with gigantic horns and angry eyes. Not only that, they were all a little insane from living in that maze for so long.

"Naturally, they didn't want to go on that way," Thea went on. "Pasiphaë had made them immortal, but Asterion was determined to get out of it. He came up with a way to destroy his scroll.

"If I recall correctly, he had to eat the scroll when the sun was shining above him." Thea tilted her head as she thought. "I don't remember the details exactly, but I know it was odd and very precise."

"Isn't it the same way to destroy your scroll?" Gemma asked.

"No, each scroll has its own set of rules for destroying it, and they are never told to the bearer of the scroll," Thea said. "Meaning, we were never told how to destroy ours. I don't even know for sure who was told, and even if I did, they would probably be long dead by now."

"How did Asterion find out?" Gemma asked.

"One of the muses told him." Thea waved her hand. "It doesn't matter. That's not the point of the story."

"Then what is?" Gemma asked.

"Pasiphaë had turned Asterion and all those other men into minotaurs centuries before he destroyed the curse, long after their natural mortal lives would've ended," Thea explained. "So the second the scroll was destroyed, they all turned into dust."

"Why?" Gemma asked.

"When the scroll is destroyed, it's as if the curse never even happened," Thea said. "And if the curse had never happened, they would've been dead and decomposed for many years. So that's what became of them."

Gemma realized that this only confirmed what Lydia had told

them earlier, and let out a long sigh. "And that's what would happen to you and Penn and Lexi if anyone destroyed the scroll."

"Exactly." Thea picked up her glass and leaned back in her chair. "So, as much as I'd like to help you, I can't help you with this. I won't do anything that leads to my sisters' deaths, or mine."

Gemma stayed where she was for a few minutes, letting this all sink in. Even if she found the scroll, it didn't mean she'd be able to figure out how to destroy it. She'd still need to find someone who knew how, and if she did that, it would turn all the sirens to dust.

"Thanks for your help," Gemma told Thea and got up. "Sorry I messed up your house."

"It's fine. I'll make Lexi clean it when she gets back." Thea smiled at her, but Gemma couldn't muster up a return smile. She lowered her eyes and was walking to the door when Thea spoke again. "It's not here, Gemma."

"What?" Gemma turned back to her.

"The scroll. I won't tell you where it is, but I can tell you that it's not here," Thea said, sounding almost irritated to be admitting it to Gemma.

"Why are you telling me this?" Gemma asked. "And how do I know that I can trust you?"

"You can't." Thea shrugged. "I'm telling you because . . ." She sighed and shook her head. "I don't know why I am. I just know that you don't have much time left before Penn replaces you, and . . . I don't want you wasting your time looking for something you'll never find."

FIFTEEN

Proxy

"Oh, my gawd, everything about this town is *horrible*," Lexi groaned as she flipped through the radio stations in Penn's convertible. "Why did you have to get a stupid classic car? We could've had satellite radio."

"You know me," Penn said. "I love the classics."

They were far enough out of Capri that the radio stations decided to just give up and turn into full-on static. Lexi flicked the radio off, then leaned back in her seat, sulking.

"At least we're getting out for the day," Penn said. "That ought to make you happy."

"No, it only makes me sadder because I get to be reminded of how awesome the rest of the world is compared to that stupid little crap fish town," Lexi ranted. She crossed her arms over her chest and stared straight ahead at the highway in front of them.

"Fish town?" Penn asked. "What does that even mean?"

"It means it sucks, and you know it." She turned to Penn, imploring her. "When we first got there, you said we'd only be there a few days. We were just supposed to look real quick and get out. Then we were supposed to go to Buenos Aires—"

"*If* we didn't find anything," Penn amended.

"Right, but we totally didn't find anything," Lexi said, then corrected herself. "Well, we didn't find what we were looking for. So we should move on."

"Lexi, I'm trying here," Penn said, trying hard to keep her tone even. "We're going to meet Gemma's possible replacement right now. I don't know what else you expect me to do."

"I know, but why do we have to wait at *all*?" Lexi whined. "Why can't you just kill Gemma and go grab this new girl?"

"Because I don't want to get stuck with another Gemma again," Penn explained as if she were talking to a small child. "I want to make sure that Liv is a perfect fit for us."

"I thought you already decided that she was," Lexi said. "I mean, that was the point of you going off by yourself to search the area for replacements. You were supposed to have already decided she was perfect."

"She *seems* perfect, but I want all of us to approve of her."

"So if I like her, we can turn her tonight?" Lexi asked.

"No, Thea still needs to meet her," Penn said.

"Ugh." Lexi groaned and leaned back in the seat. "Thea will never approve. She's so dumb."

"You're upset, and I understand that, but you *really* need to watch your tone." Penn glared over at her.

"Why don't we just kill Gemma tonight?" Lexi asked. "It was just a full moon the other day, so we have almost a month to find a replacement."

"No, that's what happened with Aggie," Penn said. "And the only reason I killed Aggie when I did was because she was going to kill us if I didn't. I had no choice, and I'm not doing it again."

"But if we just killed Gemma, we could get out of this town, and I'm sure outside of Capri there are, like, a million girls way better than her," Lexi whined.

"Lexi, we will kill Gemma," Penn assured her. "Soon. *Very* soon. Just not until I'm certain about the replacement."

"When we kill her, can I eat her heart?" Lexi asked.

"No."

"I *never* get to eat anybody's heart," Lexi pouted. "Every time we've killed a siren or another immortal, you get to eat their heart, and it makes you all extra hot and feel extra good. It's not fair. I never get to do anything."

"Yep. I get it, Lexi," Penn snapped. "I know how you feel. Now you're starting to get on my nerves."

Lexi tried to be quiet, but it only lasted about a minute before she turned to Penn. "Can I eat Daniel's heart, at least?"

Penn nearly slammed on the brakes but managed to just ask, "What?"

"Well, you were saying that you think he might be related to that Bastian guy or whatever," Lexi said. "The immortal you dated before I was a siren. If Daniel is related to him, then he probably has a better heart."

"No, you cannot eat Daniel's heart," Penn replied icily.

"Why not?" Lexi asked. "Yeah, he's cute, but who cares? You get to eat Gemma's heart, can't you just leave me your scraps?"

"No." Penn gripped the steering wheel tightly, and her words came out through her clenched teeth, which were slowly shifting into fangs. "He's mine."

"He's yours?" Lexi scoffed. "You're being ridiculous. I would expect this kind of sentimental bullshit from Aggie or maybe Thea. But never you."

"Lexi!" Penn growled. "You are annoying! I'm gonna pull this car over if you don't shut the hell up!"

"No! I will not shut up!" Lexi shouted at her. "You are annoying *me*! You and your stupid crush on an idiot human! You're being a total—"

Penn jerked the car to the shoulder and slammed on the brakes. Lexi finally shut up and grabbed on to the door to brace herself. Without saying anything, Penn turned and attacked Lexi.

She climbed on top of her, grabbing Lexi's silky hair to keep her from pulling away, and she hit her in the face over and over again. Lexi squealed and clawed at Penn's hand, but she never really fought back.

When she'd finished, Penn sat back down in the driver's seat. As she'd been hitting Lexi, her eyes had changed into a bird's. But she began to calm herself, and her eyes returned to normal.

What really worked was licking the blood off her hands. Siren blood tasted sweeter and was far more powerful than mortal hearts. In a few minutes her voice would be more enchanting and she'd be even more radiant.

Lexi sat up slowly, and out of the corner of her eye Penn could see that her face was smashed up. Within the hour, Lexi's broken face would be back to its normal beauty. Until then, she'd be in pain, and that made Penn smile.

"Now, then," Penn said as she pulled back out on the road. "I think we'll both agree that I will kill who I want, when *I* want."

"Yes," Lexi mumbled, her words slurred because both of her lips were busted open.

"Now clean yourself up," Penn continued in the same cheerful, calm voice. "You want to make a good impression on the new girl, don't you?"

"Yes," Lexi repeated, probably afraid that if she didn't say anything, Penn would attack her again. This was a fair guess, because Penn had tasted the siren blood, and she was eager to have more.

By the time they reached Auburnton, Lexi had begun to heal, but she wasn't completely cleaned. She wiped the dried blood from her face while Penn hummed along with the radio, when it finally found a station.

"There she is," Penn said as she pulled over on the side of the road beneath a maple tree.

"Where?" Lexi asked, and Penn pointed to a girl sitting at an outside café across the street.

Penn had told her they would meet her there, and the girl kept looking around, presumably checking for Penn. Her wavy blond hair was kept shoulder-length, and she chewed her lip as she waited. She couldn't be more than eighteen, and there was something wide-eyed and innocent about her.

"Shall we go meet her?" Penn asked, and without waiting for Lexi to answer, she got out of the car.

"Wait." Lexi rushed around the car and caught up to Penn as she walked across the street. "Why her? Why do you like her?"

"I chose Gemma because I thought she had siren traits—her beauty, her love of water, her strength—and I thought we could work with her stubbornness," Penn said. "Gemma didn't like us from the start, but I thought we could overcome that once she saw the gift we'd given her."

They were still half a block down from the café, but the girl had spotted them. She stood up and waved her arm wildly in the air. Penn gave her a small polite wave back.

"Now I realize my mistake," Penn said, lowering her voice. "I realize that what will make a good siren is a good follower. This girl's plain, but she'll become beautiful. She can't swim, but she'll learn. But she's the kind of girl that will do anything to fit in."

Penn smiled at Lexi. "She'll do whatever I say."

The girl walked over to meet them at the edge of the café, nearly knocking over a table as she did, and her cheeks flushed with embarrassment.

"Sorry." The girl smiled widely at them both. "I wasn't sure if this was the right café, and I've been so worried I've been waiting at the wrong one. I've been here for a half hour, but now you're here, so I'm glad that it is the right one.

"And now I'm rambling. Sorry," the girl continued without taking a breath, and then she turned her attention to Lexi. "Oh, my gosh, you are so pretty! I can't believe how beautiful you both are. Sorry. That's probably weird for me to say, and I'm sure you get that all the time, but you really are just so pretty."

"Thanks," Lexi said, then leaned toward Penn and whispered, "I think you may have gone a little heavy on the siren song this time. She's even more submissive than Sawyer was."

"I haven't even used the song on her," Penn told her. "She's just naturally this infatuated."

"Wow." Lexi stared at the girl. "She's perfect."

"I know," Penn agreed. "Lexi, meet Olivia Olsen."

"Liv," the girl said as she extended her hand. "My friends call me Liv, and I'm hoping that we'll all be good friends."

"Oh, I'm certain we will be," Lexi said with a wide smile.

SIXTEEN

Man-Eater

Gemma had snuck behind the dark velvet curtains to inspect Daniel's work on the sets backstage. She thought it might help take her mind off of her growing hunger.

Planks of wood were stacked, and a skeleton of two-by-fours was the only part really put together. Daniel obviously tried to keep his work space somewhat orderly, but not all of his equipment seemed to fit in the oversized toolbox, so some tools were lying about.

His blueprints were stacked together on top of a table. Gemma bent over them and tried to get an idea of the set. It had to be easily turned, so it could serve double duty as two sets. He also planned to create walls that could slide in to create the illusion of more private quarters, like bedrooms.

"*Thus in plain terms: your father hath consented,*" Aiden said, his voice low as he recited his lines, "*that you shall be my wife, your dowry 'greed on, and you will* . . ." He trailed off and muttered the beginnings of his speech over again.

Practice had finished up about ten minutes ago, with everyone dispersing, but Aiden had lingered behind to go over his lines again. He'd wandered backstage, his brow creased in thought, and continued to mumble to himself.

It was dimly lit backstage, so apparently he hadn't seen Gemma yet. She stayed where she was, leaning on the table, and watched him struggle. The concern in his brown eyes, as if he worried he'd never be able to learn his part, endeared him a bit more to Gemma.

So far, all she'd really seen of Aiden had been overly confident attempts at flirting with an uninterested Thea, or blundering through a scene and completely butchering his lines. It had never occurred to Gemma that he actually cared about the part or that he was even trying.

She'd assumed that he'd skated through life on his good looks and his father's name. He'd graduated from college last year, and the town had all but hailed it as the return of the Golden Boy and given him a key to the city.

But seeing him rub his temple with his battered script rolled up in his hand humanized him. For the first time, Aiden actually looked attractive to Gemma. Her stomach seemed to growl in agreement, and she swallowed back her hunger.

"Need some help?" Gemma asked, and he jumped a bit, startled by her presence. "Sorry. I didn't mean to scare you."

"No, you didn't scare me," he assured her with a grin. He walked closer to where she was standing, but the table was still between them. "I thought I was the only one here. What are you doing?"

She shrugged and looked back down at the plans. "I didn't really have anywhere else to go."

The truth was that she didn't know how much longer she could keep her appetite in control, and Aiden was looking very tempting right now.

Anxiety only seemed to make her hunger worse, and after her conversation with Thea the day before, she'd been rather dejected. She didn't know where else to look for the scroll, and wasn't sure how much good it would do her even if she found it.

On top of that she'd had something of a run-in with Alex today. Her car wasn't working, so Gemma'd been outside looking under the hood of the car, attempting to make sense of it, when Alex had come home. She'd lifted her head just in time to see him getting out of his own car, wearing his dirty work clothes.

Just the sight of him was enough to make her heart drop to her stomach. Even as much as he'd changed over the last month, she could still see the boy she'd fallen in love with, but wrapped in an even sexier package. His sleeve pulled taut on his arm, and she remembered the way he'd held her and promised to love her forever.

Then, as he was walking up to his house, he'd glanced over at her. She'd lifted her hand to offer a small wave, but he glared with such intense hate that it felt as if her heart had literally been ripped in two. It was all she'd been able to do to keep herself from bursting into tears on the spot.

She reminded herself that this was what she wanted, that this was what was best for Alex. The sirens didn't care about him at all now that he hated her.

This was the only way to keep Alex safe, and even if it meant that he'd never be able to love her again, Gemma knew that she'd made the right choice. No matter what else happened between the two of them, she could always remember the times that they'd shared together, and that had to be enough.

"Now, I don't believe that for a second," Aiden said, and Gemma looked up at him. "I'm sure you have plenty of places where you could be on a Wednesday night."

"Sadly, no," she said with a thin smile. "At least none that I'd rather go to than the dusty backstage of the theater."

"You really love the theater, then?" Aiden asked.

"I love pretending to be someone else for an hour or two," she admitted.

"Well, would you want to help me pretend to be someone else for a little while?" Aiden asked with an alluring smile.

"I'll be happy to help with the play, if that's what you're asking," Gemma said, returning his expression with a coy one of her own.

He laughed and tapped the script in his hand. "I guess I can settle for that for now."

"You seemed to be having trouble with the same bit. Do you want to try again and I'll see if I can give you hints if you get stuck?" Gemma suggested.

"Sure." Aiden handed her the script. She had her own, but his was already out. "The page is folded down. I've been getting stuck with it a lot."

She hopped up on the table, crossing her legs so he wouldn't be able to see up her skirt, and opened the book to the dog-eared page. His passages were highlighted, so she found the spot easily, and then nodded to him.

"Okay." Aiden shook his body, mentally preparing himself for the scene. "Okay." He cleared this throat, then began, "*Thus in plain terms: your father hath consented that you shall be my wife, your dowry 'greed on, and I will* . . ." He stumbled again. "*I will* . . ."

"It's not *I will*," Gemma said. "It's *and will you*, if that helps at all."

"*Your dowry 'greed on, and will you* . . ." Aiden tried again, then shook his head. "I have no idea what you'll do."

She laughed lightly. *"And will you, nill you, I will marry you."*

"Wow, Gemma, that's a pretty bold proposition," Aiden said with a broad smile. "We hardly even know each other. We should probably go on a few dates before you start making declarations of marriage."

Gemma laughed, but before she could come up with an equally flirty response, the back door to the theater slammed shut. Both she and Aiden turned to see who it was, and they heard the clack of wedge sandals on the stairs a few seconds before Lexi appeared.

"This is play rehearsal?" Lexi asked with a disparaging look around the stage. "It looks more like somebody's dirty basement and two horny teenagers."

"I'm not a teenager," Aiden said, doing his best to stand up for them, but Gemma couldn't tell if he was annoyed by Lexi's interruption or pleased by the appearance of the leggy blonde.

"This isn't play rehearsal," Gemma said. "That's over."

"Are you serious?" Lexi groaned. "Where the hell is Thea, then?"

Gemma shook her head. "I don't know. I thought Penn picked her up."

"No, Penn was busy . . ."—Lexi stopped to choose her words carefully, smiling wickedly as she did—"*entertaining* a guest. So I came down to get Thea."

"She probably started walking home," Gemma said and set Aiden's script aside.

"Great. Now I have to go track her down," Lexi said.

Gemma hopped down off the table, almost bumping into Aiden, who'd moved closer to her as she'd been talking.

"I can go with you," Gemma offered, brushing past Aiden to

talk to Lexi. "I could help you look." If she couldn't find the scroll, she could at least try to ingratiate herself with the sirens to buy herself a bit more time to look.

"I'm pretty sure I can handle it myself, but thanks anyway," Lexi said, her silken voice dripping with venom. "You can go back to playing grab-ass." She turned to Aiden then. "Watch out for this one. She's a real man-eater."

Lexi winked at Gemma, then turned to walk away. Gemma hurried after her, stopping her before she even made it to the back stairs.

"We're running lines," Gemma explained quickly. "But why don't I go with you? It's been a few days since I've gone swimming. Maybe we could all go out to the bay."

"What is with you?" Lexi whirled around to face her. "Since when do you want to do *anything* with me or Penn?"

"I—I—I don't," Gemma stammered. "I just . . . I wanted to . . . We haven't talked much lately."

"There's nothing to talk about," Lexi snapped, then she glanced around. "Wait a second. Where is that scruffy plumber or whatever that Penn is all hung up on?"

"Daniel?" Gemma asked. "He's not a plumber. He's a handyman."

Lexi glared at her. "Like I care what he does. I was just wondering where he is."

"He's at Pearl's Diner, helping Pearl fix an overhead fan," Gemma said.

Lexi made a retching sound. "He's so gross. I have no idea what Penn's problem is. She's . . ." She trailed off and shook her head. "Whatever. I should go find Thea."

"You're sure you don't want me to come with?" Gemma asked

again, trying to keep the desperation out of her voice. "I'm sure I could help."

"Honestly, I would love to leave you in charge, wandering around this tiny little shithole until you found Thea, but that would take too long," Lexi said. "I need to get Thea, and I need to get back."

"Because Penn's entertaining a guest?" Gemma asked, recalling what Lexi said earlier. She assumed that Penn had a guy over she was getting frisky with.

Lexi tilted her head. "That's what this is all about? You're trying to figure out who our 'guest' is?"

"I'm just a little curious, that's all," she admitted.

"You're worried, aren't you?" Lexi stepped forward so she was standing right in front of her. Lexi was taller than her, but thanks to the wedge heels, she now towered over Gemma. "You're afraid we might be interviewing replacements for you? That we might have *found* a replacement?"

Gemma swallowed hard. "That actually hadn't crossed my mind before."

"Well, we are. And she's marvelous." Lexi smiled. "Thea's meeting her tonight, and if it all goes well, then it's all over for you."

Gemma really didn't have anything to say to that, so Lexi just laughed. She turned and walked toward the door.

"It's a good thing I found the scroll, then," Gemma said, stopping her.

Lexi paused and narrowed her eyes at her. "What?"

Gemma swallowed hard and decided to plunge ahead. Thea wouldn't tell her where the scroll was, so there was no way that Lexi would, either. At least not if Gemma came right out and asked for it.

"The scroll that has your curse on it. If I destroy it, then I destroy all of you," Gemma said.

"You did not find it." Lexi stepped away from the door and moved closer to Gemma, but Gemma just held her ground and stared up at her.

"I did," Gemma said. "It was the second place I looked, and if you don't help me break the curse, I'll find a way to destroy it."

"Ugh." Lexi groaned and rolled her eyes. "I told Penn we shouldn't have hid it there. Once you knew who her dad was, it was, like, obvious."

"Yeah, well . . ." Gemma licked her lips. "I did meet her dad, and I got it."

"Met her dad?" Lexi smirked. "You little liar. You didn't find anything. Her dad's dead."

"I'm close, Lexi," Gemma insisted as Lexi backed away to the door. "I'm going to find it, and when I do, I'll destroy the scroll and you along with it. If you help me break it, maybe there's a way that we can all live."

"Nice try. You won't find it, you won't stop us. At least not before we replace you. You're out of time, Gemma." Lexi laughed and walked out of the theater, letting the door slam shut behind her.

Aiden started talking to Gemma, asking her what that was all about, but Gemma ignored him. He'd been standing back up on the stage, so he hadn't been able to hear everything, but he'd heard enough to know something was up.

The sirens were looking to replace her, and they were probably going to do it soon. If Gemma didn't break the curse, she was as good as dead. And the only clue Lexi had given her was that the hiding place had something to do with Penn's dead father.

SEVENTEEN

Diner

Pearl's?" Harper asked with a raised eyebrow as she slid into the booth across from Daniel. "This counts as a proper date?"

"I never used the term 'proper date.'" Daniel held up his hands defensively. "I said that we needed to get out more."

Pearl's didn't have an oceanic theme like most of the tourist traps in Capri, aside from one painting hung behind the counter. It depicted a mermaid sitting on an open clamshell holding a huge pearl, and Harper avoided looking at it when they sat down.

When Daniel had said that he wanted to go out tonight, Harper thought he meant something a bit more special, even though it was only a Thursday, and she'd tried to get dolled up. She wore a light summer dress and kept pulling it down to make sure the hem fell below the scar on her thigh.

Pearl, the owner and namesake of the diner, made her way over to their booth. The diner had other waitresses, but every time Harper came with Daniel, Pearl made a special point of waiting on them. That was probably because Daniel was always helping Pearl out, and she wanted to make sure he was treated well.

In her early fifties, Pearl was a somewhat heavyset woman. She looked a little gruff, but Harper knew that she was as sweet as her blueberry pie. Which, incidentally, matched her hair. Harper assumed that Pearl attempted to cover up her gray with some type of at-home dye kit, and it left her with bluish curls that she pinned back.

"Don't you both look nice?" Pearl commented when she reached their table and looked from Harper to Daniel. "Celebrating something special?"

Although Daniel managed to look foxy no matter what he did, Harper wouldn't classify him as looking particularly nice tonight. He wore a Led Zeppelin T-shirt with Icarus on it, and he still had the perpetual stubble on his face.

Though Harper had come to prefer his scruff to his clean-shaven look. When he'd shaved once a few weeks ago, his kisses felt different and a little alien.

"No, just hitting the town for the night," Daniel said, grinning up at Pearl. "What do you have on special tonight?"

"I have meatloaf with homemade gravy, and a chicken salad sandwich," Pearl said. "The chicken salad comes with fries. But if there's anything you want, I can make it up for you. And it's on the house tonight."

Pearl's didn't have menus. She had a few specials written on a chalkboard hanging behind the counter, but with everything else, customers were just supposed to know what she served.

"Thank you, Pearl," Daniel said. "We'd like a few minutes to think it over."

"Take your time." Pearl winked at him. "I'll check on you in a bit."

"Thanks, Pearl," Harper said, then turned her attention back to Daniel.

"What?" Daniel asked once Pearl had walked away.

"She paid you in food again, didn't she?" Harper asked.

He leaned on the table and offered her a sheepish smile. "I did fix her overhead fan, and offers of food were made, yes."

"Daniel." Harper smiled and shook her head. "You have to stop letting people pay you in food."

He shrugged. "It doesn't happen that often. I have plenty of jobs that pay me in cash."

"Really?" She was skeptical and crossed her arms over her chest. "'Cause it seems like you get paid in food or gently used sofas or a box of bootleg VHS tapes."

"That was one time." Daniel held up a finger. "And it had an entire season of the original Adam West *Batman* in it."

"You don't have a VCR!" Harper countered.

"I'll get one," he insisted.

"Well, if you wait long enough, you'll probably get paid with one."

"Haha," he said dryly, but he was still smiling.

Harper relented a bit, uncrossing her arms and leaning forward on the table. "I'm just saying. You have bills to pay, and I don't think my dad would let you pay him rent in food or videotapes."

"Don't worry. I have it covered." He waved off her concern. "The Paramount job is paying pretty well."

"How is that going, by the way?"

"Good. It's coming together, slowly but surely."

"Good. Glad to hear it." Harper rubbed at a spot on the table and, as nonchalantly as possible, she went on. "I thought something might have happened. Gemma came home last night acting kind of strange, but when I pressed her about it, she kept insisting that nothing was wrong. She just spent the whole night reading up on the mythology books I brought home from the library."

Daniel shook his head. "I had to leave early because I was helping Pearl, but everything seemed fine when I was there."

"Good." Harper smiled at him.

Pearl came back to take their orders. Harper hadn't really been thinking about it, so she just got the meatloaf and a cherry malt. Daniel apparently liked the sound of that, because he ordered the same.

Once Pearl had left to fill their order, he leaned back in the booth. He stared across at Harper and sighed.

"This is going against my rule where I said I wouldn't tattle on Gemma," he said finally.

"It's not tattling," Harper argued. "We're adults. Adults don't tattle."

"That's kind of my point." He scratched the back of his head and glanced around the diner. "When I started working on the play, I said I would keep an eye on Gemma, but I wouldn't run to you telling you every little thing she did wrong."

"I know. And I've never asked you to," she said. "I don't need to know everything she does. I just want to know that she's safe, and I trust your judgment."

"Well, anyway . . ." He sighed again. "I didn't see her much last night because I left early, but tonight, she seemed like herself. She was getting a little flirty with Aiden Crawford."

"Aiden? The mayor's son?" Harper asked, her eyes widening a little. "I thought she was seeing Kirby Logan."

"I think they broke up on Monday."

Harper scoffed and slouched back in her seat. "God, she never tells me anything."

"She doesn't want to worry you. And you tend to react like this when she tells you stuff." Daniel motioned to her.

"I'm not reacting any way," she said quickly, but she sat up straighter and tried not to look as upset. "But you were saying something about Aiden. Are you sure he wasn't just flirting with her?"

"No, guys flirt with her a lot. She usually ignores them. This time she was definitely flirting back."

"Is this a bad thing?" Harper asked. "I mean, worse than her getting involved with any guy right now?"

"No." Daniel stared down at the table and pursed his lips. "I don't know."

"What does that mean?"

"I don't know anything." He paused and glanced around the diner before continuing. "Well, Aiden used to be really good friends with my brother."

"Your older brother? So you're saying this Aiden guy is older than me and you and way, way older than Gemma?" Harper was going into high alert, but she did her best to keep her voice even so Daniel couldn't accuse her of overreacting.

"Yeah. But . . ." Daniel scratched his scruff and hesitated. "After John died, I didn't really have any reason to talk to Aiden anymore, so it's been, like, five years since we've really spoken."

"But?"

"But when he did run around with John, Aiden was not the nicest guy, and he had a really bad track record with the ladies."

"Like how bad?" Harper asked.

"I don't know." He lifted one shoulder in a half shrug and looked up at Harper. "I mostly heard about it from John, so I don't know how true any of it is. But I saw one of his girlfriends, and she had a pretty nasty shiner."

"She got it from Aiden?"

Daniel nodded. "That's what John said."

"And now Aiden's dating Gemma?" Harper asked, and by now she didn't care at all how Daniel or Gemma thought she should react.

" 'Dating' is probably too strong a word. And you have to keep in mind that Gemma is, you know . . ." He gave her a knowing look, trying to remind her that Gemma was a mythological creature capable of enslaving men. "She can handle herself."

Harper shook her head. "I don't want her to have to handle herself."

"I know. But . . ." Daniel trailed off when he noticed Harper digging in her purse on the booth seat next to her. "What are you doing?" Instead of answering, she pulled out her cell phone. "No. Harper, you can't call her."

"Why not?" Harper asked, but she'd already hit the call button and held the phone up to her ear.

"Because she'll know that I told on her, and she'll be pissed at both of us."

"I don't care." She listened to the ringing and hoped Gemma would hurry and pick up.

"*This* is why she doesn't tell you stuff," Daniel said. "You act like her mom."

Harper froze for a second. That was about the worst thing Daniel could call her. She'd been trying really hard to act more like a sister and a friend than a parent. It wasn't good for either of them if Harper kept smothering Gemma.

She was just about to hang up when Gemma finally answered.

"Gemma?" Harper said. "Sorry. Pocket dial." She paused as Gemma said something. "Yep. I'll see you when I get home." She hung up and shoved the phone back in her purse, then looked at Daniel. "There. Was that better?"

He smiled. "A little bit, yeah."

"Why did you even tell me this?" Harper asked. "You knew how I'd react."

"I thought you should be aware of the situation, so you can kinda keep an eye out for stuff," he said. "But you have to let her live her own life, make her own choices. And right now all she's done is flirt with a guy. It's not time to sound the alarm."

Harper swallowed hard and shook her head. "I don't know how I'm supposed to act or what I'm supposed to do. If I see her in danger, I'm just supposed to let her be in danger?"

"If Gemma was standing in front of a moving bus, I would expect nothing less than for you to run and push her out of the way," Daniel said. "But she's not standing in front of a bus. And we're on a date."

"I know." She took a deep breath. "I'm trying."

"I know." He reached across the table, taking her hand in his. "And I think it's sweet that you have to work *so* hard at caring less. You're like the exact opposite of the Grinch. Your heart is three sizes too big."

She smiled and blushed a little. "That was really cheesy. But also sweet."

"That's what I was going for." Daniel grinned. "I like to think that I walk the fine line between cheesy and sweet, and I always come out on top."

"Most of the time, you do."

Pearl brought them their dinner shortly after that, and the rest of their meal went well. Both of them made a point of not talking about Gemma or the sirens or college—any of the big three downers that consumed Harper's life.

When they left the diner, the sun was still up, but it was beginning its descent below the horizon. The day had been bordering on overly hot, but as it grew later it managed to hit that perfect spot of just warm enough.

Harper had parked almost a block away, which was the closest spot she'd been able to find next to Pearl's. She and Daniel began walking to her car, neither of them really speaking, just enjoying each other's company and the beautiful evening.

"What did you want to do now?" Daniel asked when they reached Harper's old Sable.

"I don't know." She leaned back against the passenger door and stared up at him. "Did you have anything in mind?"

"I was thinking maybe you could come back out to the island with me." He leaned in toward her, putting one hand next to her on the car.

"Yeah? What will we do out there?"

He pretended to think about it, his expression comically serious, and it made Harper laugh a little. When he looked back down at her, he was smiling, but it fell away to something more intent.

"I could think of a few things," he said, his voice low, and he leaned down to her.

His lips had just brushed against hers when a commotion down the street pulled her attention from him.

EIGHTEEN

Slip

Penn lay stretched out on the sofa of her living room, languidly flipping through a tabloid as Lexi paced in front of her.

"Isn't it time for Thea to come home?" Lexi asked.

Penn lifted her eyes to peer at the clock over the top of the magazine. "Play rehearsal isn't even done yet."

"But this is ridiculous. You brought Liv over last night, and everything went great with her!" Lexi sighed. "She needs twenty-four hours before she'll even discuss it with us?"

"She said she needed time to 'gather her thoughts.'" Penn let go of the magazine long enough to do air quotes with one hand.

Lexi stopped in front of the fireplace and turned back to Penn. "You should just go down and pick her up."

"I let her take the car, remember?" Penn asked.

"Why?" Lexi demanded, her tone taking on a grating whine that made it very hard for Penn not to smack her. "You always drive her."

"I didn't feel like it," Penn said as evenly as she could. "And I suggest you calm the hell down before I *make* you."

"Whatever," Lexi muttered and stormed upstairs.

Within a few minutes music came blasting out of the stereo, and Lexi sang along with it. Penn thought about yelling at her, but listening to Lexi sing was far better than listening to her complain.

It seemed to take Thea far too long to get home, mostly thanks to Lexi's choice of songs. She seemed content to put Katy Perry on repeat, and while Penn had liked the song in the beginning, by the fifteenth time in a row it began to wear on her.

Fortunately, Lexi shut it off the second Thea walked in through the front door.

"So did you make your decision?" Lexi leaned over the banister in the upstairs loft and shouted down at Thea. "You totally love her, right?"

"Is it okay if I shut the door before you start interrogating me?" Thea asked, pushing her oversized sunglasses onto the top of her head.

"*Relax*, Lexi," Penn said, all but begging her. She sat up on the couch and tossed the magazine aside. "We don't need to make any decisions this instant."

"Well, it wouldn't hurt for us to make it *now*." Lexi jogged down the stairs, but she tried to quiet the insistence in her voice. "So? What did you think?"

"Rehearsal was fine, thanks for asking," Thea muttered and sat down in a chair.

"You know nobody cares about your play," Penn said matter-of-factly, and Thea just sighed.

Lexi sat on a chair across from her, and she was literally on the edge of her seat, staring at Thea expectantly.

"I don't know how I feel yet," Thea admitted finally. She put her feet up on her chair and wrapped her arms around her knees. "It's too soon to say."

"Oh, come on!" Lexi groaned and flopped back in her seat. "You told us you would know by now! We spent the whole evening with Liv last night. She was *perfect*, and you know it!"

"She was not perfect!" Thea shot back. "She's a sycophant, and when you told her that we were sirens, she was barely fazed by it. She's probably insane." Thea turned her attention to Penn, giving her a hard look. "That was a big risk, by the way."

"I used the siren song on her." Penn brushed it off. "Liv won't be able to tell anyone, even if she wanted to. But I doubt she would anyway. There's no way she'd go back on her promise to me."

"You don't know that, Penn," Thea insisted. "You don't know *her*. And I still don't think you've given Gemma enough of a chance."

"We've given her plenty of chances!" Lexi yelled. "You're being ridiculous. This is so dumb. Liv is perfect, and you're an idiot, and we need to leave this stupid town." She stood up and crossed her arms over her chest. "Penn and I don't care what you say. We're doing what we want."

Penn shot her an icy look. "*We* aren't deciding anything. I'll make a decision. Why don't you go upstairs and let Thea and I talk, since you can't stop throwing a tantrum?"

"I'm not throwing a tantrum," Lexi snapped. Penn continued to glare at her, so she scoffed before turning and stomping upstairs to the bedroom loft.

Penn leaned forward and rested her arms on her knees, turning her attention back to Thea. "Forget Gemma. She's out of the picture. We're not keeping her, no matter what you say or what she does. Okay?"

"I think you're being a bit premature, but it's your call." Thea shrugged and kept her eyes fixed on the floor.

"When we take Gemma off the table, how do you feel about Liv?" Penn asked.

"There's just something about her that I don't trust," Thea said. "Liv rubbed me the wrong way."

"But you have to admit that she's going to follow orders much better than Gemma does," Penn said. "When I told her we were sirens, she was so excited to become one of us."

"That's just it, Penn!" Thea looked up to meet her sister's gaze. "This is a curse. She shouldn't be excited about it."

"It's an awesome curse," Penn countered, and Thea shook her head.

"You chose Lexi because of how submissive she was," Thea reminded Penn. "*I* wanted a different girl, but you kept going on and on about the handmaiden that worshipped your beauty. And Aggie sided with you to keep the peace."

"Yeah, so?" Penn asked. "That turned out great."

"Did it?" Thea arched her eyebrow. "Or is Lexi constantly getting on your nerves?"

"I can hear you, you know!" Lexi shouted from upstairs.

"No matter what you think of Lexi, you have to admit that she's worked out way better than Gemma," Penn said, ignoring Lexi. "She's been part of our group for nearly three hundred years, and she may be obnoxious, but I haven't killed her yet. So that's something."

Thea leaned closer to Penn, and when she spoke, she'd lowered her voice to just above a whisper. "I know you're not ready to leave. Whatever you have going on with Daniel, I know you're not about to give that up just yet."

Penn considered this, but didn't say anything.

"And I want to finish the play I'm in," Thea said. "I know you don't care about it, but maybe you can spend more time with Daniel, and everyone can spend more time making sure that Liv is the right choice instead of just jumping into a hasty decision again."

"You're suggesting that I wait to kill Gemma until after the play?" Penn asked.

"Yeah," Thea said. "It's only a couple more weeks."

"We don't have that much time," Lexi said, leaning over the railing of the upstairs loft so she could see them.

"We have as much time as I say we have," Penn snapped at her.

"No, we don't." Lexi shook her head. "I did something bad. By accident."

"What did you do?" Thea asked, her voice a low growl. "You didn't kill anybody, did you?"

"No, I just . . ." She sighed. "I may have let it slip where the scroll is."

"What scroll?" Penn asked. Her nose wrinkled in confusion, but then realization hit her, and she stood up. "*The* scroll? Who did you tell about the scroll?"

"Gemma," Lexi admitted sheepishly. "She tricked me last night. She said she'd already found it, and I told her that it was with Achelous, and so I think she put the pieces together. Or at least she probably will."

"You stupid wench!" Penn shouted, and Lexi cringed. "Thea's right! You are the biggest mistake I have ever made! You are so dumb and useless!"

Thea stood up, moving between Penn and the staircase as if preparing for Penn to run upstairs and attack Lexi. Penn wanted to do just that, but she stayed where she was, seething.

Her temper was barely under control, and she felt her fingers begin to elongate. Her gums had begun to itch as her teeth shifted into fangs, and her vision had already become clearer as her eyes changed into those of a bird.

"Does she have the scroll?" Thea asked Lexi, her voice calm.

"I don't know." Lexi shook her head, and Penn could see tears pooling in her eyes. That only enraged her more, and it took all her strength to keep from flying up there and ripping off her head.

"You're going to get us all killed!" Penn roared. The monster had taken over her voice, shifting it from silk to something much more demonic.

"Nobody's dead yet!" Thea held up her hands to calm her sister. "Gemma might not have the scroll yet. Lexi will go look for it, and if it's there, she'll bring it here for us to guard personally. If it's not there, then we'll go kill Gemma."

"Why don't we just go kill her now?" Lexi suggested. "Then it won't matter if she has it."

"You did this on purpose, didn't you?" Penn asked, narrowing her eyes at her. "You wanted to leave now, so you're trying to make it so we have to."

"No, Penn, I swear, it was just an accident," Lexi said.

"Penn, stop," Thea said, her words as sweet and melodic as she could make them. "Think. You don't want to kill Lexi right now. It's hard enough finding the replacement for one siren, let alone two."

Penn knew she was right, so she took a deep breath and pushed the monster back down. Slowly she felt her fangs pull back, but her eyes stayed changed. She couldn't put her anger completely to rest, nor did she want to.

She kept her power with the sirens by letting them know she'd do whatever it took to keep the power. She'd had no problem destroying anyone who stood in her way or went against her, and she wasn't about to stop now.

"Lexi, go find the scroll," Penn commanded, and her voice had returned to its normal saccharine tone. "If it's there, bring it back to me. I will take care of it."

"What if it's not there?" Lexi asked.

"You better pray it is, but if Gemma finds that scroll, you'll be the first one to die," Penn warned her. "Do you understand?"

Lexi nodded. "Yes, I understand."

She ran down the stairs, and when she raced by Penn, she gave her as much room as she could. Penn was tempted to give chase and attack her, but it would be better if Lexi retrieved the scroll sooner rather than later.

Thea waited to speak again until after Lexi had gone out the back door. They watched through the window as she dove off the cliff behind the house, where she'd land in the water crashing below them.

"What's your plan if Gemma doesn't have the scroll?" Thea asked.

"We'll stay for now," Penn said, still staring out the back window as the setting sun reflected off the bay. "I don't want another Gemma *or* Lexi on my hands, and the more time I spend being sure that Liv is the right choice, the better off we will all be.

"But we can't stay that much longer." Penn turned back to Thea. "It's only a matter of time before your precious Gemma finds the scroll, so we'll have to kill her first."

NINETEEN

Inebriated

Two doors down from Pearl's Diner was a bar frequented by the dockworkers. Harper had never been inside before because she wasn't yet of the legal drinking age, but judging by how it looked on the outside, she assumed it was a dive. Her dad had gone there from time to time, and everything he'd said about it had confirmed her suspicions.

When three men came tumbling out of the battered front door of the bar, yelling and swearing, Harper hadn't thought much of it. They made enough noise to disrupt her kiss with Daniel, but that was all.

Or it would've been, if Harper hadn't seen the source of all the trouble. Two of the men were there just to pull the third one out of the bar. They tossed him onto the sidewalk, where he'd hit his head on the cement, and that was when Harper saw who it was.

"Alex?" Harper asked. She put her hands on Daniel's chest to push him back a bit, but he'd already started stepping away.

"I'm fine!" Alex had gotten to his feet and was yelling. "That other guy was being the dick, not me!"

Harper rushed over to him, getting there just in time to catch him from falling back again. Unfortunately, he was too heavy for Harper, so he nearly took her down with him, but Daniel grabbed his arm and hoisted him back up.

"Is this a friend of yours?" one of the guys from the bar asked.

"I don't have any friends." Alex tried to push Daniel away, but Daniel kept his grip firmly on Alex's arm. "I don't need any friends."

"Yeah, we're his friends," Harper said, ignoring Alex's protests. "And we're sorry about any trouble he's caused. He's just been going through some things."

"Well, tell your friend not to come back here if he's going to be starting fights," the guy said.

"Will do," Harper promised him with a smile, and the two guys went back into the bar, leaving Daniel and Harper to handle Alex.

"I don't need your help," Alex muttered, then turned to look at Harper.

He smelled faintly of alcohol. His jeans had holes in them, and his dark bangs kept falling into his eyes. Not to mention that he'd hit his head pretty hard on the sidewalk, and Harper could see the blood through his dark hair.

"Alex, you're bleeding," Harper said. "We should take you to the hospital."

"I'm fine," he said and managed to push Daniel off him.

"At least let me look at it," Harper insisted. Alex looked like he was about to protest, so she added, "If you don't let me look at it, I'm calling 911, and they'll look instead. And I'm certain they wouldn't approve of your underage drinking."

Alex groaned but walked over to a nearby bench. He sat

down with a heavy thud and repeated, "I'm fine. I don't need your help."

"Alex, you're clearly not fine," Harper said, sitting down next to him. "You're fighting, and I've never known you to drink before. How did you even get into the bar? You're only eighteen."

He waved her off. "If you work down at the docks, they let you drink. That's the only thing that matters."

She parted his hair to get a better look, but he appeared to have only a small cut. It was bleeding some, but it wasn't serious enough to warrant stitches.

"Alex." Harper dropped her hands back into her lap and watched him. "You should really go get checked out. You might have a concussion or something."

"Oh, like you even care?" Alex sneered at her. "All you care about is that stupid bitch sister of yours."

A couple with a small child and a dog walked by just as Alex was swearing. They gave him a wide berth, and Daniel apologized and offered them a polite smile.

"*Alex!*" Harper snapped. She leaned back on the bench. "I know that's not your fault and you don't mean that, but you can't talk about Gemma that way. Not around me."

"Harper, maybe we should continue this conversation somewhere else," Daniel said, motioning to more people across the street. It wasn't late, and it was a nice night, so Capri was still somewhat busy.

Harper rubbed her temple and looked over at Alex. He had hunched forward, burying his hands in his thick hair. Despite his attempts to cover it up, Harper didn't think she'd ever seen him in more pain. Whatever was going on with him, it looked like torture.

"We can't leave him alone," Harper said at last and looked up at Daniel. "If he has a concussion, we need to keep an eye on him. And I definitely can't take him back to my house."

"My place it is, then," Daniel said.

"Why should I go to your house?" Alex asked.

"Because you just got thrown out of the only bar in Capri that would serve you drinks, and I have beer at my house," Daniel said.

With that, Alex got to his feet. "Let's get going, then."

"My car's parked down there." Harper pointed to it, but lingered behind to whisper to Daniel, "He shouldn't be drinking any more."

"That's okay, because I don't really have beer." Daniel smirked at her. "But once he's out on the island, what is he gonna do?"

"Thank you." She smiled up at him. "I'm really sorry about this. I know this wasn't what you had planned for tonight."

"I really didn't have that much planned," Daniel said. "But your friend needs you. You should take care of him."

"Thanks for being so understanding." She kissed him on the cheek.

"Are we going or what?" Alex shouted from beside her car.

Alex hadn't been that drunk in the first place, so the boat ride seemed to sober him up. With Daniel up front, steering *The Dirty Gull* across the bay, Harper and Alex sat down on the benches in the back. He leaned over the rail, letting the cool breeze and ocean spray blow over him.

"I'm sorry for being such a jerk tonight," Alex said finally. He turned back toward her, and even in the fading light she could see the pained expression on his face.

"You're not being a jerk," Harper said.

"Yeah, I'm drunk, and I'm an idiot." He grimaced. "I'm sorry I called you a bitch earlier."

"You didn't call me a bitch," Harper corrected him. "That was Gemma."

"I'm so sorry." Alex rubbed his forehead. "I don't know what I'm saying. I don't even know who I am anymore."

"What *is* going on with you?" Harper asked, realizing that now might be her chance to get to the bottom of things.

"I don't know." His voice caught in his throat. "I swear to God I wish I knew, but I don't. Everything's so messed up lately."

She'd been sitting across from him, so they both had to speak loudly to be heard over the engine. Harper got up and sat next to him on the bench. Alex struggled to hold it together, and she rubbed his back, attempting futilely to comfort him.

"Something happened, and I know it did." Alex shook his head again. "But I don't know what it was. Like I've forgotten something major."

"What do you mean?" Harper asked. "What do you remember?"

"I know about the sirens, if that's what you're asking." He stared down at his hands, absently picking at a callus on his palm. "I still remember them, and everything that happened with them."

"Everything?" Harper had stopped rubbing his back and folded her arms on her lap.

"Yeah, they turned Gemma into a siren, and then we found them and they came back here," Alex said. "I remember the fight at the docks. They killed this guy, and Gemma and I fought them. But they decided to let her live and stay here."

"Do you know why they let her stay?" Harper asked.

She knew, of course, but she wanted to figure out how much

Alex remembered. Gemma had told Harper that she'd used the siren song to get Alex to break up with her and stop loving her. But he'd barely talked to anybody since then, so Harper had no idea what Alex really knew or felt anymore.

"No." His brow pinched in frustration. "No, I don't. I remember that . . . I loved her."

"Yeah, you did," Harper admitted quietly.

"I don't know why." Alex looked up at the sky, as if searching for answers. "The thought of even caring about Gemma is repulsive. When I think about how I used to kiss her, it makes me want to throw up."

Harper didn't say anything to that. She didn't know how to respond. Alex didn't say anything for a while, either. He just lowered his eyes, his jaw clenching and unclenching as he thought.

"I was in love with her, and now I can't stand the thought of her," Alex said. "And I don't know why. I don't know what changed. You can't just wake up one day hating the person you used to love. But *I did.*"

"People change," Harper said in a lame attempt to support her sister's siren-song-enforced lie.

She wasn't sure if she agreed with what Gemma had done, but she couldn't do anything about it now. Gemma had done what she thought she needed to in order to protect Alex, and Harper could understand that.

She just couldn't imagine how painful and confusing it would be if she woke up tomorrow hating Daniel. Part of her wanted to believe that it wasn't even possible. The way she cared about him couldn't be changed by any siren song or spell.

But seeing the way this was obviously tearing Alex up, and knowing how much he'd loved Gemma, Harper had to believe that anything was possible. If a siren song could get Alex to loathe Gemma, it could probably do anything.

"It's like part of me is missing." Alex gestured to his chest. "Like something inside me has been erased. Whole chunks of me are just . . . gone."

"What do you mean?" Harper narrowed her eyes.

Gemma had been very clear that her siren song was meant only to get him to stop loving her. She loved Alex and didn't want to change anything about him. All she wanted was to keep him safe.

"Everything I used to care about, I just . . ." Alex shrugged helplessly. "I don't anymore."

"What about video games?" Harper asked. "Or storm chasing? Or your comic books?"

"No." He shook his head. "I don't hate them, but I have no urge to do anything with them. I just . . . I stopped caring. It's like everything I loved disappeared." He swallowed hard. "It's like I'm incapable of loving anything anymore."

"I don't think that's true," Harper said, but her words lacked conviction. "You just went through a really bad breakup. It takes time for these things to heal, for hearts to mend."

"I hope you're right. I don't know how much longer I can go on like this."

Once they reached the cabin, Harper gave Alex a glass of water and set him up in front of the TV. Alex seemed to be doing all right, so Daniel suggested that Harper head home for the night.

"Are you sure?" Harper asked. She stood at the doorway, talking quietly with Daniel, and glanced over at where Alex sat on the couch. "I don't want to make you take care of my friends."

"Nah, it's no problem." Daniel shrugged it off. "Besides, I think he could use some male-bonding time."

"Okay." She relented, then smiled over at Alex. "I'll see you later, Alex. Take care of yourself, okay?"

"I'll try." He forced a smile at her. "Thanks, Harper."

"I'll be back in a few minutes. Don't fall asleep while I'm gone," Daniel told him, then he walked outside with Harper.

"I won't," Alex replied.

In the moonlight, they started walking down from the cabin toward the boathouse. Daniel shook his head and let out a long whistle.

"What was that for?" Harper asked.

"Your sister really did a number on him," Daniel said.

"Yeah, she did," Harper agreed. "But Gemma had no idea what she was doing. She couldn't know that it would screw Alex up so badly."

"You can't go messing around with people's hearts," Daniel said simply. "It never ends well, no matter how good your intentions might be."

They reached the boathouse, and Daniel stopped. Harper walked a few more steps toward the dock, where Daniel's boat was tied up, until she realized that he wasn't with her. She turned around and looked back at him.

"What are you doing?" Harper asked.

"You can drive a little speedboat, can't you?" Daniel asked.

"Yeah," Harper said cautiously, walking over to where Daniel stood. "What does that have to do with anything?"

"Well, I was thinking, why don't you take Bernie's boat?" Daniel suggested. "It's technically yours anyway, since Bernie left it to you. And I don't really need two boats."

"What would I do with Bernie's boat?" Harper asked.

"You could come and go as you please." He shrugged, trying

to seem nonchalant. "You could come see me whenever you wanted."

"So . . . this is kinda like giving me the key to your place," she said.

"I think your dad already has a key to my place," Daniel reminded her. "He *is* my landlord."

"You know what I mean," Harper said. "This is like a step. A bigger commitment."

"Yeah." He smiled down at her. "But I'm ready for it."

Harper glanced back at his house, where Alex was waiting. He'd turned into a total mess after getting involved with the sirens, and it was only a matter of time before something horrible happened to Daniel.

Not to mention the fact that their date had turned out the same way they always seemed to anymore. They'd hardly spent any time together since they'd been dating, and with Harper leaving for school soon, they probably wouldn't have that much time left.

Those were all the reasons that Harper knew she should say no, that she should turn Daniel down and end things before they got any more complicated.

But somehow she found herself smiling up at him and saying, "Okay. I'm ready, too."

Right now, standing with him in the moonlight, she just couldn't give him up. Not yet.

TWENTY

Achelous

With the stacks of books spread out around her room, Gemma had to fight the urge to scream. Her frustration only seemed to be feeding her hunger. Last night at play rehearsal, she'd hardly been able to contain herself around Aiden, but she'd managed to avoid killing him or making out with him, so she counted that as a win.

It made her feel a little guilty, since it was right in front of Kirby, too, and Gemma had just ended things with him. But that was really the least of her problems.

Lexi had told her that they were about to kill and replace Gemma soon, and the only clue she had to go on was the one that Lexi had let slip: *Once you knew who her dad was, it was, like, obvious.*

Since she'd heard that, Gemma had spent all her time searching mythology books and the Internet for everything she could find about Penn's father, Achelous. Over the past couple months, Gemma had thought she'd already learned everything on him she could, and as it turned out, she probably had.

The books described an older man with a hearty gray beard

and an occasional horned form. Not much was said about him, other than that he fathered the sirens. Supposedly, Hercules defeated him over the love of a woman, but Gemma wasn't sure if that led to Achelous's demise or not.

Still, she hadn't been able to come up with anything. That was why she'd gone to play rehearsal last night. Her brain had begun turning to mush, a serious migraine gnawed her constantly, and her hunger was getting worse. She needed a break from the search to clear her head.

Of course, as soon as she'd gotten home, she dove right back into it. And yet, here she was—no closer to finding the scroll than she had been the day before.

She paced her room, figuring out what to do. The front door slammed downstairs, and she heard Harper and Marcy talking.

"Crap," Gemma whispered under her breath.

They'd made plans to brainstorm tonight after Harper and Marcy got done with work, and it had slipped Gemma's mind until now. It wasn't like she could blow them off, not without alerting Harper to how grave the situation might be.

She hadn't told Harper what Lexi had said about the scroll. It was all part of her plan to keep Harper completely out of the loop about everything from here on. There would be no need to worry Harper or freak her out. Not if neither of them could do anything to prevent her death.

If Gemma couldn't survive this, she didn't want Harper to lose her *and* the life she'd worked so hard for. If Gemma couldn't be with Harper anymore, she at least wanted to know that Harper would have a future without her.

She had to hang out with Harper and Marcy so Harper would

feel like she was doing something and wouldn't realize that Gemma was keeping things from her. Gemma had to pretend everything was okay.

"Gemma?" Harper called from downstairs. "Are you home?"

"Yeah, I'm just up in my room!"

She hurriedly closed all the books and put them away. Harper knew she was looking at them, but Gemma didn't want to let on how frantic the search had become.

"No, Marcy, I don't think that Friday the thirteenth should count as a national holiday," Harper was saying. The steps creaked under her feet as she climbed up them.

Marcy scoffed. "But Easter is a holiday."

"Easter happens once a year at roughly the same time," Harper said. She reached the landing and rolled her eyes at Gemma, showing what she thought of Marcy's latest theory. "And people actually celebrate it."

"I celebrate Friday the thirteenth!" Marcy countered.

Harper had brought up a couple cans of Cherry Coke from the fridge, and she went into her bedroom across the hall from Gemma's. Marcy followed suit, munching on a Rice Krispies treat left over from a batch Harper had made earlier in the week.

"Okay, fine, write your congressman about it, then," Harper said, setting the cans of soda on her desk.

"I will," Marcy said through a mouthful of food and flopped back on Harper's bed.

Gemma walked over to her sister's room, which was bigger than hers and had more places to sit. Harper had her bed, the chair for her desk, and a worn-out padded rocker that Nathalie had used when the girls were babies.

"So, how was work?" Gemma asked, sitting down in the old rocking chair by the window.

"Great," Harper replied absently. "I grabbed you a can of Cherry Coke, in case you wanted one."

"Sure, I'll take it," she said, and Harper walked over to hand it to her.

"Work was not great," Marcy said. "It was totally lame. We had to work on a *holiday*."

"It's still not a holiday," Harper said. She sat down at her desk and shook her head. "At least not until you write to congress."

"Sounds like you've had a fun day." Gemma smirked and took a sip of her pop. "But I don't . . ." She'd been looking out Harper's bedroom window, and she trailed off as she spotted Alex pulling into his driveway. He usually worked until after four, the same as her dad.

When he got out of the car, he was wearing ripped jeans and a T-shirt, not his usual work overalls. He walked to the house with a labored gait, and he looked like hell.

"Have you talked to Alex lately?" Gemma asked, her eyes still glued to Alex's house, even though he'd already disappeared inside.

"What?" Harper asked. "Why?"

"He's just getting home," Gemma said. "And he doesn't look so great."

"Yeah, um . . ." Harper sighed. "I think he crashed at Daniel's last night."

"Why?" Gemma finally pulled her eyes away from the house and faced her sister. "Are they hanging out or something?"

"Well. Kinda." Harper lowered her eyes. "No, not really. Alex . . . We ran into him last night, and he was getting thrown out of a bar."

"*Alex?*" Marcy asked with genuine surprise. "Geeky next-door Alex?"

Gemma shook her head. "Alex doesn't drink."

"He was last night," Harper said.

"Well, did you talk to him?" Gemma asked. "What did he say? Is he okay?"

"Not really, Gemma," Harper admitted. "I was thinking about not telling you, but . . . whatever you did to protect him, it's really messing him up. He knows he's supposed to love you, and he says it's like a part of him is missing."

Gemma didn't say anything. She just turned and stared out the window again. Alex's bedroom window was right across from Harper's, but his shade was pulled. Gemma didn't even get a glimpse at what he was doing.

"Maybe you should talk to him," Harper suggested quietly.

"I can't," Gemma said.

"He's really hurting, and I think maybe you should consider undoing it."

"I can't, Harper," Gemma said, more firmly this time. "I don't think it's possible even if I wanted to, and I don't want to. It's dangerous for him to be involved with me."

"I know how you feel," Harper said. "But if he knows the risks, you have to let him make the choice."

"Just let it go." Gemma shook her head and looked down at her can of soda. "I can't talk about this right now."

"Have you guys come up with alternate plans yet?" Marcy asked, changing the subject. She sat up straighter on the bed, crossing her legs underneath her.

"What do you mean?" Harper turned back to face her.

"The way I see it, there's three possibilities to this scenario."

Marcy held up three fingers, then ticked them down one by one as she listed the options. "One, Gemma finds the scroll. Two, the sirens have hidden the scroll so well that no one can find it. Three, they don't have the scroll."

"Gemma hasn't even had a chance to really look for the scroll yet," Harper said quickly. "We can't rule that out."

Marcy shook her head. "I'm not saying rule it out. I'm saying look into other avenues."

"That's probably a good idea," Gemma agreed. "But Lydia seemed to think they'd have the scroll. It's important to their existence."

"But maybe they left it with somebody they trusted more than themselves," Marcy suggested.

"Like who?" Harper asked.

"When I leased my apartment, the landlord didn't trust just me, so I had to have someone else put their name on it." Marcy waited a beat for it to hit Gemma and Harper. "My parents."

"You think the sirens' parents are still alive?" Harper asked.

"I don't know." Gemma shook her head, thinking back to what Lexi had said. "I don't think they are."

"Aren't their parents immortal?" Marcy asked.

"Their dad was, but I don't really know about their mom," Harper said. "I was a little confused on that."

"Who is their mom?" Marcy asked.

"Um, a muse," Gemma said, thinking. "Or two muses, actually. Thea and Penn have different mothers. I'm pretty sure the muses are immortal, too. Just not goddesses. So I think that in their regular life, pre-siren, Thea and Penn were mortal."

"But both their parents were immortal, right?" Marcy said. "Wouldn't the kids of immortals also be immortal?"

"No, I think in order to be born immortal, both your parents have to be gods and goddesses," Gemma said. "Like how Hercules was mortal. And the muses were granted their immortality by Zeus as a blessing, so they couldn't pass it on."

"But their dad was a god?" Marcy asked, and Gemma nodded. "He's definitely got to be alive, then."

"Well, not definitely, but probably," Harper agreed.

"I really don't think he is." Gemma shook her head.

"Why not?" Harper asked. "I know some of the books implied that Hercules killed him, but they also said that the sirens were dead, so I wouldn't really give that much credence."

"I know, it's just . . ." Gemma trailed off. When she'd told Lexi she'd met Penn's dad, Lexi had laughed and said he was dead, but she didn't want to explain that to Harper. "It's just a feeling I have.

"And anyway, even if he is alive, Penn really hates him," Gemma went on. "And she didn't have anything nice to say about her mother. After I first became a siren, Thea actually called the muses prostitutes."

"So it's unlikely that they would rely on them," Harper said, finishing Gemma's thought.

"And if they did, they're probably more powerful than the sirens. Hence, the title 'god,'" Gemma said. "And I highly doubt they'd want to help us kill their daughters."

"You never know," Marcy said.

The three of them sat in silence for a few minutes, thinking about what they'd been talking about. Gemma twisted the tab on her soda can and wondered if Marcy was barking up the right tree. She hadn't had much of a chance to look for the scroll yet, but even if she had, it wouldn't be bad to have a backup plan.

"You know who would want to destroy them?" Harper asked finally, and Gemma lifted her head to look at her. "Demeter."

"The chick that made the curse?" Marcy asked.

"She's not a chick," Harper corrected her. "She's a goddess, and she hates the sirens."

"Why does she hate them again?" Marcy asked.

"Penn, Thea, and the two other original sirens were handmaidens for Demeter's daughter, Persephone," Gemma explained. "They were supposed to be watching her, but instead they were screwing around, swimming, singing, and flirting with men."

"So the sirens were like guards?" Marcy asked.

"I guess." Gemma shrugged. "I think they said that their dad got them the job. From what I understand, their mothers stayed with whoever they were 'inspiring,' so the sirens were pretty much homeless from a young age."

"So they get a job watching Persephone, and they bail," Marcy said, returning the story to its main point.

"Right," Gemma said. "And then Persephone is kidnapped by Hades and taken down into the Underworld to be his bride."

"But if what Lydia says is true, that these were just powerful humans and not deities, then Hades wouldn't have been ruler of the Underworld," Marcy said. "A human—even a powerful one—wouldn't be in charge of the afterlife. So where did he take her?"

Harper lowered her eyes when the realization hit her. "He didn't take her anywhere. He raped and murdered her."

"Yeah, if I were Demeter, I'd be pissed, too," Gemma said.

"Why would she make them immortal?" Marcy asked. "If she hated them so much, why give them powers and abilities?"

"Hell is repetition," Harper said. "She wanted to make them do the same things they loved over and over and over until the things they loved the most became the things they detested."

"Do you think she would want to undo the curse she created?" Gemma asked.

"Maybe. If we can find her," Harper said. "She might think they've had a long enough run."

"How would we find her?" Marcy asked. "Or their father? Or any of the muses?"

"I can start by doing more research, but I don't know if there's really anything about sirens that I haven't read at least a hundred times already," Harper said.

"I could ask Thea, but she might not divulge much about this," Gemma said. "She doesn't like talking about their past, and she really does hate their parents."

"I could . . ." Marcy trailed off. "I don't know. What do you guys want me to do?"

"Maybe talk to Lydia," Harper suggested. "She seems to have a connection with the supernatural underground. She'd probably know something about where we could find a muse or a god."

"And I'll keep looking for the scroll," Gemma said with a heavy sigh.

"Do you have play rehearsal tonight?" Harper asked. "You could talk to Thea then."

"Yeah." Gemma glanced over at Harper's alarm clock, which said it was only a quarter after three. "It starts in about an hour. I'll be sure to talk with Thea."

"Good." Harper nodded, as if it solidified things. "So we have some kind of plan of action. That's a good thing."

"All right, so who am I asking Lydia to look for?" Marcy reached over and grabbed a notebook and a pen off Harper's desk. "I need to write it down to be sure I get it right. These Greek names are ridiculous."

"Demeter," Harper said, then spelled it aloud for her. "Any of the muses. I don't know all of their names, but Penn and Thea's mothers were Terpsichore and Melpomene."

"Okay, you need to spell those *very* slowly," Marcy said.

"And then their father," Harper said after she'd finished spelling the names.

"Who is that?" Marcy asked.

"Achelous," Harper answered.

"Like the river?" Marcy asked.

Harper nodded. "Yeah, he was a freshwater god, I think."

"Finally one I can spell," Marcy said.

And then it finally hit her. The Achelous River was located about five miles north of town. It was named by the same man from Greece who'd founded Capri, so Gemma hadn't thought anything of the name until now.

But Lexi had said, *Once you knew who her dad was, it was, like, obvious.* And the river was named after Penn's father.

If Lydia was right, and the sirens carried the scroll with them, then it would make sense they would hide it nearby. And a river named after their own father? Penn's narcissism wouldn't pass that up.

"I have to go," Gemma said and suddenly stood up.

"What?" Harper asked. "Why? Where are you going?"

"I forgot that play rehearsal starts early tonight," Gemma lied. "But it's good. It'll give me a chance to talk to Thea more."

"Okay," Harper said, but she seemed confused. "Do you want me to give you a ride?"

"No, I got it, but thanks." Gemma smiled at her. "I'll see you later."

She practically ran downstairs and grabbed her bike. Before she did, she pulled her phone out of her pocket and hurriedly texted Daniel so he'd cover for her if Harper asked about play rehearsal.

At their nightly play rehearsal and through texts, Gemma had been keeping Daniel apprised of their situation, as per their deal. He'd been giving Harper little bits of info about Gemma to keep her from getting suspicious, like telling her that Gemma had dumped Kirby and was flirting with Aiden.

But he left out all the major details—like that Thea wouldn't help her or that the sirens had found a possible replacement. Daniel had encouraged her to tell Harper about that, but Gemma couldn't. It was her turn to protect Harper for a change.

Besides, there might not be any reason to tell her about this. She still might break the curse.

Pedaling faster than she ever had before, Gemma made it down to Anthemusa Bay in record time. She ditched the bike among the cypress trees, along with her cell phone, shoes, and shorts. For once, she wasn't wearing a bikini under her clothes, so she'd have to swim in her bra, but she didn't care.

Despite how quickly she swam, it seemed to take forever to reach the mouth of the river. She didn't even enjoy the feel of the water or the current rushing against her mermaid tail. All she could focus on was getting there and finding the scroll.

Lydia had said that the paper couldn't be damaged by water, so Gemma thought that the sirens had probably hidden it somewhere underwater. Possibly underneath a rock or in a box or something buried in the floor of the river.

Following her hunch, she began to swim up the Achelous River, turning over rocks and grabbing at anything on the riverbed that looked even mildly interesting. She hadn't made it very far when the strangest thing started happening to her.

It got harder to breathe, and the scales on her tail were shifting back into flesh, but only odd patches. At first Gemma began to panic, assuming she was dying. She hurriedly swam back toward the ocean, and the odd changes stopped. She was her usual mermaid self.

That was when Gemma realized the river was freshwater—that had no effect on her. It was the same reason she didn't turn into a mermaid in the pool or the shower. Only ocean water made the change happen.

That meant that the sirens probably hadn't gone that far up the river. So Gemma focused her search on places where she could swim, staying mostly near the mouth of the river, but as the evening progressed, Gemma swam farther and farther upstream.

Once the moon was high in the sky, Gemma pulled herself up near a sandy beach next to the river. She stayed in deep enough so the water would cover her fins, and the waves splashed against her waist.

The stars were twinkling above her, and she leaned back, staring up at them. Her hands were sore from digging up the riverbed and even some of the ocean floor. Her tail ached from swimming, and the hunger made her stomach rumble.

Gemma had looked everywhere she could. The scroll wasn't there. Either it never had been, or the sirens had moved it. It didn't really matter which of those options it was. All this really meant was that Gemma had to come up with a different plan of attack, because this one wasn't working.

TWENTY-ONE

Cursed

"I love him," Penn breathed as she flung herself backward into her bed. In the three months that Bastian had been staying with them in France, Thea had heard Penn utter those same words a hundred times.

"You're being dramatic, don't you think?" Aggie asked. She sat perched on the edge of her sister's bed, watching Penn sigh and coo over her newfound romance with Bastian.

"No, I love him." Penn smiled so broadly it looked painful to Thea, who preferred to stay at the edge of the room to watch Penn's daily declarations of undying love to Bastian.

"But he doesn't love you," Thea pointed out, and Aggie and Gia immediately turned their heads to face Thea in shock.

Thea was certain that her own expression of shock and horror mirrored theirs. While she'd thought that same sentiment at least a hundred times before, it was the first time she'd actually said it aloud. Her irritation had grown to be too much, and she couldn't contain it anymore.

"He doesn't love me," Penn said, her voice flat, and then she sat up with a start. "It's the damn curse. He can't love me. We have to get rid of it."

"Get rid of it?" Gia asked. She sat on the other side of Penn, her fair skin paling further at the thought of undoing their curse. "We mustn't do that. We don't know the repercussions."

"I'm in love, Gia," Penn insisted, imploring her to understand. "I can't let anything get in the way of that."

"But Gia is right," Aggie said. "If we attempt to undo the curse, we might undo ourselves. Remember what happened to the minotaurs? When they repealed their curse, they made themselves extinct."

"Don't be so simple," Penn growled and got up. "We'll find our father or Demeter. One of them will know how to get rid of this without killing us."

"Where will we find Achelous or Demeter?" Gia asked. "They've been in hiding for years."

"Look harder!" Penn snapped. "I am in love with Bastian, and I am going to spend the rest of my life with him!"

"If you give up the curse, that might not be very long," Thea said quietly. "The muses can give up their places for love, but it means they must also give up their immortality."

"I won't have to give that up," Penn said, brushing off the idea. "Bastian is immortal, and so shall I remain."

"What if you had to choose?" Thea asked. "Between living forever or true love?"

"I won't have to choose." Penn looked at her sister like she was dumb or insane. "I can have both."

"Dear sister, but you must," Thea pressed. "The only way I know to undo the curse would be to destroy the scroll, and that would lead to our demise."

"We won't destroy the scroll," Penn said. "We will find another way. Maybe the gods can bless me the way they have Bastian."

"There are hardly any gods around," Thea reminded her. "And none of them will undo a curse to bless you."

"I am in love, my dear sister." Penn glared at her. "The gods always look kindly on love. We will find one, and that god will correct this mistake against us."

"The god would want something in return," Thea persisted. "Would you be willing to sacrifice anything for love?"

"I'm willing to sacrifice every other man on earth, and I think that's more than enough," Penn said with a wicked smile. "Now I must get ready to have breakfast with Bastian. The rest of you, scatter. Find a way out of this curse."

Penn dismissed them to do her bidding, and Gia, always the dutiful servant, immediately ran off to do as she was told. Thea, on the other hand, lagged behind, and Aggie stayed to comfort her.

"Oh, my dear sister, what is troubling you?" Aggie asked. She looped her arm through Thea's as they walked down the hall toward Thea's chambers.

Before, the house had been crawling with servants and handmaidens, but now very few remained. Once Penn had begun her affair with Bastian, she had sent away the duke and killed his brothers. She'd also killed any staff who gossiped or attempted to interfere in her relationship.

If she had been able to, she would've sent away her sisters. She wanted absolute privacy so she could begin her life with Bastian. Since she was cursed to remain with the sirens forever, she'd seemed to relegate them to staff, treating them as slaves instead of sisters.

"She doesn't love him," Thea whispered. Her voice was sweet but her tone was harsh. "She doesn't know the slightest thing about love."

"Oh, let her have her folly," Aggie said. "She's in a better mood. That must count for something."

"No, it does not," Thea snapped. "I am sick of being at her whim. I am sick of following her demands and her vanity."

"You know that she has always had a will of her own," Aggie said. "And the best way to deal with it is to bend to it."

"Why?" Thea turned to face her. "Why must I always acquiesce to my little sister?"

"Because she is your sister," Aggie said simply. "And those are your options. You obey her, or you defy her. And if you defy her, you'd best have plans to kill her. Would you rather have your sister's blood on your hands or play along with her games?"

"For once, I think I'd rather have the blood," Thea admitted.

Aggie's face contorted with anguish. "Don't say such things. You made a promise to her, to both of us, that you would care for and look after us. I know it's been many centuries since you made that promise, but it still holds true."

"Does it?" Thea asked. "Haven't I done my duty? To both of you?"

"We are sisters, and we always will be," Aggie said. "I may not understand what is bothering you right now, but I know it will pass. Everything else will pass. We are the only things that will remain. Remember that."

Thea wanted to talk more with her, but Aggie had had her fill. She turned and walked away, her footfalls echoing off the ceiling as she left Thea standing alone.

Thea went into her room, closing the heavy door behind her, and then leaned against it. Bitter tears stung her eyes.

Bastian strolled out from her bathroom. His shirt was absent, and the strings that held up his trousers were loose. He smiled broadly in the way that made his dimple pronounced, but Thea could only frown when she saw him.

"Come, now," Bastian said, doing his best to act concerned as he strode over to her. "What's all this, then?" She shook her head and wiped at her eyes. "Why is there salt upon your cheeks?"

He reached out to touch her cheeks, but she pulled away from him.

"Pay it no mind. It's simply a fight with my sister."

"Why would you fight with her?" Bastian followed her the few steps away that she'd gone, and he stood right behind her. "I hope it isn't over me."

"No, it's not." She turned back to face him. "But how long can we go sneaking around? She'll catch us eventually, and we'll have hell to pay."

"She won't catch me," he promised with a grin. "I won't let her."

"Bastian. This is serious," Thea said.

"I'm always serious." He attempted to look grave and put his arms around Thea. She rested her hand on his bare chest, the smooth muscles warm beneath her hands, and she stared up at him.

"What if I don't want to sneak around anymore? What if I want to have you all to myself?" Thea asked him.

"I would tell you that now is not the time," Bastian said. "Your sister is the ruler of this place, and her vengeance isn't something I want to cross. At least not now."

"Then when?" Thea asked.

"When it is the right time."

"Your tongue is as good at dancing around the truth as it is at singing," Thea said.

He laughed warmly. "That's not the only thing my tongue is good for."

He tried to kiss her then, but she pushed him back and pulled free from his arms, taking several steps away from him again.

"She means to break the curse," Thea said.

"Why ever would she want to do that?" Bastian stood with his hands on his hips, baffled by the prospect. "I thought she loved the power and the magic and torturing mere mortals."

"She does," Thea agreed. "But she also claims to love you, and she says that you can't love her because of the curse."

Bastian shook his head. "It's not the curse that prevents me from loving her."

"What is it, then?" Thea took a step closer to him, unable to hide the hopefulness in her voice.

"It's that she's horrible. She's a monster, and a murderer, and detests everything."

"Then why are you carrying on with her?" Thea asked. "If you know what a beast she truly is."

"I needed a place to stay," he replied simply. "I hadn't planned on being here this long. Or getting involved with you. I just wanted a warm bed for a few nights."

"So you are staying for me?" Thea asked, as he stepped close to her.

"You are one of the reasons I am staying," he admitted, smiling again.

He wrapped his arms around her waist and lifted her easily

from the floor. With one smooth move, he tossed her lightly on the bed. Then he climbed onto it. With an arm on either side of her, he held himself up, then leaned down to kiss her passionately on the mouth.

Thea allowed him to kiss her for a moment, causing heat to burn all the way through her, then she put her hand on his chest and pushed him back.

"Do you love me?"

His smile faltered. " 'Love' is not a word that I will easily throw around."

"Bastian. Please." She stared up at him, searching his blue eyes. "Every time I lay with you, I am risking my life. She will certainly kill us both if she finds us together."

"So I am risking my life the same as you. If that's not a show of affection, I don't know what is."

"Will you not say it? Will you not declare your love to me?"

"No." Bastian's voice was heavy with regret. "I cannot."

"Why?" Thea swallowed back her tears, trying not to let him see how badly that hurt her. "You said you were capable."

"You are sweeter, fairer, and in all ways more delectable than your sister." He brushed the red hair back from her forehead. "But you share equally in her bloodlust."

"Because I am a monster, that I must feed? You refuse to love me?" Thea asked.

"Come, Thea. We only have a short time until we both must be ready for the day. Can't we put these matters to bed?"

She wanted to argue more, and maybe she should have. But around Bastian, her will was weak. Within moments he was kissing her again, and all her worries were lost in his embrace.

TWENTY-TWO

Visitation

The car ride to Briar Ridge had never felt so long. The air-conditioning was out in Brian's F-150, and even though the windows were open, that only seemed to succeed in blowing more hot air into the truck. Gemma sat in the middle, wedged between her dad and Harper, and none of them said anything.

The only sound was the classic rock station, and Brian unironically sang along with "I'm on Fire" by Springsteen. But that was all.

Harper had told Gemma earlier in the week that Brian wanted to come along on their usual Saturday visit, but neither of them completely understood why. On one hand, Gemma knew she should be excited. She'd been all but begging her dad to see Nathalie since Christmas two years ago. That was the last time Brian had had any contact with their mom, not that he'd had that much before then.

When Harper learned how to drive and could make the trip to visit Nathalie on her own, that was when Brian had officially checked out. But in the years leading up to that, he'd had minimal interaction with her. It was little more than a *Hello, how are you?* when he picked up the girls or dropped them off to visit.

So it had Gemma a little freaked out that he actually wanted to do something with Nathalie, especially without any prodding from Gemma or Harper.

Brian pulled into the driveway of Nathalie's group home, and all her worries about surviving the sirens' curse were changed to simply surviving this afternoon.

"Did you call and let them know I was coming with you today?" Brian asked as he turned off the truck.

"No," Harper said. She leaned forward, her gray eyes worried. "Should I have?"

Brian sat for a minute. "No, I'm sure it'll be fine."

"We should go in," Gemma suggested, since it seemed like her dad would be content to swelter in the truck all afternoon.

"Yeah, let's go in." He nodded but didn't move.

He was tan from working outside so much, but his skin was ashen today. His blue eyes were wide and frantic, scanning the gauges of the truck like they would hold some clue about how to deal with this situation.

This was the most scared that Gemma had ever seen him look. That wasn't saying much, since he rarely showed any fear, but he was obviously terrified.

"Dad?" Harper had climbed out of the truck, but she leaned against the door, watching him. "Are you sure you want to do this?"

"No, yeah." He nodded again and licked his lips. "I need to do this. I need to see her."

Gemma reached over and took Brian's hand, his huge leathery one consuming hers, and she squeezed it gently.

"You can do this, Dad," Gemma told him.

He smiled at her, but he still appeared sick. "You're right. Let's do this."

Brian finally opened the truck door and got out. Gemma climbed out more slowly after him. Her decision to wear shorts had been a bad one. Her legs were stuck to the plastic interior, and she had to carefully peel herself off before she got out.

Harper and Brian were waiting for her, and Gemma went to knock on the door, letting the two of them stay a few steps behind her. In all the times she'd visited her mom before, she'd never felt so unnerved. This could all easily turn into a horrible disaster.

Before the door even opened, Gemma could hear Nathalie yelling on the other side, "It's for me! I got it!"

Nathalie threw open the door, already smiling exuberantly, and shouted, "My girls!"

The hardest thing about seeing Nathalie was that while the accident left her mentally impaired, she didn't look any different. She was tall and elegant, appearing more like a model than a mother, let alone someone with brain damage. Her eyes were the same shade of golden honey as Gemma's, and her smile was radiant.

The only signs were subtle, like the Harry Potter T-shirt she wore, or the bright pink streak she had running down her long brown hair, or the temporary Lisa Frank tattoos of puppies and kittens she had up and down her arm.

But to someone like Brian, who hadn't seen her in years, it had to be a shock to see her looking exactly as he remembered her. It would be easier to accept that she'd become a different person if she looked different, but she didn't.

"Hi, Mom," Gemma said.

"Oh, you look so beautiful today." Nathalie threw her arms

around her, hugging her fiercely. Then she noticed Harper and reached out to squeeze her arm. "And so do you."

"Hey, Mom," Harper said. It was a few octaves higher than she usually spoke, so Gemma knew she was freaking out a little bit.

"We brought someone with us today," Gemma said once Nathalie had finally released her. She stepped to the side so her mom could get a better look at Brian. "Do you recognize him?"

"Hello, Nathalie." He raised one hand, waving awkwardly at her.

"Is this . . . is this your boyfriend?" she asked. Then she leaned down to Gemma and lowered her voice. "Honey, he's too old for you."

"No, Mom, this is Dad," Gemma tried to explain.

"Brian," Harper clarified. "Mine and Gemma's dad. He's your husband."

"What?" Nathalie straightened up and shook her head. "No, I'm not married."

"Yeah, Mom, you are," Harper said gently.

"But he . . ." Nathalie stared at Brian, looking confused and a bit disgusted. "He's so old."

"I'm actually only six months older than you," Brian said, doing his best to keep his voice light.

She crossed her arms over her chest. "When is my birthday, then, smarty pants?"

"October sixth, 1973," Brian replied instantly.

"Lucky guess," Nathalie said, but by her expression, Gemma wasn't sure if Nathalie knew if that was correct. It was, but there was a chance that she didn't remember her birthday anymore. "What's my middle name?"

"Anne," Brian said, then pointed to Gemma. "The same as Gemma's."

"How long have we been married, then?" Nathalie asked, but her disbelief was melting. Her expression had softened into something more curious.

"It was, um, twenty years this past April." He lowered his eyes for a second, then looked back up at her.

"Twenty years?" Nathalie asked.

"This is really him," Gemma said, hoping to help convince her mother.

"It's me, Nat," Brian said simply.

"Nat?" Her eyes flashed with painful recognition, and her arms dropped to her sides. "You used to call me that. Nobody calls me that anymore."

"I'm sorry. I don't have to call you that," Brian said.

"No, you should." She reached out and grabbed his hand. "Come on. Come in. We need to talk."

She led him through the house, introducing him to the staff as her husband, and Brian would just smile politely. The staff cleared out her roommates so they could have some privacy. Nathalie sat down at the dining room table, scooting her chair close to his, and stared at him with utter fascination.

Gemma and Harper weren't sure what they should do in this situation, so they just sat down across the table and watched their parents talk.

"How did we meet?" Nathalie asked.

He'd put his hand on the table, and she was almost petting it. Gemma had never seen anything like it. It was as if she wanted to hold his hand, but she was too frantic to keep it still, so she kept running her hands over it.

"We met in elementary school," Brian said. "But we didn't start dating until high school."

"We were high school sweethearts?" Nathalie asked.

He nodded. "We were, yeah."

"You took me to the prom?"

"Yeah, I did."

"I knew it." She squealed and laughed. "What color was my dress? How did I look?"

"It was kind of a dark blue. You were beautiful." He smiled at the memory. "You always were. You still are."

"Did you propose to me?" Nathalie asked.

"I did," he said. "It wasn't very romantic. I was too nervous and I kept stumbling. You actually guessed before I had a chance to get the words out, but you instantly said yes."

She twisted the gold wedding band that he still wore on his finger, and he let her. "Where's my ring?"

"Um, the girls have it," Brian said. "Gemma does, actually."

"I keep it in a jewelry box on my dresser," Gemma said, and Nathalie glanced over at her for a second before returning her attention back to Brian.

"Why don't I wear it?" Nathalie asked.

"We wanted to keep it safe," he explained.

"Do you have any pictures of our wedding?"

"I do." He nodded. "Not with me, but I have many."

"And after we got married, we had the girls?" Nathalie looked over at them again.

"Yes, we did. They're both our daughters." Brian motioned in their direction, but he wouldn't look at them, probably afraid that they might see the pain in his eyes.

Nathalie was staring at Harper and Gemma like she'd never seen them before, scrutinizing them. "They're beautiful."

"Yeah, they are," Brian agreed with a small smile.

"Harper looks like you." Nathalie tilted her head. "She has your nose and your eyes, but hers are grayer. Yours are more blue."

"I think she's prettier, too," Brian said.

Harper laughed nervously. "Thanks, Dad."

"You visit me a lot," Nathalie said to the girls. "I see you. I remember you." She pointed to Gemma. "You swim, and . . . and"—she pointed at Harper—"you're going to college soon?"

"Yep, that's right," Harper said.

"I used to swim. But I'm acting in a play now." Gemma leaned forward on the table. "You used to be in plays. Do you remember that?"

"No." Nathalie shook her head. "Should I?"

"No." Gemma forced a smile at her. "It's okay, Mom."

Nathalie faced Brian again. She stopped petting his hand and just held it as she stared at him. "You don't visit me. Do you?"

"No, I don't." His voice was thick. "I'm sorry."

"Why not?" Nathalie asked, but there wasn't a hint of accusation in her voice.

"You . . . you don't remember me very much anymore." Brian chose his words carefully. "It's hard for me to see you and not be able to talk to you like my wife, like the mother of my children. I want to talk to you about our life together, and I can't." He swallowed hard. "You don't remember it."

"Why don't I remember you?" Nathalie asked.

"I don't know." He shook his head. "You remembered me more, after the accident, when I used to see you a lot. So it's my fault. I should've stayed with you longer."

"I wish I remembered you," she said quietly. "You seem very kind, and you have nice eyes." She reached up, her fingers touching the crow's-feet at the corner of his eye.

"Thank you," he said.

"Were we in love?" Nathalie asked when she dropped her hand.

"Yes." Brian let out a shaky breath. "We were very much in love." He pursed his lips. "And I'm sorry I let you down."

"How did you let me down?"

"I should've visited you more. I should've been here for you."

"If I loved you the way you say I did, I'd want you to be happy," Nathalie said. "And if seeing me makes you sad, then maybe it's better that you didn't."

She'd been playing with his hand, but he turned it so he was holding her hand. Tears were standing in his eyes, and he tried to sniff them back.

"I miss you, Nat."

"I wish I could say I missed you, too," Nathalie admitted. "But I don't. I don't remember you."

"I love you. I will *always* love you," Brian said. "But I can't do this anymore."

As he stood up, he bent down and kissed Nathalie on the forehead. He lingered there for a moment, breathing her in, and then he turned and walked out of the room.

"Dad?" Harper got up and went after him.

"Did I do something wrong?" Nathalie asked and looked back at Gemma.

"No, Mom, you didn't do anything wrong." She got up and went around the table, sitting in her dad's spot so she could be closer to Nathalie. "You did really good today."

"I've upset him, though." She stared at Gemma. "I've upset you, too."

"No, I'm not upset." Gemma wiped at her own eyes. She wasn't crying, but she could feel the tears forming. "It's not your fault."

"Gemma." Nathalie brushed a hair back from Gemma's face and tucked it behind her ear. "You look really pretty today."

"Thanks, Mom." Gemma laughed and sniffled at the same time. "I wish you were here again."

"What do you mean?" Nathalie asked. "I am here."

"No, *really* here. I know you're still in there, buried somewhere down . . ." Gemma trailed off as she realized something.

She glanced around, making sure that she and Nathalie were completely alone. Then she took her mom's hand in hers and leaned in close to her, keeping her voice low.

"I want to try something, Mom," Gemma said. "I'm going to sing to you, and I want you to . . . just react however feels natural, okay?"

"Okay." Nathalie had lowered her voice because Gemma had, and she nodded quickly.

"Mom, I know you're in there," Gemma sang softly, barely above a whisper. Her voice came out in a clear perfect melody, and Nathalie's expression began to relax. *"I want you to remember all the things you forgot. Everything about Harper and Dad and me. I want you to come back."*

"I . . ." Nathalie's brow furrowed. "I . . ." She grimaced and touched her forehead.

"Mom, are you okay?" Gemma reached out, touching her arm. "What's going on? Do you remember anything?"

"It *hurts*!" She put her hands on the side of her head, and her nose began to bleed.

"Oh, no, Mom, I'm so sorry," Gemma said. "Look at me, Mom. Please. Just look up."

"It hurts," Nathalie repeated, but she finally looked at Gemma with tears welling in her eyes.

"Forget my song," Gemma sang. *"Forget what I said."*

"I can't," Nathalie said, almost pleading with her. "I can't remember what you want me to. I can't be who you want me to be. I'm sorry." Then she cried out, hugging her head. "Make it stop! Make the pain stop!"

"Your head doesn't hurt anymore," Gemma sang hurriedly before the staff came running in. *"You'll never feel a headache again."*

And just like that, it stopped. Nathalie looked up at her with red-rimmed eyes and wiped at her nose with the back of her hand.

"What happened?" Nathalie asked.

"Nothing, Mom," Gemma said. "You just had a headache."

When Nathalie's staff came in to make sure she was all right, Gemma got up and went outside. If only she'd been able to do one good thing to help the people she loved, then being a siren would be worth it. But all she'd done—all she'd ever be able to do—was make things even worse.

TWENTY-THREE

Lonely

Daniel didn't want to fill the Paramount with sawdust, so he was cutting the large planks of wood out back with his circular saw. He had the board spread out across the sawhorses, and he double-checked the measurements.

The sun beat down on his back, and it threatened to be a scorcher today. He'd taken off his shirt an hour ago, and he'd resorted to wrapping a bandanna around his forehead to keep the sweat from dripping down his brow.

"They're making you work on a Saturday?" Penn asked in her sultry voice. Her words couldn't enchant him, but he could still hear how luxurious her voice sounded. "That's like slave labor."

"It's my choice to work on Saturdays," Daniel said, without looking back at her. He stayed focused on the task at hand, using a pencil to mark the wood. "It's less disruptive to play rehearsal and the businesses around here."

"I don't know." Penn walked closer to him so he could see her in his peripheral vision. "I'd find you working without your shirt pretty disruptive."

"Good thing you don't work at the law offices next door." He straightened up and finally looked over at Penn. "What can I do for you today?"

Her dress was so short, the hem didn't even reach the middle of her thigh. Her legs appeared insanely long, bronzed and taut. She wore her long black hair down, and the breeze blew it back from her face. The spectacle of her cleavage was pushed out of her low-cut top. Her full lips were turned into a small, seductive smile, and her dark eyes looked like they could unlock all the tantric mysteries of the world.

Conceptually, Daniel knew she was gorgeous. In fact, he'd venture so far as to say that she was the embodiment of sexual perfection—that no woman had ever been so beautiful or sensual in the history of the world.

And yet, as he knew that, he couldn't find himself attracted to her. Something about her flawlessness was off-putting to him, but it was more than that. Even subtracting the fact that she was evil, and counting only on physical appearance, he still found something lacking.

It was like she wasn't really there. Penn hit all the right notes, but they all rang false. She was merely the façade of a human being, with nothing behind it.

"I was taking a walk around town and I spotted you working, so I thought I would say hello," Penn said.

"Hello, Penn." He smiled at her. "Satisfied?"

"Hardly." She laughed. "You never leave me satisfied. Although I know a trick or two I'm sure you'd love."

Daniel rolled his eyes and turned away from her. "Charming."

"You say that like you don't mean it, but I think you do." Penn hopped on the sawhorse next to him as he bent over to write on the blueprints.

"Do you really?" He glanced up at her in disbelief. "What have I done to give you that impression? Was it that time I punched you in the jaw? Or when you were kicking me repeatedly in the ribs?"

He was referencing their encounter on the Fourth of July, the one and only time he'd ever hit a woman. Though he wasn't completely certain that Penn could count as a real woman. After all, she was a man-eating monster.

Penn waved it off. "That was just a little fun and games. Nobody got hurt."

"So you've forgotten how Lexi murdered your boyfriend?" Daniel asked her absently as he made a mark on his papers.

"Gemma told you about that?" Penn clicked her tongue. "I thought she kept murder a secret. Especially after what she did."

For a minute Daniel tried to ignore her. He finished checking his measurements against the blueprints, so all he had left to do was the actual sawing. He stood up and looked over at Penn, who'd been watching him with a smirk on her face.

"Okay. I'll bite," he said, tapping his pencil against the palm of his hand. "What did Gemma do?"

"She didn't tell you?" Penn asked with faux surprise. "I thought there weren't secrets between you and your girlfriend's kid sister. It's a bit strange how much time you spend with her, isn't it?"

"No. But it is a bit strange how much I spend with *you*." He walked a few steps away from her to put the blueprints under a heavy chunk of wood so they wouldn't blow away as he worked.

"You do have a point there," Penn said. She hopped off the sawhorse, but she didn't follow him.

"So . . . did Gemma do something?" He faced her. "Or was that all a lie to get my attention?"

"Oh, no, she did something." Penn smiled widely. "She killed and fed on a young man when we were staying in the beach house. I can't remember his name, but I probably never knew it. Gemma did it on her own."

Daniel shoved his pencil behind his ear and tried to remember what he'd heard about that. It had been over a month ago, and Gemma had never really spoken much about it, at least not to him.

The only thing he really knew was what he read in the paper. There had been something about a guy named Jason Way, who was in his thirties and had been convicted of rape and domestic assault. That was how Daniel and Harper had been able to find Gemma after she'd run off with the sirens. They'd been staying in a beach house about an hour from Myrtle Beach. Harper had been searching everywhere for Gemma, until Daniel found the article about Jason Way's murder.

He'd been eviscerated the same way the other sirens' victims had been, so Daniel and Harper assumed that Penn or Lexi or Thea had done it. But now Penn was implying Gemma had.

"The body they found?" Daniel asked. "The rapist?"

"Maybe." She lowered her eyes, seeming disappointed by Daniel's calm reaction. "I don't know the details."

"Well, whatever Gemma did, *if* she even did anything, I'm sure she did it to protect herself," he said.

Penn scoffed. "So that's it? She gets away with murder, literally? But I endure the cold shoulder?"

"I give you the warmest shoulder I can, Penn," Daniel said honestly.

He went on to continue what he'd been working on. He brushed past her to get his tools together.

"What is it that you're doing?" Penn asked as he made sure the extension cord was plugged into the back of the theater.

"Building the sets for the play. Thea must've told you something about it."

"She's told me too much about it." Penn groaned. "She won't stop quoting Shakespeare. It's obnoxious."

"I thought you would like that kinda thing. Isn't it from your heyday?" He came back to where she stood, since she was standing next to his saw. He crouched down next to the machine, checking the cords and blades.

"It's still my heyday. I'll never go out of style," she told him confidently.

He smirked at that. "I stand corrected."

"What's on your back?"

"My tattoo?"

Daniel's tattoo took up most of his back. It was a thick black tree, with the roots growing below the waist of his jeans. The trunk grew upward, over his spine, then went to the side so the branches extended out over his shoulder and down his right arm.

The branches appeared to be shaded, but they were twisted along the scars that covered his upper back and shoulder. The shadows were real, and the tattoo was meant to cover up the scars that he'd gotten when a boat propeller ran him over.

"Not the tattoo," Penn said. "The scars."

He was still crouched down, adjusting the blade on the saw, and he wasn't paying that much attention to her. Then he felt her fingertips gently touching the outline of his tattoo, and he jerked his shoulder back, pushing her hand off him.

"Whoa, easy there, Penn." Daniel turned back to her and held his hand out. "I don't touch you, and I'd appreciate it if you did me the same favor."

"The difference is that I wouldn't mind if you touched me." Penn smiled, and he stood up to face her. "And you don't know it yet, but you'd love it if you let me run my hands all over you."

She reached out, meaning to run her hand along the contours of his stomach, but he grabbed her wrist just before she could. He gripped hard enough that it would be painful for a human, but she only smiled up at him.

"This is your last warning," Daniel said, his voice low and threatening. "Okay?"

She licked her lips, undeterred by his apparent anger. "What will you do next time?"

Daniel didn't say anything because he didn't really know what he'd do. He didn't have that much he could hold over her head. He let go of her and walked away, wanting to put distance between the two of them.

"I was in an accident," he said finally.

"What?" Penn asked as she absently rubbed her wrist.

He motioned to his back. "That's what the scars are from. It's the same one that screwed up my hearing."

"What?" Penn asked, and something in her tone made him look back at her. "What did you say?"

"It's why I'm immune to your song." He turned to face her fully. "I know you thought it was because I was related to some ex-boyfriend of yours, but I'm not. I'm just an ordinary human with a hearing problem."

"You're certain of this?" Penn asked, her voice barely above a whisper.

"Yeah, pretty certain." He nodded. "So now maybe you can move on, put your interest in some other guy that's up to your immortal standards."

For a moment he thought she might take the bait. Penn even seemed to consider it, but then she just shrugged and tossed her hair over her shoulder.

"It's better that you're not related to Bastian anyway," Penn said. "He was a jerk."

"Lucky me." He turned his attention back down to the outline he'd been making on the wood.

"You could have a surgery to fix it." Penn leaned forward on the boards, purposely accentuating her cleavage, but Daniel barely noticed.

"I've had surgeries, and it's fine." He looked up at her, his hazel eyes squinting in the bright sunlight. "Besides, if we're being honest here, would you enjoy me even half as much if I was just another zombie under your love spell?"

"Probably not," she admitted.

"So why do you do it?" Daniel asked her directly. "Why don't you just stop and let people act the way they want?"

"I can't help myself." She lifted up one shoulder in a small shrug. "Everyone grovels at my feet, and I'm not even trying."

"That actually sounds like a pretty horrible way to live."

"It can be," Penn said, her voice sounding oddly small and far away. Then she shook off the mood and smiled brightly at him. "But most of the time life is exactly the way I want it."

"How old are you?"

"It's hard to know exactly." She tucked her hair behind her ear.

"We had different calendars back then. But the closest estimate is that I was born in 24 B.C."

"And almost that entire time you were a siren, with everyone doing anything you wanted?" Daniel asked.

"Pretty much," she replied cheerily.

He rested his hands on the sawhorse and shook his head. "That sounds lonely."

Her smile faltered for a split second, a solitary flash of a moment when Daniel realized that he'd gotten it right. This big show that Penn put on about being happy and everything being perfect, that was all it was—a big show. She was lonely.

"I had my sisters," she said, but she lowered her eyes. "And I was in love. Once."

"Bastian?" Daniel asked, sincerely intrigued by the idea of Penn feeling anything real for anybody. "The immortal that was immune to you?"

"He was also a jerk," Penn reminded him.

"You couldn't control him," he said, and she nodded. "Did he leave you?"

She licked her lips and breathed deeply before answering. "It was a long time ago."

"Why don't you spend more time with immortals? Maybe you could fall in love again," Daniel suggested.

"I doubt that." Penn brushed off the idea without really considering it. "Besides, there's hardly any of us left. Eventually, everything dies."

"Except you."

"Except me," she agreed.

"Well, if you're gonna be hanging around, I'm putting you to work." Daniel walked back over to her and picked up his saw.

"What?" Penn sounded distressed by the idea. "I don't work."

"If you don't work, I don't talk," he said. "Now hold that board."

Penn didn't look happy about it, but she did as she was told. He grabbed his safety goggles out of his back pocket, and then he went to work cutting out the set. The saw had the added bonus of being so loud he wouldn't have to talk to Penn.

TWENTY-FOUR

Allies

After the visit with their mother, Harper needed to clear her head. The ride back home had been suffocating, with Gemma seeming particularly shaken up. Both Brian and Gemma refused to talk about it, and they retired to their separate quarters to come to terms with their own emotions.

Harper decided that the fresh air would do her good, even though it was rapidly approaching ninety degrees outside. She put on the shortest shorts she felt comfortable in and a tank top, and headed out for a walk.

When she'd talked to Daniel the night before, he said he'd be working at the theater on the sets, so she decided to go downtown to see him. Maybe they could grab lunch together, but even if they didn't, it would be nice to see him after the morning she'd had.

But as she approached the Paramount and heard Penn's unmistakable laugh, she realized dourly that her day was only going to get worse.

"I told you it's not that hard," Daniel was saying as Harper rounded the corner.

His back was to her, his bare skin glistening with sweat, and Penn stood next to him. They were both leaning over a piece of wood, but Penn was leaning much too close to him for Harper's comfort.

"I've never worked a day in my life." Penn laughed again. "How was I supposed to know?"

"It's just holding a board," Daniel said. "Anyone can handle it. Even a pampered princess like you."

"You think I'm a princess?" Penn teased.

"Working hard, I see," Harper said loudly, interrupting their conversation.

Penn glared back at her, her dark eyes looking even more menacing than normal. Daniel turned around more slowly, but he broke out in a broad grin when he saw her.

"Hey, Harper," he said. "I didn't expect to see you today. I thought you were visiting your mom."

"I was." She folded her arms over her chest. "And I thought I would stop by and say hello, but I can see you're busy, so I'll go."

"Good, 'bye!" Penn said happily and waved to her.

"She's not going anywhere." Daniel shot Penn a look, then walked to where Harper stood at the edge of the lawn. "What's going on? Are you mad at me?"

"Why would I be mad at you?" Harper asked. "Just because I had one of the worst days of my entire life and you're flirting with my mortal enemy? And she is literally a monster that wants to kill you and me and everyone we know, and you're just chatting with her like old friends?"

Daniel shook his head. "That's not at all what's happening here, and you know it. You're too smart to be jealous over something like this."

"I'm not jealous," Harper scoffed, and Penn snickered from where she stood by the sawhorses. "I'd feel about the same right now if I saw you helping Hitler redecorate. She is pure evil, and you shouldn't be nice to her or hang out with her."

"I hope you'd be a little more freaked out if I was helping Hitler, because he'd be a zombie," Daniel said.

"Just never mind." Harper turned and walked away from him.

"Harper, wait." Daniel went after her, but she didn't stop until she thought they were too far away for Penn to eavesdrop. Even then she only stopped because he took her arm. "Harper."

"I told you to stay away from her," Harper said. "And I did it for your own good. She's going to kill you if you spend too much time with her. And you know it. Is it so wrong that I don't want to see you end up dead?"

"No, but is it so wrong that I want to keep her happy so she doesn't hurt you or Gemma?" Daniel asked. "Because that's all I'm trying to do. I'm just keeping the peace, Harper."

"I know, but . . ." Harper pushed back her hair. "Maybe it was a bad idea getting involved with you."

"No." Daniel shook his head. "I absolutely refuse to do this. Not today. Not ever. You can't just go into that mode again."

"What mode?" Harper asked.

"The one where you say you can't see me to protect me or some crap like that." He waved it off. "We discussed it before, remember? You don't have the right to tell me what I choose to do."

"What am I supposed to do?" Harper asked. "I'm supposed to let you flirt with the devil?"

"I'm not flirting," Daniel corrected her. "And yes, you're supposed to let me do what I need to do to keep *us all* safe. And I let you do the same."

"I don't know if I can do that, Daniel," Harper admitted.

"Look, it's really hot out," Daniel said. "Why don't you go to Pearl's, get yourself something to drink, and cool off? I'll be down in a little bit, and you can tell me about your awful morning."

"What about Penn?" Harper asked.

"What about her?" Daniel asked. "We're out in broad daylight. She's not going to eat my heart today."

"Okay," Harper relented. "I'll meet you at Pearl's in a few minutes."

"Fifteen minutes, tops." Daniel was already backing away. "I just have to put my tools away."

Sighing, she took his advice and walked the few blocks down to Pearl's. Part of her wanted to go back and help Daniel clean up his tools, but that was just to be sure that Penn left him alone.

Harper hadn't really thought Penn would hurt Daniel, not in the middle of the afternoon in public, nor did she think that Daniel had any attraction to Penn.

He was right, and in the long term it would be good to stay in Penn's good graces. But Harper just couldn't believe that any good could come from being friends with Penn.

As soon as she pushed the door open to Pearl's, the air-conditioning sent a refreshing chill over her, and she already felt a bit better. The idea to take a walk in the suffocating heat had been a bad one, but the cooler temperature of the diner was well on its way to correcting her mistake.

Harper pulled up a stool at the counter, sat on the cracked vinyl, and ordered a glass of ice water. When Daniel came in, she'd probably order something more, but for now, rehydrating and cooling off were her main priorities.

"You should take a swim," a husky voice said from beside her.

With her glass of ice water pressed to her cheek, Harper hadn't been paying attention to who was coming or going in the diner. She lowered the glass and glanced over to see Thea climbing up on the stool next to her.

"I don't like swimming," Harper replied. She sat up straighter and stirred her water with the straw.

"You really are the exact opposite of your sister." Thea set her purse on the counter. She rummaged through it for a second before taking out a hair tie. As she spoke, she leaned back and pulled her long red hair up into a ponytail. "The two of you are night and day."

"What about you?" Harper gave her a sidelong glance. "How much are you and your sister alike?"

"What can I get for you today?" Pearl asked Thea, interrupting their conversation.

"Just a cherry malt." Thea smiled sweetly at her.

Pearl smiled back at her, but seemed to flounder for a minute, like a starstruck teenager meeting her idol. Even without using her song, Thea still had the power to captivate men and women alike.

"The bonds between sisters are very complex things," Thea said once Pearl had left to fill her order. She rested her arms on the faded counter and looked over at Harper. "You must understand that better than anyone."

"I suppose I do," Harper agreed.

"You and I really have a lot in common," Thea went on. "Like you, I'm the oldest."

"Penn is younger than you?" Harper asked, glancing over at her.

"Yeah," Thea said. Pearl brought her the malt, and Thea politely thanked her. She took a long sip before speaking to Harper again. "Most people think that Penn is older. It's a common misconception."

"She's pretty bossy," Harper said.

"That's my fault." Thea smiled sadly. "Our mothers weren't around when we were children, leaving me to essentially raise Penn and Aggie. Penn was the youngest, and I overindulged her."

"I can understand that." Harper propped her chin up on her hand and watched Thea. "But that was a very long time ago. If Penn turned out to be a spoiled brat, why haven't you corrected it?"

"If you really stand up to Penn and tell her no . . ." Thea trailed off. "Well, let's just say you don't get a chance to ever tell her no again."

"Lovely," Harper muttered. "And I'm sure that Gemma is already in the habit of telling her no."

"Don't worry about Gemma," Thea said. "She's your sister, but she's my sister now, too."

Harper looked at her dubiously. "You're saying you're protecting her?"

"Something like that." Thea took another long drink of her malt. "Gemma reminds me a bit of Persephone."

"The girl that you let get murdered before?" Harper asked.

"There's one good thing about making mistakes." Thea turned to her with a smile. "You learn not to make them again."

"Why are you telling me this?" Harper asked. "What are you hoping to gain?"

"I like Gemma, and I'd like her to stay with us for a very long time," Thea said. "Lexi is annoying, and Penn is . . . well, Penn is Penn. I want someone on my side for a change."

"And you think that's Gemma?" Harper asked.

"I think she could be, yes," Thea said. "And I think the biggest thing holding her back from really committing, from really joining us, is you."

Harper shook her head. "The biggest reason she doesn't want to join you is because you're evil and Penn is a monster. *You* are a monster."

"If Gemma really commits to us and really tries, I can assure you that I'll do everything in my power to keep her safe and alive and happy," Thea said. "But if she keeps going against Penn and keeps trying to break away, I can't protect her."

Harper swallowed hard. "I can't make this choice for her."

"Maybe not, but you can let her go." Thea pulled a few dollars out of her purse and left them on the counter. "I'll see you around."

"Yeah, I'm sure you will," Harper said as Thea slid off the stool.

Once Thea was gone, Harper rested her head in her hands. For the first time, she wondered if it might really be in Gemma's best interest to remain a siren. It was a very high price to pay, but if she was alive and happy, that had to be a better choice than being dead.

TWENTY-FIVE

Pursuit

Visiting their mom the day before had completely drained their dad. In truth, it had drained all of them, but it hit Brian the worst.

The rest of the day he was out in the garage supposedly working on a project. But when Harper sent Gemma out to get him for supper, he'd just been leaning against his workbench, drinking a beer and staring off into space.

To make matters worse, the air-conditioning broke on the hottest day of the year. They only had a window unit, in the living room, so the upstairs never cooled off anyway. The air conditioner did a fairly good job on the main level, since the house was so small.

Instead of going out and buying a new AC, Brian insisted that he was going to fix their old one. He took it out to the garage, where he'd spent all Sunday morning tinkering with it, but so far there had been no results.

While Harper was out in the garage trying to convince their dad to drink water instead of beer so he didn't get dehydrated,

Gemma put her plan into motion. She'd already texted Marcy and made sure it was a go. Now all she had to do was keep Harper preoccupied.

"Hello?" Daniel answered his cell phone on the third ring.

"Hey, Daniel, what are you doing?" Gemma asked in a hushed voice. She stood in her bedroom doorway, watching the stairs and listening closely for the front door.

"Why are you whispering?" Daniel instantly sounded tense. "Is something wrong?"

"No, I just don't want Harper to hear me," Gemma said. "Listen, can you do me a favor?"

He hesitated before saying, "Possibly."

"I need you to keep Harper busy today."

"What for? What are you doing?" Daniel asked.

"I'm going with Marcy out to Sundham to visit her friend at the bookstore," Gemma explained. "We're going to see if we can figure out where the scroll might be or see if we can find Demeter or the muses or something."

"And why don't you want Harper to know about this?" Daniel asked.

"I don't want her to know about anything anymore," Gemma said. "I'm trying not to tell her anything about the sirens at all."

"So you want me to get Harper to come over so you can sneak off with Marcy?" Daniel asked. "Won't Marcy tell her what's up?"

"No, I already swore Marcy to secrecy. She likes sneaking around anyway."

Daniel sighed. "All right. I'll do it. But this isn't dangerous or anything, right? You're not going to get hurt or anything?"

"Nope. I'm just going to a bookstore," Gemma replied. "How dangerous could that be?"

After she got off the phone with Daniel, it only took a few minutes for Harper to come in the house and say she was going out to Daniel's. She invited Gemma to join, tempting her with promises of air-conditioning, but Gemma managed to decline without raising suspicion.

With Harper gone, Gemma just told her dad that she was going out to swim for a while, and he told her to stay cool and be safe. She texted Marcy, who came to pick her up in the Gremlin, and they were off to Sundham.

"This really isn't that long of a trip," Marcy said as they parked in front of the bookstore. "I don't know what your sister is so worried about."

"Well, you know Harper," Gemma said as she opened the car door. "If she's not worrying about something, then she's not alive."

Marcy led the way into the bookstore, entering underneath the perpetually creaking sign that said CHERRY LANE BOOKS. The last time Gemma had been here, they'd found Lydia back in a dark, hidden corner of the store, but today she was waiting right inside for them.

"Hey, guys," Lydia chirped. She sat on the front counter next to an antique cash register. A glittery deck of cards was in her hand, with a few cards laid out beside her.

Sitting perched at the edge like that, wearing tangerine tights with a flowered jumper, Lydia reminded Gemma even more of a pixie. She was so petite and cheery, and pink clips held her short black hair out of her face.

"Hey, Lydia," Marcy said as they walked over to the counter.

"Thanks again for letting us come in," Gemma said. "I know you're usually closed on Sundays."

"It's no problem at all." Lydia waved it off and winked at

Gemma. "I make exceptions for supernatural beings. I can't expect them to live on normal mortal time, can I?"

"I really appreciate it anyway," Gemma said.

"Sorry. I was just doing a quick tarot reading." Lydia peered down at the cards next to her for a minute, tilting her head this way and that before shaking her head and scooping up the cards. "This week looks like it's going to be busy."

"I'm sorry about that," Marcy said.

"Don't be." Lydia smiled brightly and shuffled the cards. "It's better to be busy than bored. That's what I always say."

"Marcy lives by the exact opposite of that motto," Gemma said.

Marcy nodded. "I really do."

"I know." Lydia laughed in her usual light, twinkling way, and set the deck of cards aside. "Anyway, I got the e-mail with the list of names you wanted me to look up, and I've started the search, but it may take a little while."

"Bummer." Marcy leaned against the counter next to Lydia. "But I suppose there isn't, like, a national Greek God Database like there is for missing children."

"No, there's not," Lydia said. "And it doesn't help that most of the gods and goddesses don't want to be found."

"How come?" Gemma asked.

"Humans and other immortals were always trying to capture them or kill them." Lydia pulled one knee up to her chest and leaned against it. "They wanted their power or were afraid of them or blamed them for their problems. It's a very tricky thing being so powerful."

"I would imagine it is," Gemma said.

"That's why so many of them change their names," Lydia went

on. "What do your siren friends go by now? I'm sure it's not Peisinoe and Thelxiepeia, is it?"

Gemma shook her head. "No, it's Penn and Thea."

"They're much more manageable to say and spell, too, which is an added bonus," Lydia said.

"The Greeks were lame about names," Marcy muttered.

Lydia smirked. "Well, I'm sure the Greeks would think you're pretty lame about names."

"What about Achelous?" Gemma asked. "Do you know if he's still alive?"

"I can't say for sure." Lydia gave her shoulders a helpless shrug. "Many of the gods live so far off the radar that their deaths don't even register. I've got plenty of feelers out for both him and Demeter, though."

"What about the muses?" Gemma asked.

"I did have some word on them, but none of it's good." Lydia smiled sadly at her. "The two you were looking for—Terpsichore and Melpomene—are confirmed dead, along with Calliope, Euterpe, Clio, Thalia, and Urania. The other two have been missing for centuries and are presumed dead."

"So you're saying that all the muses are dead?" Marcy asked, looking up at Lydia.

Lydia nodded. "Yes, I think so."

"Dammit." Gemma ran her hand through her hair. "I really thought they might be the key to destroying the scroll."

"Destroying the scroll is pretty impossible, even if you had a muse," Lydia reminded her.

" 'Pretty' impossible isn't 'completely' impossible," Gemma said. "Thea told me about this Asterion guy, and how he used a muse to break the curse."

"Are you talking about the minotaur?" Lydia leaned forward, her excitement piqued. "They've been extinct for over a thousand years."

"Right." Gemma nodded. "Because they undid the curse."

"And you're saying they heard it from a muse?" Lydia touched her chin as she thought about it. "That would make sense. Muses kept a lot of secrets, which is why they're likely all dead. The other reason is their almost boundless love."

"Boundless love?" Marcy asked. "Is that a nice way of saying they were prostitutes? Because hookers always seem to be targets for serial killers."

"Serial killers aren't killing immortals," Lydia said, casting Marcy a bemused look. "Muses gave up their immortality when they fell in love. They chose to be human to be able to have a relationship instead of the somewhat parasitic version they'd normally have. And then they would just die of natural causes, like any other mortal."

"So is that what happened to the gods, like Achelous?" Gemma asked.

"No. He's a true immortal—he was born that way," Lydia said. "Only those that have been granted immortality—either by being blessed or cursed—can give it up. Everyone else is cursed to live forever. Unless, of course, they're murdered."

"So if Achelous is dead, he was murdered?" Gemma asked.

"Yes. That would be the only way."

Marcy readjusted her glasses on her nose and stared at the floor thoughtfully. "It's weird that immortality is considered both a blessing and a curse."

"It is a double-edged sword," Lydia agreed.

"How do you kill a god?" Gemma asked.

"It depends on the god. If you're god of the sun, it would probably have something to do with darkness," Lydia said.

Gemma thought of Achelous, remembering how he was a freshwater god. "So for something like the god of water, it would probably involve being dried out?"

Lydia nodded. "Yeah, something like that."

"So is that how you kill a siren, then?" Marcy asked.

"No, killing a siren is a lot easier than killing a god. A god—something like Apollo or Achelous—they would be here." Lydia held up her hand above her head. "And an immortal, something like a siren or even a werewolf or troll, would be here." She held her hand in front of her chin.

"Where would humans be?" Marcy asked, and Lydia lowered her hand in front of her stomach. "That far down, huh?"

"Yeah, we're pretty fragile," Lydia said. "So anyway, lesser immortals like vampires usually have more than one way to kill them. Breaking the curse, starvation, sunlight, a stake through the heart. A god only has *one* way, and it's usually complicated and arduous."

"So there's more than one way to kill a siren, then?" Gemma asked.

"Since you were here last, I've been doing some research. I found a few ways to kill sirens, but most of them are longer-term," Lydia explained. "Starvation, having fewer than four sirens on a full moon, being apart from each other for several weeks. There's only one instantaneous way to kill them."

"And would that involve a stake through the heart or a silver bullet?" Marcy asked.

Lydia shook her head. "Unfortunately, no. It's not quite that simple."

"Of course not," Gemma muttered.

"Hold on." Lydia leaned back and punched some buttons on the cash register. It made a loud *ding*, and the drawer popped open. She dug inside, then pulled out a small, folded square of paper. "Here."

Lydia had her hand outstretched toward her, but Gemma hesitated.

"What's that?" Gemma asked.

"It's how you kill a siren. Not all of the sirens at once, but if you're fighting one hand-to-hand and need to stop her in self-defense, here's how you do it."

"Thank you." Tentatively, Gemma took the paper from her. "How do you know all this stuff?"

Lydia smiled slyly. "You could say that it's a family business. My grandma is a witch, and my father is a vampire."

"Wait." Marcy narrowed her eyes, as if noticing Lydia for the first time. "Does that mean you're a vampire? Or a witch?"

"I'm neither, actually," Lydia answered. "It just means I have an affinity, a natural inclination, towards the supernatural.

"If it makes you feel any better, my grandma is more of a good witch," Lydia said when Marcy continued to scrutinize her. "She used to help various immortals out when they were in trouble, but she was mostly a record keeper." Lydia gestured to the bookstore. "Many of these books and scrolls you see here came from my grandma, handed down generation after generation."

"Have you ever destroyed a scroll?" Gemma asked.

"No, I haven't." Lydia paused, then took a deep breath. "But if I'm being honest, I never wanted to. It's always been our job to protect them."

"Why? Some of these creatures are evil," Gemma said.

"Some humans do bad things, truly horrendous things, but

that doesn't mean that they're all evil or that we all deserve to die," Lydia said. "Though if the right creature found the scroll with humanity's curse, they might be tempted to destroy it."

"Are you implying that we are a curse?" Marcy asked, and she seemed to have relaxed around Lydia again.

"Mortality is a blessing and a curse, too," Lydia said simply.

"What if I find this scroll?" Gemma asked. "Will you help me destroy it? Or will that go against your nature?"

"My nature is to help those in need," Lydia replied carefully. "If I have the tools or information you need to protect yourself and those you care about, I will gladly give them to you."

"Do you have any ideas where the scroll might be?" Marcy asked, turning her attention to Gemma. "I know you came up empty a couple times."

"I think it might be with the sirens now," Gemma said. "It wasn't before, but I told Thea I was looking for it. I think they'll hang on to it to guard until I'm either gone or I've lost interest."

"But you aren't going to lose interest, are you?" Lydia asked.

"No." Gemma shook her head. "I can't."

"I'm sorry I couldn't be of more help to you," Lydia said, sounding sincere.

"No, you've been plenty of help," Gemma assured her with a smile. "Thank you."

Marcy thanked Lydia again, and Lydia promised she'd be in contact soon. They went outside, Gemma's head swimming with everything Lydia had told her.

"So," Marcy said once they were both sitting inside her Gremlin. "How do you kill a siren?"

Gemma unfolded the paper to find a photocopied illustration from an old book. It showed exactly what needed to be done, including a detailed diagram with suggested weapons written in English.

Marcy leaned over, peering at it. "That doesn't look so bad." Then she pointed to a particularly vicious-looking ax/spike combo labeled as a *battleax.* "It'd be easier if you had one of those, though."

TWENTY-SIX

Surrender

When Aiden had called to ask her out later that night, Gemma couldn't think of a reason to say no. Actually, she could think of a million reasons, but between the mounting hunger, the suffocating heat, and the increasing impossibility that she would find a way to save herself, she needed a break.

She knew she needed to redouble her efforts to find the scroll, but since she was pretty sure it was with the sirens, she'd have to battle to get it. Thanks to Lydia, that might be a bit easier now, although Gemma still wasn't sure she'd be able to actually go through with it. It looked brutal.

But she wanted to wait until Harper was gone. It was only a few more days until she left for college, and then Harper would be a half hour away, getting on with her life and safe from any kind of retaliation the sirens might want to dish out.

So for the next few days, Gemma's only plan was to look up ways to destroy the scroll, keep her hunger in check, and avoid the sirens—well, at least Penn and Lexi. When she looked at it that way, Aiden calling her was a bit of serendipity.

Aiden picked her up for their date, and Brian emerged from the garage long enough to vaguely threaten him not to hurt or deflower his daughter. He didn't seem to approve of the pairing, eyeing Aiden's luxury car with disdain, but he let Gemma go out anyway, probably sensing that she needed an escape.

As far as dates went, theirs went pretty well. Dinner at the yacht club overlooking the bay. It was a little ritzier than Gemma felt comfortable around, but Aiden ordered white wine and poured her a glass. She'd only ever snuck a drink of her dad's beer on a dare once before, and even though food didn't really taste the same afterward, sipping the wine felt exotic and mature.

The meal ended up running long, so they skipped the movie, and Aiden took her to one of the clubs off the beach. This Gemma did not like. It was crowded and too hot.

But the solution to that was simple—they left. Everything else was closed on a Sunday night, so Aiden took her back home. Harper's car was still gone, and the house was dark, so Gemma assumed her dad was in bed.

"I had a nice time tonight," Gemma said as they sat in his parked car. He'd left it on, so the air-conditioning was keeping them cool, and Gotye was playing softly on his stereo.

"Me, too." Aiden rested his head against his seat as he looked over at Gemma, and he smiled. There was something absolutely dazzling about his smile, and his brown eyes sparkled.

"I don't really want it to end yet," she admitted.

He reached over and used his finger to caress the back of her hand. "Maybe it doesn't have to."

"Yeah?" Gemma asked hopefully and bit her lip. "What did you have in mind?"

Aiden leaned toward her, his eyes searching hers as a confident smile played on his lips. The moment his mouth touched hers in a tempestuous kiss, his tongue tasting of cool mint from an Altoid, a strange satisfaction settled over her.

This was the physical contact she'd been craving. He fed into desires she didn't even want to admit having. His mouth was a bit too forceful, and his hands were too strong on her arms and waist, but that only added to the excitement.

Her skin fluttered, the pleasurable way it did before it transformed, but Gemma pushed it down. She silenced the monster inside her, the one that Aiden's kisses had woken up. A flush went through her, and she let out a soft moan.

That spurred Aiden on, and he reached down, hitting a button on the side of the seat so it would go back farther.

"That's better," he said in a husky whisper once the seat was lying flat like a bed, and Gemma laughed a little.

He'd climbed on top of her then, his body feeling heavy and powerful over her. Part of her was aware that there was something dangerous about this, that he had put her in a position where it was hard for her to move or fight back, but the hunger-lust was blocking out those concerns.

Gemma didn't want to think or worry about or fear anything. She just let the moment consume her.

Aiden was getting a little rougher with her than she was used to, and while it wasn't the kind of thing Gemma herself enjoyed, it drove the siren in her wild. He bit her neck when he kissed it, and it sent her skin afire. His hand knotted in her hair, pulling it slightly, and she had to use all her might to keep control of herself.

Then he slid his hand down the front of her shirt, and that was when Gemma knew she had to get a handle on things.

"Aiden, let's slow things down a bit," she whispered in his ear as he cupped her breast.

Instead of listening to her, he squeezed her chest harder—painfully, actually.

"*Aiden.*" Gemma pushed him back, and he finally let go.

"Sorry." He smiled at her, his sandy hair falling across her forehead. "I was just having some fun, but I know where the line is now."

"Okay. Just don't cross it again," she warned him, and with a cocky smirk, he promised her that he wouldn't.

When he started kissing her again, it was more gentle. Which was good, because it gave her a chance to get back in control.

But within a few moments he was back to where he had been before: kissing her deeply, his hand knotted in her hair. His other hand knew better than to go after her chest, so it gripped her side.

Gemma wrapped her arms around him. Her eyes were closed, and she concentrated on the way her body was feeling—not just the pleasure but the intensity of the fluttering of her skin, the monster inside trying to break free. Pushing it back, holding herself in check, that was the real joy Gemma got out of this.

But then Aiden's hand slid in between her thighs, and her eyes flashed open.

"Aiden," she said, but he didn't listen. He only slid his hand up farther, threatening to touch parts of her that she'd never let a guy touch before. "*Aiden.*"

"Stop being a prude, Gemma," Aiden said, his voice a low growl in her ear as he kissed her neck. "Let's just have some fun."

"I'm not having fun," she said and tried to push him off. But he was strong, and he held fast.

"Just relax and go with it," Aiden said, and she tried kneeing him in his crotch, but he deftly avoided it. He was completely in the passenger seat on top of her, pinning her there.

Her mouth began to tremble, and her fingers itched as they lengthened. As bad as this was, as much as she didn't want anything to happen with Aiden, she didn't want to kill him, either.

That was when Gemma realized too late that this was nothing like how things had been with Kirby. She wasn't in control of Aiden. She wasn't in control of the monster. She wasn't even in control of herself.

"Aiden, get off me!" Gemma screamed now and pushed against him with all her might.

He slammed against the roof of the car, and he stayed that way for a few seconds. Gemma was taking deep breaths, trying desperately to keep herself from transforming, and she let go of him, wrapping her hands together as her fingers slowly began to return to their normal form.

"You bitch," Aiden snarled, his eyes wide in a mixture of confusion and rage.

"Aiden, *no*," she managed to cry out before he wrapped his hand around her throat, but by then Gemma knew that she'd have to hurt him if she wanted to escape this.

Then the passenger door flew open, and before Gemma had a chance to understand what was going on, someone had reached in and grabbed Aiden, yanking him off her.

She sat up, gasping for breath, and she saw that Alex had thrown Aiden onto the ground. He stood over him, holding Aiden by the collar of his shirt, and he punched him twice, hard enough that she heard his fist smashing into Aiden's face.

"Don't you ever touch Gemma again," Alex growled, his arm

still cocked. Aiden tried to say something, but he just ended up sputtering out blood from his lip. "Do you hear me? Never touch her again."

"I hear you," Aiden mumbled.

"Good," Alex said, and then he punched Aiden once more.

"Alex!" Gemma scrambled out of the car. "Don't kill him."

Alex let go of his shirt, and Aiden fell back on the ground. Alex stood up straight and slammed the car door shut. Aiden got to his feet as quickly as he could, and as he got in the car, he swore at Alex and Gemma under his breath.

They both watched as Aiden sped out of the driveway, his tires squealing. Despite the heat, Gemma wrapped her arms around herself. Alex shook out his hand, which must have ached from how hard he'd hit Aiden.

"Thank you," Gemma said quietly after a few seconds.

"What the hell is going on, Gemma?" Alex asked, and she was surprised by the anger in his voice. "What were you doing with that guy? He was a dick!"

"I didn't realize he was such a dick when I agreed to go out with him," Gemma said.

"This doesn't make any sense." He shook his head and growled. "I'm so pissed off."

"It's over now, and you should go home," Gemma said.

"You don't get it." He turned back to face her and ran both his hands through his hair. "I wanted to kill him because he was hurting you. But I *hate* you."

She lowered her eyes and nodded to keep from crying. "I'm sorry."

"Why do I want to know you're safe if I hate you?" Alex demanded. "Why do I worry about you? Why am I scared that you're going to die without knowing how I really feel about you, when what I feel is contempt?"

Gemma struggled to keep her composure, and when she spoke, her words were barely audible. "I don't know."

"You're *lying*, and I know you're lying." He stood a few inches in front of her, practically yelling in her face. "Don't lie to me, Gemma. Please. Don't fucking lie about this."

"Alex, you're better off just going home," Gemma said, still refusing to look up at him. "Forget you ever met me."

"I can't forget!" Alex shouted, making her flinch. "I dream of you *every night*. Do you know what that's like? In my dreams, we're still together and I still love you. And then I wake up every morning, and I hate you, and I hate me, and I hate everything."

"Of course I know what that's like!" Gemma lifted her head and looked up at him with tears in her eyes. "I do the same thing, every day! Except I don't hate you."

"Why not?" Alex asked, almost plaintively. "Why don't you hate me? Why did we break up?"

She looked away again. "You wouldn't understand."

"Why not? If I dumped you, why wouldn't I understand my own reasoning? What the hell happened, Gemma?"

The front light switched on, and Gemma took a step back from Alex. She heard the screen door creak open as her dad came outside.

"Gemma?" Brian asked. "Is everything okay?"

"Yeah, Dad." She sniffled and wiped at her eyes. "I'll be there in a minute."

"I'll wait," Brian said. She hadn't turned around to look at him yet, but he couldn't be standing more than a few feet behind her.

"Dad, I'm okay," she insisted, but Alex was already backing away.

"You need to keep her on a short leash, Mr. Fisher," Alex said as he took steps backward. "Your daughter is hanging around with some very bad guys."

"What does that mean?" Brian asked. "Gemma? What does that mean?" He walked over so that he was standing next to her once Alex had gone into his own house.

Gemma shook her head. "It's been a long night, Dad."

"Why is there blood on my driveway?" Brian pointed to the small puddle of blood that Aiden had left behind.

Gemma sighed. "Aiden got too frisky, and Alex beat the shit out of him, okay? I had a bad, bad night, after a bad, bad weekend, and this is turning out to be the worst summer of my entire life. So if I could just please go inside and go to bed, I would really like that."

Brian stared at her with bleary eyes. His hair was disheveled from sleep, and he wore his old football T-shirt with matching sweatpants. He was not prepared for this conversation.

"Okay," he said finally.

"Great, thank you." She turned around and stormed into the house.

She raced up to her bedroom looking for solace, but it seemed like everything in it was taunting her. It was all remnants of her former life, of things she'd loved that she could never love again, of someone she could never be.

The Michael Phelps poster on her wall she ripped down, actually tearing it in half in the process. There was a picture of her mother on her bedside table and she picked it up and flung it against the wall, shattering glass everywhere. On the ceiling were fading glow-in-the-dark stars that Alex had helped her put up years ago.

Gemma jumped up onto her bed, trying to pull them down, but she couldn't reach them. She kept jumping and failing, and by then she was sobbing in frustration and anger and sadness.

"Gemma?" Brian asked, opening her bedroom door.

"Everything is ruined, Dad," she cried and fell back onto her bed. "I've lost everything that matters to me."

"That's not true." Brian came into her room and sat down next to her. "I'm still here, and I'm never going anywhere."

That only made Gemma sob harder. Brian wrapped his arms around his daughter and held her to him. As she cried into his shoulder, he stroked her hair and kept promising her that everything would be all right.

TWENTY-SEVEN

Engagements

Daniel's biggest problem with the island was that he had no cable TV. In reality, he knew he shouldn't complain, because it wasn't like he'd had cable out on the boat, either. At least now he had room to get his full-sized television out of storage and put it up.

Harper had come out to his house to escape the heat, and he was more than happy to comply. But once she'd gone home, he was left on the island alone, and he felt restless. He put in a movie, deciding that watching *Jaws* again for the fiftieth time would be better than staring at the walls.

The window air conditioner he'd put in the cabin when he moved out kept the place rather cool, but not enough. Harper had a rule that both of them kept all their clothes on when they were together, so he actually didn't mind as much that she'd left tonight, because it meant that he could shed some layers.

He stood in front of his TV, watching an unsuspecting woman swim alone in the ocean as the great white stalked her, and he unbuttoned his shirt.

"Dun dun, dun dun." Daniel was singing along with the growing intensity of the music when he heard a bang on his roof. "What the heck was that?"

He looked up at the ceiling, before realizing that was dumb and he couldn't see through it. Then he heard another bang, this one sounding like it came from the ground. He paused the movie, then went to the front door to see if he could find out what was going on.

"Of course I'm going to the front door like a stupid chick in a horror movie," he muttered. On his way to the door, he doubled back and grabbed a baseball bat from the closet. "Now I just have to remember not to go outside and ask if anyone is there."

He opened the door, fully expecting to see a raccoon, Harper, or Jason Vorhees. Instead it was just Penn, smiling in that suggestive way that she always did.

"Hey, handsome," Penn purred.

"What the hell are you doing here?" Daniel asked, but instead of answering him, she slid past him and walked into his house. "Sure, come on in. That's what I meant."

"I love what you've done with the place," Penn said as she admired the cabin. "Much nicer than the last time I was out here."

Daniel sighed and closed the door. He set the bat on the butcher's block in the kitchen. Right now it didn't look like he needed it, but things could always take a turn for the worse with Penn.

"How did you get here?" he asked. "You're not all wet, so you didn't swim."

"I flew."

Her halter dress was open all the way in the back, allowing room for her massive black wings to spread out. They were away now, so her smooth flesh appeared normal, but Daniel had seen the monster that lurked underneath.

"Oh, right," Daniel said. "You're that bird-monster thing, too. I almost forgot how friggin' hideous you really are. Thanks for reminding me."

Penn appeared unfazed by his comments. She hopped up on the kitchen counter, crossing her legs languidly and deliberately, and Daniel averted his eyes.

"Your girlfriend was out here forever. I thought she'd never leave. I was about ready to swoop down and pick her up and drop her off a cliff."

His heart stopped beating momentarily. "You didn't, though, right? Harper's alive and safe?"

"I didn't touch a hair on her pretty head," she assured him. "I knew it would put a damper on the mood if I hurt her, so I didn't."

"Mood? What mood?" Daniel asked. "And did you just admit to spying on me all night? Are you stalking me?"

She shook her head. " 'Stalking' is such a strong word."

"It's also an accurate one, apparently." He leaned back against the wall and crossed his arms over his chest.

"I was just thinking about what you said yesterday, and I wanted to talk to you about it." Penn spoke cheerily, like they were old friends catching up over Sunday brunch.

"What did I say? I don't remember anything that would imply I wanted you to stalk me."

"I wanted to talk to you alone, and I knew I couldn't kill your girlfriend, so I waited until she left. That's all that happened, okay?" Penn sounded annoyed, and Daniel decided not to push it. Things went better when she wasn't pissed off or homicidal.

"Sure. Okay," he said. "Now, what did I say that prompted this visit?"

"I'm lonely," she said, but without the vulnerability he'd seen in her before.

"I thought you had your sisters to keep you company," Daniel reminded her.

"I kinda hate them." She thought about it, then wagged her head. "Well, I don't hate Thea. I don't know if I hate Gemma yet. She's a pain in my ass, though. But I do hate Lexi. She's awful."

"Yeah, families are tough."

"But I'm lonely in a different way." She slid off the counter, her dress briefly pulling up very high on her thighs. "It's been so long since I had a real man in my life."

He held up his hands. "I have a sense of where this conversation is going, and I can head it off right here. I am not that man in your life. I never will be. Ever."

"We got off on the wrong foot, and you just need a chance to get to know me," Penn said, but she hadn't taken any steps closer to him, so that was probably a good sign.

"Well . . . Penn, I mean this nicely, but I think you're evil. So I can't see us being compatible—*ever*—because I don't think I'm evil. Or at least anywhere near as evil as you are."

"This is ridiculous. I could have anyone I want."

"Then have them. Go." He moved his hands in a shooing gesture. "I encourage you to do this. Or them, as it were."

Penn had started walking toward him with slow, measured steps. "But I don't want them. I want *you*."

"That is flattering, but . . ." He shook his head.

"Do you know how many men I've slept with?" Penn asked him.

"I don't know why you think I would find that fact appealing."

"Daniel," she snapped. She stood in front of him, staring up at him with her dark eyes. "Stop. Listen to me. Do you care about your girlfriend?"

He licked his lips. "I think you know I do."

"And you care about her sister?"

"What are you getting at, Penn?" Daniel asked, growing increasingly nervous with this line of questioning.

"I will make a deal with you. I want you to sleep with me."

"Penn." He laughed emptily. "No, I can't."

"I won't kill them if you sleep with me," Penn said, her tone seductive and velvet.

Daniel scoffed. "You think you can threaten me into loving you? Is that your plan?"

"No. I think I can threaten you into sleeping with me, and once you have, you'll never want to leave," she replied matter-of-factly.

"Penn, that's . . ." He lowered his eyes. "It's disgusting, and I won't do it."

"Really?" Penn arched an eyebrow. "I'm promising you that I would leave Harper and Gemma alone, if you have sex with me *one time.* I would spare the people you care about most, and I would give you the best night of your life."

He decided to go with a different approach to turning her down, and asked, "Do you realize how desperate this makes you sound? How pathetic this offer is?"

"Oh, trust me, Daniel, I get it," Penn said, and her expression led him to believe that she did. "But I've thought about this a lot. I want you, and I will do anything to have you."

"I'm really not that great," he insisted. "You can ask some of my ex-girlfriends. I think I'd end up disappointing you."

"Are you a virgin?" Penn asked.

He hesitated before saying, "No, but it has been a while."

"Then what I'm asking really isn't that big a deal." She smiled up at him. "Let's just do it. I can make you feel things you've never felt before." She stepped closer to him, so she was almost pressed up against him. "I'll show you ecstasy you didn't even know your body was capable of. Let me make you happy."

His shirt was unbuttoned all the way down, so he was exposed. Almost tentatively, she put her hands on his stomach, and he let her. He stared down at her, his breath coming out ragged.

Penn stood up on her tiptoes, and he closed his eyes so he wouldn't have to see her as she pressed her lips to his. She kissed him gently—tenderly, even.

At first he did nothing, but then slowly he began to kiss her back. Her body was pressed hot against his, but he kept his arms at his sides, unwilling to touch her.

She leaned in, kissing him more deeply, and he was surprised to find his body responding. As much as she repulsed him, the way she touched him actually did feel good.

Her lips traveled down, kissing his neck and then his chest. He leaned back, resting his head against the wall, and he felt her hands moving south, unbuttoning his jeans.

"Penn . . ." He pushed her hands away. She let go of his pants, but she moved her hands to his sides, still hanging on to him. "No. Penn." She tried to kiss him again, and he turned his head away. He grabbed both her wrists and pushed her back away from him. "I said no. I can't do this."

She yanked her wrists free from his and stepped back, stomping on the floor. Her eyes were yellow-green, and Daniel stayed against the wall, not wanting to set her off.

"It's because of that stupid bitch, isn't it?" Penn snarled. "If I get her out of the way, you won't have any reason to deny me, will you?"

"Don't even." He walked to her, so he could stand right in front of her and tower over her. "Right now you're just a nuisance. You've been harassing the people I care about, but you haven't done anything to me. If you hurt Harper or Gemma, then you've crossed me. Then I'll do everything in my power to destroy you, and you will *never* touch me again."

"What's the difference?" She threw her hands up in the air, but her eyes had returned to their normal color. "You're already telling me that I'll never have a chance with you. What incentive do I have to keep them alive? What reason do I have to keep you happy?"

He softened a bit and relaxed his stance. "If you care about me the way you supposedly do, you won't want to hurt me."

"I don't think you understand the way love works," Penn sneered.

He laughed darkly. "No, I think you're the one with the skewed ideas here."

"I'll be completely straight with you, okay? I'm laying it all out," Penn said. "I have been alive for thousands of years. And I used to care very deeply about things, but after a while, your heart kinda goes numb. *Everything* kinda goes numb.

"I may not love you," she went on. "I may not love anything. But you are the first thing that has held my interest in a very long time, and I will lie, murder, and devour anything to get what I want. Do you understand what I am saying to you?"

"Yes," Daniel said softly.

"So what's it going to be? Your girlfriend's head on a platter, or a night with me?" She crossed her arms and waited for his answer.

He swallowed hard. "Fine. But not tonight."

"When?"

"After Harper leaves for college."

"When is that?"

"A few days." He ran a hand through his hair. "Her classes start this Thursday."

"It's Sunday," Penn said. "So, in three days, we'll do it."

"Let's make it Friday. Give me a day to . . . get myself together." He paused. "But she can never find out, okay? Harper must never know. Gemma can't know, either."

Penn smiled. "I won't tell if you don't tell."

"Penn. I'm serious." He stared her directly in her black eyes. "I won't lose Harper, not over you."

"It's a deal, then." She smirked. "Shall we kiss on it?"

"I'll shake, but that's it."

"Fine." She held out her hand, and he took it, shaking it once.

"So I just sold my soul to the devil," Daniel said.

"I'm really not that bad." Penn leaned in to him, smiling up at him. "And once I'm through with you, you'll think you've died and gone to heaven."

Daniel stepped backward, away from her, and without looking he opened the door behind him. He motioned for her to leave.

"Thanks for stopping by, please hesitate to do it again; don't call me, and I won't call you," he said as she slid past him, going out into the hot night air.

Penn turned back to blow him a kiss, and he slammed the door shut.

Resting one hand on the door, he leaned with his head bowed. He had no idea if he'd done the right thing making that deal with her, but he definitely felt like throwing up.

"Fuck." He sighed. "I need a shower."

TWENTY-EIGHT

My Discontent

The lights were dim enough over the stage that Gemma could see clearly out into the empty audience chairs, but she wasn't really looking at anything. Her eyes were vacant, and she absently played with the silver chain around her neck. The theater stayed cool, despite the heat outside, but an odd humidity had crept inside, making it feel damp and musty.

She had stayed up late last night, crying as her dad tried to comfort her. This morning she woke up without all the telltale signs she'd spent the whole night a sobbing mess—no red eyes, no puffy cheeks, not even a runny nose. Her siren radiance was at an all-time high, but inside she felt like total hell.

Something had broken inside her. Gemma had destroyed the guy she loved in a misplaced effort at protecting him. No matter what she did, she only made things worse. All her attempts at saving herself and the people she cared about only put them in more danger.

"A pretty peat," Thea said, and Gemma was dimly aware that Thea was talking louder than she had been a few seconds ago. *"It*

is best. Put finger in the eye, and she knew why." She cleared her throat, then repeated, "*And she knew why*. Bianca?"

"Bianca?" Tom asked, his British accent filled with irritation. He'd been sitting in the front row to more objectively direct, but he stood up when Gemma didn't respond. "Oh, Bianca?"

"Gemma," Kirby said in a hushed tone, and that finally broke through, pulling Gemma from her thoughts.

"What?" She blinked and looked around the stage dazedly, trying to understand what was happening.

Thea, Kirby, and several other actors were onstage with Gemma, trying to perform the scene. They were all staring at her, waiting for her to say or do something, but for the life of her, Gemma couldn't remember what she was supposed to do.

Just offstage, standing beside the curtain, was Aiden. His lip was swollen, one eye was blackened, and he had scratches and bruises on his cheek. Everyone had made a big deal about his injuries when he came in, but he'd insisted that he'd be fine in time for the performance in just under two weeks.

He hadn't said anything to Gemma, but she'd caught him glaring at her a few times. Aiden was probably doing it more often than she noticed, though, since she was barely paying attention to anything that happened today.

"Glad to see you decided to join us onstage," Tom said with an annoyed smile. "Now maybe you'd like to say a line or two while you're here."

"Oh, I missed my cue. I'm sorry." She tried to look apologetic, but he didn't seem to care if she was sorry or not.

"I just said, *And she knew why*," Thea supplied for her.

"Okay. Um." Gemma put her hand to her forehead and squeezed

her eyes shut, trying to remember. "*Why, gentlemen, you do me double wrong—*"

"Wrong act, my dear Bianca," Tom said, barely holding back his contempt. "Of course! You have all of four lines in this scene! Why should you be troubled to learn them all?"

"I'm sorry. I'm just . . ." She shook her head. "I'm not myself today."

Aiden snorted offstage, and she glanced over to see him smirking as she floundered. That, of course, didn't help anything, and for an awful second she thought she might cry.

But then she flashed onto the image of her mother, the picture hanging outside the dressing room. Nathalie had mostly given up acting after she'd had her children, but she'd done a few more plays when Gemma was small.

While Nathalie had been running through her lines one night, Gemma had asked her what her favorite part about acting in the theater was, and she distinctly remembered her answer.

"It's all live. It's life-or-death onstage, and no matter what comes, the show must go on. You have to put on a brave face and play your part, whether you screw up or not. And there's something exhilarating about that," Nathalie had explained to her with a smile.

"Can someone help her?" Tom asked. "Or shall we stand here all day watching her flail?"

"Um, I have it here," Kirby said. He had his script rolled up in his hand, and he flipped through it, hurriedly scanning for Bianca's line. "It starts with, *Sister, content you—*"

"*Sister, content you in my discontent,*" Gemma began reciting before Kirby had even finished. It all came back to her, and as she spoke clearly and loudly, she kept her eyes fixed on Aiden. "*Sir, to your pleasure humbly I subscribe: My books and instruments shall be my company, on them to look and practice by myself."*

Last night had been awful, and things were horribly messed up, but that only meant that she had to work harder to put things right again. But she wasn't ready to give up. Not yet. She'd gotten knocked down, but the fight wasn't out of her.

"Excellent!" Tom shouted and walked back to his seat. "Now we can get on with the scene, and if we're lucky, we might make it through Act One by opening night."

"Hark, Tranio, thou may'st hear Minerva speak," Kirby said, continuing on with the play.

Gemma looked away from Aiden and focused on the action around her, trying to be present in the scene. Her exit came only a few seconds later, when the actor playing her father dismissed her offstage.

As she walked past Aiden, Gemma let her shoulder slam into him. What he'd done last night had been unforgivable. She might have been more alluring as a siren, but that didn't give guys free rein to do with her as they wished.

Thea had told her that sirens attracted rapists and pedophiles, and so far that had been a frighteningly apt description. But both Kirby and Alex always behaved themselves around Gemma, so it wasn't like she turned men into deviants who couldn't control themselves.

Shortly after her exit, Thea had hers, too, and she went backstage to where Gemma stood. Gemma had pulled out her script, meaning to go through it again before she went out for her next scene.

"Is everything all right?" Thea asked, her voice low so as not to disturb the players on the stage. "You seemed pretty out of it back there."

"Yeah, everything's fine," Gemma insisted with a smile. "I just couldn't remember my lines."

"Did Harper tell you that I talked to her the other day?" Thea asked.

"What?" Gemma's head jerked up. "Why? When? Where?"

"Calm down. It's not like I killed her or anything." Thea smirked. "We just had a nice little heart-to-heart where I told her it might be in your best interest to remain a siren."

"How do you figure that?" Gemma asked.

"So far, it's the only way I know of keeping you alive," Thea said.

"Maybe." She forced a smile at Thea. "I'm keeping a low profile and trying to get along with Penn and Lexi, just like you said."

Thea seemed surprised by that, but she smiled. "Good. I'm glad you're taking my suggestion seriously." She paused before saying, "But you need to give up your search for the scroll."

Gemma lowered her eyes. "You know that I won't."

"Well, you won't be able to find it anyway," Thea told her. "Penn has it under lock and key now."

"So she did move it, then?" Gemma asked.

Thea nodded. "She had it in a box buried at the bottom of the river. Normally we hide it in the ocean, but Penn thought a river named after our father was a sign."

"Doesn't that seem dangerous?" Gemma looked up at her. "Someone could find it."

"Nobody has gone looking for it so far," Thea said. "Until you, of course."

Thea was called back out onstage a few seconds later, and Gemma was happy for it. She didn't know how well she'd be able to lie to Thea, but Gemma had no intention of making nice and trying to play siren.

But she couldn't exactly tell Thea what she was up to. Thea had already told her she wouldn't let her have the scroll, so from here on out Gemma was on her own. She couldn't let Thea know her plans.

Practice went on fairly well, with Gemma remembering all her lines properly. She didn't have as much stage time as Thea or Aiden or even Kirby, and she found herself backstage watching them.

Toward the end of the night, she heard the back door slam. Daniel had been coming and going throughout most of the rehearsal, apparently working on sets outside so he wouldn't interrupt them. But every time he came in or out, he'd been careful to close the door quietly.

At the very back of the stage were steps that led down to a narrow hallway. One end went right to the back door, and the other led down to the basement and the dressing rooms.

Gemma left her post at the curtains to peer down the steps to see if Daniel needed help, since it was unlike him to be loud or disruptive.

She'd expected to find him struggling with a large piece of the set or something, but he was only talking to Penn. He leaned away from her, with one of his hands reaching for the door.

Her fingers were knotted in the sleeve of his shirt, and her nails had shifted into black talons that tore through the fabric. Her black eyes were locked on his, and she refused to let go of him.

They were having some kind of hushed discussion, but Gemma couldn't make out the words. Daniel's jaw was set firmly, and his eyes were stormy as he glared at Penn.

Daniel leaned down low and whispered something to her. Gemma wished she could hear it, because whatever it was he said, it seemed to make both of them angrier.

"Don't play games with me, Daniel," Penn hissed, finally loud enough for Gemma to hear.

"I think you know me well enough to know that I don't play games," Daniel said. Then he glanced up and spotted Gemma eavesdropping. "Gemma."

Penn turned to look up at her, and her expression instantly changed from frustration to her usual sultry smile. She released Daniel's sleeve, and he moved away from her.

"Sorry, I heard a noise, and I wanted to see if everything was okay," Gemma said quickly.

"Everything's fine," Daniel said. "Penn was just checking to see if rehearsal was over, but since it's not, she'll wait out in the car." He gave Penn a hard look, then attempted a smile at Gemma. "You know how Penn hates to be disruptive."

"That I do." Penn smiled at Gemma, then winked at Daniel. "See you around." As she left through the back door, she purposely slammed it behind her.

"Sorry." Daniel offered a remorseful smile. "I didn't mean to interrupt rehearsal."

"No, it's fine." Gemma walked down the steps. She stopped when she was two steps up from the bottom, so she was at eye level with him. "It's almost over anyway."

"Good." He moved toward the door. "I should get going now."

"What was all that about? With Penn?" Gemma asked, stopping him before he left.

He rubbed the back of his neck and gave a hollow laugh. "You know Penn. She's always . . ."

"No, Daniel, something's going on," Gemma insisted. He seemed reluctant to answer, so she pressed, "We agreed to tell each other everything. Remember?"

"No, actually, the deal was that *you* tell *me* everything," he reminded her, and his hazel eyes were grave when they met hers.

"Yeah, so that you can help me keep Harper safe," Gemma said. "And so you can have my back. It goes both ways, though. I can help you."

Daniel smiled bitterly. "Not this time, kid." He leaned back against the wall. "If you really want to help me, you just need to find that scroll and destroy it. That's the only way we're all getting out of this okay."

"I'm doing everything I can," Gemma said. "Lydia's looking for someone that will know how to destroy it, so once the scroll is in my hands, this is over."

"Good." Daniel rubbed his eyes and fell silent. "Do you want me to walk you home after rehearsal?"

"No, I think I can handle it. You just go home and get some rest," Gemma said. "You look like you need it."

"Can do." He gave her a half wave as he headed out the back door. "Stay safe, Gemma."

She'd been meaning to tell Daniel about her plans to go up against the sirens after Harper left for college, but after seeing him tonight, she knew she couldn't. He was already going through enough for them.

TWENTY-NINE

Photographs

So, how are we gonna celebrate?" Marcy asked, hopping on the desk next to the computer where Harper was working.

"Celebrate?" Harper asked, looking away from the monitor to Marcy.

"Yeah. This is your last day of work," Marcy reminded her. "We have to do something to celebrate."

"It's a Tuesday night, Dad's making supper, and Gemma's skipping play rehearsal tonight so we can have a family dinner," Harper said. "Does that count as celebrating?"

"Hardly." Marcy scoffed. "We have to go out and get buck-wild. Rock our socks off. Paint the town red. That kinda thing."

"I don't really feel like painting the town any color." Harper pushed the keyboard away and leaned back in her seat. "I have all my packing left to do."

"When do you officially leave?" Marcy asked.

"Classes start Thursday, so I have to leave by tomorrow so I can get slightly acquainted with the campus before getting thrown into things."

"I thought you already were acquainted," Marcy said. "Or that's what you hyped up when we made the road trip to Sundham."

"Not acquainted enough." Harper shook her head. "From what I understand, most of the other students were arriving over the weekend or yesterday. They have an orientation going on."

Marcy scooted back farther on the desk and folded her legs underneath her. "Do you have your classes all picked out?"

"Yep. I registered online. Everything on the college end is all ready. It's just everything here that feels so messed up."

"How are things with Gemma?" Marcy asked cautiously.

Harper swiveled the chair back and forth and groaned.

"I don't know." Harper shook her head. "She got into some kind of fight with Alex on Sunday night. She won't really talk about it, and what little I do know I got from Dad."

"That at least sounds like something normal and adolescent," Marcy said. "That's gotta be a good thing."

"I guess." She stopped swiveling in her chair to face Marcy. "I had the weirdest conversation with Thea the other day. She basically said she's looking out for Gemma and wants her to stay a siren."

"Yeah?" Marcy shrugged. "Didn't you already know that?"

"Kind of. But she said a few things that made me think." Harper chewed the inside of her cheek. "Do you think it would be better if Gemma stayed a siren?"

"Better in what way?" Marcy asked.

"If the only two options are death or siren, maybe she should pick siren." Harper stared up at her. "Right?"

"Right," Marcy agreed.

"But she hasn't found the scroll yet." Harper leaned forward on the desk so her elbows were on it. She rested her head on her hands and peered up at Marcy. "So I shouldn't go, right?"

"What are you talking about?" Marcy asked.

"With everything going on with Gemma, I should be here supporting her."

"She's here now and you still go to work," Marcy said. "You can't sit holding her hand every minute. If you go to college, you can still be home every night if you want. It's not that far away. You're really making this out to be a bigger deal than it is."

"I just . . . I want to make sure I'm doing what's best for everyone." Harper scowled. "And I feel like the worst sister ever."

"Or the most obsessive."

"Probably both. Obsessive *and* terrible."

"You don't need to be so dreary," Marcy said. "Me and Daniel and even *Thea* have Gemma's back. How many people do you really need babysitting your sister?"

"I know." Harper sighed. "I just wish we were closer to figuring this all out."

"Well, I've been talking to Lydia."

Harper dropped her arm and sat up straighter. "Does she know anything more?"

"Not really. I asked if she could keep an eye out for Demeter or Achelous or really any Greek-type figure. She said she would, but she doesn't know where to find them. Her specialty is shifters, which is why she's so intrigued by the sirens. She had no idea they could shift."

" '*Shift*'?" Harper repeated.

"Yeah, like shapeshifters." Marcy wiggled her body, like she was attempting to change form or having a mild seizure, and then she stopped. "Like how a siren transforms from pretty girl to mermaid to bird thing. They'd be called transformers if the robots hadn't already stolen the title. Stupid Optimus Prime, always ruining everything for everybody."

"So we're basically at a dead end now?" Harper asked, slumping forward again.

"Not completely. Lydia said that she heard some things about the muses, but she thinks they're all dead now."

"You think the muses literally being dead is not a dead end?" Harper asked, raising a skeptical eyebrow.

"Lydia knows people who knew them. So at least there's some kind of six-degrees-of-Kevin-Bacon connection," Marcy insisted.

"That would be more helpful if we were playing a trivia game instead of trying to find a way to break a curse."

"Okay, we're like Hansel and Gretel right now." Marcy turned to face her, getting more excitable as she told her story. "But instead of being abandoned in the woods and getting fat on gingerbread houses, we're following a trail of fragmented clues. And these clues will lead us to a muse or Demeter or somebody who can actually fix this shit, and that's way better than going back home with Hansel and Gretel's lame parents."

"You really suck at analogies," Harper said.

"Nah-ah," Marcy disagreed. "You suck at getting the point I'm trying to make."

"No, I get it. And you're right. I know we can do this." She sighed. "But it feels like we're running out of time."

"It's 'cause summer's ending and you're going to school," Marcy said, trying to cheer Harper up. "But you'll be home all the time, I'm sure. It'll be almost like you never left. Except that I'll have to actually start doing my job. Which is kinda lame."

"Yeah, it's gonna be you and Edie all the time until they find a replacement for me. Do you think you can handle it?" Harper smiled up at her.

"Well, it helps that she takes incredibly long lunch breaks now. Do you think she's having quickies with Gary?"

"Ew." Harper wrinkled her nose. "And she's been gone for an hour already. I wouldn't exactly call that a quickie."

"Oh, Harper, gross. Way to take it up a notch."

"Anytime."

"Hey, look." Marcy pointed at the door. "It's your handsome steed." Harper lifted her head to see Daniel walking toward the library, an old brown box under one of his arms.

She was a little surprised to see him. Yesterday she'd called him a few times, but hadn't heard from him, other than a text confirming that he was okay—just busy.

"Steed?" Harper asked, glancing back at Marcy. "You do realize that a 'steed' is a horse."

"Really?" Marcy asked, but she didn't sound swayed. "I thought it meant, like, knight in shining armor."

The chime above the door jingled, and Daniel strode over to the front desk.

"No, that's what knight in shining armor means," Harper informed Marcy.

"You must be talking about me," Daniel said. "Continue. Pretend I'm not here."

"I don't know if you noticed, but we're working, Daniel." Marcy did her best to sound bitchy, which was hard to do when she was so monotone. "This is Harper's last day, and I need her to focus and finish all the work she'd ordinarily be doing over the next nine months. So we're pretty swamped."

"*Marcy,*" Harper chastised her, but she was laughing.

"Sorry, Marcy," Daniel said. "I'll only take a couple minutes. I promise."

"Fine." Marcy sighed dramatically and got off the desk. "I'll just go back in the office and eat Edie's snacktime yogurt."

"Why are you doing that?" Harper asked.

"Because when she eats it, she gets really graphic with the spoon, and it's gross. Do you think I like peach yogurt? No. I don't." Marcy shook her head emphatically as she backed toward Edie's office. "But I eat it for all the patrons of this fair library. They should thank me. I am a hero."

Harper turned her attention back to Daniel. "Anyway, what can I do for you?"

"I know that you have that dinner with your family tonight, and I don't want to intrude on that." He'd been holding the box so it was hidden from Harper on the other side of the counter, and now he lifted it up and set it down in front of her. "But I wanted to get this to you before you left."

"You didn't have to get me anything," Harper said.

Daniel laughed and looked ashamed. "Now you're making me feel bad, because I didn't get you anything. I found this."

"What is it?" Harper asked, but she was already lifting off the top to peer inside.

"I've been cleaning out the cabin, and I found this little secret attic compartment in the top of my closet," Daniel explained. "There were a few mice living up there, and then this box, containing some memorabilia."

On top were stacks of old pictures. Some of them had been chewed at the corners, probably by the mice that Daniel had mentioned, but most of them appeared to be in fairly good shape.

"I thought we'd gotten all of Bernie's stuff out of the cabin. I was wondering why he didn't have any pictures of his wife in his old photo albums," Harper said as she sifted through the pictures.

"No, he has quite a few," Daniel said.

But she didn't need him telling her that. She'd barely even dug into it and she'd already found dozens of pictures of Bernie and his wife. Both of them appeared very young, and Harper guessed that Bernie couldn't have been more than twenty-two.

Their wedding picture was particularly gorgeous. Her dress was exquisite, and she was absolutely breathtaking. Her long blond hair had a few simple curls, and her smile was radiant. Bernie stood next to her, a young man who'd never looked happier or more dapper, but she stole the whole picture. It was almost as if the camera couldn't focus on anything else but her.

"She was so stunning." Harper admired a picture of Bernie and his wife in a modest 1950s-style bikini, then held it out for Daniel to see. "Look at her. And look at how handsome Bernie was. They were so happy."

Since she was holding it out, she could see their names scrawled on the back: *Bernard and Thalia McAllister—Honeymoon, June 1961.*

"And Thalia," Harper said. "That's such a beautiful name. I always forget it, but it's so pretty." Something occurred to her, something she couldn't quite place. "Does that name sound familiar to you?"

"No, I can't say that I've ever known any Thalias." Daniel shook his head.

"You say you found all this in the attic?" Harper asked.

"Yeah. This box was the only thing I found up there, other than mouse droppings."

"Strange," she said. "I wonder why he hid this."

Harper set the picture aside and started digging deeper into the box, where the pictures gave way to papers. Old love letters, news clippings of their wedding announcement, even one with an article about Bernie buying the island with money he'd inherited.

"What happened to her?" Daniel asked. He leaned forward, trying to read the papers upside down.

"I don't know exactly. She had an accident," Harper said, then she discovered the clipping with Thalia's obituary. "Oh, here. It says she fell off a ladder while trimming her rosebush and broke her neck. She was only twenty-four.

"They'd been married for two years," she said sadly. "That's so horrible. Can you imagine? Thinking you have your whole life together, and then . . . this. It's tragic."

"Well, Bernie seemed like he did all right," Daniel said, trying to alleviate some of Harper's unhappiness. "He had a pretty good life, up until the end."

"Yeah, he did." She nodded. "He loved that cabin. You know he built the whole thing just for her? He said that her love inspired him."

"*Pfft*," Daniel scoffed, causing Harper to look up at him. "That cabin's not so great. I'd build you an entire castle. With a moat."

"With a moat?" She grinned. "I must really be special."

"You certainly are," he agreed.

He smiled down at her, but something felt off. His smile didn't actually reach his eyes, and the flecks of blue that normally sparkled in his hazel eyes were dull. It was like he was holding something back.

Harper had been about to ask him about it when the phone rang.

"Don't worry, I got it!" Marcy called from the office. "You two just keep flirting. I'll work and eat yogurt."

"I think she's kinda freaking out that I'm leaving," Harper said.

"I can't say that I'm too thrilled about it, either," Daniel admitted.

And that was what she decided he must be holding back. He was getting a little upset about her leaving, but he didn't want her to know. Because what else would Daniel be keeping from her?

"I could always—" Harper began, but he immediately cut her off.

"No. I know what you're gonna say, and no. I'll miss you, but I'll survive. And so will you."

"Edie called," Marcy said as she came out of the office, empty yogurt container in hand. "She claims she's having some kind of car trouble. But she'll be here in ten minutes. She apologized for the terrible inconvenience."

"I'm gonna go put this stuff back with my purse." Harper put everything back in the box and put the lid on it. "I don't want to forget it, and I don't want to give Edie another reason to talk about marriage."

"Ha! I told you it was annoying," Marcy said, sounding victorious.

Harper walked to the office. "I never disagreed with you."

Marcy pushed her glasses up, and then turned to face Daniel. "What's up, hot cheeks?" she asked, completely deadpan.

"What?" Daniel asked as he laughed.

"I told Harper that I'd keep an eye on you while she's gone. I figured that without her, you'd be missing the flirty banter, so I thought I would step in and try it out. That work for you, stud muffin?"

He smirked. "That sounds great, four eyes."

"Four eyes?" Marcy was taken aback. "Really? That's the best you can come up with?"

"I don't know. I panicked." He shook his head. "Four pretty eyes?"

"You need to practice more if you're going to start flirting with me," Marcy warned him.

"Okay. What did I miss?" Harper asked as she came in at the end of the conversation.

"Just the beginning of an epic love affair." Marcy made a *rawr*-ing gesture at Daniel, who managed to look both startled and amused.

"Anyway," Harper said to Daniel, instead of addressing Marcy, "my boss will be here soon, so you should probably head out."

"All right. Sounds good."

"Thanks for bringing the box, though," Harper said. "And I'll see you tomorrow?"

"Yep. I'll be over to help you pack."

She leaned up on her tiptoes to kiss him good-bye, and he seemed to hesitate a second before leaning down himself. Then, when he did kiss her, his lips barely even touched her before he pulled away.

It was one thing to get a quick peck on the lips, but Harper wasn't even sure it had lasted long enough to qualify as a peck.

Daniel said good-bye to Marcy, then walked out of the library, acting as if nothing weird were going on. And maybe nothing was. Marcy was right there watching them, so maybe he didn't want to have any PDA. Or maybe he was just upset about her leaving tomorrow and he was pulling away.

Harper couldn't say for sure what was bothering him, but by the time Daniel had disappeared down the street, she was positive that he was keeping something from her.

THIRTY

Separation

With Harper leaving tomorrow, Gemma wanted to try to show her that she and Brian would be able to handle things without her. Even without all the siren business, Gemma knew that Harper would be freaking out about leaving. So Gemma wanted to put her mind at ease as best she could.

She'd spent all day doing the chores her sister normally did. Theoretically, Gemma was supposed to share the load, but Harper usually got to them before Gemma could.

Brian arrived home from work shortly before Harper did, and he went out back to start the grill. The end of summer was approaching, and he wanted to have a cookout for their last real family meal together.

He cracked a beer open, then stood out back, flipping burgers and brats. Harper sat outside with him, talking about her plans for the future, and that gave Gemma a chance to finish up a few of the tasks she'd left undone.

All day long she'd been working on laundry. The last load was mostly her dad's clothes, and she went into his room upstairs to put them away. Brian's room wasn't off-limits. He left the door open almost all the time, but Gemma hardly ever had any reason to go in there.

The curtains were drawn, so his bedroom was rather dark. The bed was made, and Gemma wasn't surprised to see the same bedspread he'd had for the past ten years. Nathalie had bought it before her accident, and though it was getting worn and ratty, Brian had never bothered to replace it.

Gemma sat the laundry basket down on his bed and opened up the closet. Most of the clothes inside were his—the few nice shirts he had, old T-shirts, and flannel. But a couple things that belonged to her mom still hung there.

She pushed Brian's stuff to the side so she could get a better look at Nathalie's. The wedding dress hung in a clear plastic bag that was supposed to protect it, but the train looked yellowed. Some of the pearls in the bodice had come loose.

The blue dress that Nathalie had worn in *A Streetcar Named Desire* hung without protection, and Gemma reached out to touch it. The fabric felt rough but thin. She pulled it out and held it in front of her.

The only mirror in the room was above the dresser, and Gemma turned so she could see how it would look on her. Nathalie was taller than Gemma, so the dress was a little long, and Gemma was a bit thinner. Otherwise, it looked about right.

"Gemma!" Brian called from downstairs. "Supper is done!"

"I'll be right down!" she shouted.

She took another minute to admire her reflection with the dress, and wondered what her mom would make of all this. If

Nathalie were around, would Gemma have become a siren? Would Harper have become so neurotic? Would everything have turned out so much better?

Those were questions that Gemma could never know the answers to. So she hung the dress back up, closed the closet door, and left her dad's clothes on the bed.

"We're gonna eat inside tonight," Brian said when Gemma came into the kitchen. "I was planning on us eating out in the backyard, but the heat is ridiculous. The dog days of summer are really here."

"Yeah, it's been really hot the last few days," Harper said as she set bottles of ketchup and mustard on the table.

For the next few minutes they got settled and loaded their plates up with meat and potato chips. Brian took long drinks from his beer, while Harper and Gemma sipped their soda, none of them saying anything.

"Are you all ready for tomorrow, then, Harper?" Brian asked, breaking the silence.

"Not completely. But almost," she said between bites. "I still have packing to do, but I should be done by tomorrow."

"Good." He nodded. "I thought I would take a half day tomorrow, help you get everything loaded up, then all of us could drive up to Sundham and make sure everything gets squared away."

"That sounds good," Harper said. "I know that Daniel had wanted to come. Do you think it'd be okay if he rode back with you guys? He'd ride up there with me."

"Um, yeah." Brian thought for a minute, then nodded. "Yeah. That should be fine." He looked across the table at Gemma. "Does that sound okay with you? You'll have to sit with him in the truck."

"It's fine by me," Gemma said. "Daniel doesn't bite."

"I should hope not," Brian said, almost under his breath.

"So . . ." Harper said when they lapsed into silence again. Gemma was barely touching her food, preferring to munch on chips instead of really eating. "It's the last family dinner. For a while anyway."

"Yep." Brian smiled at Gemma. "It's just me and you now, kid. Think you can handle it?"

"Yeah." Gemma smiled back at him.

"I think we'll manage," he assured them with a lopsided grin.

The conversation ran dry again. While they weren't the most chatty family on the planet, they usually talked freely. The tension of things to come was bearing down on them, though, and it was hard to make cheerful small talk.

"Part of the reason I wanted this dinner tonight was because Harper is leaving tomorrow," Brian said, his eyes fixed down on his half-empty plate. "But that's not the only reason. I knew this was my last chance to talk to you girls together for a while, and, um . . . I needed to talk."

"What's wrong?" Harper asked. "Is it cancer?"

"*Harper!*" Gemma said, appalled. "Why would you even ask that? Why is that the first place your mind goes?"

"Calm down." Brian held up his hand. "It's not cancer. I'm not sick. Everybody's fine."

"Sorry," Harper said. "Just when I hear 'sit down and talk,' I immediately think bad news."

"Well . . . stop that. Everything can't be bad all the time." Gemma leaned back in her seat, then turned to Brian. "What is it, Dad?"

"I'm divorcing your mother," Brian blurted out.

Harper and Gemma instantly fell silent and just stared at him.

"Why?" Gemma asked, and once she spoke, the questions came out rapid-fire.

"What about Mom's health insurance?" Harper asked, leaning forward on the table.

"The accident was almost ten years ago," Gemma said. "Why would you stay married to her for so long just to divorce her?"

"Where is she gonna live?" Harper asked. "You can't leave Mom out on the street."

"Is this because Harper is going to college?" Gemma asked.

"If you can't afford her insurance and college, you don't need to give me any money. I already told you not to," Harper said.

"Why did you go see her? Did you already know you were going to divorce her?" Gemma asked.

"How long have you been planning this?" Harper added.

"You both need to stop talking," Brian said calmly but firmly. "I'll explain everything to you if you just listen." He waited until they were both quiet before continuing. "Thank you. I love Nathalie. Or I did. The way I feel about her is very complicated, but . . . we're not a real married couple anymore. She's not a wife."

"She's *your* wife," Gemma said pointedly.

He shook his head. "I can't talk to her."

"Yes, you can," Gemma persisted. "We talk to her. We see her every week."

"I can talk to someone who looks like my wife and sounds like my wife, but she isn't," Brian said sadly. "I can't tell her about you, or about my job. I can't ask her questions. I can't share my worries or concerns. I can't laugh with her."

"But Dad, she hasn't changed in years," Harper said, her tone softer and less accusatory than Gemma's. "She's been like this for a really long time, and you knew that. Why now?"

"I stayed married to her partially for you," Brian admitted. "I knew it would upset you if I divorced her, and I didn't want to abandon her. She's sick. I know she is, and I didn't want to be the guy that left her or couldn't hack it."

"But you can't hack it," Gemma said, and Harper shot her a look.

"No, there's nothing to hack, Gemma," Brian said. "This hasn't been a marriage for a very long time. She is still family. She's your mother, and she will always be a part of this family. That will never change. We just won't be married."

"Why now?" Harper asked.

"You're getting older. And I see you girls, and the way you struggle to find a place. It feels like things have been in flux for a long time, like we can't move forward and we can't go back. And I need to make sure you feel like you have someplace strong, someplace safe to come back to, so you feel confident to venture out into the world."

Gemma snorted. "You think getting a divorce will make us feel safe?"

"I think it will show you that sometimes you have to move on," Brian said. "Sometimes bad things happen, and it's nobody's fault, but you can't dwell on them. You have to make the best of this life, and I don't think I've been a good example of that."

"We know you tried the best you could, Dad." Harper smiled wanly at him.

"That hasn't been good enough," he said.

"So what's going to happen to Mom now?" Gemma asked.

"I talked to the lawyer that was handling Bernie's estate, and your mom actually qualifies for more benefits if we're divorced," Brian said. "She'll be eligible for better care."

"So she's going to move?" Gemma asked.

Brian shook his head. "No, no. That was a big condition. I would never go through with this if it meant taking your mom away from you or putting her in a bad situation. I'll still be her legal guardian, and she won't move. When you girls are older, if you want to, you can step up and take over her guardianship, but I don't want to put that on you. I'm fine handling her affairs."

"I still don't understand," Harper said. "Why now?"

"I want you both to be happy. That's honestly the most important thing in the world to me. That you two are happy and healthy." He paused. "But you're growing up. You have lives of your own now. I hardly ever see either of you."

"Sorry, Dad," Harper said.

"No, don't be sorry. That's the way it ought to be. But I'm forty-one years old. Pretty soon I'll be alone in this house. And I can't still be in love with a woman who is never coming back."

"If this is what you think is best," Harper said, "then I support you."

"Thank you, sweetie." He reached out and touched her head gently.

"Gemma." Harper leaned over and took Gemma's hand. "It'll be okay."

"I just feel like everyone's abandoning her." She swallowed hard. "And it's not her fault. Mom didn't do anything wrong. She can't control who she is anymore."

"I know," Brian said. "And she's not being punished. This isn't about it being her fault. Nobody's abandoning her. I want to make that perfectly clear."

"I know it shouldn't matter, because I'm sixteen, and Mom's not even around. Nothing will really change. But . . ." She exhaled.

"Nobody will forget about her or leave her behind," Harper said. "You know I would never let that happen. Right?"

"Right," Gemma said reluctantly. "I know. Sorry." She wiped at her eyes. "I've been emotional lately, and this just . . . I don't know. I'm sorry, Dad. I know that you wouldn't take this decision lightly, and you love Mom. So if you need to do this, I understand."

And she really did. Deep down, she understood.

But just then it felt like a tidal wave was rushing over and crushing her, destroying everything in her life. And no matter how hard she tried, Gemma felt powerless to stop it.

THIRTY-ONE

Madness

Thea had begun wearing powdered white wigs to cover up the patches of hair that were missing. Nearly every moment she wasn't with Bastian, she spent in the sea outside of the house.

It was all she could do to silence the watersong, and even with that, it was nearly driving her mad. It woke her in the middle of the night, and she'd have no choice but to slip out and hope the salt water would clear her head.

Nothing really worked anymore. On top of the body aches and constant migraines, she'd begun hallucinating. She'd hear crows cawing in her room when there were none, and out of the corners of her eyes she'd see the flutter of wings. She felt on the brink of madness.

The thick curtains were still drawn, but the windows were wide open. A wind was blowing off the Mediterranean, making the curtains billow out and allowing some light into the room.

Despite the icy temperature, Thea wore only a thin sleeveless slip. Her coarse red hair had been woven into two braids along the sides of her head, carefully covering up the bald patches, until they became one frayed braid in the back.

She paced the room, alternating between gnawing on her broken fingernails and scratching at her skin. The constant hum of the watersong nearly drowned out every other noise, and she didn't hear Bastian open her bedroom door. When she realized someone was sneaking in—she'd forgotten his usual morning interlude with her after spending the night with Penn—Thea nearly attacked him.

"Thea!" Bastian grabbed her slender wrists before she beat them against his chest. She'd leapt at him as soon as he slipped inside. "What has taken over you?"

She'd been snarling seconds before, but as soon as she realized it was him, her body relaxed and she made a pitiful sob.

Thea pulled her hands from his and threw herself against him, pressing her cheek tightly to his chest. He wore a shirt, but it was undone at the top, so she could feel his warm bare skin against hers.

"I'm sorry, my love," she whispered into his chest, her words coming out in a husky rasp. It wasn't an unpleasant sound, but it was a great departure from the silk and honey her voice had been before.

"What is the matter?" Bastian grabbed her shoulders and roughly pushed her away from him. "It's as dark and cold as the dead of winter in your room."

"It's too hot outside, and the sun is too bright," Thea said.

He went over to close the windows, and Thea trailed after him, following at his heels. When he opened the curtains, she cringed in the sun, so he sighed and pulled them back again.

"Thea, you're falling apart," Bastian said as gently as he could. "You need to bathe, get dressed, and eat something. You should use this morning to put yourself together, then meet your sisters and me downstairs for breakfast."

"I am falling apart," Thea admitted with a sob. "I cannot do this anymore. I *must* eat something."

"Then eat!" He gestured widely.

"No, I need to *feed*." She whispered the last word as if afraid of someone overhearing, and hugged herself tightly.

"Feed?" Bastian cocked his head. "Haven't you been feeding with your sisters?"

She shook her head. "No. You asked me not to, and I haven't eaten in months. In the beginning it was no problem, but the last few weeks have been unbearable."

"That's what's possessed you?" Bastian asked. "The unraveling of your hair, the pallor of your flesh, the violent rages you've been prone to."

"I have not been violent," she insisted. "And it was as you asked."

"I never asked you to stop feeding." Bastian was taken aback. "I would never ask you such a thing. When I became involved with you, I knew what monster you were and what it required for you to sustain that monster."

"But I'm not a monster!" Thea yelled. "You told me before that you could not declare your love for me because of my shared bloodlust with Penn. But I have given it up. I've abstained from the evil for you."

He stared at her, his brilliant blue eyes seeming to look through her, and it was several moments before he spoke again, moments in which Thea could hear only her heart and the nagging of the watersong.

"Thea, I never asked this of you," Bastian said. "I've never asked you to give up anything. If you took my words that way, then you have misunderstood, and for that I am sorry."

"So then you care not about my bloodlust?" Thea let out a long sigh of relief, and she smiled dazedly at him. "Then there will be nothing that stands between us. I will feed this evening, and we can be on our way."

"On our way?" Bastian asked.

"Yes." Thea continued smiling as she stepped toward him. "Penn's been unable to find a way to break the curse. We've traveled as far and away as we can, and we've come up with nothing. Even the muses insist this is eternal. But if you accept that I have a monster inside me, then it doesn't matter."

"I do accept that, but I don't understand what that has to do with us leaving," Bastian said.

"We can be together. I love you, and though you haven't said it yet, I know that you love me," Thea said. "Without the curse in our way, we can be rid of Penn and move away from here."

"That may have a nice sound to it, but Aggie and Gia would never stand for the murder of your sister," Bastian said.

"They won't care." Thea leaned against him, wrapping her fingers in the soft cloth of his shirt and staring up at him. "With Penn gone, they will listen to me. If I say it's as it should be, they'll believe me."

"You want me to help you kill your sister, then run off with you and live out our existence in some kind of lovers' dream?" Bastian asked, but there was coldness in his words, something that frightened Thea.

"Yes," she said, but her smile had faltered.

"Why would I do such a thing?" Bastian asked, laughing darkly. "Why would I even want to?"

"Because we love each other." Thea searched his eyes, trying to find the warmth she'd once felt in them before.

"You've mistaken my affection for something far more than it is." He pushed his hands off her and took a step away. "I never said that I loved you, and with very good reason. I don't love you, Thea."

"Then what are you doing?" Thea asked, her voice trembling. "Why have you lain with me in my bed every day? Why have you stayed in my home for months?"

"Because I am a man, and you are a beautiful woman," Bastian said. "I have no place to live, and you are wealthy. You have been with so many, many men, Thea. I thought you understood this arrangement."

"No." She shook her head and went back over to him. "This is different. We shared something. I know that you felt something for me."

She grabbed his shirt again, clinging desperately to him, and when he tried to push her free, she refused to let go.

"Thea, let go of me. I've made a grave mistake with you, and it's time that I've moved on. I've spent far too long in this house with you and your sisters."

"You're leaving?" Thea cried. "You cannot leave. I won't let you throw everything away. I know that you love me!"

"Thea!" Bastian finally succeeded in getting her free and pushed her back so she fell to the floor. "I do not love you. I have never loved you, and I never will."

"That's not true, Bastian." She sat at his feet, weeping openly. "I won't believe that."

"My wife Eurydice is the only person I have ever loved," Bastian said. "When she died, I gave up singing, I took a new name, and I stopped loving. I gave up my heart, Thea. I cannot love you."

He turned to step away, and Thea scrambled to her feet. She grabbed his arm to stop him, but he kept going. Her bare feet slipped on the cold floor, and she stumbled and fell. He stopped, staring down at the mess that Thea had become.

"Please, Bastian," she begged. "I don't care if you love me or not. But please, don't leave me. I don't think I can live without you."

"Stop the hysterics," Bastian said, sounding disgusted. "I had no idea you were such a weak-willed woman. To think, at one time, I preferred you to your sister." He snorted.

"What do I have to do to make you stay?" Thea asked, oblivious to his insults. "Tell me what I need to do, and I shall do it."

"There is nothing you can do!" Bastian stared down at her in exasperation. "You are a whore, Thea. That's why I stayed here. That's why I slept with you. You are nothing more to me than a whore, and I thought you understood that."

He turned to walk away, and this time Thea didn't grab on to him. She sat on the floor, watching the man she loved retreat, and something snapped inside her.

In all her years, she'd never really loved anyone before, but when she'd found it, she sacrificed everything. She'd given up her health, her beauty, her sanity. And now he'd told her he'd only been using her like a common concubine.

"I am not a whore," Thea growled and got to her feet.

She didn't feel the change. There was a blind rage seething through her that seemed to block out everything. The only way she was certain that something had happened was by the look on Bastian's face when he turned back to her. His eyes widened, and he opened his mouth to scream.

Before he could, Thea dove at him. Her arm had transformed, so it was longer and more powerful, with sharp talons at the ends of her fingers. She tore through his chest easily. As she held his heart in her hands, and watched the blood dripping from his mouth, she savored the moment.

Then she opened her mouth wide and drove her jagged fangs into his flesh.

It wasn't until later, after the frenzy had faded and she sat in the pool of Bastian's blood with his corpse next to her, that she realized exactly what she'd done.

"Bastian," she said, as tears slid down her cheeks. She crawled over to him and pulled his head onto her lap. It had been mostly left intact throughout her attack, and she cradled his face, brushing back his hair with her bloodstained fingers.

As she held him, she began to wail.

THIRTY-TWO

Departure

With her bags almost completely packed and sitting on her bed, Harper still couldn't believe she was doing this. Her stomach was in knots, and she couldn't shake the feeling that no matter what she did, she was doing the wrong thing.

She'd hardly slept the night before and woke up at the crack of dawn to begin packing. It wasn't just her anxiety that made it hard for her to sleep. The heat was broaching on unbearable. The downstairs air conditioner did nothing up here, and her window fan only succeeded in blowing around hot air.

She pushed through it, though. There was a task at hand she needed to get done, so she just put her hair up in a ponytail and got to it. It was unlike Harper to put things off as long as she had this time, but the truth was that she hadn't really made a decision about whether she would leave or not.

As soon as Gemma had gotten up, she'd come over to talk with Harper. They spoke some about their parents' impending divorce, which Gemma was still having some trouble processing. But most of it was Gemma reassuring Harper that she was doing the right thing, and the world wouldn't end if she went to school fifty miles away.

Harper put her hands on her hips and stared down at the bags. All the clothes she planned to bring were neatly folded in her duffel bag and a suitcase, with the clothes she'd decided against scattered across her bed. Her toiletries had been sealed up in a Ziploc bag so they wouldn't leak, then were put in her duffel bag.

Her textbooks—all of which she'd ordered online because it was cheaper than getting them through the school—were stacked in a heavy tote next to her desk. Her computer, e-reader, and various chargers were tucked away in her laptop bag.

Everything was ready to go. Except for her.

"Hey, there." Daniel knocked on her open bedroom door.

She smiled thinly at him as he stepped inside her room. "Hi."

"You look about all packed." Daniel surveyed her room. "Am I late? I thought you told me to come over at ten."

He stood next to her, but he felt oddly distant. There was only a foot between them. When she moved, leaning a bit toward him, he moved away—as if trying to make sure she never got any closer.

The past few days, something strange had been going on with him. Harper couldn't explain it exactly, because he'd been saying all the normal things and spending time with her. But something definitely felt off.

Then again, that could just be her projecting. Her anxiety and indecision about leaving for college had to have some effect on their relationship, especially since he was a part of the reason she wanted to stay behind.

"No, you're right on time," Harper said, deciding to ignore her concerns about him. He'd come over this morning to help her pack and ride with her to Sundham, so nothing between them could be *that* off. "I woke up early and got a head start."

"That's a good thing, right?" Daniel asked.

"I don't think I can do this," Harper blurted out, and the thin veil of sensibility collapsed. "I don't think I can leave. Everybody keeps telling me that I need to do this and it's the right thing to do, but it doesn't feel like the right thing."

"Hold on," Daniel said, trying to put a stop to her panic before it completely took over. "Calm down a second. You know that no matter what you decide to do, nobody will be mad at you."

"My dad will."

"Okay, besides your dad," he allowed.

"I just feel like if I make the wrong decision, I'll ruin everybody's life. I don't want to destroy my future, but I don't want to destroy Gemma's, either." She stared up at him, her gray eyes large and pleading. "Tell me what to do."

"Harper, I'm not going to tell you what to do." He smiled sadly and shook his head. "I can't. This has to be *your* decision, no matter what anybody else says or thinks."

"I know, but . . ." Harper trailed off.

She knew she couldn't let anybody else make this decision, and she didn't really want them to, either. It just felt so impossible to choose. Her heart was being torn in two directions—looking after her sister and her family, or going after the one thing she'd been working for almost her entire life.

"Let's forget about Gemma for a second. Let's forget about her problems, or your dad, or your mom, or even me. Forget all of us." Daniel waved his hands, as if erasing everybody from her thoughts. "What do you want to do? What would you want for the rest of your life, if you didn't have to worry about anybody else?"

Harper sat back on the bed, carefully wedged between her bags. She stared down at the floor, and for the first time in a long while, she thought about what she really wanted.

"After the accident, my mom had half a dozen brain surgeries," Harper said. "And after every one of them, me, my dad, and Gemma would be sitting in the waiting room. The doctor would come in and explain to us what he did and how it went. I remember thinking, *Wow. That guy knows everything.*

"He was so calm and collected, and he made me feel calm and like everything would be okay," she went on. "Or okay-ish, anyway. I would ask him a million questions about my mom and medicine and all sorts of stuff, and he always answered every one of them. And I knew then and there that's what I wanted to do.

"I wanted to be *him*. What he did fascinated me, but more than that, I wanted to have all the answers and be able to save people. My mom is alive because of what he did."

Daniel pushed back the duffel bag, making room for himself, and sat down next to Harper on the bed.

"Sounds like a good fit for you," he said.

"Does it make me a horrible, selfish person if I say that I want to go?" She looked over at him. "That I want to do this?"

He smiled. "No, it doesn't. It's okay to go after your dreams, especially when you've worked so hard for them."

"But if I'm not here and something happens to Gemma, I'll never be able to forgive myself."

"You will be *here*, Harper," Daniel said with a laugh. "You keep acting like you're going off to war. You'll be right down the highway, and I'm sure you'll be home more often than you'll be at school."

"I know, but what if something happens and I'm a half hour away?" Harper asked.

"Then I'll be two minutes away, and Marcy will be a second away, and Thea will probably be right with Gemma," Daniel said. "I'm sure Alex would help if Gemma was in trouble, and we could even enlist your dad. Gemma's not in this alone, and neither are you. You aren't taking care of her by yourself."

"I know." She licked her lips, and finally Harper made her decision. "Okay. Then I'm going." She gave Daniel a hard look. "But you have to promise you'll watch out for Gemma."

"I wouldn't have it any other way," he said.

"I know that's kind of a big thing to ask you, since you're my boyfriend, and we haven't been together that long, and it's not your responsibility," Harper said, speaking rapidly. "It's not even really my responsibility, but I just need to know that she's safe, and I trust you."

"Harper," Daniel said with a smile, stopping her mid-ramble. "I know. It's okay. And I would never let anything bad happen to you or Gemma."

"Thank you." Harper leaned in, meaning to kiss him, but before she had the chance, Daniel stood up and took a step away from the bed.

"Did something happen? Did I do something?" she asked him.

"No." He scratched the back of his head and avoided eye contact with her. "Why would you say that?"

"It seems like you don't want to kiss me."

Daniel laughed, but it sounded flat. "Why wouldn't I want to kiss you?"

"I don't know." She stared up at him, fearing the worst might be true. "That's why I'm asking you."

"I just . . ." He shrugged and paced the room slowly, walking the length of her bed in front of her. "You know, you're leaving . . . It's an emotional time, and I don't want to make you do things."

"What are you talking about?" Harper asked.

"There's just a lot going on." He motioned with his hand, making a big circle to represent the "a lot" that was going on.

Her heart dropped. "Are you breaking up with me?"

"What?" His eyes shot up, looking startled, and he shook his head. "*No*, no, God, no. I . . ."

She waited a few moments for him to finish his thought, but when he didn't, she stood up and pressed, "What is it, then?"

Daniel lowered his eyes. "It's nothing."

"If something's happening . . ." Harper tilted her head, trying to meet his gaze.

"No. I'm just . . ." He sighed, and finally he lifted his hazel eyes to meet hers. "I'm going to miss you."

"I'll miss you, too." She stepped closer to him and put her hands on his chest, and this time he didn't pull away. "But I'll still come down for weekends. So we'll see each other a lot."

"I know," he said, but there was something pained in his eyes, something more than simply missing her.

"Is there something else bothering you?" Harper asked. "I feel like you're holding something back."

"No," he said. "I'm just thinking about what I'm going to do when you're gone."

"You'll get more sleep, and you'll have more time to work." Harper tried to make a joke of it. "That'll be good, right?"

"Yeah. It will."

"I'll probably call and text you so much you won't even notice I'm gone."

"No, I'll definitely notice." Daniel put his arm around her waist, his hand strong on the small of her back, and with his other hand he tucked a lock of hair back behind her ear. "You know how much you mean to me, right?"

"Yeah. Of course," she said. "And you mean a lot to me, too."

"And I would never do anything to hurt you." His voice had gone low, sounding husky and thick. His hand lingered in her hair, the rough skin of his thumb caressing her cheek. "I never want to disappoint you or let you down."

"And you don't, Daniel," Harper told him earnestly. "You impress me all the time, with your patience and kindness and strength. The things you do for other people, that you do for me and my family . . ."

"I would do anything for you, to keep you safe, to keep you happy." His eyes were searching her face, almost studying it, and he swallowed hard.

"I know."

"I love you," Daniel said softly.

Harper stared up at him, too stunned to say anything at first. The weight of the words hit her, and there was something both warm and terrifying about them.

Then Daniel was kissing her, his mouth pressing deeply against hers, and she didn't have to respond. It was almost as if he didn't want her to, like he was afraid to hear what she might say. She wrapped her arms around his neck, pulling him closer to her, and hoped that would be answer enough.

If he'd been holding something back before, he certainly wasn't now. His hand stayed on her face, his fingers tangling in her hair. His arm around her waist was all but holding her up.

She'd been standing on her tiptoes, leaning up to kiss him more forcefully, but they stumbled backward. He put both his arms around her waist to steady her. Her shirt had ridden up, so his hand gripped the exposed flesh, sending heat through her.

He stepped forward, pushing her back, their mouths still pressed together, until she felt the bed hit the back of her legs and they tumbled onto it. A pile of clothes bulged underneath, forcing her to arch her back, but it was actually better that way—it pushed her closer to him.

The feverish way he kissed her, making his scruff pleasurably scrape her lips, wasn't enough anymore. She wanted more of him, *all* of him, really. Her hands slid underneath his shirt, digging into the powerful muscles of his back, as she held him to her.

Under her fingertips, she felt the bumps and dips of his scarring, and realized that her fingers were on the outlines of his tattoo.

Daniel had an arm on either side of Harper, trying to hold himself up so he wouldn't crush her. But she leaned up, pushing her body against his. She raised her legs so her thighs were pressed into his waist, and he moaned against her lips.

Brian coughed loudly, interrupting the moment so Harper's flush of heat switched from pleasure to shame.

Daniel rolled off of Harper, and as she sat up, she readjusted her shirt. Nothing had been up or off, but things had gotten rumpled. Her dad stood in the doorway of her room, but he was staring off down the hall, probably not wanting to accidentally see something he could never unsee.

"I just wanted to let you know that I'm home from work now,"

Brian said. "I'm going to go help Gemma with her car before we head out. But you two might want to come down or hose yourselves off."

"Um, thanks, Dad," Harper mumbled, looking down at the floor. "We'll be down in a second."

"That'd probably be good," Brian said, then walked away.

THIRTY-THREE

Broken

Gemma knew part of the reason her dad was working on the car was out of penance. Not that Brian really had anything to atone for. He was an adult, and he had every right to terminate his marriage, especially since he had obvious reasons for it.

She shouldn't be hurt over it, but she was anyway. Brian knew that, too, so he was doing his part to make her life a little easier. He also probably figured that she had enough trouble this summer, and he'd promised to fix her car every time it broke down.

That normally wasn't that big a chore, but with the heat the way it had been the last few days, any amount of time spent outside wasn't fun. The sun beat down, and the humidity smothered them.

"Do you think you can fix it, then?" Gemma asked. She leaned back against the closed garage door while her dad had his head under the hood of her car.

"Yeah." He'd been twisting something with his right hand, but now he just leaned forward, staring at the jerry-rigged abyss. "But I'll have to get a part for it."

"Sorry." An awkward silence fell between them, so she asked, "Is Harper about ready?"

"Oh, who knows?" her dad muttered.

"Didn't you check on her?"

"Yeah." Brian snorted. "She said she'd be down in a minute, but I came outside, so I don't know."

"Oh." She didn't know what that was about, but Brian didn't seem to want to talk about it. "Thanks for taking a look at my car, Dad."

"No problem." He straightened up and wiped the grease off his hand with a rag. "Hey, what do you think of that Daniel kid?"

"Daniel? He's a good guy."

"He treats your sister all right?" Brian looked at Gemma, watching her.

"Yeah." Gemma nodded. "As far as I know, he treats her really well."

"Good." He wiped harder at the grease. "Are they getting serious, do you think?"

She shrugged. "Maybe. I know Harper really likes him."

"Ah, hell." He sighed, then shoved the rag in his back pocket. "I knew eventually it would happen."

"What?"

"Both of you, dating boys." Brian squinted up into the sunlight so he wouldn't have to look at his daughter. "I always kinda hoped at least one of you would end up an old spinster."

She smirked. "Sorry, Dad."

"And here comes more trouble." He motioned next door, and Gemma looked over to see Alex walking toward them.

He wore his regular clothes as opposed to his work overalls, but his Boba Fett T-shirt appeared a bit too small. It hadn't been a few weeks ago, but now it pulled snug across his chest and biceps.

His hands were shoved in the pockets of his jeans, and he kept his head down. His thick hair cascaded across his forehead.

"Hello, Alex," Brian said, his voice firm but not exactly hard. "I haven't seen you at work the last couple days."

"Yeah, I haven't been feeling very well." He glanced up at Brian, but only for a second, then turned to face Gemma. "Hey, Gemma, can I talk to you for a minute?"

She stood up straighter, but stayed leaning against the garage door. "Sure."

"Gemma?" Brian said, studying the two of them. "I can stay out here, looking at a few other things on your car."

"No, it's okay, Dad. I've got it." She tried to smile reassuringly at him.

Brian hesitated before nodding. "All right. I'll go check on Harper. But we do have to get going soon."

"Okay. Thanks, Dad," Gemma said.

They stood in silence until after Brian had gone into the house. Alex finally lifted his head and looked at her. She wanted to brush his brown hair back from his forehead, so she could search his eyes for the warmth that had once been there.

But she didn't. Not so much because she was afraid of how he would react if she touched him—but because she was afraid that she might not find any warmth left inside him.

"I need you to be honest with me," Alex told her.

"Okay. I'll try."

"No, Gemma," he snapped. "Not *try*. Completely honest. If you ever loved me, I need you to be honest."

She swallowed. "Okay."

"I loved you," Alex said, and she couldn't look at him. "And I think I loved you for a long time. Well, maybe I really liked you for a long time, but once we started dating, I was head over heels for you."

"I don't know why you're telling me this. I have nothing to be honest—"

"Because I loved you with everything in me, and now I can't stand you," Alex said. "Except that's not even true. It's like I'm supposed to hate you. But I don't think I ever really can."

"I'm sorry," Gemma whispered.

"I've thought about it and thought about it. But I can't think of a single reason why my love turned into hate. I don't even remember breaking up with you. Do you?"

"Of course I do," she said, but that was sort of a lie.

Alex hadn't broken up with her. What she remembered—and she did remember it vividly—was her using the siren song to cast a spell on Alex and convince him that he didn't love her. She thought about it every day, and even though she knew it kept him safe, she wished she could take it back.

"What did I say? What were my reasons?" Alex demanded.

"You . . . you said . . ." Gemma stumbled, trying to come up with a reason for their breakup.

Until a few days ago, Alex had never asked why. He hadn't even spoken to her in a month. So she'd never had to make up an excuse for why their relationship had ended.

"I didn't break up with you, did I?" Alex asked. "None of this was my idea. You used your song on me."

"No, I—"

"Gemma!" Alex yelled, sounding exasperated. "I know you did. I just want to hear you say it."

She stared down at the driveway, but she felt his eyes burning into her. "It was for your own good."

"For my own good?" He laughed darkly. "You had no right to do that. *No right!* To control my feelings, to mess with my heart and my head. Do you understand what you've done to me? I can't enjoy anything. I'm miserable all the time. You took away all of the love I had inside me."

"I didn't mean to." She looked up at him, blinking back tears. "I only wanted you to stop caring about me so you'd be safe, so the sirens wouldn't go after you anymore. I never meant to hurt you."

"It doesn't matter what you meant!" he shouted, and she flinched. "Did you ask me if I wanted this? Did you even talk with me about this before you did it?"

"No, I knew what you would say."

He scoffed. "You knew what I would say, and you did it anyway?"

"I couldn't let you get hurt or killed over me!"

"Gemma, I would rather die than feel the way I do now. Do you understand that?" He leaned toward her, his face inches from hers, and his dark eyes burned with rage. "Death would be far better than being unable to love ever again."

"I didn't know it would be like that," she said. "I thought you'd just forget about me. Alex, I never wanted to hurt you."

"What am I supposed to do now?" Alex asked. "How am I supposed to live the rest of my life?"

"I don't know." She shook her head. "Maybe I can sing to you and undo it."

"*No.*" His eyes widened. "That's what broke me in the first place! Don't come anywhere near me with that song. You have no idea how to control or use it. You could end up killing me next."

She nodded, secretly feeling relieved. Alex was right. She didn't completely know how to use the song, and after the way she'd accidentally hurt Nathalie before, she didn't want to try with Alex. If she hurt him more, she'd never be able to forgive herself.

"I know, I'm sorry," she said again.

"Sorry doesn't cut it, Gemma!" Unable to control his anger any longer, Alex lashed out, and punched the garage door right next to Gemma's face. She flinched but didn't move. "Are you scared of me?"

"No." She stared into his deep brown eyes, and behind the anguish and confusion there was a flicker of warmth—a hint of the Alex she still loved desperately. "Should I be?"

"The worst part of all this is that as pissed off as I am, as much as I hate you, somehow I'm still in love with you, too," he admitted softly. "There's parts of me that even your siren song can't touch."

He leaned in and kissed her. Gemma had expected this new, angry Alex to be rough and forceful, but he wasn't. While he wasn't as gentle as he'd once been, it was because there was a sense of urgency to his kiss. Like he understood that he only had a few precious seconds when the wall could come down, when he could really love her and hold her again.

She wrapped her arms around his neck, but that snapped him out of it. He grabbed her arms and pinned them back against the door. His breath came out raggedly, and he stared at her with a mixture of yearning and contempt.

"I can't do this," Alex said finally. He let go of her and stepped back.

"I'll find a way to help you," Gemma said. She moved away

from the garage door but didn't go after him. "I'll fix this mess that I made."

Alex turned and jogged back to his house, and she let out a deep breath and leaned back against the door. She didn't know how she'd do it, but she'd do everything in her power to fix what had happened to him.

Harper, Daniel, and Brian came out of the house a few minutes later, and Gemma had apparently collected herself enough, because nobody commented on her emotional state. Daniel rode up with Harper in her car, while Gemma sat in uncomfortable silence with her dad in his truck.

When they arrived at Sundham University, Gemma felt a bit strange. All the other students appeared settled into their dorms, and Harper had a small caravan of people carrying her few belongings past them as they went to her room.

All the bigger furniture was being provided by or rented from the dorm, so Harper only had to bring her personal belongings. She'd chosen a loft bed with a desk underneath, and while it was already in her room, it hadn't been put together.

Harper's roommate was already in her room, hanging up a Florence + the Machine poster on the wall, when Gemma came in with Harper. Her back was to them, and her wavy blond hair was pulled up in a loose bun. As Brian and Daniel began the struggle with putting together the loft bed, she came over to introduce herself to them.

"You must be my new roommate," the girl said. Her brown eyes were wide and surprisingly innocent, but there was something about her smile that made Gemma ill at ease. "I was beginning to think you weren't coming."

"Yeah, it took me a little while." Harper smiled sheepishly.

"Well, that's okay." The girl grinned broadly. "My gramma always said the best things in life are worth the wait."

"Well, I hope so," Harper said. "I'm Harper Fisher, and this is my little sister, Gemma."

"Hi," Gemma said, taking Harper's roommate's outstretched hand. "It's nice to meet you."

"I'm Olivia Olsen, but my friends call me Liv," she said, smiling even wider. "And I hope we're going to be friends."

THIRTY-FOUR

Ramifications

Gia had heard her wailing. Aggie and Penn were out for their morning swim already, so far out into the Mediterranean that they couldn't hear Thea completely losing it after slaughtering the only man she'd ever truly loved.

When Gia came into her room, Thea was sitting on the floor, drenched in blood, as she cradled her lover's corpse. Thea might have stayed that way all day, until Penn came in and finished her off for killing Bastian.

If it hadn't been for Gia, Thea wouldn't have been able to get her wits about her. Since she'd fed, she was thinking clearer than she had in weeks, but her devastation completely overrode that and clouded her judgment.

Fair and soft-spoken, Gia didn't even ask Thea what had happened or why it had happened. She simply gathered her up and took her into the bathroom to clean her, and then Gia went back out and wrapped Bastian in a bedsheet.

She sent the servants to fetch buckets of water, and when they returned, Gia began sopping up the blood off the floor with blankets and towels. Once Thea had cleaned most of the blood off herself, she joined Gia, kneeling down and scrubbing it from the floor.

Then the two of them went out, carrying Bastian with them. They dove into the sea and took him as far and deep as they could. They weighted his body down with a small boulder, knowing that the fish and the tides would take care of the rest.

When it was all finished, all the blood cleaned off them both from the sea, all the bedding and the body disposed of, Thea offered Gia a small thank-you, but Gia simply brushed it off and went into the dining room to join Aggie and Penn for a late breakfast.

Thea had always thought it was a shame that Gia had become one of them. They referred to her as their sister, since the sirens were a kind of sisterhood, but she wasn't really. Unlike Thea, Aggie, and Penn, Gia's parents were mortals. She'd gotten a job as a handmaiden for Persephone, and by all accounts she'd been doing a fine job until the other three girls showed up.

In fact, if Penn, Thea, and Aggie hadn't dragged her away that day, Gia would've been content to stay behind and guard Persephone. She loved to listen to Gia sing as Gia braided Persephone's hair.

But they had dragged Gia away. Then Persephone had been raped and murdered, and her enraged mother had cursed all four of them forever—even sweet Gia, who had the most beautiful singing voice imaginable.

It didn't take long for Penn to notice that Bastian had disappeared, and she went berserk. Initially, she suspected foul play, since she couldn't believe that anybody would leave her. But after days of Thea, Aggie, and Gia placating her, Penn had eventually come around to the idea that Bastian had left.

That didn't do anything for her rage, though. She stormed around the house, breaking things, yelling, throwing fits. She tore apart several servants simply for looking at her the wrong way.

The one good thing about her preoccupation with Bastian was that Penn hadn't noticed the change in Thea. Her radiance was back, her hair was once again lush, and she wasn't so frenetic anymore. Her voice was still husky, and Penn taunted her about that—the way she'd been taunting her for months.

None of the other sirens had understood why she'd stopped feeding with them, although Aggie seemed to support it and cut down herself. Not nearly as much as Thea had, because it was maddening and painful, but she'd made an effort, at least.

Penn's rage came to a head less than a week after Bastian had died. She was tearing apart his room, looking for any clues as to where he might have gone so she could find him and kill him. The other three tried to stay out of her way, and spent the afternoon in the sitting room.

Gia had taken to playing the piano and singing. Aggie was sitting in a chair, working on her needlepoint, which had been her favorite pastime for over a century. Thea sprawled out on a chaise, attempting to read a book, when Penn burst into the room.

"Which one of you did it?" Penn snarled, and Thea's heart froze.

"What?" Aggie asked.

"Bastian." Penn had some pieces of paper crumpled in her hand, and she held them up for all to see. "I found this in his room. Which one of you wrote this?"

"Whatever are you going on about?" Aggie asked, but Thea already knew.

As soon as she'd seen the papers, she understood what Penn

was talking about, and she cursed herself for being so stupid. She thought she'd been so careful and had cleaned up any evidence of Bastian's murder, but she hadn't thought to erase signs of their affair.

"These!" Penn threw the papers to the ground. "And don't play dumb. I know one of you did it."

Aggie set aside her needlepoint, and she got up from the chair. She picked one of the pages up from the floor, smoothing it out.

"*Bastian, my dearest love, I cannot wait until our next moment together. Every moment we are apart, I fear I will not survive until I can feel your embrace again,*" Aggie read. She looked up from the paper and shook her head. "Forgive me, dear sister, but I do not understand. What do your love letters have to do with anything?"

"Those aren't my love letters, you nitwit," Penn hissed. "I never wrote those. One of *you* did."

Thea sat up on the chaise, but she said nothing and tried to keep her face expressionless. She could feel Gia watching her from the other side of the piano, but Gia didn't speak up, either.

"How do you know one of us wrote them?" Aggie asked reasonably. "These could be from the servants or any of Bastian's old lovers. They could even be from his wife."

"No, no, no." Penn shook her head and knelt on the floor to tear through the letters. "This one. Here." She held it out for Aggie to read.

"*Your siren song, it calls to me in the night. Even when I am with your sister, I assure you, I am thinking of you,*" Aggie said.

Internally, Thea winced, but she remained motionless. She and Bastian used to slip each other love notes under their bedroom doors. Thea would often carry his in the bodice of her dress so she could take them out and read them over and over again.

But in the process of making love, her dress often came off, and the notes would get lost or left behind. That one she'd apparently left in Bastian's room after one of their trysts.

"See?" Penn asked, her eyes blazing. "One of you was trying to steal him from me!"

"Penn, even if one of us did sleep with him, and I'm not saying one of us did, I know that I have not," Aggie said. "That means nothing. Bastian left you. He didn't run off with one of your sisters. He left us all behind."

"No." Penn shook her head and got back up to her feet. "One of you drove him away. One of you was having an affair with him, and you scared him off. You went behind my back, and you chased away the man I love. One of you has to pay."

"Penn, calm down," Aggie said. "You don't want to do anything rash."

"Which one of you was it?" Penn shouted, ignoring Aggie. In fact, she wasn't even looking at Aggie. She glared at Thea, and then at Gia.

Thea met her gaze evenly, her heart pounding so loudly in her ears that she heard nothing else. Penn's eyes flitted over to Gia, who immediately lowered her eyes. She'd done nothing wrong—she simply cowered anytime Penn came at her.

But Penn took that as a sign of guilt.

"It was you!" Penn roared and ran at Gia. "You did this, didn't you?"

"No, Penn, I would never—" Gia tried to argue with her, but Penn wrapped her hand around Gia's throat and slammed her back into the wall.

"Penn!" Aggie got to her feet. "Stop it! Put her down!"

"She destroyed my only chance at happiness," Penn growled. "And now I'm going to destroy her."

Gia's blue eyes were wide, and she pulled at Penn's hand. By then Penn had already begun the transformation into the bird. Her legs were shifting underneath her gown, and she grew taller, with the feet and legs of an emu sticking out below.

Her arms were elongated, and her fingers had hooked talons at the ends. Her silky black hair thinned out as her head bulged and changed shape to adapt to the mouthful of fangs. The wings burst through the back of the dress, flapping as they unfurled and partially blocking Thea's view.

Gia never changed, though. Her eyes stayed blue the entire time, so none of her shifted into the bird-monster that could've protected her.

Thea had many years to think on this day in the future, and she never came up with a satisfactory reason why Gia didn't. There were only two reasons she could come up with. Perhaps Gia didn't believe what was really happening. She didn't think Penn would actually hurt her, so she didn't want to defend herself and upset Penn more.

Or maybe Gia wanted to die. She'd never really wanted this life or belonged in it in the first place. So maybe she welcomed Penn's reaction, and that was why she never fought back or betrayed Thea's confidence.

With one quick motion, Penn reached in and ripped out Gia's heart. Aggie screamed for her to stop, but it was already too late. Gia opened her mouth, but no sound came out. She just moved her lips soundlessly, like a fish underwater. When Penn began tearing off her head, Thea closed her eyes.

Thea lowered her head, but she still heard the sound—the tearing of flesh, the cracking of bone, and the wet thud as Gia's head fell to the floor. Those would be the sounds she'd hear in her nightmares for years to come.

Throughout the whole ordeal, as her sister murdered Gia for a crime that Thea herself had committed, Thea had said absolutely nothing.

THIRTY-FIVE

Determined

The curse of the minotaur and Asterion stuck in Gemma's head. When he had destroyed the scroll, all the minotaurs had turned to dust. It had been like the curse had never existed.

As soon as they got back from dropping Harper off at college, Gemma knew she had to find the scroll—at any cost. It wasn't just about her anymore—Alex needed her to do this, too.

She had some time with her dad, who seemed to be taking Harper's leaving a bit harder than any of them thought he would. They went out for dinner at Pearl's after they'd gotten back, and Brian had floundered with the conversation. He seemed kinda lost.

After supper, they went home, and Gemma had immediately called Thea. It was in the guise of going for a late-night swim, but she really wanted to find out what the sirens were up to, and see when the best time would be for her to sneak in.

Thea hadn't been interested, but in between complaining about Lexi and talking about play rehearsal, Thea made a confession—they were going out of town the next day to feed. It had been a while since Thea had eaten, and she was growing restless.

Gemma tried not to think about what that meant, that somebody would have to die to feed the sirens. She knew that they had to eat, and the small comfort she could take from it was that they'd cut down and they were going outside of Capri to find food.

But the sooner she found the scroll, the sooner she could stop the sirens, and then nobody else would ever have to die. And she had finally found her chance.

Gemma woke up Thursday morning with a renewed sense of purpose. She waited around the house for as long as she could. Thea hadn't told her what time the sirens planned on leaving, but she imagined that Lexi and Penn weren't exactly morning people, so she waited until early afternoon.

When she finally decided it was late enough, she hopped on her bike and rode down to the library at the center of town. She wore a dress, so she pedaled carefully but quickly.

She'd left without telling Daniel—specifically going against their agreement that she would tell him everything. But he seemed to have something heavy weighing on him, and if this went well, none of them would have to worry about the sirens for much longer. It would be better if she just dealt with this on her own and got as few people involved as possible.

The skies overhead had been darkening all morning, and Gemma felt a few sporadic raindrops as she pedaled. Not that she minded. The air was thick and warm with humidity, and it would be nice if the rain came and cooled things off.

Gemma locked her bike up outside the library, and when she opened the door, it felt like stepping into a refrigerator after being outside. The library was relatively busy, thanks to the combination of stifling heat and the impending storm.

Marcy sat at the desk, her head tilted back as she attempted to balance a pencil on the spot between her top lip and her nose. She was apparently oblivious to the patrons around her and didn't even notice Gemma until she walked right up to her.

"Hey, Marcy."

Marcy lost her concentration and the pencil dropped. She shrugged and sat up straighter, and Gemma leaned on the desk.

"Are you here applying for the job?" Marcy asked. "Because we have a vacancy now, and one Fisher sister is probably as good as another."

"That's actually not a bad idea," Gemma said. "Remind me to apply when I have more time."

"You don't have time now?" Marcy arched an eyebrow. "Then what are you doing here?"

Gemma smiled at her. "I came to ask you a favor."

"I'm not buying you booze or cigarettes," Marcy replied immediately. "Harper would kill me if I did, and they're both lame habits. If you want to get a tattoo, though, I know a guy who does underage tattoos."

"How do you know a guy?" Gemma asked, momentarily distracted from her mission. "Do you have a tattoo?"

Marcy stood and lifted up her shirt. She angled herself to the side so Gemma could see the tattoo right above her hipbone. It was of Ursula from *The Little Mermaid.* Her tentacles were twisting over Marcy's hip, and Ursula smiled broadly with blood-red lips and winked.

"You have a Disney character?" Gemma asked in shock.

"She's a sea witch, and she's badass, okay?" Marcy pulled her shirt down, then sat back in the chair. "Hey, are there such things as sea witches?"

Gemma shook her head. "I'm pretty sure there aren't."

"Lame." Marcy scowled in disappointment. "It would've been sweet if you could just make a deal with a sea witch. I mean, you'd give up your voice to stop being a siren?"

"I would. But I don't think that's going to be an option."

"Life would be so much simpler if it worked out like a cartoon," Marcy said, her monotone sounding wistful for a moment.

"It certainly would," Gemma agreed. "Back to the favor I wanted to ask you."

Marcy narrowed her eyes at Gemma. "You can ask, but I reserve the right to say no."

"Obviously. It's not a huge one, though," Gemma said. "I just need a ride up to the sirens' house."

"Up on the cliff?"

"Yeah, my car isn't working, and I just wanted to go up there real quick before the sirens get back," Gemma explained. "It's a short car ride, but the bike ride up the hill would take too long."

"Where are the sirens?" Marcy asked.

"I don't know for sure," Gemma said. "Thea said they were going out of town to eat, and she didn't think they'd be back in time for play rehearsal tonight. I wanted to have as much time up there as I could, and I wanted to be able to get out of there really fast."

"Understood. When would you wanna go?"

"The sooner the better."

"So I'd have to leave work?" Marcy asked.

"I could wait until—"

"Hey, if I have to go, then I have to go," Marcy cut her off and got up. She grabbed her car keys out of a drawer. As she walked around the desk, she called back over her shoulder to the office, "Edie, I'm heading out! I have to help a friend! It's life-or-death!"

"When will you be back?" Edie asked and came out of her office in time to see Marcy and Gemma departing out the front door. "Marcy?"

In the short time that Gemma had spent inside the library, it had already dropped ten degrees outside. It still wasn't really raining, but the wind had picked up, and Gemma was even more grateful that Marcy was driving her. Riding uphill on her bike, against the wind, would've taken forever.

Even in Marcy's Gremlin it was still almost a fifteen-minute drive through town and up the winding road through the pines. Gemma directed Marcy to park a little ways down from the house, closer to the overlook where Gemma had taken Alex before.

"Thanks, Marcy," Gemma said and unbuckled her seatbelt. "I don't know how long I'll be gone, and if you get tired of waiting, you can bail."

"I'm not gonna bail." Marcy scoffed. "I should go with you up to the house."

"I don't know." Gemma shook her head. "I don't know when the sirens are coming back, and if they find us both there, they will probably be awfully pissed."

"Then maybe I could be a lookout or something," Marcy suggested. "You don't know when they're coming back, so I could warn you." Gemma bit her lip, debating, so Marcy pushed on.

"Come on, Gemma. Harper will kill me if I let something happen to you. You can at least let me watch the door. That's what Fred and Thelma always leave Shaggy and Scooby to do, and if it's good enough for Shaggy, it's good enough for me. That's my life's motto."

Gemma smirked at that. "Okay. But if you see a siren, stay out of the way, especially if it's Penn or Lexi."

"Agreed," Marcy said. "My mama didn't raise any fools and she didn't raise any heroes."

Marcy and Gemma got out of the car and snuck through the densely wooded area that separated the overlook from the sirens' house. The wind was blowing through the trees, stirring up pine needles and making a howling sound through the branches.

The house was centered in the middle of a small clearing right at the edge of the cliff. The driveway was empty, so presumably the sirens had already left for the day. Just to be on the safe side, when Gemma went up to the door, she knocked and rang the doorbell. When nobody answered, she decided the coast was clear.

The door was unlocked, but Gemma hadn't expected any different. Penn didn't think anybody would dare to steal from her, and even if they did, she didn't care that much since none of the stuff was really hers anyway. She could replace it all with little or no effort.

Gemma left Marcy waiting outside with instructions that if any of the sirens showed up, she was supposed to ring the doorbell and then take off into the trees. Gemma would hear the doorbell, then sneak out the back door. That was the plan, anyway.

After doing a quick once-over on the main floor, Gemma went upstairs to the loft, which was where she'd thought they'd hide it anyway. Assuming they even had it hidden here.

The second level was one massive room, having been designed as the master suite, but Penn, Lexi, and Thea all appeared to share the space. Two king beds fit easily in the room, with a twin bed shoved off to the side. Based on the small pile of hot pink panties sitting on the smaller bed, Gemma guessed that one was Lexi's.

Skylights in the ceiling let Gemma see the dark clouds swirling above. They were nearly black now, and she flicked on the closet light. She didn't want to turn on the main bedroom light in case the sirens came home. They'd be able to see that from the driveway.

The walk-in closet was large and overflowing with clothes. On hangers, in drawers, in piles on the floor. It had been customized with plenty of drawers and storage, which meant that Gemma had a lot to sort through.

The sirens had an endless supply of shoes. Stilettos, wedges, boots, flats in every style and color. She started taking out shoes and rifling through drawers, hoping to find a false bottom or some kind of hidden compartment.

Thunder rolled overhead, and the closet went black. Gemma froze, afraid that someone had turned off the lights, but then she realized that the wind had just knocked the power out.

It was too dark to search properly in the closet, so she went into the bedroom. She moved over to the bedside table and began rooting around the drawer, hoping for a sign of the scroll, but she would've settled for a flashlight at that point.

A loud crash against the skylights startled Gemma so much she nearly screamed. She looked up to the windows and saw that the rain had finally started, coming down in torrential sheets. It pounded against the glass and roof, the sound echoing through the room.

She was about to recommence her search when she heard a clatter downstairs. She stayed where she was, listening carefully, but it was hard to hear clearly over the rain. Then she heard a bang, and this time she was certain that it hadn't been the storm.

The doorbell hadn't rung, but Gemma realized belatedly that the power was out. If it was a wired doorbell, that meant there would be no sound. Walking quietly and slowly, Gemma went toward the railing at the edge of the loft.

It wasn't until she'd made it all the way to the edge and looked straight down that she saw what had made the noise.

Lexi stood staring up at Gemma. Her long blond hair was dripping water in a small puddle at her feet, and she wore a bikini. She was completely in human form, save for one finger on her right hand. Her aqua eyes sparkled in the dim light, and her smile was happy and playful, without a hint of malice, which made it all the more creepy.

Her left hand was gripping hard on Marcy's ponytail, yanking her head back sharply. Marcy's glasses were smashed on the floor, next to the pool of water from Lexi's hair. A cut ran across her eyebrow, with blood trickling down her temple, and Marcy's eyes were wide with fear.

She didn't move or scream, and Gemma instantly saw why. Lexi's otherwise humanoid hand had one longer finger with a razor-sharp talon at the end, poking right into Marcy's jugular. If she moved or even yelled, it would slice right through her neck.

"Hello, Gemma," Lexi said sweetly in her singsong voice. "I know you were playing hide-and-seek, but I have a better game. Why don't you come down, and I'll show you how to play?"

THIRTY-SIX

Trepidation

Liv had shown Harper where all her classes were, as per Harper's class schedule. Liv was from a neighboring town in Delaware, but she'd moved into the dorm a week ago. The extra time, as well as orientation, had really given Liv a good idea of where everything was and how the college worked.

While Liv was incredibly helpful and nice, there was something almost *too* nice about her. If Harper told a joke, no matter how lame it was, Liv laughed really hard at it. She also told Harper she was pretty and smart about a hundred times.

The other weird part was that Liv kept making vague references to these "super adorbs" new friends she'd made. It was like she was trying to impress Harper, but whenever Harper tried to ask more questions about them, Liv completely shut down and changed the subject.

Still, Liv had been good for distracting her, and Harper had managed to avoid calling Gemma or Daniel a million times. Though she did text them a few times to make sure everything was okay, and they both claimed it was.

Even though Liv had taken the time to point out every one of her classrooms, Harper was so preoccupied that she forgot everything Liv had shown her. She was late for her first two classes, and the only reason she was on time for her third one was because it was with Liv, and she physically led her to the classroom.

They sat next to each other, and when the teacher passed out the class syllabus, Harper was both relieved and surprised to see that she'd actually read some of the texts in high school. The day was starting to take a turn for the better when Harper started feeling a weird pain in her chest.

She took a deep breath, hoping that would ease it somehow, but the pain only intensified. Her chest tightened, and nausea washed over her. Then the terror hit her. It was intense and unrelenting, and adrenaline surged through her.

Other people would've thought they were having a panic attack, and that was probably what a doctor would've diagnosed. But this was different. As soon as the fear hit her and a shooting pain stabbed through her stomach, Harper knew what it was.

"Gemma," she whispered.

"Harper?" Liv asked, leaning in closer to her. "Are you okay? You don't look so good."

"No, I gotta . . ." She took a deep breath. "I gotta go."

She stood up quickly, knocking her books to the floor with a loud clatter. Everyone turned to look at her, and she just mumbled an apology as she scrambled to pick up her things. The teacher asked if everything was okay, but she didn't answer.

Harper rushed out of the classroom as fast as her legs could carry her. In the hall, she had to stop and lean against the wall for support. The terror and pain were too strong, and it almost brought her to her knees.

"Harper?" Liv asked. She'd followed her out of the classroom and went over to see if she was all right. "What's the matter?"

"I need to get to my car," Harper said. "I have to go home."

"I don't think you're in any shape to drive," Liv said.

"Please." She looked up at her, imploring her. "Help me to my car. I have to get home. *Now.*"

"Okay." Liv nodded, then looped her arm around Harper's waist to help steady her.

As they walked, Harper reached into her pocket and dug out her phone. Gemma's name was first in her contacts, and she hit call. The phone rang and rang, but Harper only got her voice mail.

They stepped outside of the building into the pouring rain. Harper had only gone to class a few minutes ago, and it hadn't been raining then. Now it was coming down so hard she could barely see.

That didn't deter her from dialing the phone, though. She kept calling again and again and again. But Gemma never picked up.

THIRTY-SEVEN

Liberate

Daniel had made an important decision—he had to tell Harper. After days of going back and forth about it, he'd finally come to terms with the fact that Harper needed to know about the deal he'd made with Penn.

Once he came to that conclusion, he only had to figure out when would be the best time to tell her. Part of him thought it would be easier to wait until after the fact, because then it would already be done.

He knew if he told Harper before he slept with Penn, she might try to talk him out of it. That wouldn't be so bad, except that she might succeed.

It wasn't that he wanted to have sex with Penn—in fact, quite the contrary. When it came down to it, he wasn't completely sure he'd be able to perform, although the other night when Penn had been kissing him had him partially convinced that it wouldn't be an issue. No matter what his heart and mind felt, his body seemed to respond to certain things.

But Penn was guaranteeing the safety of Gemma and Harper. He couldn't turn that down.

Of course, he knew that this wasn't an indefinite guarantee. If he did sleep with Penn, one of two things would happen afterward. Either she would immediately lose interest in Daniel, and then probably kill him, Harper, and Gemma just for fun. Or she'd like it, and continue to blackmail Daniel into seeing her.

There was a third option, one where Daniel also enjoyed and actively pursued a relationship with Penn. While she seemed certain that was the way things would end up, he was highly dubious. He didn't think anything in the world would feel good enough for him to want to be with her.

The best-case scenario was that Penn would keep blackmailing Daniel, promising him protection for Harper and Gemma as long as he was sleeping with her. His only hope to defend the people he cared about was to become some kind of indentured prostitute.

And that was why he had to tell Harper before he went ahead with it. He didn't want to sneak around behind her back repeatedly cheating on her, no matter how good the reason might be. She needed to know what he was doing so she could decide for herself if she wanted to continue a relationship with him.

Daniel knew full well that he might lose her over this. Even though he was doing it for her, because he loved her, he knew it would be a hard thing to accept.

But if he had to choose between losing her forever to keep her safe and happy or being with her and watching her suffer and die, then he would gladly choose the former, no matter what the cost was to him.

Since he and Penn were set to seal the deal tomorrow, he thought he'd better have the conversation with Harper today. He didn't want to have it over the phone, though, and he didn't have a car.

So that led Daniel to Alex's house, where they stood in the driveway next to Alex's blue Cougar. The sky was dark above them, but it hadn't begun to rain yet.

"Are you sure?" Daniel asked as he took the car keys from Alex. "I don't want to put you out."

"No, it's fine." Alex shook his head.

"Are you gonna be able to get to work okay?" Daniel asked.

"I haven't been working lately," Alex admitted.

Daniel eyed him. It'd been a week since he'd last seen Alex, ferrying him over from his island to mainland Capri. Alex had been rather hungover then, but even factoring that in, he seemed to be doing better.

It wasn't until they'd been talking for a little while that it finally occurred to him. Every time he'd run into Alex during the past month, Alex had been looking at the ground or staring off at nothing. This was the first time in a long while that Alex was actually looking him in the eye.

"Oh, yeah?" Daniel asked. "Are you quitting?"

"Maybe, if I haven't already been fired." Alex shrugged. "I just need to do something different. Working out on the docks isn't for me."

"Did something happen?" Daniel asked.

"I don't know." He furrowed his brow. "I think I need to take some time off and figure things out. I've been in a weird place lately, and . . . I don't know. I feel like things might be turning around."

Thunder cracked overhead, and Alex looked up, staring at the heavy clouds swirling above them. The wind blew his hair back from his eyes, which had a look of total fascination in them, like the storm was entrancing him.

"I should be out there tracking this," Alex said quietly, almost to himself.

Daniel joined Alex in staring up at the sky. "It looks like it's gonna start storming soon."

"There's something big on the way, that's for sure," Alex agreed.

"Yeah, well, I should probably get going if I'm going to head up to Sundham before the storm really rolls in," Daniel said, looking back at Alex.

Alex nodded. "All right." He waited until Daniel turned to walk away before saying, "Hey, Daniel. Are you . . . You're talking to Gemma a lot?"

"Um, kind of, I guess," Daniel answered uncertainly. "Why?"

"I can't . . ." Alex shook his head, as if struggling to find the words. "Right now I can't protect her the way I want to. Things are . . . not right between us. But I want her safe."

"Yeah, I get that," Daniel said.

"Can you watch out for her?" Alex asked, looking at him. "Just until I can get this mess under control. Can you keep an eye on her for me, make sure everything's okay?"

"Yeah, of course." Daniel nodded.

Alex looked relieved and smiled. "Thank you."

"No problem," Daniel said. "And I'll have your car back in the morning."

"Yeah, that'd be fine," Alex told him. "Take as much time as you need."

Without any further warning, it started to rain. Earlier, when Daniel had been walking over to Alex's, he'd felt the occasional sprinkle. But this was as if the sky had opened up and poured water on them.

"I'm gonna run inside," Alex said, and he was already backing toward his house.

"Yeah, sure." Daniel hit the remote unlock on the keys and reached for the car door. "Thanks again!"

He jumped in the car, already dripping wet. It had only been a matter of seconds that he'd been outside in the rain, but it was coming down hard enough that he was nearly soaked. He ran his hand back and forth through his hair, trying to shake off a few excess drops.

Daniel knew how to drive, but he'd never driven Alex's car before, so he took a few minutes to acclimate himself. One of the hardest things about driving a strange car was figuring out how to get the windshield wipers working at the right speed.

Once he got that straightened out, he backed out of Alex's driveway. Daniel hadn't even made it to the end of the block when his phone started vibrating in his pocket. When he pulled the phone out, the ID said it was Harper, so he took a deep breath and decided that now was as good a time as any to invite himself up to visit her.

"Hey, Harp—" Daniel began, but that was all he could get out before she was shouting frantically in his ear.

"Where's Gemma? Are you okay? Are you with her? What's going on?"

"What?" Daniel had just reached the stop sign at the end of the block, and there were no cars behind him, so he decided to wait there until he could figure out what Harper was freaking out about. "I'm fine. I don't know where Gemma's at. I'm just in a car."

"What car?" Harper asked. "Where are you going? Have you talked to Gemma?"

"I borrowed Alex's car," Daniel said. "I thought I would come out and visit you tonight, and I haven't talked to Gemma today."

"No!" Harper shouted. "You can't come out tonight! Something's wrong. Something's going on with Gemma. You have to find her."

"Slow down, Harper," Daniel said. "I can barely understand you."

"I've been calling and calling, and she's not answering her phone," Harper said. Her voice was trembling, and it sounded like she was on the verge of tears. "And I just know it. Something's happened, and I don't think I'll make it there in time."

"Are you driving right now?" Daniel asked. "Harper, you need to pull over until you calm down. You're bordering on hysterics, it's torrential rain, and you're on the phone. You're gonna get in an accident."

"No, I'm fine, Daniel," Harper insisted. "I just need you to find Gemma."

"Yeah, I get that, and I'll go look for her as soon as you pull over," Daniel said.

"Daniel, *please*!" Harper sobbed. "She's hurt! I can feel it, and she's hurt!"

"Okay, calm down," Daniel said, keeping his voice as even as he could. "I'll go look for her. Do you have any idea where she's at?"

"No, but she's probably with the sirens," Harper said, and that sounded like a safe bet to Daniel, too.

"I'm going out to their house now." Daniel pulled away from the stop sign. "You need to take a deep breath and slow down. I'll find Gemma and make sure she's safe. As soon as I do, one of us will call you, okay?"

"Okay." Harper exhaled, and she did sound a bit calmer. "Thank you. And I'm sorry for calling you. I just didn't know who else to turn to."

"No, it's no problem," Daniel assured her. "I'll take care of it."

"Thank you," Harper repeated. "And be careful, okay? I don't want you getting hurt, either."

"I will, and drive safe. I'll talk to you soon."

Daniel tossed the phone on the passenger seat and sped up. Harper's worst fear was coming true, and she hadn't even been gone for a day.

He briefly considered that this might just be her paranoia flaring up, but he immediately dismissed it. Harper and Gemma had that weird psychic bond, and if she said that Gemma was in trouble, then Gemma probably was.

Whether or not the sirens were involved with what was happening with Gemma was another story. Daniel didn't think Penn would go back on their deal, not when it was so close to happening. But she'd only promised that *she* wouldn't hurt Gemma or Harper. That didn't mean the other sirens wouldn't.

He raced across town, ignoring speed limits and red lights whenever he could. When he started up the hill, things got a bit trickier. It was raining so hard the streets were flooded, and the wind had picked up. The car couldn't get traction, and the storm nearly blew him off the road several times.

When he finally made it to the driveway of the sirens' house, the car skidded in the mud and ended up getting stuck in the water-slogged grass under a tree. Daniel didn't care, though. He just jumped out of the car and ran toward the house.

Before he even stepped inside, Daniel knew things weren't good. One of the front windows had been smashed out, letting the rain pour inside, and he heard an unearthly roar—a sound he'd only heard once before, when Penn had been trying to kill him as the bird-monster.

"Gemma!" Daniel shouted and threw open the front door.

He'd never been inside the house before, so he had no real frame of reference, but it was obviously demolished. A couch had been upended, a coffee table snapped in half. Even the fridge had been pulled away from the wall and tipped on its side, with the food and beverages spilling out, looking like an eviscerated appliance.

Marcy was lying on her stomach, half hidden by the couch, and Daniel couldn't tell if she was dead or merely unconscious. He didn't have time to check on her or even to think about it, though, because there was a much bigger problem at hand.

Gemma was crouched down underneath the stairs, using them to shield her. She had a fire poker in one hand and held it pointed at the awful monster standing in front of her.

Lexi had her back to Daniel, her massive golden wings completely unfurled, so a large part of his view was obstructed. Her legs had grown much longer, so Lexi stood at least two feet taller than she had been before.

The smooth bronze skin of her legs had changed into blue-gray scales, and the knee jutted out backward. Her feet had clearly become those of a bird, her five toes converging into three, with long, sharp claws at the end of each one.

Her head had expanded and elongated as well, so her blond hair no longer covered her scalp evenly. It had become stringier and mangier, billowing out in thin wisps when the wind blew through the room.

The Lexi creature had heard him come inside, so she turned back to face him. Her large eyes were the yellow of a bird's, and her mouth was overflowing with rows of jagged, pointy teeth. Her lips had peeled back around them to make room, and her jaw extended out farther than it had before.

Instead of saying anything, Lexi just threw back her head and laughed when she saw him. The sound came out more like a crow cawing than a human laugh, with a demonic undertone reverberating through it, and Daniel knew that that definitely could not be a good sign.

THIRTY-EIGHT

Reticence

Gemma had been holding off Lexi as best she could. That was hard to do when she refused to let herself shift into the monster, and Lexi had become a much larger, much stronger creature on a murderous rampage. Lexi had gotten a few good kicks in to Gemma's stomach, and if she didn't have siren healing powers, Gemma'd have been worried about internal bleeding. That's why Gemma had hidden under the stairs—she clearly couldn't fight her head-on.

"Just who I was hoping to see today," Lexi told Daniel in her awful monster voice.

With Lexi's back to her, Gemma stood up and drove the poker right into her shoulder. She wasn't really sure where else would be a better place to stab her, since Alex had already proven that stabbing her through the heart did nothing.

Lexi roared in anger and grabbed the poker with her long, skinny fingers. Gemma slid out past her, running low to the floor to avoid Lexi's wings as they flapped in rage.

"Daniel, run!" Gemma shouted, and she started to charge toward him.

Then she remembered Marcy, turned, and doubled back toward her. By the time she had turned around, Lexi had already gotten the poker free, and she threw it across the room. Daniel ducked, and it narrowly missed his head before it clattered against the wall.

Lexi stood between Gemma and Marcy, so Gemma swallowed hard and took a step back toward Daniel. Lexi lowered her head, her eyes narrowed, and when she stepped forward, her head made a bobbing movement that reminded Gemma of a robin looking for worms. It wasn't nearly as cheerful an image, since Gemma and Daniel had become the worms.

"What's the plan?" Daniel asked as Gemma moved toward him.

"I don't really have one," Gemma admitted.

"I have a plan for you," Lexi said, her lips stretching in a distorted smile. "I plan on killing and eating both of you, and then getting the hell away from this town. The two of you are the reason I've been stuck here for so long, and once I get rid of you, I'll be free of this godforsaken shithole."

"Penn won't like that," Daniel said.

"Yeah, well, there won't be much she can do about it once you're dead," Lexi shot back, and she ran at them.

Her legs were long and frighteningly fast. She looked clumsy and oversized, but she was agile and quick.

Gemma grabbed Daniel's hand and bolted out of the way just in time to get out of Lexi's grasp. They'd been standing by the broken window, and Lexi's feet slipped in the water from the rain, so she skidded across the floor and crashed unceremoniously into the wall.

It would only be a matter of seconds before she was back on her feet again, which didn't leave Gemma enough time to grab Marcy and get out of there.

They needed to come up with a game plan. Gemma ran to the only place she could think of where she and Daniel could at least grab a few seconds to gather their thoughts.

She led Daniel into the pantry and slammed the door behind them. It wasn't a huge space, and it was totally dark, but both of them could fit in there easily. The door wasn't the strongest, but at least it was something standing between them and Lexi.

"This is your plan?" Daniel panted as they leaned against the door.

"This is more like my plan before a plan," Gemma said.

"Let me in, let me in," Lexi cajoled in the silkiest voice she could manage. The tone wasn't quite up to her usual standards. Something about being the bird-monster made it impossible for her to sound sweet.

Her talons ran up and down the door, making a scraping sound that gave Gemma the chills, but she wasn't really trying to get in. At least not yet. The eerie clawing at the door was for effect.

"Not by the hair of my chin," Daniel shot back, and that made Lexi cackle loudly again.

There was complete and total silence for a few seconds, which Gemma didn't like. She didn't know what Lexi was doing out there, but it probably wasn't good.

"You're supposed to let me know before you do shit like this," Daniel reminded Gemma.

"Sorry." She grimaced as she pressed her weight against the door. "I thought I could handle it."

"Why don't you turn into the monster?" Daniel asked, keeping his voice low in case Lexi was listening.

Gemma shook her head, even though he couldn't see her in the darkness. "I can't."

"Sure you can."

"No, maybe I can, but I can't control it once I do. I might hurt somebody," she insisted.

"That's kinda the point, though, isn't it?" Daniel asked.

Ever since Lexi had started attacking her, Gemma had actually been fighting to keep the monster down. It was her body's natural instinct to transform into it, to try to defend herself, but she was afraid that if she let it out, it would completely take over again.

Lydia had even given her the instructions on how to kill the sirens, but Gemma wasn't sure she could do it. Well, she knew for certain she wouldn't be strong enough to do it in her human form, and as a monster, she wasn't convinced she'd be able to control herself enough to do it.

"I did it once before and I don't even remember it," Gemma told him. "I wasn't in my mind at all. I was a complete monster, and I killed someone."

Suddenly Lexi slammed into the door. Gemma and Daniel had simply been leaning against it, but now they pushed back on it with all their might, trying to hold it shut.

"Again, that doesn't sound so bad, given the situation," Daniel said through gritted teeth as Lexi ran into it again.

"Yeah, if I hurt Lexi, but what if I hurt you or Marcy?" Gemma countered. "No. I can't risk it."

"Well, we've got to do something or Lexi is going to kill us pretty quickly," Daniel said as the door began to crack. "Can you at least do a partial change? I've seen the other sirens do that."

"I don't know how." Gemma pushed against the door, but she

knew it was going to give soon. "I've tried, but so far it's been all or nothing."

Lexi's hand smashed through the door. It was a small hole, just enough room to fit her slender wrist, and wood poked up at Gemma with jagged edges and splinters. Lexi's long taloned fingers reached out, feeling around for either Gemma or Daniel.

"Open the door!" Daniel commanded, and when Gemma didn't do it immediately, he shouted again, "Open the door, Gemma!"

She was on the side by the door handle, while he'd been holding the side with the hinges, and Lexi's hand was right in the middle, grasping for them.

While Gemma didn't understand what Daniel's plan was, she pulled open the door. Lexi's wrist was caught in the wood, so when Gemma pulled it, she took Lexi with her.

Lexi stumbled into the pantry, knocking canned foods and spices off the shelves as she did. There was hardly enough room for her, and one of her wings was actually stuck outside. As Lexi screeched and struggled to pull free from the door, Gemma dropped to the floor and crawled between Lexi's legs, barely avoiding getting stepped on.

Daniel followed Gemma, but he was less lucky. Lexi's legs lashed out, and she kicked him in the ribs. He cried out, but he kept moving.

Gemma was running toward Marcy, hoping to reach her before Lexi freed herself, but Daniel was moving slower, thanks to Lexi's kick. Gemma didn't see him, but she heard him yell, followed by the sound of shattering glass.

When she turned back around, she saw one of the large back windows had been broken out, and Daniel was gone. Lexi stood in the center of the room, smiling pleasantly at Gemma. She'd grabbed Daniel and thrown him through a window toward the edge of the cliff.

"Lexi, you bitch!" Gemma growled and charged at her.

But Lexi was lightning-quick. She swung her arm out, hitting Gemma painfully in the chest. She fell back to the floor, and while Lexi towered over her, cackling like a bird, Gemma reached out and grabbed one of her legs.

Pulling as hard as she could, Gemma managed to throw Lexi off balance. She stumbled backward, flapping her arms and wings like mad and sending papers billowing around the room, until she finally fell backward.

Gemma scrambled to her knees and crawled over to her. Remembering the picture that Lydia had given her, Gemma climbed onto Lexi. She sat on her bare stomach, straddling Lexi.

As soon as she did, Lexi reached out and grabbed Gemma. Her long fingers wrapped tightly around Gemma's throat, cutting off her air supply. Gemma balled up her hand and punched Lexi as hard as she could in the stomach, hoping her fist could break through Lexi's soft flesh.

Lexi squawked and threw Gemma off her, causing Gemma to crash painfully against the fireplace.

Gemma coughed and gasped for breath, and she knew she had to come up with a better plan. There was no way she could stop Lexi with her bare hands. She needed to find a weapon, unless she turned into the monster.

Unfortunately, Gemma didn't have time to do either before Lexi was on her. Lexi reached out for her, and Gemma narrowly slid underneath her grasp. The golden wings were outstretched behind her, and Gemma grabbed one, yanking on it as hard as she could.

But Lexi was stronger. She flapped her wings and sent Gemma

flying back on the floor. Lexi ran back over to her, running as quickly as her long bird legs could carry her, and when she reached Gemma, she kicked out at her.

Her clawed foot connected with Gemma's stomach, tearing into the tender flesh, but that wasn't the worst part. Lexi kicked her so hard that when Gemma flew backward and collided with the wall, everything went black for a moment.

She had no idea how long she was out, but when she opened her eyes, her head throbbing painfully and her vision blurred, she saw Lexi standing over her, cackling at her pain. Gemma tried to move, but she wasn't getting up so easy this time.

"I'm going to go outside and finish Daniel off," Lexi said as she stepped back. "But don't worry. I'll be back for you in a few seconds, after I eat his heart."

THIRTY-NINE

Massacre

Daniel had landed facedown in the mud among shards of broken glass. He rolled over onto his back—slowly, because he had a feeling that Lexi had cracked one of his ribs. The rain was pouring down on him so hard, it felt like needles stabbing his skin.

He squinted up and saw Lexi climbing out the window. She had to fold her wings against her back to make it through.

Daniel tried pushing himself up, but flying through a glass window had knocked a lot out of him.

Lexi walked over to him, her legs taking long, rather elegant strides. When she stood over him, her outstretched wings worked as a partial umbrella. She cocked her head, staring down at him.

"I cannot wait to eat your heart," Lexi said, and flicked out an odd, serpentine tongue.

"Well, you're gonna have to."

Daniel rolled back and pulled his legs up to his chest, then he pushed them out as hard as he could, kicking her in the chest with both his feet. Lexi stumbled backward, barely managing to keep her balance in the mud, and she flapped her wings to steady herself.

He got to his feet just as Gemma came out the back door. She stumbled a bit as she walked, and one arm cradled her stomach, where he could see the blood seeping through her shirt. Gemma stood in between Daniel and Lexi, glaring up at her.

"That's enough, Lexi!" Gemma shouted.

Daniel was standing behind Gemma, but he saw it start to happen. Her fingers were stretching out, and her nails were shifting into long black talons. Her mouth began to twitch, and he knew it was going to become filled with those awful teeth.

But before Gemma completed the transformation, Lexi flapped her wings. She leaned forward, deliberately hitting Gemma with her wing, and sent her flying over the edge of the cliff.

"Gemma!" Daniel yelled, and he ran after her. He barely stopped in time to keep from sliding off the edge himself, and one of the toes of his shoes actually did hang over.

He was too late to do anything other than watch as Gemma crashed into the rocks below. The waves were beating against the cliff face, turning a frothy white, and Gemma was lost instantly in them.

"You'll be joining her soon," Lexi said. "But first your heart is mine."

She was taller than him, so it made for a strange angle, and he had to jump up to be able to punch her. But his fist connected, landing squarely in her temple.

As the bird-monster, her torso had elongated, and her ribs protruded grotesquely. Underneath that, the soft tissue of her belly was completely exposed, and Daniel punched it as hard as he could.

She squawked and stumbled back, so he stepped forward,

punching her again with his other fist. Her wings flapped to keep her balance, and the powerful gusts of air from that motion nearly made him fall back, but he kept his footing.

His mistake came when he tried to punch her in the head again. She was leaning forward, trying to correct her stance so she wouldn't fall back, and the opportunity seemed too good to pass up. So he threw a right hook, hoping to connect with her jaw, but instead her head snapped to the side and she clamped her teeth right on his forearm.

Daniel cried out in agony. Lexi's mouth was filled with hundreds of narrow teeth, sticking out haphazardly like needles in a pincushion. He could actually feel some of them going all the way through his arm and coming out the other side.

When she let go, Daniel collapsed to the ground on his knees. The rain was pounding against his arm, mixing with the blood and running down into the mud.

"Not so tough now, are you?" Lexi asked.

He tried to get back on his feet, but Lexi kicked him in the chest. It was even harder than she'd kicked him before, and the blow sent him flying. He landed on his back and skidded a few feet in the mud.

Lexi had knocked the wind out of him, and it was several painful seconds before he was able to take a breath again. He coughed hard, his lungs screaming as he gasped for air.

He tried to sit up, but then he felt Lexi's foot on his stomach, pinning him to the ground. The claws from her toes pierced the fabric of his shirt and drove into his skin. He grabbed her ankle, her skin feeling reptilian under his hands, and tried to push her off him, but she wouldn't budge.

"It's over, Daniel," she assured him. "I'm going to kill you now."

Lexi bent down, reaching her long fingers out toward his chest. He steeled himself for the inevitable, and the biggest regret he had was that he'd let Harper down. He promised her that he wouldn't let anything happen to Gemma, and he had failed.

He stared up at Lexi, unwilling to look anywhere else but her eyes. If she was going to kill him, he wanted to make her see it. Her wings were sheltering him from the rain, so he could look up at her without squinting.

Then suddenly Lexi pulled her head back and let out a tortured squawk. Her wings moved, and icy rain splashed into his face. He closed his eyes against it, and then he felt something warm mixed in, dripping on his skin.

The foot disappeared from his stomach, and Daniel lifted his arm, shielding himself from the rain as he sat up.

Lexi had taken several steps back from him, and one of her wings was flapping wildly. The other one . . . wasn't there. Blood was spilling out from her shoulder as she wailed.

Penn stood in front of him, looking completely human, except for her arms. She had the same arms as Lexi, complete with the clawed fingers. In one of her hands she held Lexi's golden wing, but she tossed it aside like it was an old piece of garbage.

"What's your problem, Penn?" Lexi screamed at her. "I was only playing around!"

"I warned you to leave him alone," Penn said. She stepped toward her, and Lexi took another step back, edging toward the cliff. "I said don't hurt him or those stupid Fisher girls. And what did you do?"

"I was just fooling around, Penn!" Lexi insisted, but Penn didn't seem convinced.

Lexi kept trying to back up, and her feet slipped in the mud.

She fell back to the ground, her head hanging over the cliff edge while her body remained safely on land. Her one wing flailed horribly, but Penn was on top of her, pinning her down.

Penn sat on Lexi's stomach, straddling her, and she wrapped one hand around Lexi's throat. Lexi made a gurgling sound and began clawing at Penn's hand. Lexi's legs kicked aimlessly, unable to reach Penn.

With her free hand, Penn tore into Lexi's stomach, going up underneath the rib cage to get to her heart. Lexi screamed louder and flailed even more, but it was to no avail. Penn pulled it out, holding up the small, black heart in front of Lexi, showing it to her.

Lexi gnashed her teeth and tried to push Penn off, so Penn tightened her grip around her throat. Lexi's yellow eyes looked like they were going to bug out of her skull, and finally Penn tore through the flesh and bone. She ripped off Lexi's head and let it fall, crashing down into the ocean below.

FORTY

Liability

Gemma had hit the rocks first, snapping her back. The waves had crashed over, pulling her underneath before she had a chance to scream.

On land, she'd been giving in and was letting herself shift into the monster, and that became a problem once she hit the water. Her fingers had lengthened, and her feet had morphed into three-toed avian feet.

Not only did this make for horrible swimming, but the beginnings of transformation seemed to make it harder for her to change into a mermaid. She was frozen midshift, unable to become fish or fowl.

Her body wasn't healing, either. Pain tore through her back, and she couldn't feel her feet. But that wasn't even the worst of her troubles. She couldn't breathe, and the waves were pulling her out. She was drowning.

After she'd frantically clawed her way toward the surface, the salt water began to affect her. The flutter ran over her legs, and her clawed feet shifted into fins. Her lungs burned, but the pain in her back subsided. Her body was healing itself.

When Gemma was about to lose consciousness, air finally flooded her lungs as she could breathe underwater. Her tail pumped frantically behind her, and she burst through the surface of the water, breathing in deeply.

The waves had taken her a little ways from the cliff, and she swam toward it. When she reached the rocks that jutted out of the water, she found a large one and crawled onto it.

That was easier said than done. The rock was slick and wet, and the waves and rain kept beating against her, trying to push her down. Not to mention that her mermaid tail was like dead weight as she clawed her way up.

Gasping for breath, she sat perched until her tail shifted back into legs. She thanked her lucky stars that she'd worn a dress today, but she still had bigger problems.

It would take her too long to climb up the face of the cliff. Daniel was in trouble, and if she didn't get up there fast, Lexi would have him for dinner. She closed her eyes and tried to will the transformation.

The problem was that any other time she had started to change, it had been because her life was threatened. It was something that happened by instinct. And while she cared about Daniel and wanted to save him, her body didn't have quite the same reaction.

"Come on, just do it," she whispered to herself, her hands balled into fists on her lap. "Just change, dammit."

Then finally she began to feel something. Not in her eyes or fingers, which were usually the first things to alter. Her shoulders were itching, and then she felt a sharp sting. Unlike all her other changes, this was painful. The wings broke through her skin, and it actually felt as if bone and feather were tearing through her flesh. She had to bite her lip to keep from crying out.

Two massive copper wings spread out behind her. She turned her head from side to side and watched them beating in the rain. The rest of her transformation seemed to halt, and while she would've preferred becoming the full monster so it would be easier to fight Lexi, she'd settle for this.

Flying seemed to come naturally, like swimming with her fish's tail or ripping out Jason's heart. With a little concentration on her part, the wings were flapping and lifting her up off the rock.

As she was flying up toward the top, a bloody head came falling down past her. Based on the stringy blond hair attached to it, Gemma guessed it was Lexi's, and she flew even faster.

When Gemma made it up to the top, Daniel was half sitting up and appeared conscious and mostly okay. Gemma hovered in the air, surveying the scene before deciding whether to land or grab him and take off.

Penn was climbing off what was left of Lexi, both her hands covered in blood up to her elbows. Thea was inside the house, watching through the broken window.

"I told you we shouldn't have let Lexi stay behind today," Thea was saying. "I knew something was up with her."

"Yeah, yeah, you're always right." Penn licked some of the blood off her hands, then held them out so the rain would wash away the rest of it. "Thea, come out here and drag this body in the house before we lose all the blood. We'll need it to make another siren."

Thea groaned, but came outside to collect Lexi's body anyway.

Gemma landed gently on the ground next to Daniel, and he looked up at her. A cut on his forehead left blood streaming into one eye. He smiled crookedly when he saw her, appearing both relieved and rather dazed.

"Thank God," he said. "You're not dead."

"No, I'm not. How are you holding up?" Gemma asked as she looked him over.

"And you've got that whole thing." He motioned up to her copper wings and ignored her question.

She crouched down next to him and spread her wings out wide, shielding both of them from the rain. "Are you okay?"

"Yeah, he's fine, no thanks to you," Penn said. She walked over to them while Thea was dragging Lexi into the house through the back door. "What the hell were you doing? How did you let it get this far?"

"I was trying to fight back," Gemma said. "But she threw me off the cliff, and I have no idea how to control this monster thing."

"You should've just let it take over," Penn said. "Then *you* could've killed her." She waved it off, then turned her attention to Daniel. "Are you okay?"

"I have a few scrapes and bruises." He held up his arm, which was covered in holes from Lexi's teeth. "But I should live."

"Do you think you'll be well enough for tomorrow?" Penn asked.

"What's tomorrow?" Gemma asked, bewildered.

Daniel kept his eyes fixed on Penn, and ignored Gemma. "I said I would be."

"I want you at your best," Penn said.

Gemma looked from one of them to the other. "What are you talking about?"

"You owe me," Penn said, and at first it seemed like she was only talking to Daniel, but then she pointed to Gemma. "Both of you owe me. And I will collect."

With that, Penn turned and stalked back into the house, leaving Gemma outside to deal with Daniel.

"What was that about?" Gemma asked him.

"Nothing." He shook his head and wouldn't look at her.

"Holy shit!" Marcy shouted from inside the house, apparently conscious and moving around again. "What the hell is that?" Presumably, she'd just encountered Lexi's decapitated, eviscerated bird-monster corpse.

"We should grab her and get out of here," Gemma said.

"Yeah," Daniel agreed.

He started to stand up and winced, so Gemma reached out and put her arm around his waist to help him up. He carefully put his arm around her shoulders, mindful of her wings, and leaned on her for support.

As they walked toward the house to collect Marcy, Gemma said, "We'll have to tell Harper about this, but when we do, we really need to play down how much danger there was."

"Oh, yeah. She would lose it if she knew what really happened." Daniel looked up, admiring Gemma's wings. "Those are pretty awesome."

"Yeah, they are." She sighed. "Now I just need to figure out how to put them away."

FORTY-ONE

Revelations

It really wasn't that bad," Daniel insisted for the hundredth time, playing down his injury.

"You keep saying that, but it doesn't make me believe you any more," Harper said.

He leaned against the counter in her kitchen, his arm held out in front of him while Harper cleaned up his bite marks from Lexi. The cut above his eyebrow was already taken care of, covered with a couple Band-Aids.

Harper had almost reached Capri when Gemma called to let her know that everything was okay, but she'd been scant on details. Harper had arrived home just as Marcy was dropping off Gemma and Daniel, so she'd seen exactly the state they'd made it back in.

While Gemma had appeared fine, her dress was covered in blood in the back, and the fabric was torn up around her shoulders. Daniel lacked Gemma's healing powers, so he looked like hell.

They'd both given Harper an abbreviated story about what had happened with the sirens, and she knew they were trying to downplay how perilous things had gotten. When they'd finished, Gemma went upstairs to shower off the blood and dirt and change into dry clothes.

Daniel didn't have anything to change into at her house, so he settled for letting Harper dress his wounds. When she poured alcohol over the holes in his arms, he winced.

"Sorry, but I have to clean it out," Harper said. "You have no idea where Lexi's mouth has been."

"I know. The alcohol just stung a little."

"Most of these holes go straight through." She tilted his arm to get a better look. "You really should go to the doctor."

"I'll be okay."

She gave him a stern look. "Daniel."

He tried to match her seriousness but smirked a little. "Harper."

She rolled her eyes and went back to washing off his arm with an alcohol-soaked paper towel. "You're covered in drying mud, and your clothes are wet. You really should shower and get into something dry."

He watched her cleaning his arm, grimacing when she poked at a hole. "Are you going back to school tonight?"

"No. After tonight, I don't know if I'm ever going back."

"Harper." He pulled his arm back from her so she'd look up at him. "The one thing we proved tonight is that we can handle things without you."

"Look at you, Daniel!" She gestured to his bloody, ripped-up shirt. "You're all torn up, and you almost died!"

"But I didn't," he said reasonably. "I'm fine, Gemma's fine. We survived."

Harper scoffed. "Barely."

"Things will be calmer for a while."

"How do you figure?" she asked skeptically.

"With Lexi dead, I think things will be quiet."

"You're sure she's dead?" Harper asked.

"Lexi? Yeah." He nodded. "She's dead."

"Why did she do it? Why did Penn kill Lexi to save you?" Harper stared at him, studying his response.

Daniel lowered his eyes. "I don't know."

"Is there something you're not telling me?" Harper asked, and she had the strange feeling she'd had before, that Daniel was pulling away and keeping something from her.

He seemed to hesitate before answering, "No."

"Daniel." She stepped closer to him and put her hand gently on his chest, the fabric of his shirt damp against her skin. "If there's something going on, I should know about it. Whatever it is, you can tell me. We're in this together."

"I know." He smiled at her, but there was something in his eyes, something dark he was trying to mask. "And I'd tell you."

"Good," Harper said, not knowing how else to push the issue. If he insisted that nothing else was wrong, she had to trust him. She cared about him, and he'd never given her any reason to doubt him. "I do love you."

He leaned in, kissing her gently on the mouth, and then smiled at her. "I know."

The front door banged open, and she heard Brian's heavy work boots thud on the floor as he took them off. She glanced over at the microwave to see that it was after four, meaning that he was home from work for the day.

"Oh, shit. My dad's here," Harper said, realizing that she had no idea how to explain the situation to him.

She had pulled away from Daniel by the time her father was

standing in the kitchen doorway. His hair and coveralls were wet from the storm, and he did not look happy to see them.

"Hey, Dad," Harper said as cheerfully as she could.

"Hello, Mr. Fisher," Daniel said. He'd straightened up and tried to look presentable.

"What's going on here? Was there an accident?" Brian asked, eyeing Daniel.

"Uh, yeah. Kinda," Harper said. "Daniel's just having some troubles."

"What are you doing home?" Brian turned his attention to her. "Shouldn't you be at school?"

"Yeah, I just . . ." She rubbed the back of her neck. "Daniel called and let me know about the accident, so I thought I'd come and . . . help."

"Accident?" Brian stepped farther into the kitchen so he could get a better look at Daniel. "What kind of accident leaves holes in your arms?"

"It's kind of a long story, Mr. Fisher," Daniel said.

Brian crossed his arms over his chest. "You're getting stitched up in my kitchen. It seems like you have time."

"That's fair." Daniel floundered for a second, then turned to Harper. "Um, Harper, do you want to explain to your dad what happened? You're so much more eloquent than I am."

She smiled thinly at him, then started with, "Well, Daniel was . . . he was out on his island and . . ."

"You know that I know this is clearly bullshit, right?" Brian asked. "You're not even trying to cover it up."

"Dad, some things are . . ." She sighed. "I don't need to tell you everything."

"When you're in my house, you do," Brian countered.

"I'm not sixteen, Dad." Harper crossed her arms over her chest and tried to appear defiant. "And I don't even technically live here anymore."

"Technically, yeah, you do," Brian said. "Harper, cut the crap. There has been something going on for a long time now. Not just this but with your sister and Alex. Something is happening, and it's about damn time somebody tells me what's really going on."

"Dad . . ." Harper trailed off, trying to think of a way to explain this to her dad that didn't sound totally insane.

"I'm a siren," Gemma said, and Harper and Brian looked over to see her standing in the doorway.

Harper was aghast. "*Gemma!*"

"He knows something's up, Harper." She shrugged. "All this lying is getting dumb, and I'm sick of hiding things from you guys. So I'm laying it all out on the table."

"You're a siren?" Brian had turned around to face her. "The mermaid thing that sings?"

"There's more to it than that, but yeah, that's the gist of it," Gemma said.

Brian stared at her, not saying anything. Harper watched him nervously as he furrowed his brow and narrowed his eyes at Gemma.

"Dad, she's telling the truth." Harper broke the silence, hoping to lend some credibility to her sister's revelation.

"I would sing for you, but I don't want to hurt you," Gemma said. "I messed up Alex, and I don't want to do that to anyone else again."

"Bernie did always tell me to watch out for sirens," Brian said finally.

"What?" Harper and Gemma said in unison.

"He said that eventually the sirens would come, and I had to be on the lookout for them." Brian shook his head. "I just tossed it up to an eccentricity, but I guess I should've been paying more attention. Not that I ever would've suspected my own daughter."

"Dad, what are you talking about?" Harper asked.

A knock at the front door interrupted their conversation, but Harper's attention didn't waver from her dad.

"I'll get it," Gemma said and left to answer the door.

Harper was about to press her dad for more information when she heard Gemma at the front door saying, "Thea. What are you doing here?"

As soon as she heard Thea's name, Harper darted out of the kitchen. She wanted to push Gemma out of the way and tell Thea to get lost, but she stayed a few feet behind, waiting to see what Thea wanted before getting involved.

"I got your boyfriend's car out for you," Thea said. She was standing on the doorstep, and she motioned behind her to Alex's mud-splattered Cougar parked in the driveway. "I figured it was the least I could do after the day you had."

"Thanks," Gemma said. "Is Penn really pissed off?"

"Not really. I think she was looking for an excuse to get rid of Lexi," Thea said.

"So you just came to bring back the car?" Gemma asked, since Thea was still standing there in the pouring rain.

"No." Thea reached into a large purse she had over her shoulder and pulled out a rolled-up beige tube. "I came to give you this."

"Is this . . ." Gemma took it from her and stared down at the worn papyrus. "This is the scroll." She gaped at it, then looked up at Thea. "Why would you give this to me?"

"You've been looking for it, haven't you?" Thea asked wryly.

"Yeah, but . . ." Gemma sighed. "If I destroy this, you'll die, too."

"Yeah, probably," Thea agreed bleakly. She looked away from Gemma and stared at the pouring rain. "I've watched Penn kill three of my sisters with her bare hands. Lexi I didn't care for that much, but Gia and Aggie . . ." She trailed off and swallowed hard.

"Aggie wanted to destroy the scroll." Thea turned back to meet Gemma's eyes. "That's why Penn killed her. Aggie thought we'd lived long enough, we had enough blood on our hands." She paused. "I'm finally starting to realize she was right."

"Thank you," Gemma replied quietly.

"Yeah, well, I don't know how to destroy it, and the damned thing never did me any good." Thea gestured toward the scroll. "But maybe you'll have more luck." Then she turned, walking off into the rain, and leaving Gemma and Harper standing in the doorway.

The Watersong series continues with

Elegy

Coming soon